FIRST LOVE

Hugh huffed in exasperation. "Why are you taunting me when I am only attempting to make peace with you? I feel it is quite necessary that we arrange matters so that we can rub along tolerably well together until I am married and until you are gone from my house! You might at least attempt to cooperate! And why are you smiling? Do anything but smile!"

"Hugh, try as I will I cannot be so decorous in this moment, or so indifferent as you appear to wish me to be," Merry said. "Being back at Hathersage has put me in mind of how it was between us, and that so forcibly, that I suppose I have merely fallen back into a familiar manner of speaking with you and laughing with you, and well . . . a lot of other things!"

Hugh leaned forward in his seat. "You—we—must forget the past. Until you arrived here, I promise you that the past was forgotten, completely!"

"Not completely," she said, looking hard at him, also leaning forward. "Surely not? Though you may be marrying Miss Youlgreave, you cannot tell me all of our adventures of so many summers ago are forgotten to you?"

Hugh seemed to grow momentarily disconcerted as he looked away from her. He stared toward the windows for a long moment. "No," he responded at last, very quietly. "I suppose you are right in that. Never forgotten. We did have a great deal of fun, didn't we?"

"Yes," Merry breathed, caught up in remembering how it had been. And for that reason she found she could say nothing more. Her heart was full of love for him.

ZEBRA'S REGENCY ROMANCES
DAZZLE AND DELIGHT

A BEGUILING INTRIGUE (4441, $3.99)
by Olivia Sumner

Pretty as a picture Justine Riggs cared nothing for propriety. She dressed as a boy, sat on her horse like a jockey, and pondered the stars like a scientist. But when she tried to best the handsome Quenton Fletcher, Marquess of Devon, by proving that she was the better equestrian, he would try to prove Justine's antics were pure folly. The game he had in mind was seduction — never imagining that he might lose his heart in the process!

AN INCONVENIENT ENGAGEMENT (4442, $3.99)
by Joy Reed

Rebecca Wentworth was furious when she saw her betrothed waltzing with another. So she decides to make him jealous by flirting with the handsomest man at the ball, John Collinwood, Earl of Stanford. The "wicked" nobleman knew exactly what the enticing miss was up to — and he was only too happy to play along. But as Rebecca gazed into his magnificent eyes, her errant fiancé was soon utterly forgotten!

SCANDAL'S LADY (4472, $3.99)
by Mary Kingsley

Cassandra was shocked to learn that the new Earl of Lynton was her childhood friend, Nicholas St. John. After years at sea and mixed feelings Nicholas had come home to take the family title. And although Cassandra knew her place as a governess, she could not help the thrill that went through her each time he was near. Nicholas was pleased to find that his old friend Cassandra was his new next door neighbor, but after being near her, he wondered if mere friendship would be enough . . .

HIS LORDSHIP'S REWARD (4473, $3.99)
by Carola Dunn

As the daughter of a seasoned soldier, Fanny Ingram was accustomed to the vagaries of military life and cared not a whit about matters of rank and social standing. So she certainly never foresaw her *tendre* for handsome Viscount Roworth of Kent with whom she was forced to share lodgings, while he carried out his clandestine activities on behalf of the British Army. And though good sense told Roworth to keep his distance, he couldn't stop from taking Fanny in his arms for a kiss that made all hearts equal!

Available wherever paperbacks are sold, or order direct from the Publisher. Send cover price plus 50¢ per copy for mailing and handling to Penguin USA, P.O. Box 999, c/o Dept. 17109, Bergenfield, NJ 07621. Residents of New York and Tennessee must include sales tax. DO NOT SEND CASH.

Merry, Merry Mischief

Valerie King

ZEBRA BOOKS
KENSINGTON PUBLISHING CORP.

To Bob and Nancy Collins, for all your
support and encouragement

A merry heart doeth good like a medicine.
Proverbs 17:22

Author's Note

Abbot's End in Derbyshire, and its environs—including the great country house of Hathersage Park—are strictly inventions of my imagination.

Valerie King

Chapter One

Merry Fairfield rubbed her chilled, gloved fingers together for the hundredth time and peered anxiously through the dark, cloudy night. She was anticipating at any moment the approach of a certain travelling coach for which she and her two companions were waiting. Fortunately, midnight, in early December, 1818, lay heavily upon the Derbyshire countryside, obscuring her presence to any who might be alert for highwaymen on the roads.

Tonight she was a highwayman, dressed in the guise of a young man wearing a dark blue coat, waistcoat, breeches and top boots, overlayed by a warm cape. Atop her long, black curls, she wore a short, black wig, a black beaver hat and a half-mask. Was she truly here, in the north of England, at last? Was she truly preparing to waylay Lord Rayneworth's coach? What if she was captured? She could be hanged for so heinous a crime as thievery on the King's highway.

But thick clouds overhead, a narrow country lane choked with ancient trees, and dense shrubbery lining the lane had all united to protect her. In a word, she was concealed perfectly for robbing a nobleman of wealth and consequence and for exacting from the sixth viscount, Lord Rayneworth, a few guineas to help relieve the sufferings of the poor. If he proved unwilling, she might just exact a kiss from him as well!

Of course Lord Rayneworth had not been a nobleman when

she had become acquainted with him four and a half years earlier. At that time, he had been merely Hugo, brother to her dear friends Judith and Constance Leighton, whom she had met at Miss Teversall's Select Seminary for Young Ladies of Quality when she was sixteen. In truth, he would never be an exalted *Lord Rayneworth*. To her, he would always be her darling *Hugh*, the man she loved.

Now she meant to play the highwayman and to rob him. Or at least to help steal his purse, since it was not she who had planned tonight's attack upon the viscount, but rather a famous outlaw known throughout the North Midlands as the White Prince.

Generally, highwaymen were no longer a threat to the traveller in these modern times. Well-guarded mail coaches and lighter, quicker carriages had all but eliminated the persistent menace of highway robbers who, even thirty years ago, had been the terror of the roads.

But the White Prince, who stood a few yards from her with one of his regular soldiers in attendance upon him, was not an ordinary highwayman. He was her very dear friend, Laurence Somercote, a man who had been the salvation of the destitute all over Derbyshire and in other parts of the North as well, for the past two years. Times were hard for everyone, but especially for the poor. Because of the unhappy results of the Corn Laws, bad harvests of late, and the displacement of cottage industries with large, mechanized textile mills, a growing poverty had come to the land. Numerous families had been left without sustenance or the means of earning a living. It was for them that Laurence, acting as the White Prince, demanded his highway tolls, selecting his coaches carefully from those travellers whom he knew to be well-shod.

She had arrived at the village of Abbot's End earlier that afternoon with the sole intention of paying a visit upon the nearby Hathersage Park—home to Lord Rayneworth, his four sisters, and his brother, Kit. But before sending a missive to Judith and Constance informing them of her presence in Derbyshire, she had left the Cat and Fiddle Inn at which she was staying to take the air. It was then that a lame beggar named Gates had accosted her. So careful was the beggar's speech, costume, and mannerisms that nearly ten minutes of conversation with the interesting creature actually passed before she knew that he had some mischief brewing. He then tricked her into accompanying him to the smithy where he was employed, gave her a fright by pretending to abduct her, and afterward revealled his astonishing identity to her—he was none other than Laurence Somercote.

How astonished she had been!

But hours of delightful conversation had ensued. No, he had never gone to Virginia as was believed of him. Yes, he enjoyed immensely his ruse and his robberies. Was his army a large one? Hardly, but he did have splendid support among the townspeople and throughout the villages of Derbyshire. Many would rise up to protect him if the militia one day captured him.

He then persuaded her to cast all caution to the wind and join him on one of his adventures. She had been intrigued from the first, having always been of an adventurous turn herself. When she learned that his next victim was Rayneworth, how could she resist?

He explained his reason for choosing to rob the viscount. "I know he has struggled mightily to restore his own estates—his father was grossly improvident, a great gamester by all accounts. I also know that there is not an estate in all of Derbyshire whose farmers have fared as well as his because of his efforts at improving his lands. But Merry, he has neglected to exert his influence on those of his class who have increased the misery of the North Midlands, instead of eradicating it. I want Rayneworth to know he has failed to serve his title, even though I am aware he has set an excellent example where his estate is concerned."

Merry had not been at all certain what Laurence meant by Hugh failing to *serve his title*, but whatever his reasons, her course was fully decided—she would dress herself as a young man and play the highwayman.

So, here she was now, midnight upon the land, butterflies dancing riotously in her stomach, her heart straining into the darkness, longing for Hugh's coach to appear. She stamped her booted feet and slapped her arms to keep the cold from creeping into her bones.

Drifts of snow lined the lane leading to the viscount's ancient home of Hathersage Park. She again searched the gloomy, shadowed vista before her, through thick stands of oak and beech trees which swarmed about the lane like dancers in a crowded ballroom, seemingly permitting passage only upon a whim. When would Hugh's carriage lamps flicker through the trees and announce his arrival?

Perhaps if she stared and wished hard enough her wait would be over and the man she had so longed to see again would appear suddenly before her. But no matter how fiercely she attempted to part the darkness with her gazing and wishing, and wishing a little more, nothing appeared magically to dispel the gloom.

A gust of cold December wind shivered through the leaves of the tall, majestic branches overhead, a laughing sound as though the trees were mocking her for arriving in Derbyshire uninvited.

What folly!

Much she cared any longer if it was folly to pursue a man. Let the trees laugh, and the night yawn at her in its darkness—she would be with Hugh once more and that was all that mattered! She was willing to set aside her pride in order to discover why he had stopped corresponding with her so suddenly only five months earlier. And why he had told her to get herself a husband!

She didn't want another man to take as husband!

She wanted only him and for that reason she had journeyed from her home in the South of England, near Brighton, to the colder, more forbidding North.

A fevered excitement rushed through her as she thought of Hugh, wondering if he would be glad she had come to Derbyshire to see him, yet fearing he would reject her. But whatever the outcome, she was happy to be so very near Hathersage Park at last.

Something caught her eye. A light in the distance, a coach-lamp which behaved like a shivering candle in the wind, extinguished then relit a dozen times as the carriage moved forward, emerging from behind one tree then disappearing behind the next.

"Laurence!" she whispered. "A coach is coming. It must be Rayneworth!"

Laurence moved away from his soldier and drew near to her. "Is your mask secured?" His query was a command. "Make certain of it! If anyone recognizes you—and for all we know Rayneworth could have an entire party in his coach—there will be the devil to pay, make no mistake!"

Merry felt for the knot of her half-mask and knew that the ribbons were securely tied. She could see quite well through the slits of the mask, but hoped and trusted that in the dimness of the light provided by Hugh's coach lamps, he would be unable to discern the emerald green of her eyes. If ever he caught a good glimpse of the color, he would know her at once. Since childhood, the unusual, deep color of her eyes had been remarked upon time and time again.

But would he know her by her lips, by her smile, by the evenness of her teeth? Her half-mask only disguised the upper portion of her face just past her nose.

As the carriage lamps drew closer, the cadence of her heart increased, beating strongly in her breast. Would she truly be seeing Hugh after so many years of waiting? It did not seem possible. She felt her knees tremble and she forced herself to take a deep breath, realizing she was scarcely breathing at all. It would not do one whit to swoon at the very moment she needed all her wits about her.

The lane switched back and forth causing the light from the

lamps to dance wildly about. Closer the carriage came. She could hear Rayneworth's horses now, trotting steadily over the familiar, hard-packed road, his postillion calling out encouragement to his horses.

Hugh Leighton, sixth viscount Lord Rayneworth, looked out the window and into the night, letting the black outlines of trees and shrubs lull his mind. He had for a long time recognized that when his eyes were busy and his mind at rest, he was able to solve even the most intricate of difficulties. Presently, he had several dilemmas to resolve in connection to his estates in Derbyshire. For one thing, he was considering reopening an ancient mine on his property from which he would be able to extract the extraordinary Blue-John—a mineral found exlusively in his county. To his knowlege, Blue-John did not exist anywhere else in the world, save Derbyshire.

But the investment required to reopen a mine!

The labor!

He could not begin to fathom the costs involved nor the risks!

But the profits! That was something to consider, indeed!

How strange that his life had taken such a turn that he had begun thinking as much like a man of trade as a nobleman.

In his right hand he held a brass-handled walking-stick which he planted firmly on the floor to keep his balance in the often pitted, dirt roads of the North Midlands. The lanes all about his home of Hathersage Park as well as the several villages scattered about the countryside near Abbot's End, had not yet experienced the renewing effects of macadamizing which many southern highways enjoyed. So twenty jolts here and there, and here again, could mean a bruised body by the time he arrived home. His walking stick seemed to help keep the bumps to a minimum.

If he sometimes felt like an old man because of the stick, he ignored the passing sentiment. Far better to be of a practical turn of mind where travelling was concerned; after all he was a man of business now, and travel had become as critical to the successful renewal of the Rayneworth fortune as was his dogged attention to his estates.

In addition to the mine, he had been contemplating the prospect of cutting down part of his vast home wood in order to increase the farmable land. Selling the timber would certainly help fill his coffers as well, but a good crop-producing farm was what was needed to increase the long-term wealth of his estate. Many farmers throughout the kingdom were struggling to turn a profit, but his tenants had fared better than most. For the past three years he had been involved in the rebuilding of his estate, and during that time he had studied the latest farming methods and had been able to improve his own home farm as well as the farms on his estate.

Somewhere in the far reaches of his mind, he knew that many farmers in Derbyshire were barely surviving, but he couldn't be concerned with them, only with his own tenants. He smiled thinking he was now as much conversant with manures as he was with the conduct expected of a gentleman in a drawing room. In the spring, he intended to journey to Norfolk where he meant to study Mr. Coke's methods, a famous gentleman who had made amazing strides with his own lands. Perhaps a few more lessons in husbandry would serve to complete the reparation of the Rayneworth fortune.

A long road, he thought with a sigh. He was all of seven and twenty, yet felt nearer to forty if the truth be told. He had left his boyhood long ago and with another deep sigh realized he would never again know the joys and freedoms of those years, of galloping into the wind and taking a hedge or drystone wall without the least concern for his safety. The years now stretching before him would be filled with rising early and removing after a hasty breakfast to work in his study. Day after day, he would examine his estate books, meet with his staff, argue out priorities for needful repairs about his home and his outbuildings with his trusted bailiff, try to make wise decisions about the development of his lands—this was the portrait of his future now.

All these thoughts, mingled with the concerns for reopening the mine, moved through his mind in a tempo fixed to the steady clip-clop of his horses' hooves along the packed dirt of the lane. He would be home soon.

Home. Hathersage Park. Honoria.

Why did these thoughts bring a heaviness to his heart instead of joy?

Merry's knees were trembling now. She knew a sudden impulse to turn around and bolt away, but she stilled the panic rising in her chest, reminding herself that this was Hugh's carriage fast approaching. Another deep breath.

He was nearly upon them now.

The last bend in the lane showed long shadows of trotting horses, the reflections of the carriage lamps rising and falling against a darkened, snow-shrouded hedge of rhododendrons and blackthorn, and upon grassy weeds thick at the base of the shrubs. The horses came into view first, light from behind casting the postillion's face in blackness, the interior of the travelling chariot shadowed and gray. Merry's gaze seemed fixed to the box-like glass lamps on either side of the front of the coach, her limbs frozen as Laurence, his pistols primed and ready, suddenly moved past her, his attending soldier following quickly behind to take up a station in the center of the road.

The boy, so slight of frame, seemed oddly confident in this moment as he squared his stance in front of the oncoming horses and fired one of his own pistols into the air, then leveled the second at the oncoming coach.

Rayneworth's horses started at the sound of the pistol-shot, leaping into the air as the postillion called sharply to them. He brought the leader to earth with a sharp, downward tug on the reins. The entire equipage came to a jerking halt.

Laurence marched quickly toward the horses, refraining

from speech as he held the pistol at the postillion's head. The postboy's response was delivered in a slow nod, his gaze never waivering once from Laurence.

Laurence turned and gestured for Merry to move forward. She began walking toward the coach, her knees still shaking ominously and for a second she thought the dizziness which had assailed her earlier might now cause her to swoon. She swallowed hard and took another deep breath, the movement of her feet helping the sensations of fainting to disappear.

She passed Laurence, then the second team of horses. She could not resist looking through the front window-glass of the coach. The face of the occupant was fairly impassive save a curious lift of his brows, but the features were familiar—her beloved Hugo, and he was alone.

Merry watched him intently as he returned her gaze in full. Even in the palest of lights, with the midnight shadows casting his features in strong relief, she could see that he was still as handsome as ever. His thick auburn hair was cut simply *á la Brutus* and brushed forward to sweep lightly over his temples. Thick, arched auburn brows accentuated clear, blue eyes. His complexion was extremely fair and unmarred by even a hint of a freckle. His chin was firm and proud, his lips determined. His shirtpoints seemed to deepen the hollow of his cheeks, enhancing the high curve of his cheekbones, perhaps his finest feature. His aquiline nose gave strong indication of an ancient and proud lineage reaching back into the days when reckless tribes and remnants of a Roman invasion marched across England, when the Danes overran the Midlands and Derbyshire became part of the great Danelaw, of an England when warfare was accomplished with the skill of bow and arrow, by Anglo-Saxon and Norman. Her gaze was again drawn back to his blue eyes, eyes which still regarded her intently, the blueness masked by the dark of the night.

What was he thinking? she wondered.

Chapter Two

Hugh had been attempting to comprehend why he suddenly felt unhappy about being so near to home when the sound of a pistol shot brought his reveries to an abrupt end. His horses had leaped into the air and afterward his postillion had brought them to earth. Just as abruptly, his coach came to a jolting halt. Only the brace of his walking stick against the coach wall in front of him kept him from sliding from his seat.

"What the devil!" he had cried, leaning forward to peer through the front window of his coach. He took in quickly the sight of an arrogant youth stationed in front of his cattle, pistol in hand, of a taller, more commanding fellow holding his pistol to the postboy's head, and of a smaller man moving slowly from behind him.

For a moment, his gaze had been drawn back to the taller man. What a fine pair of shoulders he had and a bearing like a prince. He could be none other, Hugh thought, than the White Prince. He had frequently heard the servants speak of the famous outlaw in voices of awe and respect. Even Mr. Belper, who held the living at Hathersage Park and who was not given to expressing many opinions, said that the White Prince ought to have been with Wellington at Waterloo in '15—surely then a great many lives would have been saved, for a more able officer one could not find than a man who could attract an army to him as the White Prince most surely had.

But as the smaller man had come from behind the outlaw, Hugh's attention had been quickly diverted. It would seem a youth was to perform the honors this night.

Who was he, he had wondered. A new man, most likely, by his hesitant manner.

Hugh narrowed his eyes.

Man?

Hardly a man, he decided suddenly, as the young outlaw swept up a fine hand to adjust the strings of *her* black half-mask. And certainly not with lips like those, he thought, as the soldier appeared within clear view of his window. Light from his carriage lamps illuminated her countenance and exposed kissable, cherry-red lips. A female, most decidedly, and a deuced pretty one too, if he was any judge of ladies sporting half-masks!

When she stopped to scrutinize him through the window-glass as well, he had been slightly amused at first. Then a rather odd feeling crept over him, as though the past had suddenly risen up from the grave of his mind and had begun pouring one memory after another over him. He began to recall in swift succession days spent in the saddle, afternoons swimming in the river to the south of Hathersage, descents down the hundred steps at Bagshawe's Cavern, all with a feisty young lady in tow.

"Fairfield," he whispered into the cold, dark night air, as the soldier moved away from the window-glass to the door. Now why had he thought of Merry Fairfield? Somehow, the young soldier had put him forcibly in mind of her. Was it possible Merry was in league with the White Prince?

Impossible. Merry was safely ensconced in Sussex and perhaps engaging the interest of one of her numerous beaux, just as he had told her to do in his last letter to her. By now, she might even be married.

He heard the latch lift and thoughts of Merry dissipated as quickly as they had come. Of the moment, he ought to be more concerned with the fact that very soon this young woman would attempt to rob him. What ought he to do?

Several schemes shot through his mind. The most promising

one remained, but would he be wise to implement it? He thought it very possible he could hold the woman captive and force the White Prince to let him pass, on pain of her death, then turn her out of the coach a half mile or so down the road. But the smatterings of gossip he had heard regarding this out-law and his army had led him to believe that more than just these three were involved in the attack. A score of the White Prince's army could be hidden in the trees and shrubs sur-rounding the lane. He had no reason not to believe, given the current unrest throughout England, that the outlaw's army was both numerous and well-mounted. He strongly suspected his coach was all but surrounded.

For that reason, he decided to submit to the young woman's attack, but when the door opened an inch, a spark of mischief flicked within him and he could not resist giving the door a shove with his walking stick, an action which gave the female a decided start, as she jumped away from the door. She was not, however, easily overset. She returned to the doorway, a soft smile on her face as she clicked her tongue at him.

"I'll 'ave thy purse, m'lord," the soldier said in the peculiar manner of Derbyshire common folk. "An be quick about it!"

He looked at her face carefully, trying to peer through the slits of her mask in order to determine the color of her eyes. But the night was too dark, permitting him only to see a glittering of pure pleasure cloaked deep within the slits.

He lifted a brow, and smiled faintly in return. "You'll have to come into my coach and get it," he responded simply.

Again she clicked her tongue. "Dunna think to be wrestlin' wi' me, m'lord. That be the White Prince, in case thee were mistakin' him fer an 'alfling. He wouldna like it above half if thee were to do me harm."

Wrestling with her! Now there was an image which again forced a dozen memories to surge forward, of a summer he had been trying desperately to forget for the past five months. The woman before him disappeared entirely, as one memory in particular rose above the rest. Gone was the night, gone were all the horrific events of the past three years since his parents' deaths, gone was the terrible weight upon his shoulders.

It was summer. An idyllic summer, with a pungent forest of oak to the east, a sheep-dotted hillside to the west and in between a dale rich with busy farms, hay and a trout-laden stream. Bad harvests had not yet taken a toll on the land.

He felt young, without the smallest care weighing him down, reckless, free. With Merry galloping along beside him, he was in the saddle, riding hard, a warm, August sun on his face and a cool breeze blowing over him which quickly dried the sweat from his brow. The next moment, he was flying from his horse—why, he couldn't remember—and then sinking into the slithery bank of a small stream. He regained his feet to Merry's laughter, his breeches soaked and streaming with muddy water, a sharp pain pulsing low in his posterior and radiating at least five vertebrae north.

Merry had looked down at him, swinging her horse around to get the best view of his predicament, arrogantly safe in her saddle, unsympathetic to the last, her face and voice lit with an amusement that rankled sorely.

In truth, she had been in the habit of laughing at him quite frequently, completely unimpressed by his station and future prospects—her deep green eyes a sparkling reflection of the summery landscape all about them.

There was nothing he could do but pull her from the saddle, into the brown mud beside him. She was outraged and immediately let the mud fly. He responded, wrestling with her, until they were both completely covered.

Of course he had kissed her. More than once that summer.

Of course they had exchanged fledgling vows of love.

But she had been so young, a chit not yet out of the schoolroom. He had determined in his mind to let her grow up, unfettered by what was probably a mooncalf sort of love between them anyway, knowing that it was likely she would forget him before even a twelve-month had separated them.

But he had always hoped to meet her one day in London,

during her first season; then perhaps he would approach her with the hope of discovering if her womanly heart could love him.

She was so unlike any young lady he had ever known. He wondered if she had changed, if she had adopted those artifices all too familiar to him from his own earlier visits to the Metropolis—the mincing steps, the fluttering fans, the quickly-batted eyelashes. Lord, he hoped not. Surely she would never be so missish, and undoubtedly wasn't, especially if all that Judith and Constance had reported to him was true.

But his life had taken a sharp turn when his parents died. He had not been to London for her first season, or any season following. Now it was too late. Would he ever be able to forget her?

He blinked, the memories suddenly dissipating as the soldier extended her hand to him and again commanded, "Thy purse, m'lord!"

The young woman came sharply into focus.

He looked at her, at the half-smile on her lips, at the glitter of her eyes behind her half-mask and knew she was delighting in the robbery. As he watched her, a sensation of longing so desperate welled up in him that it was all he could do to keep from pulling the soldier into the coach and holding her fast, as though in doing so he could for just a moment recapture the summer shared with Merry. Only with the strongest of efforts did he repress the impulse, swallowing hard as he took firm hold of the young woman's outstretched hand, and turned it palm up. He was a little surprised that she didn't flinch at his touch, nor did the smile diminish from her lips.

She certainly had pluck, this one!

He withdrew his purse from the pocket of his coat, placed it on the palm of her hand, then folded her fingers up about the small, leather pouch.

How sweetly the damsel smiled for him then, a full, glorious smile, her task complete. He released her hand, but before he knew what was happening, she climbed quickly into his coach and fairly threw herself into his arms, embracing him fully.

The feel of her young, warm body against his was like having all the pain of the last several years stripped from him for the barest moment. He found himself holding her fast, encircling her with his arms, returning her embrace. She drew back slightly, yet still clung to him, apparently wanting to look at his face. How tenderly she smiled!

What would she do next, he wondered. He found himself utterly dazed by her reckless, heedless conduct. When she pressed her lips to his, he was stunned not less so than by the extraordinary sensations which began quickly to devour him as he responded to the young woman's kiss. He shouldn't be feeling this way toward a complete stranger. Why was he taking such pleasure in her soft lips and in her youthful body? Perhaps so many sudden memories of Merry Fairfield had simply overwhelmed him as he gave himself thoroughly to a veritable whirlpool of inexplicable emotions and powerful physical desire. He returned her kiss passionately, his arms holding her fast, his hands and fingers grasping at her cape in fevered strokes. His lips were hard upon hers as he thrilled to her eager response, her own hands no less clutching as she pushed back the binding capes of his greatcoat and slipped her arms tightly about his neck.

He thought she heard him whisper his name, *Hugh*. Was it possible he knew her?

How long he kissed her, he could not know. Time seemed to become all tangled up in his mind. But it was undoubtedly longer than the White Prince could tolerate, for his voice alone, as he called for his soldier to leave the coach, forced her to draw back from him.

With her hand still secured about the back of his neck, she whispered again in her common voice, "A fair payment, I expect, eh, m'lord?"

She then tried to pull away, but he found himself not wanting to let her go, and kept her close to him. Only after he had kissed her again, did he answer her question. "A fair payment, indeed," he responded hoarsely.

With that, she drew away from him, turned around and leaped lightly to the ground. She gazed back at him steadily, her hand upon the door, as though she wanted to say something to him. She chose instead to offer him a salute and afterward gave the door a quick shove, shutting him up tightly inside.

Almost as quickly, his postillion set his team in motion. His coach quickly rolled past the young soldier and the White Prince. The third man had already disappeared into the woods.

The robbery was over.

Hugh leaned his head against the squabs and squeezed his eyes shut. When the young woman had closed the door upon him, he had felt as though she had sealed him up in a tomb. What a peculiar sensation. Coupled with his inexplicable unhappiness about returning home, a nauseating panic overcame him, as though he was indeed trapped in a tomb and couldn't breathe. In a moment of revelation, he knew that some cruel force had just revealed to him a portrait of the life he should have had in painful contrast to the existence he was currently enduring. His chest grew tight with sadness and fear.

Had he been a wild animal he would have let out a great, savage roar.

But there was nothing he could do about the path stretching out before him. Nothing. His commitments and responsibilities were sealed and had been sealed from his birth. He had now only to endure with grace the hardships assigned to him.

As he had done many times before over the last three years, he clenched his jaw tightly shut, and intoned a phrase which he repeated several times whenever he felt so keenly the loss of his hopeful, idealistic youth. *For Hathersage, for my heirs.*

Chapter Three

Merry joined Laurence and his compatriot as they moved quickly onto the narrow path which wended its way through the beech wood beside the lane. They moved briskly, away from the site of the robbery, deeper into the woods.

She tossed Laurence the purse, holding back the happy laughter which rose up in her throat, but which if released would have exposed their position. She knew the rule—a speedy, silent retreat was absolutely essential to the success of any given attack. But she didn't want to keep silent—not by half. She wanted to turn about in circles, to squeal, to cry out, to exclaim the depths of her joy, her happiness.

She had not erred afterall in coming to Derbyshire. Tomorrow, she would go to Hathersage Park and present Hugh with his purse, then kiss him again by way of explanation. Surely he would then confess he loved her, that he had been in love with her all these years, that he wanted to marry her. Surely!

She felt Laurence take her elbow and give her a slight shake. She sensed something was amiss and turned toward him. The other man passed them by upon Laurence's signal. A few seconds later they were alone.

Laurence began in an urgent, low voice, "Merry, why didn't you tell me you were still in love with him?"

"I know it was wicked of me to kiss him," she returned hurriedly, also in a whisper as she tried to explain. "But I couldn't resist. Please don't come the crab over me. You've no idea how happy I am! And don't scowl so! It is most unbecoming!"

"Damme, how do you know I'm scowling when it is so dark I cannot even see the smallest glimmer in your eyes? But that's not important. Merry, didn't you know? Rayneworth is not free to give his heart to you."

Merry shook her head. Laurence wasn't making the least bit of sense to her. "Whatever do you mean, *Rayneworth is not free.* I know he is greatly concerned about his estates, that he spends most of his waking hours engulfed in business, but—"

"—you mistake my meaning," he said somberly, his hand still upon her elbow.

A pause ensued, a silence which in quick stages brought Merry's high spirits plummeting to earth. She again shook her head. "I don't understand," she reiterated.

"I wish I'd known," he murmured. She could see by the silhoutte of his head that he had turned away from her slightly. "Damme, Fairfield!" he continued, clearly agitated. "I thought you knew. I swear I did. The fact is, Rayneworth is betrothed. To Miss Youlgreave, Honoria Youlgreave. They are to be married in little more than three weeks—Christmas Day, in fact. I'm sorry. I suppose I was too enrapt in my own schemes of the moment to realize that your motives in attending me tonight were not entirely selfless. Dash-it-all! You would have made him a fine wife! A very fine wife, indeed! But you are come too late!"

Merry felt as though the breath had been knocked from her. Her mind was a blur of disjointed thoughts. The darkness of the hour suffocated her.

She drew in a deep breath and forced herself to think.

Hugh to be married.

Merciful heavens, *Miss Youlgreave!*

Honoria Youlgreave!

"The coldest fish in all of England," she murmured. "To marry my Hugo?"

"Yes, yes!" he whispered. "Now not a word more. We must catch up with Am—that is, my soldier. Now not another word!"

The White Prince insisted that those who numbered among his soldiers would never know one another and so names were not to be employed. Merry only vaguely realized Laurence had almost revealed the identity of his compatriot, but the knowledge fell quickly from her thoughts, unable to compete with the devastating news he had just imparted to her.

She fell into step behind her friend, the younger soldier leading the way to where the horses were hidden. She felt numb and oddly ashamed for having kissed a betrothed man with such abandon.

Hugh to be married.

Her heart felt as though heavy iron weights had been attached to the bottom of it and she was being drawn down into a deep, dark well.

She had waited for years for Hugh to come to London during at least one of her first seasons. For years she had been anxious to rekindle the brief vows of affection they had exchanged four and a half years prior. He had told her then that she was far too young to accept his hand in marriage when she had not even enjoyed her first season. She had known even then that what she felt for Hugh was not merely a schoolgirl's silly *tendre*, but a love which would abide forever. But she had submitted to his wishes knowing that for the most part it seemed like a sensible course to take. She had swallowed her disappointment, had returned to her home in Sussex near Brighton like an obedient child, and had had her first season—and her second and her third, but still Hugh had not come to her!

His correspondence to her, since the death of his parents, had been most discouraging. In the few letters he had sent her, she had not recognized the man she had tumbled in love with that idyllic summer so many years ago. But how could he have remained so high-spirited and carefree when from all accounts, the Rayneworth estate had been left in shambles. And worse followed a year later when his sister, Amabel, only fourteen at the time, suffered a serious injury while driving out with him in his curricle. Since that accident she had not left her Bath chair.

His last letter, nearly five months old now, had been short and to the point—she should marry one of the handsome young men he had heard tell of from Constance and Judith.

But that was absurd. In the three years since she had come out, not a single gentleman had come close to stealing her heart as Hugo had.

Now he was to be married.

As she tramped along silently into the woods, tears began to slip down her face. She pulled her hat from her head and tore the half-mask from her face in order to swipe at the tears with the sleeves of her coat. She felt as though she was caught in the midst of a horrible nightmare. Why had she waited so long in coming to Derbyshire? Why? Surely the man who had just returned her kisses a moment ago was not a man entirely enraptured of his bride-to-be! Why then had he offered for Miss Youlgreave? If only she had come to Hathersage sooner? If only . . .

Merry awoke slowly to the sound of traffic rolling along Abbot End's High Street. Her bedchamber on the first floor of the Cat and Fiddle Inn faced the street. She found the crunch of carriage wheels on cobbles and the clip-clop of horses hooves a soothing rhythm as she slipped from sleep into that netherworld just before waking.

In the queer turns of her sleepy brain, she believed she was back in Sussex, in her own bed. Dreamily, thoughts of Hugh filled her mind as they had nearly every morning since she had first met him so many years ago, of his auburn hair and aquiline nose, of his charming smile and handsome face.

She lay on her side, her hand tucked between her cheek and her pillow. She opened her eyes lazily and saw the white linen pillowslip, and the gray woolen blanket. How odd. Her bedcovers were not gray at all, but a beautiful rose silk.

Well, never mind that. She closed her eyes and culled from her memory one of her favorite remembrances of Hugh, of descending the hundred steps of the Bagshawe Cavern, practically clinging to his coattails. She wished she was in Derbyshire, at Hathersage Park even now, instead of home in her bed.

It rained so often at Brighton, near the sea.

But snow lined the lanes.

Yet there was no snow in Brighton, especially so early in winter, if at all.

Snow. Hugo. Hathersage Park.

Why did she suddenly begin to feel uneasy? She opened her eyes, trying to bring her vision and her mind into focus. A very pretty alphabet sampler in blues and yellows hung on the wall. Now who had stitched that piece of work, she wondered. She knew she had not performed the task. And what was it doing in her bedchamber?

Her sense of anxiety grew. She rolled onto her back and stared up at the ceiling. A white plaster ceiling, cracked in places, stared back at her instead of the beautiful rosette of rose-colored silk which adorned the canopy over her bed.

An ugly sensation of panic ripped through her as the last vestiges of sleep drifted away from her mind. She sat bolt upright, feeling ill and only with the strongest of efforts did she keep from casting up her accounts. Memories of the night before surged through her in heavy waves—happiness at being kissed so thoroughly by Hugh striking her one moment, then grief at the news of his betrothal slaying her the next.

Rayneworth.

Honoria Youlgreave.

A Christmas wedding!

She flew out of bed as though each successive thought had tightened up a spring within her and uncoiled abruptly upon the word *wedding*.

She had to do something and be quick about it or her heart was likely to burst! Or even worse, she might dissolve into a pitiful watering pot, like so many other silly females she had known over the years.

But what could she do? Good Lord in heaven she had wracked her poor brain the entire distance home, from the lane in the woods near Hathersage Park, dipping down into the valley of Abbot's End, to the well outside the village where she had changed her clothing quite scandalously behind a large pine tree. But no clever plan had come to mind.

She crossed the chamber quickly to stand before her wardrobe, jerked the doors open and surveyed the numerous gowns she had brought with her from Sussex. They were all of the finest fabrics and shaped into the latest fashions by a skilled Frenchwoman, all designed with a single purpose—to attract Hugh's notice.

But she was too late! He was betrothed.

She had to think of something, concoct some way of reawakening his heart toward her.

But he was betrothed! Even if his heart could be won, he was not free to love her!

As she pulled a gown of dark blue velvet from the wardrobe and slid it over her head, she again tried to conceive of some scheme by which she might harnass hope and lay claim to some chance of a future with Hugh, but her imagination seemed dull, unequal to the challenge.

But then, how could a scheme emerge when her mind was positively beleaguered by thoughts of Hugh's betrothal? For one thing, why had he offered for Miss Youlgreave when surely he could not have forgotten the vows of love they exchanged so many years ago?

But they had been younger then—she, not yet seventeen while he was only three and twenty. Now, four years and more had passed, he had failed to come up to scratch and he was betrothed to the last woman on earth Merry believed could ever make him happy.

What had happened to Hugh that he would have begged for the hand of Honoria Youlgreave—of all creatures? Of course there were the many obvious answers. She was well-born, well-bred, well-connected, sufficiently dowered and quite pretty. But even Judith and Constance agreed she was about as lively as a tree stump. And Hugh could never be happy with someone so prosaic, so dull, so, so dutiful!

She moved to the window, near the wardrobe, ignoring the cold wood floor beneath her bare feet, and touched the cool glass. She whimpered out of sheer frustration especially in light of the worst truth of all, that she had only herself to blame for the betrothal. She should have come to Derbyshire sooner! Every instinct even as early as a year ago had been urging her to make the trek north from Sussex. Decorum alone—well, perhaps mixed with a little pride—had held her back. After all, it was most improper for a lady to invite herself to a gentleman's home.

In the midst of her hapless reflections, her stomach rumbled, demanding attention. She realized she was very hungry after her night's adventure. Besides, she never succeeding in solving even the simplest of difficulties until after she had breakfasted. Perhaps a tray of food would serve to enliven her imagination along with a warm fire on the hearth.

A few minutes later, she ordered a meal brought to her bedchamber and requested the services of one of the maidservants for her morning toilette.

A half hour later, after her gown had been properly buttoned, her long, black curls styled with the use of curling tongs, and a tidy fire lit upon the hearth, Merry was prepared to begin the day. She sat before an ample meal of sweet oatcakes, thin slices of Yorkshire ham, a baked apple, and a cup of chocolate. She ate heartily, unwilling to permit even the direst of predicaments to prevent her from enjoying a finely cooked meal. Besides, Derbyshire fare was among the most delightful.

When she had savored the last morsel of ham and rolled a final swig of chocolate slowly about her tongue, she set her mind to considering the grave difficulty before her. Her thoughts still seemed chaotic. But at last she was able to place them into some semblance of order. She needed more information before deciding what she ought to do next.

Immediately she penned a missive and had it sent to Hathersage Park. Judith and Constance would be able to provide her with just such details as she required. Before she entered Hugh's home, she needed to know as much of his betrothal and of Honoria as possible. For one thing, if Hugh had actually tumbled in love with Miss Youlgreave, then she had only a single course open to her—to congratulate him on his betrothal and to wish Miss Youlgreave well.

But if circumstances alone had prompted the betrothal, well then, perhaps something might yet be done.

She took up a vigil upon a winged chair of colorful chintz near the window, a poem of Lord Byron's open on her lap and her feet planted upon a footstool. She could do nothing until she received an answer to her letter.

All she could do now was wait.

She laughed, thinking how ironic it was that she had waited four years and look where *waiting* had gotten her—in the most desperate quandry of her life!

Chapter Four

Constance Leighton gripped her twin sister tightly about the waist. She was trembling at the thought that she and Judith were about to confront their eldest brother, Hugo, regarding a Christmas ball—a former tradition at Hathersage Park which they hoped very much to restore. Since the death of their parents, Hathersage had become a dull place, bereft of most of the occasions which had made life in the great country house a joyous, vibrant affair. Constance, along with Judith, wished for even a little of that joy to return to their home. To have all the attendant festivities of a Christmas ball ringing from the rafters would be a wondrous experience. But Constance thought Hugo was as like to agree to the ball as he was to agree to cut off his right thumb.

Judith in turn slipped her arm in support about Constance's waist and gave her a squeeze. "Don't be so henhearted!" she whispered. "He is only Hugo after all, and not likely to bite our heads off for intruding! If he does not like our request, he may simply tell us nay?"

Constance shuddered and moaned faintly. "He will scowl at us and you know I cannot bear the way he draws his brows together when he is displeased. Then he will set about reminding us of how selfish we are being to request anything, when isn't it clear to the whole world how he has struggled and slaved to bring our family about!"

"However did you get to be my sister," Judith retorted, clearly disgusted with Constance's theatrics. "If Hugo were to sneeze, you would swear he was giving you a dressing down! You have far too much sensibility—"

"—and you have far too little, else you would comprehend my quakings and would not make me enter his office so early in the morning!"

"Very true, but for the moment please try to have a little courage."

Constance smiled weakly as her sister scratched quietly on the door to Hugh's study on the ground floor of the great house.

Wealth, of a great and extensive sort, had belonged to the house of Leighton and the viscounts Rayneworth for over two centuries until the mid-eighteenth when Constance's grandpapa developed an uncontrollable passion for the turf. Her own dear father had apparently been no less enthralled with the performance of the four-legged beasts upon a set course and if his accounts were accurate, the whole of her male forebears were mad for cards, for hazard, for gaming of every sort.

Their enthusiasm escaped her entirely, though she strongly suspected the same blood ran in Hugh's veins, or once did. Her memories of him before their parents were drowned in a yachting accident were of a fearless young man who loved riding and hunting, swimming and fencing, every manly art that existed. She had even seen him engage one of the footmen in a bout of fisticuffs—all in fun, of course!

But Hugh was greatly changed, especially from the time he overturned Amabel in his curricle. Indeed, she vowed she hardly knew him at all anymore.

She could scarcely blame him, however, for the change. After all, it would seem her dear papa's penchant for betting on the horses had run amuck and his passion for gaming extended to the East End hells as well. When Hugo inherited Hathersage Park, only the strength of his will had kept the estate from being sold out beneath the family in order to discharge their father's enormous debts.

Poor Papa, and Mama!

Poor Hugo!

Her sympathies, however, were drawn up short quite abruptly by Hugh's voice. "Come!" was the curt invitation to enter, a muffled bark behind the exquisitely carved oak door of his private study across from the rose and green drawing room.

Constance's courage failed her. She whimpered and tried to pull away but Judith held her fast. "Henhearted grouse!" her sister cried, giving the door handle a sharp turn. She threw the door wide and gave her sister a push into the commodious chamber.

Constance fairly stumbled in. Her brother sat at his desk at the far end of the panelled, rectangular chamber. He was scratching at his estate books, which he frequently did. He paused, glanced briefly up at his sisters, dipped his silver-handled pen in the inkwell, and resumed scratching.

Constance started to speak, but he lifted his left hand in a swift, silencing movement, which caused her to clamp her mouth shut and to take a nervous step backward.

"One moment," he said, not unkindly, his pen continuing to scratch as he spoke. "Permit me to finish this entry and I will hear you out." The scratching of his pen became a kind of music to Constance's ear. She began tapping her foot, hearing in her mind a Bach prelude she had only this morning been practicing on the pianoforte.

She waited, but the scratching continued.

Judith spoke, trying to gain his attention. Judith had less patience than anyone. But again the left hand was thrown up. Judith grunted her disapproval, then took up a seat in a black and gold Empire chair near the fireplace to the left of Hugh's desk.

Constance did not want to sit. She had been sitting at the pianoforte for over an hour and she was quite content to move about for a while.

Her gaze drifted to the antiquated map desk of burnished mahogany which sat in the very center of the room, perched

upon a black and red Aubusson carpet. Several of the numerous
flat drawers of the desk were open. Hugh no longer used the
drawers for the ancient seafaring maps which had belonged to
one of their ancestors—a notable admiral of the seventeenth
century—but his own detailed geophraphic maps of the lands
belonging to the Rayneworth estate.

Something about the desk gave Constance pause. She moved
to look at the map spread out on top of the desk and held down
by small, cylindrical pewter weights. Shortly after Hugh had
taken up his duties as the sixth viscount Rayneworth, he had
established a pattern of riding out early each morning, in fair
weather or foul, and examining the whole of his property, one
square acre at a time.

She was still amazed at his having entered upon so enormous
an undertaking, for the Rayneworth lands were extensive. But
beyond the sheer size of the area to be covered, the terrain was
even more formidable. Derbyshire was not in any manner a
flat, comfortable land but rather sat at the base of the Pennine
Mountains and rose in ridge after ridge of newly-birthed hills.
Each hill dipped down to a river and dale only to rise and dip
again to another hill, river and dale.

Hathersage Park was in just that place in the county that the
north half of the estate bore some of the more rugged character-
istics of the hostile high country, while the southern half enjoyed
lower elevations and better farmland. Hugh's land was as varied as Derbyshire itself, dotted with woodlands of beech and
oak, riddled with streams, nestled in a lovely dale which travelled north and magically transformed into rugged hills and
crags which made for fascinating walks. Many of the crags were
steep and treacherous, dropping to rivers below. One of the
crags even had a terrible history of a young lady who, after
being jilted by her betrothed, threw herself from the top.

Constance shuddered in terrifying delight at the mere
thought of being so enamored of a gentleman that death was
preferable to life without him. Judith had always snickered her
disgust at such a silly goosecap of a female, but Constance had

thought her brave and had made up a whole story about the famous maiden. She had one day even hoped to have the story published, but she had failed to finish it. At the very moment the heat of the story was upon her, a most intriguing invitation had come to her and to Judith from a schoolfriend in Hampshire. A regiment had been billeted near the young lady's home and, well, she had to go with Judith to Hampshire and somehow it became impossible to concentrate on such a sad story when so many handsome young officers were running about!

She sighed, her attention again drawn back to the map. She never had that sort of fun at Hathersage. Hugh was too busy to entertain their friends and acquaintances. Still, she was very proud of his efforts even if she did long for a return of at least some of his liveliness.

As she looked at the map, she recognized her brother's hand in the numerous notes—a bog here, a slide of rock there, a mine shaft, a quarry now a lake, references to quail and grouse, the word Blue-John and a question mark following after. A certain awe overcame her, a respect for her brother which, instead of hindering her tongue, loosened it.

"Hugh, have you completed the final acres? Oh, wouldn't Papa be proud of you!"

Her brother had been hastily dipping his pen in the inkwell, but instead of lifting his left hand again to silence her, a faint smile touched his lips. He held the pen silently in his hand as he looked up at her from his desk.

"No, but nearly so," he responded. "Only eleven acres more."

"The treasures you must have unearthed in all that time!"

He nodded. "Indeed, and did I tell you I believe we found another of those curious mounds near the old mine. Siddons believes it is ancient—perhaps two thousand years old or more—bits of pottery and bones inside. I suppose it is not too great a stretch of the imagination to believe that this island has been inhabited for a goodly number of years."

"Mr. Belper showed me his collection of articles he discovered in the caverns only last week. Bones carved into odd shapes. Remember when you and I found that bone in one of the limestone caves with one side whittled to cutting-sharpness?"

"Indeed, yes, and before we had got half out of the cave you had concocted a complete dramatic play of murder and revenge among ancient cavedwellers."

Constance saw his taunting smile and she sniffed, "Well, it certainly could have happened, especially since the murder took place within a family, and the family was large—like ours. Even in this house I can comprehend any manner of motive for wishing to do injury to one's family members—"

"—like a brother wishing to take the ceremonial bone to his sisters because they disturbed him during his projections of how large the deer herd had grown from the following summer and whether or not there would be sufficient food to see the family through the winter?"

At that, Constance grew grievously alarmed, "Hugh, are matters come to such a pass that we might starve this Christmas season?"

"Constance, your imagination is grown far too lively! I was speaking metaphorically regarding interruptions, not food supply."

"Oh, well I am relieved. In which case, er, Judith has something she wishes to ask you. It is of the utmost importance."

Hugh glanced at Judith and saw that she was looking up at the ceiling. To Constance he said, "I believe your sister has already decided that you are the one to broach the subject with me—whatever that subject might be."

"Must I, Judith?" she asked in a small voice. "I know you say he would prefer to hear the request from me, but—"

Judith rolled her eyes at her wavering sister, then approached Hugh's mahogany desk on a sure tread. Constance moved to stand just behind Judith's right shoulder. "Hugo," Judith began in her firm, brusque manner. "Constance and I have been giving the matter a great deal of thought and we believe the time has come to return Hathersage to its most sacred tradition."

Hugh lifted a brow. "Chapel services each morning?" he queried facetiously.

Constance bit her lip as she watched an expression of horror suffuse Judith's face. "Chapel services!" she exclaimed, dumbfounded. "Whyever would you think—! Oh—oh, you are teasing me! How vexing you can be, Hugo!"

"Well you did say *sacred!*"

Judith huffed a little in exasperation. "You know very well I would never ask you to hold chapel services. As it happens, it is a Christmas tradition. At least Mama made certain that such an event occurred each year at Yuletide."

Constance peered at her brother over the safety of Judith's shoulder. She could see the wary light in Hugh's blue eyes and the manner in which his brows were slowly drawing together into his famous scowl.

She sighed, holding no hope whatsoever of a happy outcome. He and Judith would be brangling soon—which was all they ever did. Hugo was as he always was, absorbed completely in matters of business and not in the least concerned that either of his twin sisters would very soon dwindle into ape-leaders if they did not take care!

She listened to Judith presenting her careful arguments for the Christmas ball in her increasingly harsh voice, and she could not but keep from turning away from Judith's back. She found herself facing the map table again, her imagination drifting off to the limestone cave, with its blackened ceiling caused by ancient tribal fires, and the tale she had woven of murder and revenge. She felt very sad of the moment, though she did not know precisely why. She was certain it had something to do with how hard Hugh had been working for so many years and how, after all that work, all he had were these maps to show for it.

Of course that wasn't entirely true; he had Honoria. But at the mere thought of her, Constance shivered mightily, the way she did whenever she was about to contract a putrid sore throat. She wondered vaguely if Honoria ever got sick. She doubted it. Somehow, she didn't believe any form of illness would dare to approach such a humorless creature lest upon introduction, the illness would fall dead.

She giggled to herself. Poor Honoria! Poor Hugo!

If she had any intention, however, of continuing the sympathetic trail of her thoughts, Judith's rising temper forbade her.

"But whyever not!" she heard her sister exclaim. "We are permitted no amusements in this house. But then of course this is *your* house, isn't it! Your siblings might just as well go to the—that is, we might as well not exist! I think you are selfish and mean and—and a care-for-nobody!"

At that, Constance could not keep from turning back to look at her brother. His complexion was high, his blue eyes wide with astonishment. "Care-for-nobody?" he exclaimed, rising from his seat. "Do you think for one moment I wished for this life? Or that I haven't thought a dozen times of selling all and buying a parcel of land in—in Virginia!"

"You have?" Constance cried, greatly surprised.

"Virginia?" Judith exclaimed. She blinked several times and with each blink her countenance grew more subdued. Her eyes lost their fire, her shoulders settled down and a frown wrinkled her forehead. Her voice was considerably abashed as she continued, "You cannot mean what you are saying."

Constance bit her lip. She had never thought of her brother as unhappy but in this moment she believed he was, more than he would ever own.

Hugh sat down, his complexion paling. "Pray forget that I have uttered such an absurdity. I would never seriously contemplate such a scheme, I assure you." He was silent for a moment before reverting to the subject at hand. "As for holding a Christmas ball, try to consider the matter from my perspective and from our good Mrs. Penistone's vantage point. I am to be married in a little over three weeks time and though it is to be a small affair, how easily can Mrs. Penistone have Hathersage

Park prepared not only to receive a new mistress but to have an entire house gleaming with beeswax for a Christmas ball?"

Judith spoke bitterly. "And of course *Honoria* would expect her to have all twenty bedchambers gleaming."

"Judith!" Hugh returned, stunned, staring at her in wide-eyed astonishment. "You would dare speak such an unkindness about the woman who is to become not only my wife but your sister? I cannot credit my ears. When did your heart become so embittered? How can you speak so of Honoria when she is all that is considerate, sweet and—and generous!"

"Generous?" Constance queried, surprised. Though her heart beat strongly in her breast at having chosen such a tense moment to agree with her sister, she felt compelled to continue, "Though I do not mean to give you pain, Hugo, and though Judith has given her opinion more harshly than perhaps she ought, I have seen nothing in your bride which lends me to believe she is as openhearted and generous as you wish us to believe.

"When I told her I was taking a hamper of food to one of the poor in Frogwell, she lectured me for some few minutes, saying that I was only adding to their distress by helping them more than was necessary, that they would become overly dependent upon my beneficence and refuse to labor as was required by their station. I still cannot conceive of what she meant by it.

"She would not even change her rather strident opinion when I explained that Mr. Rugeley had broken his leg a fortnight ago and could not work in the textile mill where he was currently employed for several weeks and poor Mrs. Rugeley was, well, she was bearing her eighth child—though I know it was indelicate of me to say so. Honoria nearly turned purple with embarrassment that I would mention it.

"But Hugo, I still don't see how I was doing more than offering a much-needed assistance. If a man is unable to work and his wife is in child-bed, and the Corn Laws have raised the price of bread to truly unmanageable heights, what more can a family do? He was too proud to ask for help and I only learned of their unfortunate circumstances from Mrs. Penistone, who knew Mrs. Rugeley when she was a child. Honoria could not give me an answer except to say that her uncle believes that the poor are simply a lazy lot and the kingdom needs to be protected against such laziness. But then, I have never liked Sir Rupert. Never!"

Constance watched her brother place his hands upon his cheeks, his elbows upon the desk. He sighed heavily then said, "I cannot possibly begin to judge the situation to which you refer, Constance. I will only say in defense of my betrothed that I have always known her to speak kindly where the poor are concerned. But as for giving a Christmas ball, I must refuse your request for the reasons I have stated. Mrs. Penistone does not need a parcel of work placed upon her shoulders when she is about to receive a new mistress. And now if you will excuse me, I have a great deal of business to attend to."

"Is that all you will say?" Judith asked, her lips pursed tightly together, her shoulders squared against her brother's obstinance.

"Yes," he said flatly, again setting his pen to the paper before him quite vigorously.

Judith wheeled around, giving her skirts a flip and taking Constance by the arm at the same time. Once on the other side of the door, Judith pulled a face in the direction of her brother, huffed once and said, "We will have our ball—all we have to do is set our minds to it! There must be a way! There must! And I don't give a fig if Honoria likes the scheme or not!"

"But Judith," Constance whispered, unwilling to have her voice travel through the door and back to her brother, "Hugh won't have it! You heard him. He is quite set against a ball, or any amusement, as he has been for three years now."

"Well, it is time he changed."

"What do you mean to do?"

"I don't know," Judith responded, placing her hands upon her hips, her expression more determined than ever. "But I will think of something! See if I won't!"

At that moment, Siddons, the butler, appeared bearing a silver salver upon which a missive rested. Constance felt goosebumps suddenly rise upon the nape of her neck and travel in a delicious trail all down her back. An unexpected missive in the early morning hours of an early December day presented every happy prospect of adventure—particularly since neither she nor Judith were expecting to hear from any of their usual friends and acquaintances.

Judith picked up the letter, but before she opened it Siddons said, "Lady Hucklow's carriage is just coming up the avenue. Miss Youlgreave is with her. I thought you might wish to know."

"Thank you, Siddons," she responded. When he moved to scratch upon the door of Hugh's study, she added, "And don't bother his lordship, I will tell him the good news."

Constance suppressed the laughter which rose in her throat. Hugo despised being disturbed by his betrothed and her aunt so early in the day. The entire staff knew as much and it was with some relief that Siddons replied, "Very well, Miss Leighton, as you wish."

When Siddons moved away, she broke the seal, and Constance peered over her sister's shoulder. She read the delightful scribbles along with Judith and, once they realized who the letter was from and that Merry Fairfield was actually in Derbyshire, the twins shrieked in unison, hugged each other and danced about in circles several times.

A moment later, Hugo threw the door open, the expression on his face confounded as he said, "What the devil is going forward!"

Both young ladies stopped abruptly. Constance stepped in front of the missive still held in Judith's hand, and exclaimed, "I am sorry Hugo. I was just, er, just telling Judith the funniest thing that, er, Mr. Belper told me. Pray go back to your study." Then she smiled, a sensation of pure devilment taking her over. "Oh, Siddons was just here and informed us that Miss Youl-

greave is just now coming up the drive, along with Lady Hucklow, of course."

The annoyed expression that overtook his eyes gave her
enormous satisfaction and she turned quickly about, caught
Judith by the wrist and hurried her away.

Once out of Hugo's earshot and having reached the fine
entrance hall, Judith stopped her abruptly. "You quite stole my
thunder, didn't you? I wanted to tell Hugo myself the truly
charming news that his beloved has ignored his wishes yet
again. I wonder what crisis has occurred this morning that must
needs bring the ladies to Hathersage Park."

"It is possible Honoria cannot decide between a gown of
figured muslin or velvet for her nuptials and simply must have
Hugh's opinion before she dares to venture to have the fabric
cut."

"How is it, Constance, that our dear brother chose such a
mealy-mouthed creature to take as wife?"

"Well, she is quite pretty."

"Yes, but then," here she smiled mischievously, pausing
before she continued, as she waved the letter before her sister,
"so is Merry Fairfield."

Constance squealed again. "Merry is come to Abbot's End!
We are saved, Judith! We are saved at last."

"Indeed, we are!"

With that, they dashed up the stairs, neither young lady
wishful of having to endure either Lady Hucklow or Honoria's
arrival!

Chapter Five

Hugh returned to his desk annoyed. He had already spoken several times with his betrothed, requesting that she and her aunt restrict their morning calls to the afternoon. Surely by now Honoria understood that during the first half-dozen hours of each day he must attend assiduously to his ledgers and estate business in order to accomplish all that must be done for Hathersage. The fact that she seemed to simply ignore his wishes on this score distressed him for it meant he would have to confront her yet again.

Upon each previous occasion, when he had addressed the delicate conflict between them, she had most profusely apologized expressing her horror at having caused him distress. At the same time, she attempted to convey her opinion that she would not have disturbed him were it not of the utmost importance.

He was having some difficulty, he mused, helping her to see that deciding between an apricot silk-damask for the morning room or a flowery chintz was not precisely a matter of the utmost importance.

She disagreed, stating that the appearance of his ancestral home was the full expression of his labors. Silk-damask and chintz were critical, as was the planting of a new rose garden beside the maze, as was the purchasing of a Chinese bowl, very *de riguer,* for the mantel in the library. He had been studying a treatise on manures when she had arrived early to discuss the bowl. His thoughts had run in a truly vulgar train and he had had to check his tongue several times to keep from telling her what she might do with her pretty blue and orange bowl.

For now, for the several minutes required for Lady Hucklow's coach to draw up to the front door of Hathersage Park, for the footman to let down the steps for his bride-to-be and her aunt, for the ladies then to be escorted into the rose and green drawing room, and for Siddons to personally convey to him that Lady Hucklow and Miss Youlgreave awaited him in that august chamber, he determined he had at least ten minutes of solitude.

He seated himself at his desk, and again picked up his pen. He saw to his dismay that when he had heard his sisters shrieking in the hallway, he had let his pen drop, which in turn had left a frightful blot on the middle of the page before him. He carefully rewrote the information covered by the splotch of ink, then continued his work, transcribing his notes from his ride of the day before.

Only eleven acres left. He could not credit he was nearly done with a task that was now three years old.

He read the next series of notes on a severely tangled underwood at the edge of the home wood. He read it again. The words seem to run all over the small scrap of paper he held in his hands.

Severely tangled.

His vision blurred. A black silk mask. Fine even teeth. A warm, youthful body.

He gave himself a shake. When had memories of the night's adventure crept into his thoughts?

When would such memories cease creeping up on him?

Why, only a few minutes ago, when Constance had been touching his maps, he wondered if her fingers were upon the lane where the White Prince had waylaid his coach and where the young woman had thrown herself upon him, and kissed him. She had kissed him in the same way Merry had once kissed him, fully, passionately. Good God, had it really been four and a half years since he last saw her! Impossible.

What was she doing, he wondered. Had she fallen in love yet as he had bid her to in his last correspondence? Odd that he couldn't bring himself to tell her he had become betrothed.

And who was it he had kissed last night? Why was he filled with longings he could not put into words?

He again gave himself another shake and concentrated on the piece of paper before him. A tangled undergrowth. Possibly the home of a tribe of rabbits. Soft white rabbits. Soft skin and lips. Her body responsive. He closed his eyes and finally gave in to the call of the memories and felt his arms enfold the young soldier again.

When he had kissed her, he had known the strongest impulse to shut the door fast upon her, and to keep her with him forever. Not that he would have risked the life of his postboy for her, but the impulse, the desire, remained with him yet. Indeed, he had awakened to that desire this morning and for the first few moments of waking, when the gray and rose-pink of dawn was bidding him to begin his day, he had thought of running about at midnight, again, in hopes of provoking another attack by the White Prince and by the young woman whose warm, lithe body had somehow brought old, haunting dreams and desires to the forefront of his mind.

A sharp rapping upon the door pierced through his reveries like a cannon brigade and he drew in a quick breath.

"Come!" he called out, setting pen to paper and pretending to make an entry with a pen that proved dry. Had the ladies already settled themselves in the drawing room? Surely Siddons had not yet seen them disposed upon the sofa in the drawing room.

He looked up and was immediately on his feet, feeling somehow as though he were a little boy caught dipping his sister's braids in the inkwell.

"Honoria!" he exclaimed, not having expected her to come directly to his study.

"Good morning, Rayneworth," she said in her quiet voice as she took a small step forward and smiled sweetly upon him. "I can see that I have caught you by surprise. Have I interrupted you?"

"No, of course not," he began politely, still stunned by her sudden appearance. She was gowned in a pelisse of light pink silk trimmed with gold braid and a matching bonnet, a color that complemented her dark brown hair and brown eyes. Remembering his need, however, to speak to her about letting him work in peace during the morning hours, he added hastily, "That is, yes, you have interrupted me—you know of my need to attend to Hathersage during these first hours of each day—" he saw her shoulders droop slightly "—but it is the nicest sort of interruption."

"I would not have troubled you if the matter were not quite important," she said, in defence of her assault upon his study.

He knew the role he must play, and quickly rounded the desk to take her left hand in his and to place a dutiful kiss upon her cheek.

He grew confused however, and the memories which had been dogging him since the early morning hours suddenly rushed over him. Without thinking, he drew his betrothed into a crushing embrace and kissed her full on the mouth. Every hunger he had been suppressing for years seemed to rise up and demand to be fed. He held her close to him, his lips searching hers fervently.

"Honoria, my darling," he whispered, kissing her cheek. "To think we are to be married in only three weeks time. How I long to be with you." Again he kissed her soft, warm lips.

But the body he held in his arms did not yield to him, nor was there the least answering response of a kindred desire. She felt in his arms as though she had been like a rabbit caught suddenly in mid-path by rushlight, frozen and frightened.

He knew he had erred. He slowly uncurled from about her and because he feared he had fairly frightened her out of her wits by his ungentlemanly conduct, he slowly placed a tender kiss on her cheek, then backed away from her.

"My aunt awaits us in the drawing room," she said haltingly. Clearing her throat a little, she continued more evenly, "I had wanted only a private moment with you to see if you approved of my design for a small table for the morning room. I cannot quite like the carved legs of the several presently in the chamber. There is something vulgar about acanthus leaves on the legs of tables and chairs. I prefer a straight line, which I believe is a better reflection of the solidity of such a house as Hathersage. Wouldn't you agree?"

He felt just as he had when the young woman had shut the door upon him not ten hours earlier. He again felt as though he had been closed up in a tomb.

Honoria crossed the room and presented to him the sketch to which she had been referring. He felt numb as he sat down again behind his desk and mechanically extended his hand to the outstretched drawing. He glanced at her briefly. The only visible signs she emitted, giving indication that she had even recognized his amorous attempt, were that her complexion seemed a trifle paler than usual and her hand shook a little as he took the drawing from her.

He swallowed hard and through a blur of thoughts gazed down at a drawing he could not see. He nodded, "Very nice. You have my fullest approval." Only when he handed it back to her did he realize he had been holding it upside down. Would she even notice or care? He knew he ought to pursue the subject of this ill-timed visit with her, but somehow he had lost heart entirely. Something larger than her disinclination to respect his need for solitude during the early morning hours had just presented itself. He did not know next what to say or do.

Did he even know Honoria?

"You surprised me," she ventured in a whisper, addressing the difficulty between them.

He looked up at her, feeling hopeful suddenly, but she would not meet his gaze.

"I didn't expect to be kissed, otherwise, I would have prepared myself—"

He could see she was acutely embarrassed and he rose hastily to his feet and again rounded his desk to draw near her. It pleased him that she did not back away from him when he took her hand in his, even though he sensed she wanted to bolt from the room. A great tenderness toward her was born in him at that moment as he realized she was a woman with very little experience.

"I was far too hasty," he said quietly. "My love for you can be my only excuse. But will you forgive me for being so precipitous?"

At that she finally looked up at him and smiled faintly. "Of course, I will, Rayneworth." He could not convince her he wished to hear his Christian name on her lips. "But it is my duty to you and I promise to do better next time."

"You are the very best of women," he replied and placed a passionate kiss on her fingers.

She pulled her hand from his clasp and finally stepped away from him. "Now do come meet my aunt," she said, again smiling faintly. "She was very keen on my sketch though she suggested ball and claw feet, but as I said before, I believe a straight, simple leg would by far reflect the order and splendour of your home. Only do tell me your true opinion, for I—I don't believe you had quite enough time to see the sketch as I would have wished you to."

The thought of having to judge between a table leg designed with a ball and claw or a straight foot so bored him that he merely responded, "I shall always defer to your superior judgement in such matters, my dear. I have told you as much before. You will be mistress over my home and as such, you may rely upon me to support your decisions. Besides, you are a woman of excellent taste and refinement."

She seemed satisfied at last and turned to leave the room. As he stepped into the hallway beside her and closed the door upon his study, she said, "Rayneworth, I was very curious about something. When we first arrived, I heard the strangest squealing sound. Do you know what that was?"

He offered her his arm and when she placed a gloved hand upon his sleeve, he said, "Ah, that would be my sisters, I fear. Some anecdote of Constance's set them both to, er, squealing."

"Really," she began in just that tone she employed when she was preparing to gently criticize one of his siblings. "I didn't know such a noise could be heard on the other side of such a heavy front door. It was quite remarkable and my aunt vowed she had never before heard of young ladies being permitted to run screeching about a house. When Siddons opened the door for us—and I do hesitate to mention it for fear of being guilty of actually *tattling*—but Rayneworth, they were running up the stairs! My aunt nearly suffered a spasm! I myself was never more shocked in my life."

Hugh sighed. "I shall speak with them."

"Thank you. It is not my place to correct your sisters, but they do set a truly dreadful example for little Beatrice. When we are wed, I hope they will know that I simply won't tolerate children running about the house without a proper respect for their breeding and station. It is most unbecoming, especially in Judith and Constance who ought to know better."

Hugh found himself irritated, even though when he had heard their shrieks he too had determined he needed to speak with his sisters about their conduct. He did not believe it was proper either. But having Honoria state what she would and would not tolerate at Hathersage was coming it a bit too strong.

He chided himself, for that was not true. She was well within her rights to demand that he speak with his sisters. After all, once Honoria was his wife, she would then be mistress of the house and her wishes would be paramount. But even more so, her desires in everything were supposed to be his first object. With only the strongest of efforts did he repress a sigh.

When they arrived at the rose and green drawing room, Honoria decorously took up her station beside her aunt. After Hugh had bowed low over Lady Hucklow's proferred hand,

Honoria handed the sketch of the table to her aunt and stated that Hugh had found the design charming, indeed that he preferred straight legs to the ball and claw which Lady Hucklow had recommended. Lady Hucklow smiled coldly at Hugh, and nodded her head in acquiescent defeat to her niece.

Hugh sighed inwardly, wondering how it was a sense of strong impatience had returned to him. He feared if the morning continued in this fashion, he would soon be snapping at the servants's heads out of sheer exasperation. Mentally, he decided he had best plan to ride out on his final exploration of the estate as soon as he saw Lady Hucklow's carriage rolling back down the drive toward her home, Dovedale Manor.

He seated himself opposite his bride-to-be. Since the ladies were quickly caught up in a vital discussion of the merits of having two tables made instead of one, since Honoria would be likely to get a reduction in price on the second table were she to have them made at the same time, Hugh found he was able to let his thoughts wander at liberty.

They quickly found an object in Honoria.

Truly, she was an elegant creature. Her figure was tall and almost ethereal in appearance, her limbs graceful and thin, her carriage and countenance very much the lady. Her complexion was so pure it seemed a perfect blending of apricots and cream. Her eyes were the softest doe color and shape, a rich brown and quite round, and should have been her loveliest feature. But there was something in her expression, a calculativeness perhaps, which diminished the beauty of her eyes. Her cheeks were high and well-rounded, her face wide at the brow, drawing to a chin which on a livelier female would have been considered adorable. As it was, the heart shape of her face was perpetually hindered by the coolness and objectiveness of her gaze and by the fact that she rarely smiled.

He wondered why that was, why she did not smile or even laugh very often. Of course, she was of a quite serious and dutiful turn, which was after all the chief reason he had chosen to offer for her.

The business of his life at Hathersage would involve many, many years of hard work and he could ill afford to be wed to a frivolous woman who would pout through the long winters and springs, angry that the little season and the spring season would be forbidden her. When he had stated to Honoria the nature of his needs in a wife, she had seem immensely pleased and had responded with a quite simple statement that her attendance of any of the London gaieties had been only from a sense of duty. "How very ironic," she had added, "that I would be spared such a duty by the necessity of performing another duty much more to my liking here, at Hathersage."

As he propped his elbow onto the arm of the chair in which he sat, supporting his chin with his thumb and resting his fingers against the temple of his brow, he continued to watch her. She had only one real flaw of person, her nose was a deal too aquiline to be accounted beautiful. She wore her dark brown hair in a becoming array of ringlets across her forehead, with the remaining lengths bound into a careful chignon atop her head. He had imagined unwrapping her coiffure—something he certainly intended to do upon his wedding night!—and holding the pretty mass in his hands.

But would she permit him such a liberty?

What an odd thought, yet she was so reserved that somehow it came to him that it was quite possible she would not encourage such an advance. His gaze dropped from her face to fall to the pink silk slippers upon her feet. A feeling very much like disappointment assailed him, but he quickly gave himself a shake, reminding himself that until he was married to her, he would not truly know how she would respond to his touch, to his embrace, to his love.

Yet if the spontaneous kiss he had placed on her lips just a few moments ago was any indication of what his future with her would hold, he could not allow himself to be content. He then reminded himself that love was not his primary objective in marrying Honoria, or anyone. He had a duty to his family name to fill up his nursery, and he had a duty to his estate to provide a careful mistress over his house so that one day his heir would enjoy the benefits of all his labors.

"And what is your opinion, Rayneworth?" Lady Hucklow's melodious voice called to him. She was dressed in a purple velvet pelisse trimmed with ermine. Both her bonnet and her muff were made of the same fabric and trimmed in the same expensive fur.

Hugh blinked twice and smiled, "I do beg your pardon, but I was not attending precisely. My opinion on what subject? The table-leg?"

"No, no, upon the White Prince, of course. Hucklow is becoming daily more determined to bring the scoundrel to heel. The sooner the better, I say. No one is safe upon the road. I shall never forget, when I was accosted by the outlaw, how my heart resounded in my ears until I thought I should be deaf ever afterwards—or swoon, which fortunately I did not since I held my vinaigrette beneath my nose the entire time."

Hugh released his chin from the light grasp of his thumb and straightened in his seat. Lady Hucklow was a woman of short stature who made up for this deficiency by holding a strident opinion on any subject presented to her. Her manners were perfect if not gracious, she governed her temper well, and she was in every possible, outward respect, a lady of quality. Her connections were respectable, her fortune equally so, but her marriage had been one of convenience. She had been wife to Sir Rupert for over twenty years, a childless union which somehow he knew did not displease her.

She winced whenever children were about.

She had for some years been Honoria's guardian and mother since Honoria's parents had died when she was but a child. Her hair was black and peppered with gray and her complexion such that he believed the light rouge upon her cheeks a necessity. She had a birdlike nose, small round blue eyes, an oval face and straight, black brows. She might have been considered a pretty woman in her youth, but the firmness of her opinions had long since replaced her beauty with a hardness of feature he thought less than attractive.

Though he had never truly considered the matter before, he realized suddenly that he did not like Lady Hucklow.

He cleared his throat. "I'm 'fraid that I have very little opinion to offer you." He felt oddly self-conscious, his neck growing warm beneath the swirls of his neckcloth, as he revealed his adventure of the night before. "The fact is, my coach was waylaid last night, coming back from Chesterfield. The White Prince and two of his soldiers took my purse." He did not mention that one of the soldiers had been a young woman.

Both ladies gasped and he immediately regretted having said anything to them.

What a complete nodcock he could be!

"Were you injured?" Honoria asked, her hand pressed tightly against her bosom.

Hugh lifted a hand in protest. "No, of course not, you can see I am perfectly well. They stopped the coach by firing a pistol in the air, then demanded my purse. After I gave it to one of the, er, soldiers, my coach was free to leave. I believe the White Prince uses the money to feed a score of local families. Quite harmless, the whole of it, so pray give it no further thought."

"No further thought?" Lady Hucklow queried, indignant. "You seem completely unperturbed by the fact that you were robbed last night." She rose quickly to her feet, "Come, Honoria! I must tell my husband of this at once! He will want to know of this latest theft. And as for you, Lord Rayneworth, I don't hesitate to say that your indifference to an act of highway robbery is the chief cause that the rest of us are left to endure frights and spasms, to live in sheer terror day after day wondering when we will next have our coaches plundered and our lives become forfeit."

"Surely not forfeit," Hugh said, rising to his feet, deeply concerned that Lady Hucklow was exaggerating the situation far out of proportion. "Everything about the *attack* was conducted with expediency and respect. I never once felt my life endangered. The White Prince and his lot are not after all a band of Vikings come to pillage Abbot's End. Though the outlaw's methods are suspect, I believe his intentions are honorable."

Lady Hucklow stared hard at him down her beak's nose, her small blue eyes opened wide in astonishment, her hands shoved deeply into her muff. "You are beginning to sound like a veritable Jacobin and I won't listen to another word. It must be your youth that would permit you to speak of robberies with such admiring indifference. I mean to send Hucklow to you as soon as I can. He will explain the gravity of the situation to you, since it is become alarmingly clear to me that you haven't the faintest notion that we are all being held hostage by this outlaw's ability to evade capture! I beg you will have my coach brought round at once!"

Hugh found his temper rising and was only able to quell the sharp retort which lit up the end of his tongue when he caught sight of Honoria's imploring expression as she followed behind her aunt.

To add to the awkwardness of the situation, Siddons appeared at that moment bearing a tray of refreshments for the ladies. But Lady Hucklow was adamant. She must leave at once to seek her husband's counsel even though Hugh pressed her to partake of a cup of tea before leaving.

Siddons disappeared back down the hall with the tray in hand. In quick fashion, probably owing to the butler's assessment of Lady Hucklow's temper, the coach was soon heard rolling across the gravel.

When Lady Hucklow crossed the threshold and headed toward the coach, Honoria held Hugh back with a slight pressure on his arm. "Thank you for not speaking your mind to her," she whispered. "She means well and to some extent I cannot help but agree with her—you seem amazingly indifferent to your adventure of last night. Perhaps we can speak of it later."

"Will you be coming to dinner tomorrow night?"

"Yes, as planned."

He possessed himself of her hand and would have lifted her fingers to his lips, but she pulled her hand quickly away, her cheeks flaming. He led her to the coach and when he had closed the door upon both ladies, he returned to slowly climb the shallow steps leading back to the door.

If his heart was heavy with concerns for his future happiness, he ignored the sensation knowing that a return to his duties would, as it always seemed to do, restore his equanimity.

Chapter Six

One hour later, having become completely absorbed in reading Lord Byron's exotic poem, *The Corsair*, Merry fairly jumped from her skin when a rapid knocking resounded on her door.

A silly, schoolgirl's image leapt to mind, of Hugh opening the door to her summons, of Hugh's blue eyes brimming with love and wonder as he met her gaze, of Hugh running to catch her up in his arms, of Hugh kissing her again.

Goodness, what an absurd goosecap she had become!

She stilled her heart and ordered her mind, rebuking such foolish unreasonable thoughts. Only when she was able to breathe deeply and calmly did she respond to the second round of rapid knocks which assailed her bedchamber door.

After bidding her caller entry, two bright, pretty faces appeared, peeping one above the other as the door opened just a crack. Both young ladies, so familiar and so beloved to her, bore mischievous smiles.

"Merry!" they chimed in perfect, delighted unison.

Merry rose quickly from her seat, tossed her book on her bed and crossed the room with her heart full of joy at the sight of her dear friends. When the twins pushed the door wide, she caught each of them up in an embrace—Judith first, then Constance, since that was the acknowledged order for the sisters.

After gazing into their eyes, she burst into laughter along

with them. They had shared too many pranks together at a school they all considered a dead bore for any of them to stand upon ceremony or to behave with perfect politeness and decorum.

Merry took a step away from them, that she might take hold of a hand of each. "But how well you both look in green velvet and military epaulettes!" she exclaimed. "How utterly dashing! Kit must be envious. Does Hugo still keep him about, kicking his heels? I had thought by now he would have enlisted as a common foot soldier rather than remain at Hathersage a moment longer than necessary! He is eighteen, isn't he?"

The sisters looked at one another and grimaced. "Yes, but it doesn't matter, not by half!" Judith cried, turning back to look at Merry. "Things are come to such a wretched pass, you've no notion!"

"Hugo has persuaded Kit to enter the church!" Constance announced. "Yes, well you may stare! I was never more shocked in all my life when Kit told us of his decision a year ago!"

"It is true," Judith cried, probably in response to the gape of Merry's mouth. "Our brother is to take Holy Orders!"

Merry blinked several times, unable to credit what the sisters had just told her. "Holy Orders?" she queried, disbelieving her ears. She released each of their hands and continued, "We are speaking of Christopher, are we not? The young man who once locked you both in the Jericho for an entire afternoon? The same devilish creature who set off fireworks in the caverns? Who disappeared for two days and was finally found trapped in the old mine and came out of his adventure laughing? It cannot be!"

The sisters nodded, their expressions growing dark and somber. Constance closed the door upon the cold draft from the hallway. Judith addressed the difficult matter.

"A clergyman!" she reiterated in disgust. "Oh, Merry, can you imagine Kit becoming a somber vicar, saying prayers over the departed, tending to the sick, preparing sermons for a congregation? All that when he was made to wear a uniform!"

Merry was at first too astonished to give her answer. She was in entire agreement with Judith. In her opinion, Kit was no more fit for the church than a badger to flying on the wing!

"I don't understand," she put forward finally. "But pray, do come in and curl your feet up on the bed if you wish for it. I shan't complain to Hugo about your conduct!"

At that the sisters giggled, some of the weight of the subject at hand lifting for a moment. They disposed themselves comfortably upon the bed, kicking off matching green velvet slippers and unbuttoning warm pelisses almost simultaneously. Had they been a pair of horses, Merry observed—as she watched deft fingers quickly relieve the buttons of their constraints—they would have been considered matched to a shade.

She took up her seat in the winged chair of flowery chintz which was situated opposite the bed. She found, however, that she could not be easy and therefore perched herself on the very edge of the chair, a dozen questions vying for supremacy in her mind all at once. She had so much to discover that it was all she could do to keep her thoughts in some semblance of order. But uppermost among her numerous concerns was what could it possibly mean that Kit had actually agreed to serve in the church instead of His Majesty's Royal Army?

She was anxious to place her questions before the sisters, but she withheld her queries while they removed their outer garments.

Judith and Constance peeled off their pelisses, revealing woolen morning dresses of a light green beneath. Judith caught sight of the volume of verse Merry had tossed onto the bed when her friends had arrived. She picked it up and showed it to Constance. Both girls feigned swooning backwards, falling onto Merry's pillows.

"The Corsair," they breathed together, then rose back up to sitting positions, giggling all the while.

"Oh, how I've missed you both!" Merry cried. "And the season is always too short!"

"Always," Judith agreed, beginning to remove her bonnet which matched her pelisse. Merry noted that the green wool of the twins' morning gowns set off to extreme advantage the auburn richness of their hair.

"I think the season ought to be at least five months long, instead of less than three," Constance echoed, untying the white satin ribbons of her bonnet.

Merry smiled fondly at the sisters. They shared the same color hair as Hugh, each glorious crown of auburn ringlets coming into view as the bonnets were fully removed. Beneath prettily arched auburn brows, light blue eyes twinkled and danced, set in charming oval faces of symmetrical beauty, their Venusian charms hindered only by the *retrousse* noses gleaned from their mother.

Merry adored the Leighton twins.

Judith frowned slightly as she looked at Merry. "Of course, though I sadly miss all my friends in London, the experience of leaving is made far worse by the prospect of having to come home to Hathersage and to Hugo."

"So we try not to come home at all, if possible. Aunt Phillips always invites us to Bath for the summer—"

"—though a hundred times," Judith continued, picking up the thread, "we tried to persuade her upon the beneficial effects of the sea-bathing at Brighton—"

"—which we know you prefer—"

"—still, we could never move her from her plans," Constance finished. "She adores Bath."

The girls sighed together.

Merry set aside the twins's wish that they could be with her in Brighton during the summer and instead addressed the more poignant remarks regarding Hathersage and Hugh. "But I had no notion you disliked coming home. I mean, I noticed you were not particularly anxious to speak of Hu—that is Rayneworth or of Hathersage but I had always supposed it was because you were so enraptured of London."

The twins exchanged a glance full of meaning and purpose.

Judith pulled at an auburn curl near her right temple and, without directing her gaze toward Merry, said, "And you were always so pointed in your questions regarding *home.*"

"Yes," Constance added. "You always asked after Judith's health, then mine—"

Judith continued, "—and of course of the health and spirits of Amabel, Kit, and Beatrice—"

"—then the progress of repairs at Hathersage—" Constance broke in.

"—then regarding the state of the poor in the dale—"

A brief pause ensued followed by the twins declaring in unison, "—and then about Hugo!"

Merry clasped her hands tightly upon her lap as though in doing so she could prevent her friends from learning what they already apparently knew or suspected—that she was in love with their brother. She felt the tips of her ears burn and quickly drew in a deep breath in order to subdue her rising embarrassment. She knew if she did not, her face would soon betray the precise state of her feelings by turning a brilliant crimson red!

"I don't know what either of you mean except that I have always had a fondness for Hathersage and—and your entire family."

"Especially Hugo," Judith stated firmly. She slid off one side of the four-poster bed, and at the same time Constance slid off the other.

"Dearest Merry!" Constance cried as both young ladies crossed the small chamber and sank to their knees in front of her. "We had always supposed Hugo would one day come to his senses and marry you. All of Abbot's End and every village hereabouts could see he had tumbled violently in love with you, and of course there could be no doubt on any score precisely where your sentiments lay. It was utterly charming, so you needn't be in the least mortified, what with the pair of you running wildly about the countryside every morning when Judith and I were still abed—smelling of April and May—"

"—not to mention," Judith added, "stealing off to the yew maze in order to share a kiss or two."

"Hush! The both of you!" Merry cried, releasing her hands suddenly and pressing a palm to each hot cheek. "You make me sound so very wicked."

"Well, you are wicked!" Judith said with a smile, afterward resting her head on Merry's knee. "That is why we have always been such famous friends—"

"—and always shall be—" Constance added.

"—and why you must come to Hathersage and spend Christmas with us."

Merry blinked, staring down at the top of Judith's head. "Spend Christmas with you?" she asked, stunned. She had of course wished for an invitation—indeed, hoped for one—but the offer, having arrived so tidily, took her by surprise.

Constance spoke softly and sweetly. "Well, that is what you wanted, why you came to Derbyshire, isn't it? To be near Hugo? To see if you might rekindle his affections for you?"

Judith peeked up from her reclining position and winked at her. "Well, isn't it?" she asked, her blue eyes twinkling mischievously.

Constance leaned against Merry's arm and regarded her beseechingly, again prodding her. "Yes, isn't it?"

Merry placed an arm about Constance's shoulder and a light hand upon Judith's head. "I shan't pretend otherwise any longer. Clearly I have not been so very clever all these years in concealing the depth of my regard for . . . for Hugh. When your brother did not attend the season last spring, a feeling rather like panic began rising within me and his last letter—"

Judith sat back on her heels abruptly. "What did it say?" she asked, her brows drawn tightly together.

Merry sighed. "Only that he hoped I should soon find a husband and that he did not know if he would have occasion to write again." She remembered having read those painful words, how a cold feeling had swept over her, how even with the sun shining she was certain the drawing room in which she had been standing had turned quite dark, as though a cloud had passed overhead. "Yet, he did not tell me of his betrothal. I only learned of it once I arrived here in Abbot's End. I wish you would tell me of Miss Youlgreave and how it all came about."

The twins eyed one another, two pairs of shoulders slumping in sullen, pouting unhappiness. "Honoria!" they breathed together.

Judith pressed a sympathetic hand upon Merry's arm. "By July of last year I could have told anyone how it would be. She had come to live with her aunt, Lady Hucklow, in late May and it seemed to me the moment she crossed the portal of Hathersage, she behaved as though she meant one day to rule over us all."

"Oh, Merry, you cannot conceive how dull a place the Park is become! Honoria has convinced Hugo that the strictest housekeeping economy is the nearest to God's blessing. He permits only one small fire in the drawing room each evening and none in our bedchambers!"

"And in the mornings when you dress?" Merry asked, stunned.

The girls shook their heads.

Merry stared at the opposite wall, unable to credit her ears. She tried to imagine the man his sisters were portraying to her, but she could not.

"It must be all her influence then," she murmured, not realizing she had spoken aloud.

"Not entirely," Judith said. "I will be fair in this—Hugh was greatly altered before Honoria arrived. You will not know him—I am convinced of it. But won't you come and spend Christmas with us? We need you to set everything to rights, if you can. Hugh shouldn't marry Honoria. No matter how well-bred and accomplished she might be, she will never make him happy. Never! Do say you will come to Hathersage!"

Merry shifted her gaze to Judith's worried eyes. "I will accept your invitation. Indeed, I had hoped you would ask me to come. But as for setting everything to rights, I can make no such promise. I only wish to see for myself whether or not Hugh will be happy with Miss Youlgreave. If I determine he has even the remotest chance of finding a life of happiness with Honoria, I shan't interfere."

Constance bit her lip a trifle before saying, "Well, whatever you do, will you grant me one favor?"

Merry could not imagine what she would say next. When she nodded, Constance continued, "We wish to have a Christmas ball—which Mama and Papa held every year when they were alive, inviting the whole countryside for miles around to attend—but Hugh of course will have none of it. He says it is because the housekeeping staff cannot possibly manage both a ball and his nuptials. But if you knew what a poor affair his wedding breakfast promises to be, you would laugh at his having said such a bad thing about Mrs. Penistone. She in turn fairly clapped her hands with glee when we told her we meant to beg Hugo for a Christmas ball. Mrs. Penistone always took enormous pride in her preparations for the ball. Its success was her greatest pride. But Hugo would not even consider it. To own the truth, I believe he is afraid a ball would overset Honoria."

"She cannot be so poor-spirited as to not wish for a ball at this most joyous time of year?"

"Poor-spirited hardly begins to describe her," Judith responded firmly, her jaw hard and unyielding. "But you will discover all when you come to Hathersage. And now," she added, rising to her feet and opening the doors of the nearby wardrobe, "I intend to help you pack all your belongings for we shall not leave the Cat and Fiddle without you!"

"You should beg Hugh's permission first," Merry said, feeling suddenly anxious. The description both sisters had presented to her of Hugh did not lend her a great deal of confidence that the sixth viscount would see her presence in his home as anything more than a nuisance.

Constance rose to her feet as well and spread her hands out before Merry in a pleading manner. "If we behave with every propriety and consideration in this matter, which is what you are suggesting we do, I tell you now the battle as well as the war will be entirely lost—and that without the enemy having once been engaged. Surprise is of the essence. We can always retreat if necessary, just as Wellington was wont to do once he had gained a foothold on the Peninsula. But if Hugo refuses a request that you stay with us before you have even passed through the gates, how will you then get into the house? I promise you, it would be impossible! No! I am fully persuaded that once you are there, he will be completely unable to send you away."

Merry swallowed hard and considered this piece of what she felt to be very sage advice, and slowly rose to her feet. "The portmanteau is beneath the bed," she said at last, "besides the two trunks there against the wall."

Constance suddenly looked all around her and cried, "Merry, where is your companion?"

Merry looked a trifle conscious as she replied, "I left her in a hotel at Derby. I know I set several proper tongues to wagging by travelling alone and actually taking a room here without benefit of a chaperone, but poor Miss Yarlet is grown quite old and to own the truth, she pinches at me so! Besides, her sister, who has a very large family, resides near Derby."

"And she would never have permitted you to accept of our invitation, would she?" Judith suggested.

Merry glanced from one to the other, then shook her head. "No, she most definitely would not have approved."

Judith smiled wickedly upon her. "Then you were very right to have gotten rid of her!"

Chapter Seven

Merry stood between Judith and Constance. The twins each had an arm about her waist as the three of them stared at Siddons and waited for him to recover. When the good butler, his complexion high even to the top of his receding hairline, did not seem capable of responding, Merry intervened.

"How do you go on, Siddons?" she queried politely.

Siddons was staring at her as though he was looking at a spectre, his mouth slightly agape, his small brown eyes opened in wonder.

"Miss Fairfield!" he cried, at last. "Why, it's been of an age! I confess we had all hoped—" he fell into a brief fit of coughing as he hastily bowed to her, his complexion darkening further still.

Merry felt a warm rush of sentiment rise up and envelope her heart. Though Judith and Constance might have encouraged her to come to Hathersage Park, their motives were not entirely selfless. And being giddy sort of girls, she could not rely entirely on their judgement—Kit may have indeed experienced a remarkable change of heart, Hugh may not be the unhappy husband-to-be which they had portrayed him. But to see the surprised delight in Siddons' eyes, and to watch him blush with embarrassment at having nearly revealed his opinion that she had been the staff's hopeful at one time, so encouraged her that she felt tears burn her eyes.

Why had she waited so long in coming to Derbyshire?

"I know it is a terrible imposition at this time of year," she began politely but pointedly, "to come to Hathersage since I understand a wedding is in order. But when Judith and Constance invited me, how could I refuse?"

"Indeed, Miss, you could not, and I heartily approve. I will have the baggages sent to the same chamber you occupied on your last visit."

She took in a deep breath, her heart beginning to hammer loudly in her breast at the next question she must ask. "And where is his lordship? Would you be so kind as to inform him of my arrival?"

Siddons again looked very conscious and cleared his throat. Straightening his shoulders and composing his countenance, he replied somberly, "I believe his lordship went into the gardens—near the yew maze. If you would care to—" he let the remainder of his hint rest in the air.

"Very good, thank you," Merry replied promptly.

"I trust you still recall the way?"

"Of course," she responded, smiling in spite of her wish not to. The butler bowed to her and quickly walked away.

Judith and Constance turned to her, their faces alive with smiles of sheer mischief and meaning.

"You must go to him—now," Judith stated in her decisive manner.

"How perfect!" Constance breathed. "The yew maze!"

The sisters then giggled. After stating their intention of seeing that roses were brought round from one of the succession houses for Merry's bedchamber, they turned and disappeared down the hallway following in Siddons' wake.

Merry waited on the black and white tiles of the expansive entrance hall for a long moment, trying to compose herself.

The yew maze!

She swallowed hard, a dozen memories rolling over her, each more profound than the previous one—of stolen kisses and laughter, of running and running only to be captured. Oh, how hard she had tumbled in love with Hugo!

She lifted her gaze from the tiles of the floor and looked about the entrance hall. It appeared just as it had so many years ago, displaying two sixteenth century chairs of carved mahogany upholstered in a deep royal blue and appearing very much like thrones. A round inlaid table sat in the very center of the entrance hall above which light from upper level windows reached down to drench the space below. The square staircase rose into the upper levels.

Only the light was different from her visit four and half years earlier. She had been at Hathersage in the height of summer and the entrance hall had appeared like a vivid, warm reflection of August heat and life. Now in winter, how cool, how reposed the panelled walls, the classical floor and the wood stairs were. Beautiful still, magnificent certainly, but subdued by winter's snowy light.

A few Christmas greens, she thought absently, on the wooden handrail, tied up with red ribbons. And some pine boughs and holly berries arranged on the beautiful table in the center of the tiles. Perhaps Hugh's succession houses were blooming with red roses!

What thoughts were these?

She gave herself a shake and moved into the rose and green drawing room. She was struck by Lady Rayneworth's artistry—the formal receiving room was decorated with rose silk on the walls, and as an underdrape upon each majestic window, of which there were five. Over each window was a gilt cornice overhung by an elegant loop of green velvet. The effect was stunning. The carpet was of geometric patterns in shades of rose and green and the furniture, all in the elegant Empire style—Egyptian sofas in white and green strips, black lacquer chairs covered in green velvet, the fireplace of white marble and bearing juxtaposed caryatids at each end of the mantel. A portrait of the family by Laurence adorned the space above the mantel, the painting some seven years old, since Beatrice was only an infant, her gown three times as long as her height in a fine, sheer muslin.

Here, Merry's attention was fully caught. All eight members of the family enjoyed the same beautiful and quite thick auburn hair, a striking phenomenon to say the least. But more than just the beauty of so much red entreated the viewer to keep looking. There was something in the shared expression of all that kept her gaze fixed upon the portrait. A certain lively mischieviousness characterized the whole of the Leighton clan. How happy she was to be back at Hathersage at last. Somehow, she felt at home, a sensation which made her purpose in coming to Derbyshire seem even more urgent.

She passed through the maze of furniture into a connecting antechamber which housed Judith's harp. Beyond the antechamber was another long, elegant receiving room, decorated in a fine crimson and gold silk-damask. From this chamber, the ballroom had been added in one direction and a long gallery in another.

She was about to pass into the long gallery when she stopped abruptly at the sight of another portrait near the ballroom entrance which she had never seen before.

She breathed in sharply, tears brimming in her eyes as she saw the man she had known some four years ago smiling at her—a warm, welcoming smile. Hugh's blue eyes were filled with laughter, as they always had been when they were together. Her heart reached out to him, longing for him, hoping he was not so changed that he would have forgotten completely the vows of love they had exchanged.

But even if he did remember, and still held in his heart some affection for her, what did it matter now? He was betrothed. Still, she had to see everything for herself. So long as she knew he would be happy, she could be content. Well, if not content, then at least she could be easy in her mind.

She moved into the long gallery which was adorned by a series of more portraits, many of them quite old—two hundred years and more—of Rayneworth ancestors. In the middle of the gallery, overlooking the formal garden, was a series of tall French doors which allowed much of the gallery to be bathed in northern light. The doors were a necessary contrast to the dark, occasionally gloomy portraits staring down from the walls along the impressive length of the chamber.

When she opened one of the doors, she realized that there was not a great deal of difference in temperature from the gallery to the air outside. She was grateful she wore a fur-trimmed red woolen pelisse and slipped her hands back inside her fur muff.

She closed the doors behind her as she stepped onto a wide brick terrace which was guarded by topiaries trimmed in the shape of chess figures and settled into huge pots. She paused and looked all about her. So little had changed, she realized, but through December's eye how different everything appeared. The home wood rose in the distance climbing a hill and disappearing beyond. A herd of deer lived in the wood and during summer could be seen in early morning and early evening, feeding in the meadows at the edge of the wood.

Directly before her, the formal gardens spread out in a geometric pattern of diamond-shaped beds, one after another. A light dusting of snow lay on the gardens. She could see the depressions Hugh's footsteps had made in the snow and she immediately began to follow the path he had taken, a straight line to the yew maze.

Would she even remember all the turns to the center?

Now that she had committed her feet to walking down the path, now that she would soon be seeing Hugh, she began to move briskly. She could feel the cold air brightening her cheeks and she wondered if her complexion, by the time she reached the center of the maze, would ressemble the dark red color of her woolen pelisse. She smiled at the thought. Hugh had never seen her in winter's light, or in winter's cold. What would he think of her now? Did she appear more womanly now that she was twenty? Would he think of her as grown-up or would he remember only the schoolgirl he had kissed?

Her heart began to race like the wind as she reached the opening of the maze. Her hands were cold. They shouldn't have been since she wore soft, yellow kid gloves. But then her fingers were always cold to the bone when her heart was beating in such strong anticipation.

Left, pass the first opening. Right, then right again, pass two left openings, to the end. Left, a quick right, a quick left and left again. Her feet crunched through older snow that had been frozen from many nights before and which could not melt since it was held in the shadows of the tall yew walls day and night. Pass an opening, right. One more.

She remembered precisely how to arrive at the center which now loomed before her. Hugh was there.

His back was to her when she reached the archway leading into a small, private central square. He stood in front of a snow-covered stone bench, one booted foot propped up on the bench. He wore his black great coat, pulled up high upon his collar. His shoulders were straight even though one arm rested on his knee.

A thousand memories tugged at her, each demanding to gain prominence in her thoughts. She was dizzy with pushing them all back and trying to force herself to see the man before her. She had forgotten he was so tall. She whispered his name. How odd! She had meant to speak his name aloud, but her voice had not responded properly to her inward command. He moved slightly, his arm and hand coming up off his knee.

Had he heard her?

How could she speak to him, when so much love seemed to be rushing over her that her voice would not even respond to her will?

She took a deep breath, then stepped into the snow-decked square—three small steps.

"Hallo, Hugo," she said at last, her chest rising in full anticipation of watching him turn around. Would he be glad she had come?

* * *

Hugh heard Merry's voice and whirled around abruptly. Had he imagined she was with him because of last night's adventure and because of all his unsettling thoughts of the morning?

No, he had imagined nothing.

For there she was, dressed in a cherry red pelisse, so pretty against the snow-dusted yews.

"Merry," he called to her. "Is it you, really?" How funny he would say that, of course that was her. Just as he remembered her from her visit of four years ago, only a woman now, possibly even prettier than ever, and quite fashionably dressed.

She approached him slowly, her lips parted, her green eyes fixed upon him as his must have been upon her. He couldn't have torn his gaze from her if he had wanted to.

"Yes, 'tis I," she returned, a soft smile beginning to light up her face.

He knew the oddest sensation that he had a hundred things to say to her, to tell her, to share with her. He realized that whatever else they might have been to each other—as young as they were—they had been friends first.

He wanted to speak, to begin telling her the numerous thoughts which jumped to the front of his mind, but all he could do was stare at her in wonder, in amazement.

"I've missed you, Hugo," she said, quickening her steps and taking one of her hands from her muff. She then let the muff fall in the snow, and it was at that moment he began walking toward her. Before he knew what was happening he had caught her up in his arms and was holding her fast, the warmth of her body, the feel of her in his arms, the joy of having her with him again causing his heart to take flight and rise up into the heavens, like a bird on the wing.

If he could have placed a name to the sentiment that poured through him upon holding her in his arms, he would have called it hope.

Dear, sweet hope.

He knew he shouldn't be holding her, he knew he should release her. But how she clung to him! He even felt the softness of her lips upon his neck. Pain engulfed him, as though all the difficulties of the past four years had somehow collapsed together and met in this one embrace.

"Merry," he whispered, her red velvet bonnet pressed into the side of his head.

"Have I come too late, Hugh?" she asked. "You should have sent for me, silly man."

"I couldn't ask you to come," he responded, unable to do more than whisper. "You don't know what difficulties have beset me since Mama and Papa perished. And not once could I imagine you here beside me, suffering through the years."

She pulled back from him finally and looked up at him, her brow knitted, her hands resting on his arms. "You did not believe me equal to the task?" she queried.

"You were very young," he said simply. "Just turned seventeen and later, I grew to need a different sort of—" He was unable to complete his thought.

"Wife?" she asked.

He drew in a long breath. "Precisely so."

"Well," she responded. "I believe I comprehend you completely and though I will not pretend that I had hoped matters would have fallen quite differently between us, I promise you I blame you for nothing. We were friends, first and always, and I shall wish you joy." She released his arms and extended her hand to him. Hugh took it, looking down into her face. Her clasp was firm, the expression in her green eyes was one of complete affection. He believed her sincere.

"Thank you, Merry. Your approbation means everything to me." He was going to say more, he meant to say more, to begin enumerating Honoria's many virtues and how she would be the perfect mistress for Hathersage Park, but he was caught suddenly by the emerald color of Merry's eyes. He was looking into them and suddenly he had no thoughts at all, except wondering whether Merry was in love with another man and how much he would enjoy planting such a man a facer, and how beautiful the crimson of her bonnet set to advantage the beauty of her eyes and the blackness of her hair. Her nose was straight and not in the least aquiline like—well, like many other women he had known—and her lips were lovely and parted and always so welcoming.

His gaze became fixed upon her lips. Thoughts of the night before now swarmed over him. He closed his eyes, remembering the young soldier in his arms, her warm body against his, her arms about his neck, her mouth upon his.

He didn't know he had been leaning toward Merry, but the next moment somehow she was in his arms, and her warm, youthful mouth was upon his and her arm was about his neck. He held her tightly to him and felt her lips part. The invitation was so complete and he was so lost that he kissed her thoroughly, even roughly, his heart straining toward her. He heard a soft kitten's sound issue from her throat, as her body moved against him, into him with such hope and delight.

So unlike the kiss he had forced upon Honoria.

Thoughts of Honoria brought reality crashing down upon him. He pulled away from Merry, stunned and dismayed by his conduct. "Good God!" he whispered hoarsely, shaking his head in utter confusion. "I don't know why I importuned you! Merry, I do beg your pardon!" He took two steps backward and with a brushing movement of his hand waved her away. "You should go. Indeed, you should! I have betrayed my dear Merry—I mean, my beloved Honoria."

Merry looked at him, a chuckle rising in her throat. The sight of Hugh backing up so awkwardly and swiping at her with his hand was more than she could bear and she began to giggle.

"Why are you laughing?" he asked, his brows drawing up into a frown.

"Because you are being quite absurd! You did not importune me. I will go, however. I must see if my portmanteau has been properly unpacked!"

"What?" he asked, astonishment now lighting his face, his breath a misty cloud in the air.

She turned around and moved to retrieve her muff from the

snow. She picked it up and began brushing off the clinging flakes which turned watery as she wiped them from the fine fur. She turned back to him with a teasing smile. "Oh!" she cried, pleased that he appeared dumbfounded. "Did I not tell you? Your sisters have invited me to spend the holidays with you. But there is one small matter I feel I ought to address before I seek my bedchamber—Judith and Constance begged me to ask you if they could please have their Christmas ball. It would mean ever so much to them and since I am come to stay until past the New Year, I should be happy to manage the whole affair and even share in the expenses if you wish for it. I understand that your most pressing objection is the trial such an event would place upon your overworked housekeeper. I only wonder that Honoria did not offer to help, since your sisters clearly wish for the ball so very much. But I am here, and I can certainly take the burden from Mrs. Penistone, so I don't see now that there can be the least obstruction to the scheme. I shall tend to it all myself. Good day!"

She then hurried away because she had achieved precisely the effect she wished for—his mouth was agape, a brutish sort of anger had stitched his auburn brows together, and he was clearly preparing himself to do battle.

She was experienced with him, however, and a retreat—just as Constance had suggested—was clearly in order. The moment she was out of sight of Hugo she began to run, her heart picking up its cadence loudly in her ears.

She giggled again when she heard Hugo bellow, "Merry Fairfield, come back here this instant! If you think you've come to Hathersage to work your devilment, you are greatly mistaken!"

She knew the yew maze well, however. Hugh had not known that on her first week at Hathersage, she had not only come out to the yew maze at night to study it, but she had made drawings of every niche in the intricate shrubberies. She found the three successive turns she was looking for and hid herself. She heard

Hugo bellowing his complaints about her speech as he passed her by and eventually exited the maze.

She heard his feet crunching on the path of gravel leading to the back terrace and she knew she was safe. "Damn and blast, Fairfield!" he cried. "Where the devil—I mean, dash-it-all, where are you?"

Merry smiled to herself, exceedingly satisfied. "That is the Hugo I know," she whispered. "Perhaps he is not beyond redemption after all." She leaned against the shrubbery intending to wait a full quarter hour before emerging from the maze. Besides, she had a great deal to ponder, not least of which was the kiss he had just placed upon her so willing lips.

Surely he is meant for me, surely.

But a more disturbing notion rocked the hope which had begun sailing about in her heart.

Perhaps Honoria enjoys his kisses, too.

Chapter Eight

After Merry knew she would not be caught by Hugh, she left the safety of the maze and returned to the gallery where she found Mrs. Penistone awaiting her. The housekeeper was a thin woman in her later forties who was a spinster but, in keeping with the tradition abounding throughout the country, she had adopted a married prefix, indicating a husband who had never existed. She had brown eyes, dark brown hair streaked with gray, a narrow though not unattractive face and was well-known among the parishioners of All Saints in Abbot's End to be in possession of a fine, lilting soprano voice. She and Cook, whose contralto voice was the envy of many lesser skilled ladies, were known to deliver the prettiest duets and sometimes sang at wedding breakfasts for families about the market town.

Mrs. Penistone led Merry to her room and made her feel even more welcome than Siddons had. She tried not to be encouraged by these attentions to her arrival, but she couldn't help it. She was enormously flattered by the housekeeper's delight that she had come to stay through the New Year.

Surely she was meant to be here always! Surely!

The housekeeper presented her with a maid who would attend to her toilette throughout her stay, a pretty young woman by the name of Jeannette who dipped a shy curtsy and peeped at her from round, pretty gray eyes fringed with thick black lashes. Mrs. Penistone then informed her that nuncheon

was being served shortly in the morning room and that Miss
Leighton and Miss Constance had expressed their wish that she
join the family at her convenience.

Merry again thanked Mrs. Penistone for her kind attentions
to her. "For I know you must be frightfully busy," she said.

Mrs. Penistone opened her mouth as though to speak an
impulsive thought then clamped her lips shut.

Merry lifted her brows. "What is it?" she asked quietly,
glancing askance at Jeanette. When she saw that the maid was
unpacking her trunks and performing her task in utter astonishment at the sight of her exquisite gowns, she pressed the housekeeper. "Please," she whispered. "You were about to say?"

Mrs. Penistone looked quickly behind her since the door was
still open to the hallway. In a low voice she said, " 'Twere no
trouble at all, Miss Fairfield. And all that I intended to say was
that I am not such an overworked creature as *some* would have
you believe." She nodded briskly, her hands clasped tightly
before her. "So if you are needful of anything, please do not
hesitate to come to me!"

Merry was a little surprised but agreed readily to make any
request she might have known to her. The housekeeper seemed
satisfied and after instructing Jeannette to take great care with
Miss Fairfield's belongings, she quit the chamber, closing the
door behind her.

When Merry had removed her bonnet, handed her wet muff
to Jeannette, exchanged her pelisse for a crotched shawl of the
finest white cashmere, saw any clinging snow brushed from the
hem of her dark blue velvet morning gown, and had her black
curls tidied, she finally felt prepared to greet the rest of the
family.

A few minutes later, Merry stood upon the threshold of the
morning room and smiled. The whole family was gathered for
nuncheon—save Hugo—and she savored the moment since it
reminded her of so many meals shared with Hugh's family
during her first sojourn at Hathersage. Five handsome crowns
of beautiful auburn hair turned toward her since the siblings

were already seated at the table. Each welcoming face lifted up to look at her and returned her smiles—Judith, Constance, Kit, Amabel in her Bath chair, and young Beatrice who had been little more than a babe in leading strings when she was last at Hathersage.

"I had forgotten how remarkable it is that you all share the same color hair. What a delightful portrait you make."

Everyone babbled at once, calling out greetings to her. Kit rose from his chair and made his best bow. How tall he was and how very handsome. She insisted he retake his seat and that the ladies remain where they were. "I want to look at all of you, just in this way! I have been gone far too long!"

She knew Judith and Constance were speaking that they were agreeing with her completely and complaining that they had been such simpletons not to have insisted she visit sooner.

But Merry's attention was drawn away from the chatter at the table as she glanced about the large, high-ceilinged chamber.

The morning room was quite cheerful and, though large, in its way quite cozy. A large, brick fireplace sat on the west wall and she could imagine in her mind the now empty hearth burning brightly with a Yule log. She wondered why no such log adorned the fireplace yet.

Her gaze drifted quite of its own accord to the tall, Elizabethan window facing south. The chamber was situated at the west end of the long gallery with one window on the south side overlooking the formal gardens and a matching window facing the west, but stationed on the other side of the fireplace. Both windows were hung with red silk-damask, a fabric used upon the walls and the sofas as well. Behind the drapes, a thin, airy underdrape of white muslin permitted southern and afternoon light to flood the family's favorite room.

The view through the western window was exquisite, a perfect composition of the best of Derbyshire—a snow-drifted lawn sloping down to a low, drystone wall, and beyond, a dale rich with green farmland in the summer, though at present appearing like a pretty white quilt stretched in odd-shaped patches from one drystone wall to the next. The distant rise of a tall steeple marked the hamlet to the south of Abbot's End, a small village called Frogwell, and on the far horizon a craggy outline of hills traveled northward in a determined rise to the Peak district. Above the horizon, snowclouds shrouded the land, promising more cold and more snow and thicker coats for the wool-producing sheep of the higher elevations. Everywhere clumps of oak and beech dotted the landscape, a strong indication that forest had once dominated the land. Hidden, ice-crusted brooks were everwhere and at the base of the tors and crags, the River Wye eased through the lowest point in the dale.

How different Derbyshire was from Sussex where the downs rolled softly through the south and the sea pressured the edges of the land reminding the coastal inhabitants that England was an island. But in Derbyshire, it seemed as though the land went on forever, in a cascade of everchanging terrains.

"I am Beatrice," a child's voice called to her, interrupting her reverie.

Dear Beatrice.

Merry returned her attention to the family, and to the youngest of the Leighton children. "Of course you are," she responded, again smiling. "I could never forget you, although when I last saw you, you weren't quite so tall."

Beatrice immediately deserted her chair and moved across the room to stand directly in front of Merry. She was fully seven and clearly full of her own thoughts as she placed a hand upon each hip.

"Judith and Constance want you to marry Hugo but he is already betrothed to Honoria," she stated firmly, her confident posture and pointed manner of speaking putting her forcibly in mind of Judith.

"Beatrice!" the twins chimed, instantly reprimanding the youngest Leighton sibling.

"How old are you now, Beatrice? Eight or nine?" Merry queried, hoping to change the subject quickly.

"I am seven, but I am tall. Everyone says so. Are you really going to stay here and make everything better?"

The twins groaned and muttered promises of vengeance to which the feisty Beatrice merely pulled a face.

"Well," Merry returned. "Do you wish me to make things better? Ought I to stay? And if you wanted something better, what would that be?"

"I want Hugo to stop coming the crab so much and to smile more. He is quite sad, you know, though he pretends he is not."

"Well, I did speak with your brother earlier in the yew maze, and do you know he came the crab over me, too. I think he's just caught up in a truly dreadful habit. It might be a bit tricky to break him of it but I think we can."

"We could roll up the *Times?*" Beatrice suggested hopefully, her blue eyes wide.

Merry laughed. "Whatever do you mean by that?" she asked, taking Beatrice by the hand and leading her back to her chair.

"We used to have a dog named Puppy—but he ran away. When he was very little, he was quite naughty and Hugo would roll up the *Times* and when I asked him what he was doing, he said he was breaking Puppy of a bad habit."

Merry laughed as did the rest of the siblings. She was just pushing Beatrice's chair back into the table when the laughter in the chamber stopped suddenly.

She looked up and saw that Hugo was now standing in the doorway, as magnificent as always, but a rather piercing, disapproving expression on his face. She felt a blush begin to creep up her cheeks, realizing he had probably heard every word. She refused to be undone, however, by his disapprobation and began composing herself.

Thankfully, he did not address her immediately, but merely regarded her with narrowed eyes for a moment, then sauntered into the lofty chamber.

She had an opportunity therefore to scrutinize his appearance and found her heart quickening within her breast. He was devilishly handsome and not less so after having shed himself of his greatcoat and hat and after combing his auburn hair. He was dressed with immaculate precision, his shirtpoints moderate in size, his neckcloth worn in a subdued but intricate fashion known as *trone d'amour,* his blue coat fitting neatly upon his broad shoulders, his white silk waistcoat showing little more than an inch below the cutaway of his coat, his buff breeches tucked into gleaming top boots. Everything about his costume bespoke the hand of a skilled tailor. The work of Weston, perhaps, though she could not imagine when he found time to visit the famous London clothier.

"The *Times,* eh?" he queried at last, moving to stand behind his chair at the head of the table.

She stole a glance at him beneath her lashes as she slipped Beatrice's napkin onto the young girl's lap. She knew that his siblings were tense, clearly waiting for an argument to ensue, but she saw something more, something which gave her courage. Yes, there it was—a twinkle in his eye.

"Indeed, if necessary," she responded with spirit, unblinking. "Or worse, if I could possibly contrive it!"

"And to what bad habit were you referring?" he asked,

All eyes were upon Merry as she faced his lordship squarely.

She was about to give him an answer when Siddons arrived, along with two footmen, each bearing a large tray laden with the results of Cook's morning labors. As the servants began arranging dishes from the trays onto the sideboard nearest the servant's entrance, Hugh bid her speak.

"Are you certain I should?" she asked, directing her gaze toward the the butler and the footmen for a brief moment, then back to him.

He smiled faintly. "I daresay there is not one among my staff who is not fully conversant with all my faults. Pray, speak your mind. I am not afraid of you."

Hugo's brows were raised in a haughty challenge, one she did not hesitate to take up. "Your wretched habit, to which I was referring, is that you brangle with everyone, coming the crab, as Beatrice so astutely put it, and that you ought to stop doing so. We are not your enemies, Hugh, honestly we're not!"

Hugh seemed a little surprised and glanced around the table. Merry watched him meet the gaze of each of his four sisters and his brother. He even caught Siddons's gaze, who apparently could not keep from staring back at his master for a forceful moment, the expression in his eyes full of meaning, before returning to his labors.

"Is that the way of it then?" Hugh asked, obviously stunned. "Am I become such an ogre?"

The silence in the room was deafening in its accusation. He let out a sigh of frustration and moved to the side of the table where he held out a seat for Merry next to Amabel.

"Come," he said gently. "I promise I won't bite your head off for sitting down—or for giving me such an incisive dressing down!"

Merry rounded the table eyeing him warily in an exaggerated manner which made him growl playfully at her in return.

"Thank you, sir," she said as she seated herself. At this kinder interchange, a soft giggling went round the table.

He took up his seat, Amabel sitting on one side of him and Constance on the other. Beatrice sat between Kit and Constance and Merry, sitting across from Kit, found that he was watching her closely.

"What is it?" she queried, as Siddons held a platter of cold, sliced chicken at her elbow. She lifted a slice onto her plate then returned her gaze to Kit.

"You're deuced pretty, Merry!" he cried out impulsively, then blushed. "I say, that didn't sound quite proper."

Assuming a more dignified manner, one which Merry thought it likely he had been practicing as a necessary part of taking Holy Orders, he continued, "What I meant to say, was that when you were here so long ago, and we played at ducks and drakes, I remember enjoying your company so much it never occurred to me that you were a—a diamond of the first stare—but so you are!" He glanced nervously up the table at Hugh as though seeking his approval. Merry wondered what his reaction might be to Kit's observation, but Hugh was leaning close to Amabel and speaking quietly to his invalidish sister.

Merry returned her attention to Kit and after thanking him for his compliment launched into a cataloguing of their various adventures, from playing at ducks and drakes, to exploring the nearby limestone caverns, to entering the abandoned mine only to race out of it when they were certain they had heard ghosts within, to marking corks with paint and letting them float into the underground river, then racing downstream to watch them appear a half mile away above ground where the river re-emerged. Kit's eyes became filled with a light which had clearly been absent before they began their reminiscing.

During that time, Siddons presented her with an additional variety of fare, from roast beef to lobster patties, partridges, peas, and artichokes. An assortment of fruits accompanied the meal, along with fresh-baked bread, butter, jellies, creams, nuts and sweetmeats.

Her plate full, she asked Kit gently how it had come about he had decided to forsake his military career in favor of the church.

His initial response was quite candid. "It was Hugo's idea, and a good one," he said, peeling an orange. "I have taken great pains with my studies and Mr. Belper—do you remember the vicar? But of course you could not, for he has only been here a little over a year. At any rate, he is quite knowledgeable and is tutoring me in Latin and mathematics. I hope to enter Oxford in the next term."

"I see. You still ride, though, don't you?"

"Not as much as I was used to," he said, appearing a little conscious. She could see he was trying very hard to uphold the dignities of his hoped-for office. "My interests are—are quite different than when you were here last."

She smiled faintly, thinking this was not the young man she had met four years ago and a very nervous sensation came over her. Judith and Constance had indicated that Kit was so altered that he was no longer human, but what she saw before her was a man of devotion and principle. She thought he might benefit from a little more exercise since his complexion was decidedly pale, but otherwise he most certainly could have experienced a sobering realization that he was more fit for the church than the army. In truth, she did not know what to think of him.

She glanced up at Hugo and saw the attentiveness with which he spoke to Amabel and to Beatrice. What was here that was not proper, good and acceptable? Or was it possible her recent remonstrances had already had a happy effect? She glanced at Judith, feeling that all was not as bad as the twins believed.

Judith gathered up several peas upon her fork. Somehow she must have sensed Merry's waivering for she whispered, "Do not be fooled." Then she slipped the fork between her lips, chewed and smiled at Merry.

Merry stared back at her and gave her head a small shake. Clearly affection, principle and family devotion reigned in this home. Would she be doing what was right if she made a push to overset Hugh's household? She didn't know.

When the meal was concluded, Hugh rose and carefully drew Amabel and her Bath chair back from the table. Since Merry stood up at the same time, she found herself turned to face Amabel directly. She remembered her as perhaps the most willful of the Leighton children and for that reason considered it a great irony that Amabel had been confined to a Bath chair—most likely for the remainder of her life. How did she bear it, she wondered?

But as she looked at Amabel, she was struck by the healthful appearance of her complexion. Roses could bloom on cheeks so rich with color. In addition, her blue eyes were bright, her lips a pretty shade of pink and even her hair gleamed in the early afternoon light. She was as unlike most invalids Merry had known as she could possibly be.

As though somehow discerning the trail of her thoughts,

Amabel lifted her chin to Merry, her blue eyes suddenly sharp and piercing.

A challenge? But why? What could Amabel mean by it?

Then the expression passed, like the sun drifting behind a thick, dark cloud.

"How do you go on, Amabel?" she asked politely, her gaze never wavering from her face.

"Very well, thank you," Amabel responded, in a quiet manner. Too quiet perhaps, Merry thought, but to what purpose? "I am glad you have come to Hathersage," she continued in a breathless voice, as though she found breathing a great difficulty. "You were always a favorite of mine and I can now thank you for all the books you have sent me over the years and the musical compositions, though I daresay you will be grievously disappointed that I have not made greater progress at the pianoforte."

"I shall be disappointed in nothing," Merry responded sincerely. "But while I am here, permit me to push you about out of doors as frequently as you wish for it. If I recall correctly, you were rarely in the house the last time I was here."

"You are very kind," Amabel said, smiling feebly. "I do enjoy the gardens and the woods." She closed her eyes and appeared to be sinking with exhaustion. She turned back to her brother and said, "Hugh, I am very much fatigued. Would you please take me to my bedchamber?"

"Of course," Hugh responded gravely, his voice purposefully low as though he was afraid of hurting her ears by speaking too loudly.

As he passed by Merry, he said, "Will you await me in the library? I believe we have something to discuss."

"Certainly," Merry responded.

Once he was gone, both Judith and Constance pounced upon her. "Will you ask him about the ball?" they chimed.

"I already have," she replied.

"Indeed?" Judith exclaimed, shocked. "I knew we could rely upon you!"

"What did he say?"

"I ran away before he could tell me no, but somehow I believe he means to refuse my request! If you will excuse me, I intend to remove to the library and prepare myself for battle."

Kit spoke as he rose from the table, a frown knitting his brow. "Honoria will not like a ball," he said earnestly. "Her feelings ought to be considered. After all, she is to marry Hugh in but three weeks time."

The twins turned toward Kit and glared at him.

"What have I said?" he asked, taking a step backward.

"You have been far too buried in your books and not half attentive to our crisis. Hugo should not even marry Honoria. She will make his life a misery—"

Kit's jaw grew rigid with disapproval. "What you mean to say," he interrupted her, "Is that she will make your life a misery. You are thinking only of yourself when you say she will not bring Hugh happiness. But I believe she has helped Hugh tremendously and that she will make him an unexceptionable wife. What do you say, Merry? You were always sensible, and for all of Beatrice's inappropriate remarks I know that you have not come to disrupt Hugh's wedding. Where the ball is concerned, wouldn't you agree Honoria's sentiments ought to be of prime consideration?"

Merry's former belief that the family was not in so sad a state of disrepair as Judith and Constance wished her to believe came flooding back to her. She tried to speak her heart honestly without betraying to Kit the depth of her sentiments toward his elder brother. "I most certainly have not come to make Hugh in any manner unhappy, of that I most heartily will assure you, and certainly not to disrupt his nuptials. But as for the ball, I am concerned that Honoria has not heard her future sisters' wishes and in some manner tried to accommodate them. Seeing to the happiness of my future sisters and brother would be my first object, tell me what you think?"

Kit looked away from her, his blue eyes fixed upon the linen tablecloth now scattered here and there with dishes, silver and crumbs from the recent repast. "You are speaking what you feel from your heart and I do believe you would make us your object. But Honoria is not like you. She is of a more delicate temperament. I will not say she cannot attend to Judith and Constance's wishes, only that when she does it will probably not be in a manner which would most please them. That she would dislike a ball, therefore, I will not construe as a disinclination to support her future family, but rather merely a reflection of her quieter demeanor and spirit, her dislike of gaiety."

Merry smiled suddenly, "How very unkind of you to speak so wisely, Kit. Almost you persuade me not to push for the ball."

Since Judith and Constance immediately set up a furious caterwaul in their fright that Merry would now desist from taking up their cause, Merry reassured them that she had every intention of discussing the matter fully with Hugh.

Shortly afterward, Merry quit the morning room and headed for the library with Beatrice in tow. The young girl had demanded to attend the interesting Miss Fairfield and suggested that if Merry wished to read her a book, she would have no objection.

Chapter Nine

On the way to the library, which was on the first floor of the mansion, Beatrice chatted happily about everything and nothing. Merry had been surprised that Beatrice wanted to accompany her to the library and even more so when she took her hand and held it the entire way. They were mounting the stairs when Merry reached just that stage of conversation with the happy seven-year-old where her mind started to drift. Her responses became confined to the less than erudite, "Oh, yes," or, "Oh, my," or the even more profound, "Indeed!"

She was settling in nicely to the one-sided dialogue, apparently sustaining her part to Beatrice's satisfaction, when the young girl brought her attention sharply round again.

"I hope we have a ball," she stated.

Merry looked down at her, very curious as to why Beatrice wished for an event which by its nature she would not be permitted to attend, or would observe only for a little while. "And why is that?" she queried.

Beatrice changed the subject. "Can you take the stairs two at a time? Judith and Constance do whenever Hugh is not looking, or Mrs. Penistone."

"I suppose I would be able to if I wanted to," she replied.

"Don't you wish to? I think it is famous fun." She glanced up the stairs, then down the stairs and, seeing that no one was around to spoil her mischief, immediately lifted her skirts of bright pink velvet and began stretching her legs to reach every other step.

How could Merry resist such an invitation?

She didn't even try, but lifted her own dark blue skirts and began mounting the stairs slowly, keeping pace alongside Beatrice, as they quite scandalously skipped alternating steps.

Beatrice giggled. "Judith said you were a right 'un, and so you are!"

Achieving the first floor was no simple task, since the ceilings on the ground floor were quite high. Merry found herself decidedly breathless by the time she reached the upper landing.

Beatrice seemed less affected by her exertions and once they began down the hallway she again took up Merry's hand. She reverted to the original subject. "I hope we have a ball because I like to watch Honoria dance. She is the prettiest dancer I have ever seen. She is even better than Constance. But Judith does not appear to advantage on the ballroom floor."

It was obvious to Merry that the child had grown up around adults, for her mode of expression was mature beyond her years.

"She does not?" Merry queried.

Beatrice shook her head. "No, she is far too jumpy. Both Constance and Honoria glide even in the most difficult of movements. When I am older, Hugh has promised I might have a dancing master of my own. When I go to London, I want to be the best dancer of them all."

"Then I'm sure you will be," Merry responded.

They arrived at the library and upon entering the large, well-stocked chamber, cold air greeted them. For all the magnificence of Hathersage, the great house was far too grand to be entirely comfortable, especially without fires burning in any of the grates. Still, the long, lofty room was a pleasure to behold.

Three tall Elizabethan windows ranged across the length of the wall opposite the door and were hung with green velvet Empire valances supported by brass rods, along with matching panels which hung to the floor and were tied back with gold braided ropes and tassels. The remaining three walls, each climbing thirty feet in height and serviced by three rolling ladders, were lined with bookshelves which rose to an exquisite plaster-work ceiling. The bare spaces between the intricately carved white plaster-work were painted a rich yellow the color of lemons. The wooden floor was partially covered by three large Aubusson carpets in floral patterns of green and gold. The furniture had been chosen for comfort and was grouped primarily around the fireplace which was situated in the center of the wall shared by the hallway beyond. All the pieces were upholstered in the same green velvet—two winged chairs and two small sofas. Several footstools in a fine needlework, each depicting a basket of roses, were placed near the fireplace for the ladies's convenience. Occasional tables of mahogany gleamed beside the chairs and sofas.

The bookshelves had been the effort of a master craftsman and were constructed of a beautifully grained oak. The fine leather of the thousands of books lining the shelves, as well as the fragrance of beeswax and turpentine used to keep the oak shelves in excellent condition, lent the chamber a rich aromatic quality that always smelled to Merry of learning, of pleasure, and of at least one stolen kiss.

Goodness! She hadn't realized until she had returned to Hathersage precisely how frequently Hugo had stolen kisses from her. She remembered now that he had been chasing her about the maze of sofas and chairs that punctuated the room, caught her beneath one of the ladders, then had kissed her soundly—their first kiss. How surprised she had been! Stunned, really! But not more so than by her own conduct, because after he had stammered out an apology, she had quite spontaneously caught him up in her arms and planted another kiss upon his lips, only to dash away from him, quitting the house altogether to conceal herself in the nitch in the yew maze.

The whole of their flirtation had been filled with so much fun and delight that it was no wonder no other young man had been able to tempt her since.

She had had dozens of suitors—some truly enamored of her and of the quickness of her mind and of her liveliness. Some, of course, had been enchanted by her tidy fortune and estate which would come to the man she married. But not once had she been in the least tempted by the young men who had pursued her.

No, her heart had been lost to Hugo many years ago and still was as she glanced toward the ladder, toward the very spot where he had first kissed her.

When she felt Beatrice tugging upon her white cashmere shawl, which kept the chill of Hathersage from overtaking her, Merry gave herself a shake and turned toward the young girl.

"Will you read this to me?" Beatrice asked. "Honoria has been teaching me to read and I can comprehend most of the words, but I had by far rather have you read to me."

Her choice of books made Merry smile. "Oh, *Arabian Nights*! My very most favorite. Come, sit on my lap and we can look at the illustrations together. Do you use watercolors? When I was quite young, I used to make a large copy of the illustrations with my pen and then carefully paint between the lines."

"Oh, that sounds like marvelous fun," Beatrice exclaimed. "Maybe we could do that after Hugo gives you his dressing down."

Merry laughed, sitting down in a winged chair of green velvet. She pulled the child onto her lap, and settled her into her shoulder. "What makes you think your brother means to give me a dressing down?"

"Because he spoke to you in just that tone which he always uses when he means to give one a dressing down. Now, read!"

Merry obeyed Beatrice's command and for the next fifteen minutes she was lost in the enchantment of a book which was beginning to pull apart at the binding from that most honorable of reasons—overuse!

When she reached the end of the first tale, both she and Beatrice sighed with satisfaction. She would have begun discussing the story with her had not Hugh's voice interrupted.

"How kind of you to read to my sister," he said.

Merry looked up from the book and to her surprise saw that Hugh was seated across from her.

"How long have you been there?" she cried. "I vow I don't recall your having even entered the chamber."

"I heard fully half the story. When I arrived at the library, I heard Beatrice's laughter and then the rise and fall of your voice. I knew you were in the midst of giving one of your readings so I stole in as quietly as possible. It appears I succeeded. You were always so accomplished at reading with expression! Even Papa liked to hear you after supper. Do you know how frequently he picked up his glass of port and his box of snuff from the dining table, and carried it into the drawing room in order to join you, Mama and my sisters so as not to miss even a single word? Of course Kit and I followed equally as enthusiastically."

"I didn't know that!" Merry cried, with great satisfaction. "And I truly had not the least awareness that I pleased your family so. But I am glad of it."

She looked deeply into his eyes, wondering yet again how it had come about he had actually offered for another woman. Feelings of panic at the promised loss she must endure when he married Honoria on Christmas Day brought her throat constricting so tightly she had to force herself to breath and to swallow.

When he continued to simply stare at her, his thoughts inscrutable, she whispered to Beatrice that she must leave now for, if she remembered, Hugh must give her a dressing down.

Beatrice grimaced up at her. "I don't want to go. I want you to read another tale and then we shall do illustrations and watercolors together."

"Go," Merry said firmly and gave the child a gentle shove, sliding her easily down her suddenly straightened legs. "I'll come to you as soon as I have spoken with Hugo."

Beatrice made full use of the slide Merry's legs had provided for her. When she landed at Hugh's feet, she rose up to stand before her brother and wagged an accusing finger at him. "You must be kind to Merry, for I want her stay. We are going to have fun together and don't come the crab, or . . . or I'll put a spider in your bed tonight!"

"Beatrice!" Merry cried. "What a naughty thing to say."

"Come now, scamp," Hugh responded. "I will promise to behave but I must speak with Merry and you must leave us in peace. Now! Give us a kiss!"

Beatrice slipped her small hands about Hugh's neck and kissed his cheek.

Placing his hand upon her back, Hugh directed her toward the door and gave her a friendly little push. "Off with you now. But no more talk of spiders!"

Beatrice raced toward the door all the while explaining to Merry that she meant at once to hunt down her watercolors, although she said she wasn't certain whether they were in her bedchamber, the nursery or the scullery, where one of the footmen had been painting horses for her, a skill he had mastered quite neatly.

"Merry, do you think the footman should join us? You would like his horses. Indeed, you would!"

"Go!" Hugh cried again, as Beatrice waited by the door and shuffled her feet.

"Oh, very well, but don't keep her forever, Hugh!"

When the door closed behind Beatrice at last, Hugo turned his attention to Merry and smiled faintly. "I promise I will not *come the crab,* as you and Beatrice are so fond of insisting, but we have several matters to discuss, don't we?"

Merry nodded, but said nothing in response. Hugh rose to his feet, crossed to the fireplace near Merry's chair, then retraced his steps to pace the length of the sofa, and then returned to the fireplace. She could see that he was having some difficulty either ordering his thoughts or knowing how to begin. She was content, however, merely to watch him and remained silent. For one thing, once he did begin speaking she was certain he would not be lost for words.

After settling his elbow on the mantel he turned to hold her gaze steadfastly. "Though it would seem," he began with a pinched frown between his brows, "that I cannot precisely turn you out of doors at this late hour since my whole family would most likely commit mutiny and perhaps hang me from the top bannister, I think we ought to achieve an understanding, you and I. For you must know that had I had the smallest inkling my sisters meant to invite you to stay under my roof I should have forbade it entirely."

Merry blinked at him. "Why is that, Hugo?"

He grimaced at her slightly. "You know very well why! Don't play the innocent with me. But first, I do apologize for kissing you. It was most ungentlemanly of me."

"Apology accepted," she responded brightly, folding her hands primly upon her lap, hoping to irritate him.

After rolling his eyes slightly, he slid his elbow off the mantel and turned more fully toward her. "I cannot precisely account for why I suddenly embraced you as I did, but I believe it had more to do with what used to be between us than what currently is. Therefore, I am fully persuaded I shall not be experiencing any such absurdly youthful impulses again."

"Certainly not!" Merry agreed heartily, trying to keep her countenance.

"Oh, do stubble it, Merry," he retorted. "If you think for a moment I am completely unaware of what you are trying to accomplish with your pert remarks and silly mannerisms, you much mistake the matter. Now, permit me to speak and at least try to attend me with a little dignity."

"As you wish, *m'lord!*" she continued as before.

He huffed in exasperation, "Now why are you taunting me when I am only attempting to make peace with you? I feel it is quite necessary that we arrange matters so that we can rub along tolerably well together until I am married and until you are gone from my house! You might at least attempt to cooperate! And why are you smiling? Do anything but smile!"

"Hugh, try as I will, I cannot be so decorous in this moment, or so indifferent as you appear to wish me to be. Being back at Hathersage has put me in mind of how it was between us, and that so forcibly, that I suppose I have merely fallen back into a familiar manner of speaking with you and laughing with you, and well . . . a lot of other things!"

At that he seated himself opposite to her as he had been when she was reading to Beatrice. He leaned forward in his seat and clasped his hands together tightly, as though to implore her. "You—we—must forget the past. Until you arrived here, I promise you that the past was forgotten, completely!"

"Not completely," she said, looking hard at him, also leaning forward. "Surely not? Though you may be marrying Miss Youlgreave, you cannot tell me all of our adventures of so many summers ago are forgotten to you?"

He seemed to grow momentarily disconcerted as he looked away from her. He stared toward the windows for a long moment. Merry wasn't certain if it was so, but she thought his shoulders fell slightly. "No," he responded at last, very quietly. "I suppose you are right in that. Never forgotten." He directed his gaze back to her and the sad smile on his face fairly broke her heart. "We did have a great deal of fun, didn't we?"

"Yes," she breathed. She was caught up in remembering how it had been and for that reason found she could say nothing more. Her heart was full of her love for him.

He searched her eyes, the smile fading entirely from his lips. She saw that he was remembering too, for his blue eyes had taken on a sharp, piercing quality so familiar to her that the expression nearly forced the breath from her lungs. She extended a hand to him and whispered his name.

His gaze dropped to her hand. He stared at it for a long moment, his thoughts inscrutable. "No," he whispered at last, as he rose to his feet and moved to stand by the windows.

He was silent for a long time, his back to her as he looked down on the grounds below.

Merry's heart plummeted. If he had taken her hand, she

knew that a moment later he would have pulled her into his arms.

But then what? Perhaps that was what he too was pondering. Then what? He was betrothed to another woman.

When he spoke, he changed the subject completely. "I know your offer to assist Mrs. Penistone in preparing for a ball was kindly meant, and that you believed such an offer might alter my decision, but I truly cannot support your wish to see that my sisters have their Christmas *fête*. To own the truth, it is not a matter solely because I believe Mrs. Penistone has enough to occupy her days." Here he turned back to her, his demeanor somber. "I simply don't believe a ball is appropriate in my house at this time. I could place the blame upon Honoria knowing that she would not wish for it. But I confess to you Merry, I simply haven't the heart for it. I don't wish to hear my house full of sounds which will only serve to remind me of former years when Papa and Mama would twirl beneath the hundreds of candles in the ballroom chandeliers. It will be many years before I can hope to restore that sort of vivacity and wealth to Hathersage."

Merry wanted to say that had he offered for her, instead of Honoria, even now he could be planning how to make best use of her considerable fortune in repairing his estate, but she knew the point was moot. At the same time, she thought she understood his sentiments. Instead of addressing them directly, she said, "I can see now why Kit has grown into a man of sense. Earlier he gave me another such sound argument—though on a different subject, of course—and I could not answer him, just as I cannot answer you now. You've spoken your heart honestly and perhaps you have even given me the one reason for resisting the notion of a Christmas ball which I can understand." She rose to her feet, and taking a deep breath said, "Would you compromise with me then on one thing?"

"I will try," he said, approaching her, a smile relieving the soberness of his expression.

"Well, my request is this—will you permit me to decorate the entrance hall with a few Christmas greens and red ribbons, along with the morning room? I know it would give great pleasure to your sisters, as well as to brighten these early snowy days. We do not get quite as much snow in the south, you know."

His smile deepened. "To think I feared you meant to ask for a *soirée* instead of a ball. Of course you may place a few greens about both rooms."

"Oh," she cried. "There is just one more thing—"

"Just as I thought," he cried, lifting a hand in mock horror.

Merry laughed. "No, no, it is nothing so bad as whatever oddities are coursing through your brain. Merely, do you have an objection to my going in search of a Yule log? The fireplace in the morning room is certainly large enough to hold a quite massive one. It would, of course, mean taking your sleigh out for an afternoon jaunt through the home wood, with your brother and sisters. What do you say? You could even come with us, if you wished."

"I haven't the heart of the moment to refuse you," he stated simply. "And Merry, if my obligations weren't fixed elsewhere I most certainly would have enjoyed a jaunt through the woods."

"Thank you, Hugo," she returned quietly. She wanted to say more, to tell him she loved him, that she was so happy to have him near her after so many years that her heart was near to bursting, that she wished the clock turned back. Instead, she merely smiled and quit the room.

Once in the hallway, she began to consider just what manner of decorations she meant to introduce to Hathersage. The truth was, she had just told Hugh a whisker. She had no intention of restricting her efforts to a *few* decorations—not by half! Instead, her mind was already conjuring up the prettiest wonderland of them all—the morning room alive with greens, trimmed with red satin and trailing across the mantel, over the windows, all about the chandelier, and gracing every table in the room, but most especially the dining table.

Hugh would be stunned, and probably a little angry, but only at first . . . at least she hoped so.

At the top of the landing looking down the stairs she saw Siddons pass into the rose and green drawing room. An idea occurred to her. She wondered how well Siddons, Mrs. Penistone, Cook and the head-groom sang together. Judith had told her they were all in the church choir at Abbot's End and vied for chances to display their abilities before the parish at every possible opportunity. Surely they could perform a few Christmas carols for the children. Surely!

Chapter Ten

Merry was in the mursery with Beatrice, copying the illustrations found between the covers of *Arabian Nights,* when Judith and Constance found her. They immediately pounced upon her, demanding to know whether or not there was to be a ball. Merry was sorry to disappoint them, especially when both young ladies became instantly blue-devilled.

Surprising tears even welled up in Judith's pretty blue eyes. "It is not only because the ball would have been such a delight," she said, folding her arms and hugging herself against the cold of the nursery, "but now we won't have anything happy to think about for days and days."

Merry, who was seated at a well-worn wooden table, frowned in concern at Judith, who moved to stand beside the window and stare out at the grounds below. The nursery was on the second floor of the mansion and the view of the dales to the east and the home wood to the north were magnificent.

For the first time since her conversation with the twins at the Cat and Fiddle Inn, the thought occurred to Merry that Judith was very unhappy—not just dissatisfied at the lack of amusements at Hathersage, but truly without joy.

Merry tried to explain her brother's refusal. "Hugh said that his reluctance to give such a ball was because not only would he be unable to host such an event in the future, but the occasion would serve to remind him most painfully of your parents. He seemed quite distressed about the whole of it."

Constance drew forward a chair, placing herself close to both Merry and Beatrice in order to observe Merry's sketches. She seemed less affected by the news than her older sibling, but a long sigh gave strong indication that she was disappointed as well. "I don't mind not having the ball," she said, "but I really miss how it used to be. I am only sorry that Hugo wants to forget the past. Perhaps we err in wishing to recreate it, but I don't think so. Beatrice, your choice of colors is quite lovely. A pink and orange horse. How very clever!"

Beatrice did not respond. She was far too busy with her paints and paintbrushes to even acknowledge the compliment.

Merry addressed the twins. "Would you care to join me in an excursion tomorrow to Abbot's End? I believe then you might not think yourselves completely forsaken. As it happens, I find I am in sudden need of yards and yards of red satin ribbon."

Judith looked back at her over her shoulder, her eyes brightening a little, probably at the thought of a five mile journey to the busy market town. "Red satin ribbon?" she queried. "Whatever for?"

Constance leaned over Beatrice's shoulder and, holding her hand, guided the paintbrush in such a manner as to create a more realistic tail for the horse. "Yards and yards?" she queried, glancing at Merry with her brows raised.

"About fifty, I should think, or perhaps a hundred!"

"*A hundred!*" the twins exclaimed in unison.

"Well, yes of course," she stated. "For several years now I have been in the habit of placing greenery and red satin bows on all the mantels in my home during Christmastide. It is quite pretty, and since I am not at home, well . . ." Here she paused, looking from Judith to Constance, then back again, smiling all the while. "Your brother has given us permission to decorate the morning room. Oh, and to go in search of a Yule log as well!"

Even Beatrice turned to stare at her.

After a moment's silence, Constance was on her feet and the twins were fairly jumping up and down. Judith returned from the window and hugged Constance, then the pair of them descended upon Merry.

"Oh, Merry!" Judith exclaimed, hugging her. "Thank you! Thank you ever so much!"

"We shall have Christmas after all!" Constance cried, adding her embraces as well. "Merry, you truly are the best of friends."

Beatrice did not apparently find the information quite as enchanting. "Honoria will not like it," she stated. "And now, if you please Merry, I am ready for the next sketch."

But Judith would have none of Beatrice's indifference and began tickling her youngest sister. "We don't give a fig whether Honoria likes our Christmas greens or not! When she is mistress here she may do as she pleases but until then, it is still our morning room. And as for you, if you don't tell me you are delighted, I shall tickle you until you cry!"

Beatrice was laughing so hard by now that she was fairly screaming for Judith to stop. "I am delighted! I am delighted!" she squealed. "Pray stop, Judith, you are hurting my sides!"

Judith ceased attacking her then caught her up in a quick hug. Beatrice pushed her sister away, scowled at her for having interrupted her painting, and again demanded another sketch from Merry.

When the twins's jubilation had subsided, the hour for departure on the morrow was agreed upon and Merry could again concentrate on Beatrice. She passed a quiet afternoon, enjoying her time with the youngest Leighton, learning carefully the names of each of her pets. The nursery—very much Beatrice's domain—was populated with a variety of feathered, scaled, and furry friends who at one time enjoyed a much larger place in the family's daily life. It would seem Honoria had some few weeks past insisted that Beatrice's collection of caged animals refrain from visiting the morning room, a source of pain to the young girl. She had a lizard named Freddy, a frog named Daphne, two birds—Tweet and Pete—and a white rabbit known affectionately as Hugo. Once Merry had mastered an extensive knowledge of each pet and Beatrice's nurse suggested for the third time that Beatrice ought to permit Merry a few moments respite before dinner, only then did she leave the nursery.

After dinner, the evening passed swiftly. All the ladies joined in to make plans for the morning room—including Amabel. Kit sat nearby trying to become engrossed in translating a passage from Latin. Hugh remained with the family for only a few minutes, saying that he had a great deal of business yet to attend to. He then reminded everyone that he would be leaving the day after next in order to spend two days in Derby.

When Amabel asked what particular business took him to the county town, he replied, "I am to see a man about the costs involved in reopening the Blue-John mine," he explained. "The mineral is experiencing a considerable popularity just now, but I need a great deal more information before I can determine whether or how to proceed."

"The expense would be enormous, wouldn't it?" Merry queried.

"Precisely so!"

Kit lifted his head from his book. "Merry, do you remember when we went into the mine, but soon came running out because we thought we heard ghosts?"

"I thought you were translating your studies?" Merry queried, smiling at him. The result of her teasing, however, was not what she expected. Even Kit's ears turned red as he mumbled out a guilty explanation that he should have been attending to his Latin and that he was grateful she had reproved him.

Merry stared at him, distressed that she had evoked such a guilt-laden response. Next time, she promised herself, she would take greater care how she went about teasing Kit. She had certainly not meant to embarass him.

She chanced to catch Hugh's eye and saw that he was puzzled, even a little distressed by his brother's reaction. What did it all mean, she wondered. It was obvious Kit was trying very hard to be worthy of his calling, only was it the right calling for him?

On the following morning, Merry, Judith, Constance and Beatrice clambored aboard the barouche and headed to Abbot's End. But before they had gotten beyond the gates, Sir Rupert Hucklow's travelling chariot drove past them. Merry had not met the baronet before and as he nodded to the occupants of the barouche, she caught only a glimpse of white hair beneath a black silk hat, and very dark eyes.

Hugh sat at his desk in the study, reviewing the ledgers from one of his tenant farmers—a precise accounting of last summer's poor oat harvest and the amounts received from other smaller crops taken to market. The figures were not nearly what he had hoped to see.

And he was thinking of reopening the Blue-John mine!

How impossible everything seemed! Yet he had come so far in three years and he knew that though progress seemed painstakingly slow, he *was* making progress.

He was about to open his minerology book when Siddons interrupted him with Sir Rupert on his coattails.

Sir Rupert did not wait to be announced but passed by the butler and began speaking at the very same moment. "Rayneworth! What is this news my wife tells me of your having had a skirmish with the White Prince! Why didn't you come to me at once! A dastardly business when a man is not safe in his own lanes!"

He pulled off his gloves, sloughed off his greatcoat, and jerked his hat from his head, afterward loading all upon Siddons. The butler's tightly compressed lips expressed a strong disapproval of the baronet's manners.

Hugh could forgive Sir Rupert his manners, but not his indiscretion. Had Siddons not already been informed about the attack upon his master, the baronet's loose tongue would have performed the office. He would have confronted Sir Rupert,

but his wish to return to his labors as quickly as possible su-
perceded his desire to rebuke a man who would soon be related
to him by marriage to Honoria.

He therefore gestured for Sir Rupert to sit in the chair in
front of his desk. "Do you wish for some refreshment?" he
queried. "Coffee, perhaps? Tea?"

But the baronet shook his head. "I can't stay very long," he
said. "I'll be heading to Abbot's End next to meet with the
militia. But first I want to hear of your encounter with the
outlaw."

Hugh, realizing he still held his pen in his hand, returned it
to the silver tray in front of him. He had been so preoccupied
with Merry's sudden arrival, as well as with his own business
concerns, that he had all but forgotten the recent attack.

"There isn't a great deal to tell, really," he began, clasping
his hands loosely together on the desk. "There were three
soldiers in all, or at least only three that I could see, and the
White Prince held a pistol to my postboy's head. The whole
affair was conducted with stark efficiency. One soldier stopped
the coach by firing into the air, another soldier relieved me of
my purse, and the next moment my coach was flying down the
lane. It was midnight, very dark, very cloudy. I could not see a
great deal and I certainly did not recognize the identities of any
of the men involved." He could not bring himself to say that
one of the soldiers was a young woman. A protective instinct,
he thought absently. Whatever her motives in having joined the
White Prince, he could not like the image of a noose about her
neck.

He looked at Sir Rupert and saw that the baronet was watching him fixedly, his small, black eyes glinting like a man caught
up in the thrill of the hunt.

Sir Rupert was a tall, thin man, wiry in stature, tense in
movement. His hair was a pure, vivid white in contrast to his
age, which had only that year touched half a century. His nose
was decidedly aquiline, lending a hawkish appearance to his
countenance. Deep lines ran in arched grooves from his nose to

his thin lips. But his eyes, even though they were small, dominated his face. They were as dark as shadows on a moonless night.

"Then you did not see the White Prince clearly enough to know him?" Sir Rupert queried, his eyes narrowed.

"No, not at all," Hugh responded. "I was only able to observe that he had the bearing and command of an officer, carrying himself with dignity and confidance. But no, I did not see his face, nor did I discern anything about him that seemed in the least familiar."

"I see." The baronet's alert attentiveness faded as his thoughts drew inward for a moment. He stroked his chin with his hand. "I appreciate your candor and willingness to speak with me. Lady Hucklow was quite overset by what I am certain she misunderstood you to have said." He affected a smile, but Hugh sensed it was a mere attempt at politeness. The disparity in their respective stations prevented Sir Rupert from delivering his remarks in the manner to which he was accustomed—in the form of a lecture.

"Indeed," Hugh remarked, leaning back in his chair and narrowing his eyes slightly. "I don't recall having expressed my opinions hesitantly or in vague terms. In what manner did you feel your good wife had misunderstood me?"

If he expected Sir Rupert to be at all rebuffed by his words or his posture, he was mistaken. The baronet leaned forward and stated, "I shall not mince words, Rayneworth. You've a deal too much intelligence to be told anything but the truth, and the truth is that the White Prince is using his supposed compassion for the poor to garner a fortune for himself."

"A fortune?" Hugh queried, surprised. "To my knowledge, no one has parted with more than a hundred pounds at any given time and usually the amount is considerably less."

"Indeed you are right! But if you add up all the robberies, the estimate of the combined amount is somewhere in the vicinity of three thousand pounds. And though to you, I'm sure that must seem a mere pittance—"

Hugh lifted a hand in protest. "It does not, believe me!" he said.

"Ah, just so," the baronet nodded. When Hugh had sought Honoria's hand, he had naturally found it a matter of honor to reveal to Sir Rupert the precise condition of his purse and his estates. The man before him knew nearly everything about his father's horrific gaming habits, as well as his own momentous efforts in restoring prosperity to Hathersage.

Sir Rupert continued. "As I was saying, to many the sum of three thousand pounds would be a lifetime's wages!"

Hugh conceded that Sir Rupert's reasoning was sound, but responded that he found it hard to believe that a man would risk his life, nearly every day, for such a reason.

Sir Rupert nodded. "I am convinced the White Prince enjoys making a cake of the local militia by evading capture. But no matter what his motives, I am determined to see that the rascal is brought to justice—to hang him, if necessary—in order to restore the byways of our county to their former safe and peaceful condition. The more I learn of the White Prince's movements, the more I have begun to see a pattern, a mode of operation which I believe will be his undoing—which is also why I urge you to relay to me even the smallest scrap of information you might have, or in the future might uncover, regarding this man. Do I have your support?"

Hugh saw nothing to object to in the baronet's request. "Certainly you have my support," he said. "I would only ask that when the time comes and the White Prince is captured, that the normal order of justice should prevail. I do not want to see him hanged without a proper trial. At this juncture, even I am curious to hear his explanations and to have an accounting of the disbursal of the monies he stole."

"As to that, I am certain everyone would wish for a sedate trial, but tempers among the militia and others wishful of seeing the White Prince answer for his crimes do not always allow for the letter of the law." Withdrawing a watch from his pocket, he rose to his feet. "I must take my leave of you if I am to be in Abbot's End on time."

Hugh rose to his feet as well. He would have extended his hand to the baronet, but Sir Rupert had already executed a bow and turned on a booted heel to leave. A curt "good day" tossed over his shoulder was almost an afterthought.

As the coach and four rumbled loudly across the ancient bridge over the River Wye, the small market town of Abbot's End came into Merry's view. The town was nestled just beyond the river in a sheltered valley surrounded by wooded, rolling hills now covered with snow. Most of the buildings of the town had been constructed of a warm, brownish stone, lending a continuity of appearance Merry found particularly pleasing to the eye. Above all the roofs rose the charmingly crooked spire of the Parish Church of All Saints.

The journey from Hathersage Park had been accomplished speedily, the snow having stayed on the ground so that the lanes had not yet turned to a deep mud. It seemed to Merry that the farther the barouche rolled away from the Park, the happier, more bouyant, and more joyous the inhabitants of the coach became.

Once arrived, the ladies descended the barouche at the Cat and Fiddle Inn, where they left the coach in the hostler's capable hands. After ordering a nuncheon to be enjoyed later, they were free to roam about the shops at will, heading along Church Street adjacent to the High Street.

Merry thought Abbot's End a delightful town which enjoyed a prestigious historical association—nearly one hundred and fifty years earlier the Parish Church of All Saints had been attended by no less a personage than Charles the First.

Two stately almshouses—Dovefield and Peggs—also adorned the town, along with a second, lesser inn called the Dolphin. There were many ancient stately homes along the street, a triangular green laden with snow, and by the river a

mill. Merry had the impression that time had stopped in
Abbot's End and she would not have been surprised if men in
velvet tunics and hip boots suddenly emerged from the taproom
of the Dolphin sporting wide, black-plumed hats.

The dressmakers' shop was the first order of the day. The
milliners' followed, which happened to suit Merry's purposes to
perfection, for the shop possessed all the red satin ribbon, in a
variety of widths, the ladies could wish for. If they did not
purchase a hundred yards, they came close to acquiring nearly
seventy-five, all of which the ladies were certain they could put
to good use.

When their arms were laden with bandboxes and packages,
they returned to the Cat and Fiddle where a light nuncheon of
fruit, cold chicken and beef, aged cheese and lemonade was
served. Afterward, they savored freshly baked Ashbourne gingerbread whose history was as intriguing as the flavor of the
biscuits was exquisite. It would seem that earlier in the decade
three hundred French soldiers had been billeted in Ashbourne
and one of these had brought along a recipe for the biscuit.
Since then, Ashbourne had become famous for the delightful
gingerbread and Abbot's End had quickly followed suit, providing its citizens and guests with a sampling of the unique biscuit.

Just as the ladies had seen all their purchases loaded back into
the barouche, Merry chanced to turn and see a man waving at
her.

The beggar!

Her heart picked up a quick cadence and as she saw Beatrice
carefully stowed opposite the twins, she said, "I must give that
poor man a shilling or two. Do you see him there? When I was
last at the inn I heard his very sad tale—he is quite lame, you
see—and I do so want to help him. Will you wait a moment?"

If the twins eyed her curiously, they readily assented. After
Merry told the postboy to stay the horses, she quickly crossed
the cobbled street and approached the beggar.

"How do you go on, my good man," she said quietly, dipping
into her reticule and withdrawing a shilling.

"Wery well, miss," he replied in a hoarse, gutteral voice. "Be thee well?" he queried.

"Quite well! I am no longer residing at the Cat and Fiddle, however."

The beggar nodded toward the barouche. "The Park, is it?"

"Yes," she smiled, pressing the shilling into his hand.

"T'lord bless thee for thy kindness to a stranger." Beneath his breath, he added, "I hope you know what you are doing."

She smiled, and as she moved to return to the coach she whispered, "And you, Laurence. Pray be careful." She then hurried away.

Clamboring aboard the coach, her thoughts were driven back to the day of her arrival in Abbot's End. She had had no idea Laurence was even in the small market town—nor that he actually lived among the inhabitants of Abbot's End as a beggar.

She remembered how he had tricked her so completely her first afternoon in town. She had just emerged from the Cat and Fiddle Inn when an unfamiliar, quite haggardly beggar accosted her.

At first she was stunned by the man's persistence in accompanying her along the street, but as he kindly explained the difficulties of his circumstances, she was moved to great pity. He asked only for a tuppence for a little bread, refusing her offer of more, but requesting that she do him the honor of accompanying him to the blacksmith's shop where he performed odd jobs for the smithy, who he said was his cousin.

"Thee would please me, Miss," he said, using the peculiar Derbyshire form of address. "What dost thou say?"

She had responded with a smile, accepting his arm, and replying as she had heard the townspeople reply. "I'm willing."

He smiled in return and she was a little surprised to see a fine set of even, white teeth smiling back at her. How very curious those perfect teeth had been, belonging as they had to a man who in every other respect appeared to have been whittled away by life.

His hair was scraggly, stiff and gray over which—and quite low on his brow—he sported a worn, limp hat. His knitted mittens were ragged, and he walked on a halting step, stamping a gnarled walking stick heavily down on the sidewalk with each step. She had been certain at one time he must have been a fine figure of a man, for even in his hunched appearance, he was taller than she.

Only as they neared the smithy did she begin to suspect some manner of mischief was abroad, for his steps began to quicken and he had taken hold of her elbow as if needing support. She began to feel quite anxious when he drew her down a narrow alleyway, explaining it was a quicker route to the blacksmith's forge. But before she knew what he was about he had drawn her into the deserted stables behind the smithy, shut the door and caught her up in a quite scandalous embrace—or so she thought.

She began kicking at him and would have screamed, but he clapped a hand over her mouth and spoke in his real voice. " 'Tis I, Fairfield! Don't you know me! Laurence! Laurence Somercote!"

Only then did she stop kicking at his shins, and leaned away from him to peer past the carefully placed grime on his face, the black patch over his eye, the scruffy hair.

"Merciful heavens!" she had cried, pulling away, yet holding onto his arms as though fearing if she let go, he would disappear. "Am I viewing a spectre?" she cried. "I had thought you were in the Colonies! When did you return? I don't understand! And why are you dressed in these rags?"

Instead of paying a morning visit upon the inmates of Hathersage as she had originally intended, she spent the entire afternoon in one of the stalls of the stables, speaking in low tones to one of her dearest friends. He explained his situation to her—how it had come about that he had taken to the highways of Derbyshire as a sort of modern Robin Hood. He explained that upon the death of his parents he had been cheated out of his inheritance by his uncle, Sir Rupert Hucklow. Sir Rupert had falsified a will stating that Laurence had fallen into ill-favor with his father, having married an opera-dancer, and that he and his offspring were to be disinherited.

"A pack of lies, of course. But since I had been living in London for several years—though I had never so much as given an opera-dancer a *carte blanche*, nonetheless married one!—Sir Rupert was believed. He produced witnesses, you see. And before I could so much as blink, all my funds were cut off. I could not even hire a solicitor to defend myself. But I will have my revenge. There is one man in town who can redeem me— one of the witnesses still lives here, and I have befriended him. Apparently, Sir Rupert has not been kind to him."

"Then you hope he will one day speak the truth."

"His conscience troubles him—he has even gone so far as to confide the truth in me."

"How terribly ironic," she had responded. "But Laurence, are you aware of the danger in which you are living? I have heard some of the militia bragging that they intend to see you hanged before Christmas Day!"

"It will never happen," he returned, taking hold of her hand and squeezing it reassuringly. "I am far too careful to be caught by such braggarts. And, I have far too many who support my cause in this town and the work I am able to do among the poor. You can have no notion! The generosity of these people is astounding. When I am finally become master of Dovedale Manor, I most certainly will see that the poor are tended to beyond just the meagre, however beneficial, help the alms-houses are able to bestow."

Her fears were eased a little with the mention of the support he had in the town. "You are beloved, Laurence. Truly! You are spoken of everywhere among the laborers, farmers and many of the shopkeepers with the greatest affection. I had only to listen, while enjoying my breakfast, to the various conversations and arguments which rose up all about me the moment your name was mentioned. Does anyone know who you are?

That the beggar is both the White Prince and Laurence Somercote?"

He shook his head. "Only the blacksmith who has passed me
off as his impoverished cousin from Cornwall. And he had to
know in order to take my part, because the vagrancy laws would
not otherwise have permitted me to reside here in Abbot's
End."

She nodded, comprehending the difficulties of the situation
perfectly. "Then you are reasonably safe," she stated, again
wanting him to reassure her.

"As safe as I ever wish to be," he returned.

Merry smiled again, recognizing in her friend a kindred
spirit. Laurence would never wish for his life, his existence, to
ever be entirely easy. That was when he had asked her to join
him in his attack on Rayneworth's coach. How could she have
refused? The whole of the adventure was precisely what appealed most to her.

And then she had dressed as a young man, had joined Laurence and his compatriot on their midnight robbery, and she
had kissed Hugh.

Now she was with his sisters, living beneath his roof, wondering what she ought to do next and whether or not she should
disrupt his betrothal.

She sighed as she directed her gaze out the window. Judith
and Constance were busy trying to determine how to make the
prettiest bows from the red ribbon. Beatrice was leaned against
her shoulder, falling into a doze, so that she was unhampered
in her reflections.

Since their discussion in the library, Hugh had been polite
but very distant with her. Nor would she be free tonight to
engage him in any manner of private conversation in hopes of
determining whether or not his heart ought to be rekindled
toward her. No, not tonight.

Tonight, Honoria was coming to dinner.

Chapter Eleven

Hugh watched Honoria's complexion pale, the apricot color disappearing from her cheeks entirely. "Miss Fairfield should not be here. It is improper," she stated in the strongest voice Hugh had ever heard her employ.

He stood with his betrothed and Lady Hucklow at the entrance to the rose and green drawing room, for they had just arrived for dinner. He had informed them that Merry was a guest at Hathersage through the New Year and though he wanted now to explain that she been invited by his sisters to come to his home before he could advise them against such a scheme, Lady Hucklow prevented him.

"Most improper and incomprehensible!" she echoed brusquely. She drew quite near to him and from her short stature craned her neck back to look up at him, her small, blue eyes opened wide with disapproval. "I am most seriously displeased, Lord Rayneworth. The whole of the arrangement is a blow to my niece's consequence, not to mention a stigma upon your own reputation. But tell me, did you even know that she was coming, for I vow I don't recall your having mentioned to me that you were expecting visitors. Really, I am utterly astonished!"

He was so taken aback by their swift expressions of displeasure that he could do little more than beg them to enter the chamber and to make themselves comfortable. He suspected that no matter what his explanation, a brangling of sorts was destined to ensue not least of which was because Lady Hucklow—and to some extent, Honoria—did not believe he took enough command of his siblings. Yet because he already felt more at odds with his brother and sisters than he ever thought he would, he knew he was crammed quite neatly between a rock and a hard place.

"Really, Rayneworth," Honoria said quietly as she sat down and disposed her skirts of lavender silk upon the green and white striped cushions of the sofa. "I cannot conceive how such an arrangement came about. I am greatly disappointed." The tip of her nose was pink with cold and she pulled her dark purple wool shawl, overlaid with white lace, closely about her throat.

The sofa on which she sat was positioned near the fire, but he could see that she was chilled, as was Lady Hucklow who sat next to her. Lady Hucklow drew a white kerchief from the sleeve of her royal blue silk gown and dabbed at her nose, sniffling all the while, afterward keeping the kerchief held tightly in her hand.

Hugh did not immediately sit down but rather moved two screens close to his guests in order to try to direct the meager warmth from the logs about them. He frowned at the smallness of the fire glowing upon the hearth. Honoria had praised him for not letting a grand blaze waste his resources on the estate. It wasn't just that he was preserving his trees in the home wood, she had explained, but he was sparing the necessity of having one of the footmen tend to the fires in order to keep them burning properly.

But seeing that Honoria's nose was growing pinker by the second, he thought another log or two would not undermine his economies overly much. He was just about to ring for Siddons when Merry appeared at the entrance to the chamber.

"I am terribly sorry I am so late, Hugo, but Beatrice would have me read to her another of the Arabian tales before she could be persuaded to clamber between the sheets. Her nurse is a darling, however. Hallo, Miss Youlgreave! It is has been of an age since we last met in London two seasons ago, I believe. May I wish you well? You are getting a good husband in Rayneworth, as you very well know."

She approached Honoria and extended her hand. Honoria responded by giving her two fingers and bowing slightly in response to Merry's greeting.

Merry shot a quick, questioning glance toward Hugh then back to Honoria, querying, "Will you present me to your aunt? I don't believe I have had the pleasure of making her acquaintance."

"That much is true," Lady Hucklow stated baldly, before Honoria could perform her office. "I have never in my life seen you before."

Hugh saw the indignation in Merry's eyes and sighed inwardly. For a woman who professed to value manners and breeding above all, Lady Huckow could be quite rude when she chose. For that reason, he stepped forward. "Permit me, Lady Hucklow, to present an acquaintance of mine as well as a most beloved friend of Judith and Constance, a confidant who they hold in the deepest affection, almost as a sister. Merry Fairfield."

He did not mistake the approving light in Merry's eye as he turned to smile at her, though he thought the deep curtsy she presented to the baronet's wife a deal too facetious to permit him to keep his countenance without turning away and checking the laughter which rose in his chest.

When he turned back, however, he saw that the curtsy had had a profound affect on Lady Hucklow.

"Prettily done," she commented, almost smiling. Merry's irony was most fortuitously lost to her. Addressing Hugh, she said, "Now do pull a chair forward for Miss Fairfield. I should like to know more of her family and connections. And where are your sisters and brother?"

Hugh drew a chair near the fire for Merry who in turn answered Lady Hucklow's question for him. "Kit is helping

Amabel with her Bath chair and both Judith and Constance forgot the hour. They were busily employed on a most interesting scheme—which I have promised not to reveal on pain of death for the present—and will be downstairs momentarily. They do beg your forgiveness."

Lady Hucklow nodded, but scowled in disapproval. "Rayneworth, I recommend you get a proper companion for your sisters who can instruct them. They lack a mother's firm, guiding hand. Such manners should never be tolerated."

Hugh glanced toward Honoria and took up a chair across from her. "They will have a *mother* very soon," he responded, smiling gently upon her. "And one who I hope will best know how to encourage and direct my sisters—especially the younger ones."

Honoria's complexion began to rise. But he could not tell if she was pleased with his compliment or despairing. She did not look at him, but instead clutched her shawl more closely across her bosom.

"Is this receiving room always so cold in the evenings?" Merry queried, distracting Hugh entirely from his perusal of his betrothed's face.

"Well, no—that is yes, I suppose it is," he responded.

"I don't like to see too many fires," Lady Hucklow said. "The cost of keeping a house can run riot if one lets it. This chamber is perfectly warm for my comfort." She sniffed her nose several times, then lifted her kerchief to dab at it again.

Hugh was about to disregard the opinions of the Lady Hucklow and request a footman to build up the fires when he saw that Merry was peering at Honoria's nose. After two seconds, she sat back in her chair and turned to glare at him.

"What have I done now!" he cried, defensively.

"If I must explain it to you, then you are utterly hopeless." She rose as she spoke and, after begging the ladies to excuse her, she quit the chamber.

"Why, I have never observed such paltry conduct in all my life!" Lady Hucklow exclaimed, outraged. "Did you see how she stared at my niece! And you are permitting this hoydenish creature to stay beneath your roof?"

"I have already told you that she is a particular friend of my sisters," he responded, irritated at Lady Hucklow's perpetually high tone. "So long as my siblings live *beneath my roof* I will encourage them to have their friends about them. As for Miss Fairfield's manners, she perhaps might be a trifle unpredictable, but I believe her intentions are quite kind and considerate." He knew perfectly well she had gone to fetch a servant and a little more firewood, but thought the effort would be lost on a lady— perhaps two ladies—determined to dislike her. He therefore turned the subject and begged Honoria to tell him if she had more sketches of tables or chairs to show to him.

Conversation proceeded quite adequately until five minutes had passed and a huge commotion was heard in the hallway. Two footmen burst into the chamber, each bearing a load of wood in their arms, followed by a third man who held a bundle of several sizes of kindling. Merry begged pardon for the interruption and Hugo hid his smiles at the sight of Honoria and Lady Hucklow staring at her in shocked disapproval.

Merry took up a station beside Hugh and upbraided him. "I have never known you to be so heartless, Lord Rayneworth. How could you permit your bride-to-be and her nearest relation to shiver in their slippers from the cold! When did you become so . . . so thoughtless?"

He lifted his hands palms upward in a hopeless gesture and refused to give answer. Within another five minutes, a fire literally roared in the high, arched ancient hearth, the earlier logs and the kindling creating a perfect birthing place for leaping flames. The warmth which radiated from the fire soon spread over the ladies in a fine heat, causing Honoria to shed her purple woolen and lace shawl and for Lady Hucklow to tuck her kerchief back up her sleeve.

Hugh could not keep from exchanging a smile of mischief with Merry. But to his enormous surprise, the fire had an unlooked-for effect that he believed would serve as an example to him the remainder of his days, for very soon all three ladies were quite relaxed and chatting amiably. He would never have guessed such a result would accrue from the building of a tidy blaze in his hearth, but so it had and for that he found himself grateful to Merry.

As he watched Honoria, he saw a distinct softening of her habitually reserved expression, and thought that if she could learn to smile a little more she might even be accounted as pretty as Merry Fairfield.

That the fire seemed to light up Merry's black hair and dance upon the ringlets which surrounded her face and clung to the elegant curves of her neck was a vision he found difficult to ignore. Frequently, she drew him into their discussions of poetry and poets and of the astonishing works of Turner, the famous watercolorist. Before long, as Merry led quite to perfection the comfortable paths of their conversation, he found himself relaxing, as well, particularly when Siddons appeared bearing a bowl of traditional Christmas punch which was passed round and received—even by Lady Hucklow—with great pleasure! Merry must have requested the punch at the same time she had gathered up the wood and the footman to increase the fire.

He was proud of her in that moment—a surprising response to her simple efforts, efforts which he believed constituted the very best of *manners*. He only wondered that he had been lulled into such an indifferent state that he had not overridden his betrothed's protests against fires, and provided his guests with comforts more worthy of his affection and relation to them.

When Mr. Belper arrived, the vicar too responded enthusiastically.

"Your home is quite full of Christmas cheer, Lord Rayneworth, and what a magnificent fire! What? Christmas punch? Yes, most willingly will I accept a cup at your hand." He was a big man, narrow in the shoulders, broad through the chest, and gave every promise of devloping a paunch in later years.

His features were uniformly congenial. He had large brown eyes, a straight if somewhat wide nose, and a warm smile.

The vicar then entered the small circle about the fire and bowed low over Merry's hand upon being introduced to her. She watched him, scrutinizing each of his features in turn, with an expression with which Hugh was quite familiar. There was nothing unkind or impertinent about it—she simply enjoyed people. He remembered she had once told him that she was fascinated by everyone she met, bad or good, and took great delight in learning their histories. "For you would be astonished to know how varied everyone's childhood is. Did you know, for instance, that when I was but five, the Prince Regent caught me up on his horse one morning and rode me several times about the Steyne pretending I was his daughter, the Princess Charlotte? He was so amusing and kind. I adored him then and still do."

He did not realize he was staring at her until he noted that her expression, as she watched Mr. Belper give something to Honoria, changed. Her features seemed arrested and if not confused, then poised in a state of waiting to see what next would happen.

He found himself intrigued and, shifting his gaze from Merry to Honoria, saw that a warm smile was on his bride's lips.

He was stunned, for he had never seen her smile so sweetly before. How pretty she was, even beautiful! An uncomfortable thought occurred to him—why had she never smiled for him so prettily? He remembered how embarrassed she had been when he had kissed her. Perhaps she was more comfortable with the kindly Mr. Belper than her future husband.

As his gaze dropped to her hands, he saw that she was holding a small lavender and white crotched cross. Mr. Belper was explaining his gift to her. "My housekeeper was so moved by your having admired hers that she made one for you and hopes you will accept it as a token of her affection."

"Most thankfully, I will. How very kind of her and of you, Mr. Belper."

Hugh found his interest waning. Mr. Belper had for several months now showed Honoria every manner of attention befitting the lady who would soon be mistress of the living to which he was attached. Glancing back at Merry, he saw that she was now looking into the fire, her expression inscrutable.

How deuced lovely her complexion was by firelight. A most traitorous thought overtook him suddenly. He wished he was alone with her. Not to kiss her, of course, but merely to be with her, to take pleasure in her company. He found himself longing to know how she had busied herself over the past several years. Yes, she had written to him frequently, but letters could only impart a trifling of one's activities and thoughts. Did she still enjoy sea bathing as much as she always had? Did she have another clever anecdote to relay about the most famous sea bathing assistant of all—old Martha Gunn? What was she thinking, he wondered.

Merry watched the flames dance about the logs, her gaze flicking from one log to the next, in response to the sudden quickening of her heart. The expression on Miss Youlgreave's face, when Mr. Belper had given her the cross, had been so enchanting that she could not help but be filled with renewed hope. Was it possible Miss Youlgreave was in love with the vicar? Or did she just wish it to be so? Was she grasping at straws or did there seem to be a bond of affection between Mr. Belper and Hugh's betrothed?

Only one thing was certain, she had every intention of encouraging such a bond, whether it existed or not, whenever the occasion permitted.

Chapter Twelve

Two days later, Merry pressed her mittened hands together within her fur muff and sighed with deep contentment. She was seated in an ancient sleigh among all of Hugh's siblings, tightly pressed between Beatrice and Kit in the back seat while Constance and Judith protected Amabel from the cold by sitting on either side of their invalidish sister in the front seat. The sun shone on freshfallen snow from the earliest hours of the morning, and the snowdrifts sparkled, vivid against the green of the looming home wood and the deepness of the blue sky above. Even the horses seemed to appreciate the adventurous nature of the outing, picking up their hooves in a lively manner as the coachman hurried them over the drifted lane, their silver bells jingling in a lively tune with each prancing step they took.

The gentle rise and fall of the sleigh as it progressed down the lane lulled Merry into a fine reverie. Her thoughts were drawn back to the dinner two nights earlier with Honoria and Lady Hucklow present. Once seated at the dining table, all had proceeded much as Merry would have expected it to—Lady Hucklow scowled upon the children, each in turn, time and time again. Honoria merely winced when anyone spoke too loudly. Hugh seemed fairly oblivious to his siblings's unhappiness, attending, as he always did, quite solicitously to Amabel throughout the meal.

Merry's attention, however, had not been focused upon the

family. Mr. Belper's gift to Honoria had so greatly fascinated her that she spent almost the entire progress of the meal observing him. By the time he had let his gaze rest upon Honoria for the tenth time, and after a tenth sigh had escaped his lips, she concluded the vicar was half in love with Hugo's betrothed.

Was it possible or even likely that Honoria Youlgreave could return his regard? And how was she to encourage such a match, especially when Honoria was one of the meekest young ladies she had ever known? She supposed that her temperament had been shaped to a large extent by Lady Hucklow, whose short, thin frame completely belied her enormous strength of will. An overbearing guardian upon Honoria's gentle spirit had undoubtedly served to crush her will, if not completely, then in part. Even if Honoria was experiencing an awakening toward the vicar, what chance did love have to bloom when Lady Hucklow was there to smash it to bits the moment she caught scent of it?

The worst of it was she had but three weeks to effect a change—if a change could truly be effected. Goodness! Never had three weeks seemed so infinitesimal an amount of time!

When she heard Kit ask, "Merry, are you attending me?" she realized she had been ignoring her companions.

Giving herself a mental shake, she turned toward him. "I beg your pardon, Kit, I was spinning air dreams, I fear. What were you saying?"

"I was only speculating on whether or not Hugo was like to swoon at the sight of the morning room. When Judith told me you had purchased a few ribbons and candles with which to decorate the chamber, I expected to see a little holly, bound up by bows on the mantel. I did not credit my eyes when even the chandelier above the table was draped with yew branches and red silk!"

Merry glanced askance at him and smiled. "Hugh is very like to faint, isn't he?" She had spent the entire day yesterday laboring over the family's favorite room along with the twins and Beatrice. Amabel had been too ill to leave her chamber to join in the decorating, but had informed Judith that she was saving her strength for the sleigh ride on the following day. She and the twins, with Beatrice gamboling about their heels the entire time, had hauled a mountain of cuttings to the morning room from the yew maze and from one the holly hedges near the home farm. It was fortunate Hugh had left for his trip to Derby that morning because by midday the morning room appeared more like an unkempt garden than an elegant chamber in a viscount's house. But they had eventually bound up all the greens into garlands and wreaths, laced them with streamers of red ribbons and bows, and in the end brought the full glory of Christmas to the morning room. Hugh was supposed to return sometime this afternoon and like Kit, she wondered how he would react to the extent of their decorations. "Only tell me what you thought of it?" she queried.

"Very jolly," he responded at once. She noticed how he sat so very straight and proper even in the sleigh. He had most assuredly taken Mr. Belper's lead in every aspect of his hoped-for calling. She felt suddenly wistful, remembering the days of a wilder, more exuberant young man. She watched him sigh faintly, his gaze drifting easily over the pretty wooded forest, his thoughts turning inward. After a moment, he continued, "Mama was used to seeing all the principal chambers dressed for Christmastide. I didn't realize until I walked into the chamber—upon Constance's invitation to inspect your final efforts—just how much I missed the gaiety of former celebrations. I thought the effect quite lovely."

Judith, seated directly in front of Kit and apparently aware of his conversation with Merry, tossed a comment over her shoulder, "I wish Hugo would permit us the ball—then Hathersage would truly be as in former times."

But Kit was still not of her mind and returned curtly, "He is right to respect Miss Youlgreave's wishes in this matter."

Judith took the rebuff in silence and asked Amabel if she was sufficiently warm. Muffled to her cheeks in warm blankets, Amabel murmured in a weak voice that she was quite comfortable. Merry was glad the invalid had felt sufficiently well to join them on the outing. Of all the siblings, Merry had the least occasion to speak with Amabel. And even when she did, it seemed to her that after a few minutes conversation Amabel grew visibly fatigued. In spite of her evident weakness, Merry hoped in the coming days she would become better acquainted with her. Amabel was even more altered than Hugh—probably due to her confinement to the Bath chair. She had once been the most adventuresome Leighton, always game for a lark. To see her now, so thin, so weak, distressed Merry. She only wished that there was something she could do to help her. But Hugh had told her that no less than eleven surgeons had come to see her, and not one had been able to effect a cure.

Merry's thoughts had begun to affect her spirits, so she shook them off and addressed Kit regarding their former subject. "I only hope your brother does not enter the chamber until we have the log lit and all the candles placed about the room as well."

"I counted the candles!" Beatrice added on a squeal. "I forgot to tell you! There are thirty-three and that is not including all the ones in the chandelier. Are we to light those as well?"

"Of course, at least for the first night," Merry returned. "But now I am beginning to quake. Thirty-three! Good heavens! The walls will be dancing with candlelight and Hugh will not like it at all."

Judith turned back to look at Merry and trilled a bright ripple of laughter. "Isn't it famous fun! Hugh will take a pet and I shan't care a trifle."

Amabel, who rarely spoke, said, "You are both mistaken. Hugh will not dislike it at all."

Silence fell abruptly as astonishment settled over the swift sleigh. The trees shot past in a snow-laced blur of leafless trees and scattered evergreens. Merry leaned forward slightly, placing her hand on the back of the front seat for support, her lap rug slipping away from her as she addressed Amabel. "Do you really think so, Bella?" she queried, greatly surprised by the invalid's opinion. Something within her heart beat strongly at Amabel's belief, a feeling very akin to hope.

Amabel was quiet for a moment, as were all the other Leighton children. Everyone waited to hear her opinion. "Yes. For all his harshness these many years, he is still Hugo. I used to think he enjoyed Christmas more than any of us. I believe he will again one day, perhaps beginning this year."

Merry resettled herself against the squabs and drew her carriage blanket back up on her lap. She felt odd tears sting her eyes. Amabel had said so much in those few words, more than she would ever know. Hope now burned brightly in her heart. *Perhaps beginning this year.* Constance and Judith might have told her Hugh was not beyond redemption and that with a little encouragement he could be brought round, but hearing Amabel's steady voice and opinion affected her more deeply. Why, she wasn't sure, but Amabel had always possessed a keen intelligence.

Beatrice began expressing a similar opinion about her oldest brother and before long Kit put forth an example of a particular memory he had of Hugh. "He set out quite early one morning, before the house was even awake, in order to find a Yule log. Just as the family was sitting down to breakfast in the morning room, we heard the strangest sound—Hugh was singing 'Joy to the World' in his loudest voice. He had the stable boy, riding on the back of a big brute of a horse, pull the log to the sloping lawn outside the morning room. Hugo was standing up fully, waving and singing to us. Papa and Mama laughed and laughed. He was always such a game 'un. I threw open the window—it was frightfully cold—and would have joined him except—"

But Kit was unable to complete his thought since at that very moment a muffled shot broke the silence of the forest.

"Good God!" he cried. "Who is hunting in our home wood?"

Constance turned around to face Merry and Kit. "Do you

suppose it is poachers?" she whispered, a hand to her cheek, her eyes wide with fear.

"Pull up there!" Kit called out to the coachman. As the sleigh quickly drew to a halt opposite a clearing, the source of the rifle shot came into view. At the far edge of the clearing, a man, quite disheveled in appearance, was bending over his kill. Because his head was bound tightly by a knitted muffler, apparently he had not heard the sleigh bells, or Kit's voice.

"Oh, dear God," Merry murmured under her breath.

Before anyone could speak or prevent him, Kit leaped from the sleigh and was swiftly covering the distance between the sleigh and the poacher.

"Kit, wait!" Merry cried. The girls began calling to him, fearing for his life, but he ran steadily onward, oblivious to their pleas that he return to the safety of the sleigh.

Kit felt each cold breath burning his lungs as he pressed toward the ragged man who was quickly working a rope about the young buck's legs. Steam rose from the body of the fallen animal, a red stain seeping into the snow. Kit knew a fury he had rarely experienced. How dare anyone steal onto his family's lands and take one of their herd. Poaching was a terrible crime. He had discussed the matter with Mr. Belper several times and had concluded that such lazy men—as poachers most assuredly were—deserved only the harshest of punishments.

He was finally within eight feet of the man, surprised that the poacher had not yet attempted to flee. His worn hat was strapped tightly to his head by a brown knit muffler and further wound about his throat. It was possible he had simply not heard the sleigh or his sisters and Merry screaming at him from the sleigh.

Finally, the poacher became aware of his pursuer, lifting horrified black eyes to Kit, eyes sunken into a thin face that showed a straggly stubble. The man fairly leaped away from his task and from the buck, the ropes falling into the snow. His weapon, an old-fashioned blunderbuss, remained behind.

Like a startled hare, he shot into the woods and Kit realized however close he had come to quickly bringing his quarry to earth a moment ago, he was now in for the devil of a chase. Already his lungs ached with the effort he put forth to keep up with the man who was heading to the east in a trail it would seem he knew quite well. He was about to give up, as the man increased the distance between them, but something within his spirit—pride perhaps—suddenly broke free. It was as though a renewed energy was released into every part of his being, his head first, then his lungs, then his arms and legs. He no longer ran over the snow, he flew, his legs pumping like the slats on the wheels of Trevithick's mighty steam engine that propelled the heavy, monstrous machine to begin moving faster and faster. Thus moved his legs and his arms. He felt like a machine. He felt like he had not in many years. The exhilaration, particularly as he began to quickly close the distance to his prey, rolled over him in wave after wave of extraordinary, heady pleasure.

Then he leaped into the air, flying at the man, and brought him to earth with a heavy thud into the snow, his arms trapped about the poacher's waist. He expected a fight and got one. The man would not be caught, he knew what the price would be—hanging. Sir Rupert had posted every possible warning regarding the punishment destined for the next poacher caught in the midst of his wretched activities.

The body beneath Kit was thin, and he thought it would take so little to break a bone or two. But the man squirmed and slid, turning over in one easy motion bringing a bony knee hard into Kit's stomach. The pain was like a burst of light in his brain but he did not let the man go. He would not! Instead, he rose up over him and brought a fist into the side of his head. But the muffler protected him and for the next few minutes the men were rolling in the snow, arms and legs flailing as they punched at each other's faces.

Finally, Kit was able to throw him on his stomach, catching his arm at the same time and twisting it hard up his back. One mighty tug and the thin arm would break, he thought, but the man's entire body fell suddenly quiet and he cried out a single word, "Give."

The battle was over and though Kit heard the united tramping of feet from behind him, the sound of his hard breath along with the poacher's filled the shrubbed space all about them. Between gasps, the man pleaded, "I've six babes to feed and not a job nor poor relief enough to do it. Pray, Lord Rayneworth, let me go. I'll not poach on thy lands again."

"I'm not Rayneworth," Kit puffed in response.

The man turned around to eye him, then dropped his face back in the snow. "So thee are not. Thou art Master Kit, then. I was away so long, I didn't see thee grow up." He swallowed hard and said nothing more.

Kit frowned, his hand still pinning the man's arm up his back. "So you know who I am? How do you know me?"

"Pa were the smithy at Frogwell. I'm his second son, Jacob."

"Jacob Wright?" Kit cried out, astonished. "But your family has always been upright, proud, hard-working. Why aren't you following in your father's trade?"

The man laughed bitterly. "I lost both hands at Waterloo."

Kit recoiled from the man's words, releasing his arm at the same time, his eyes flying to the bemittened stub. If he thought the man would run, he was mistaken. The fight had completely gone out of him. Jacob rolled onto his back, sat up and presented his hands for Kit to inspect. Only a thumb and forefinger remained on his left hand while the right was gone from the wrist—a mere stump.

"You receive army's pay."

"Nay. The government provides nought. I've nothing."

"Poor relief, then," he added, a sensation of panic rising within in him.

" 'Tis not enough to feed eight," he responded simply.

By now, the coachman was within a few yards and called out his assurances to Judith and Merry, who followed behind him, that Master Kit was unharmed.

Kit felt nauseous, in part from the chase and in part from the horror of the sight of the man's hands. He did not want either his sister or Merry to see what he had seen, and he quickly helped the man replace his mittens. He met Jacob's gaze, and an understanding passed between them, man to man. All that Kit could think now was that however fine Mr. Belper's arguments had been, he had neither looked into Jacob Wright's sunken, starving eyes nor seen the horribly scarred remains of his hands.

Just as the ladies arrived, he reached down and offered Jacob his assistance. Jacob lifted his arm to Kit, and Kit took it at the elbow, easily drawing him to his feet. He didn't weigh very much, less than Kit, and he was easily four inches taller.

"Well, then," Jacob said in a resigned, clear voice, never once taking his gaze from Kit's face. "I suppose thee'll be wishful to take me to Sir Rupert. He'll be the man wanting to put the rope about m'neck."

Merry stepped forward and placed a hand on Kit's arm. "Kit, you cannot," she said. "Pray do not."

When Judith added her plea for mercy, Kit said, "I have no such intention of delivering him into Hucklow's hands. I might have done so a few minutes ago, but—but not now. Only, what's to be done? Even if we vow to remain silent about this incident, you know what Beatrice is—she will blurt it out to someone, and then where shall we be?"

Merry looked at Kit and at the poacher. With a smile, she suggested, "Perhaps he could receive the deer as payment for helping us to find a Yule log. Undoubtedly he knows the woods well. Surely, he can serve as our guide?"

Kit's face brightened. "And if ever Sir Rupert hears gossip about a poacher, we can tell him it was no such thing! Very well!" He turned to Jacob and said, "In my opinion, you have earned your buck and I daresay a thousand such deer as well, for your service to the Crown. But Miss Fairfield's suggestion is a sound one—I'll pay you with the deer if you will find a Yule log for our home. I trust you are adequately familiar with the forest to know precisely where one might be found?"

Jacob clapped Kit on the shoulder with his bound-up stump and said, "Thou art a good lad and I know just t'one, if thee and thy man will come wi' me. 'Twere a magnificent oak struck by lightning two years past. Shattered it were, leaving a thick, wide trunk."

The poacher bade the coachman, who was smiling in obvious approval at this unexpected turn of events, to bring one of the horses along to pull the tree stump, informing all that the log was but a half mile off. After giving the coachman a general sense of the location of the log, he and Kit began trudging down the path, their combined footprints marking a clear trail for the servant.

Merry and Judith returned to the sleigh where Amabel and Beatrice had remained seated and Constance stood at the horses' heads, patting them, talking soothingly to them and holding their bridles in a tight hand.

Later, when the sleigh was heading back to the house, the log in tow, Merry's heart was so full she could hardly speak. Before they arrived home, she squeezed Kit's hand and told him he had conducted himself magnificently.

Kit responded that he had only done what any decent fellow would have done. "Besides, he—he had been badly wounded at Waterloo and receives no assistance from the government. Merry, I didn't want you to see—that is, he lost both his hands in battle. I didn't know until he showed me and then I didn't want you or—or any of my sisters to see. To be so crippled and destitute! I am utterly revolted by the whole of it. All the arguments I have heard, sounding so sensible about laws and justice and crimes needing to be punished—well, they hardly made one whit of sense in the face of that man's suffering."

"I quite agree," Merry responded quietly.

He then laughed, exclaiming that he had not meant to dampen the spirit of the party and began to sing "O Come All ye Faithful," an effort which clearly pleased the ladies for they immediately joined him.

Chapter Thirteen

"This is certainly a mystery," Hugo said, a frown between his brows. "But is it only the laborers then who appear to be rallying behind the White Prince?" He stood by the fireplace in the library, holding a glass of sherry between his thumb and middle finger, absently rocking the small glass in slow circles. The sun was making a slow descent, but because clouds had begun rolling in from the northwest, already the chamber was growing dim and the light from the windows fading fast.

Honoria, her aunt and her uncle were with Hugo, each partaking of the nut-flavored wine. Both Lady Hucklow and Honoria were seated directly across from the fireplace, still wrapped in their warm pelisses, though their bonnets had been removed. Their slippered feet rested upon needlepoint footstools.

Hugo's gaze was fixed upon Sir Rupert who sat in the green velvet winged chair nearest the empty hearth.

The baronet regarded him from intense black eyes as he sipped his sherry. "You may imagine my surprise," the baronet said in a steady, firm voice, "when the militia reported to me that several of the tradesmen actually proclaimed their support of the White Prince's efforts and that if he was caught they would sorely protest his hanging."

Hugh observed that whether he was enraged or amused, the pitch of Sir Rupert's voice never waivered, as though in the

ordering of his voice he could command his world. As the rich
wine bathed the sides of Hugh's rocking glass, he wondered
why Sir Rupert had settled in Derbyshire when he could certainly have enjoyed a career in London among the Tories. His
white hair only served to add to his appearance of command.
He was made for politics, at least in his presence and in his
voice. His connections, however, were not nearly so fine as
his demeanor. The baronet completed his thought, again in his
even voice. "I was never more shocked."

"I don't know that I quite comprehend taking such a position
either," Hugo returned. His own views regarding the White
Prince differed somewhat from Sir Rupert, but he certainly did
not condone aiding the outlaw. The only real difference between his beliefs and the baronet's was that he felt hanging as
a form of justice was utilized far too frequently throughout the
kingdom, especially for stealing. Only last month, a poacher
had been caught near Chesterfield and after a quick, brief trial,
had been summarily hanged. Of course he knew poaching
could become a terrific problem if it was not checked—but
hanging a man, that was another matter entirely! For himself,
he would much rather see such criminals transported to New
South Wales than hanged.

The baronet nodded his agreement with Hugo's remark. "I
don't know that I understand it either," he said. "But this I do
know—which is what I wanted to tell you most particularly
today—we are very close to capturing the White Prince."

"Indeed?" Hugo queried, greatly surprised.

Sir Rupert nodded. "Very close. I can't tell you how satisfied
I will feel when an outlaw who has been tyrannizing our families all these months and years is finally taken in hand."

When the baronet launched into yet another recital of all the
reasons why Hugh must support his efforts and why he should
not in any manner be sympathetic to the outlaw, Hugh found
his mind wandering.

He recalled how he had felt when he had given over his purse
to the young woman. He would not have described *her* attack

as tyrannical, he thought, barely suppressing a smile. He turned slightly away from his guests, especially from the penetrating view of his bride-to-be, and felt the memory rush over him again like a strong, cool breeze sweeping through the valley on a late summer day. No, there had been nothing tyrannical about the kiss she had placed on his lips.

Then another memory, unbidden, asserted itself, of holding Merry again in his arms in the yew maze, of feeling her warm instantly to his touch, hugging him hard, kissing him wildly in return. Why were his thoughts slipping about so randomly? Perhaps it was the sherry, or the steady rhythm of Sir Rupert's voice. Whatever the case, the next moment he recalled how great his anticipation had been the entire drive from Derby to Hathersage—how anxious and excited he had been about coming home!

It had been a long time since he had experienced such a yearning to cross the portal of his house. At first, he tried to tell himself that his enthusiasm was because he would be married soon and that he was looking forward to having a wife. But that wouldn't fadge! Only a few days earlier, when he had been traveling home from Chesterfield he had found himself dreading his return.

Then he tried to tell himself it was because Merry and his sisters were placing a few sprigs of holly in the entrance hall to dress it up for Christmas and he had always delighted in the day when greens and red satin bows were splashed about the entrance hall and the major rooms of the house. But somehow he could not quite credit that the strength of his wish to return to Hathersage was because of a few yew or holly branches.

Next, he tried to tell himself that since Merry had come to his house he had softened some of his attitudes toward his siblings, and therefore he was looking forward to seeing each of them again. But howevermuch he loved Kit and Amabel, Judith, Constance and Beatrice, he knew they were not the real reason his heart had beat strongly the last mile of his journey home. Only when his travelling chariot rolled onto the gravel drive did he finally own the truth—he wanted to be home because Merry would be there.

Merry would be there.

Was he still in love with her?

No, of course not.

He repressed a sigh. She had been dear to him once, yes, that much would always be true. But he wasn't in love with her. He loved Honoria. It was just that Merry's arrival had aroused so many forgotten memories within him that he couldn't help but experience a revival of them all. He found himself wanting to relive them with Merry. Once he was married, however, he was certain that these memories would disappear like a long-burning candle which eventually must melt away and gutter, the flame extinguished forever. His day-to-day obligations would be like the flame to these memories.

However clever his mental arguments, he still found himself straining for the sounds of sleighbells. Siddons's first duty when Hugh arrived home was to inform him that his siblings and their guest were still hunting for a Yule log but were expected back shortly.

"Rayneworth," he heard Honoria address him gently. "You are not attending to my uncle."

Hugh turned quickly back to Sir Hucklow and said, "I do beg your pardon. I am just a trifle concerned about my brother and sisters. They are not yet returned. One hour more and night shall have fallen."

"Ah," Sir Hucklow nodded. "Yes, yes, of course. I share your concern and should night fall, I shall be happy to go with you to meet them on the road."

"Thank you. You are very kind. But for the moment, rather than let my imagination run riot, pray continue. I promise I shan't let my thoughts wander again."

Sir Rupert smiled faintly. "May I count on your support? May I tell some of the tradesmen that you are in whole agreement with my schemes to bring the White Prince to heel? I believe then that we will have a better chance of seeing Abbot's

End united against this rogue, for you must know that your influence would tip the scales. It would seem the progress you have made among your tenanted farmers has not gone unnoticed. You are spoken of highly wherever I turn."

Hugh lifted his brows. "Really?" he queried. "I had no notion. I am very pleased, though. But tell me, precisely what is your scheme?"

Sir Rupert finished his glass of sherry before answering. He appeared very solemn. "We have mapped the last several attacks, including the one upon your coach, and have been able to discern a clear pattern. The White Prince tends to work the countryside like the spokes of a wheel, a very simple method really of covering a large space of land without wearing out his welcome in the local villages. We believe we know where his next attack shall occur and I mean for it to be upon my coach. It would seem that the White Prince has a particular fondness for robbing me. I suspect he is conversant with my efforts to undo him, which must account for it. I have not spoken of it before, but I have been relieved of my purse no less than seven times. It would appear as though I am a particular target of this outlaw." He laughed faintly, before adding, "Almost I feel as persecuted as the Sheriff of Nottingham. Quite silly, when I think of it. But his preference for my money as opposed to that of many others whose wealth certainly exceeds mine, also makes our White Prince more vulnerable. I may just prove to be his Achilles' heel. I can't give you more of the particulars, because we haven't decided yet which night we mean to proceed. But very soon I will be putting it about that I am leaving Dovedale Manor for a day or two and then we shall see. There is only one thing I wish you to know—the next attack will not be far from Abbott's End."

Hugh drained his own glass and set it on the round, inlaid table beside Sir Rupert's chair. He found nothing unexceptionable in the scheme and nodded. "You have my full support in this. I will never condone the White Prince's conduct these many months and more, regardless of his motives. Your niece and I are agreed on that score." He turned toward Honoria and smiled gently upon her. She answered with an equally kind smile and his heart grew soft toward her. He had the sensation that were she to extend herself toward him just a little, he could love her exceedingly well.

"Very good, very good," Sir Rupert said, his voice still firm and even. "I—well now, that is a welcome sound! Do but listen—sleighbells."

Honoria was immediately forgotten as Hugh caught the jingle of the sleighbells faintly through the windows facing the avenue of beeches. He quickly left his station by the hearth, the jubilant sounds of "O Come All Ye Faithful" greeting his ears, the melody delivered by the occupants of the sleigh in full voice.

Something within his heart rushed about madly, swelling his chest with pride and affection. It had been some time since joy of this magnitude rang through his home. And they did sound joyful, his siblings and Merry.

When he reached the window, he could not resist throwing it wide. Tears burnt his eyes at the sight before him. In the growing dusk, the coach lamps on either side of the sleigh emitted golden fans of light on the snowladen drive. The cold air rushed over him and he smiled and waved as the verses continued. The sounds of Christmas and the delight of every Christmas past poured over him one joyful note upon the next. Behind the sleigh, there to his amazement was Kit, scrambling to his full height as he rode the Yule log somewhat precariously.

"He will fall!" Honoria cried. "Surely! Do make him get off, at once!" She had taken up a station beside him and expressed her fears.

"Kit will not fall!" Hugh responded with a cry of familial pride. "He was always the finest athlete of us all, his balance is superb." To prove his opinion, Kit began walking the length of the log and crying out several whoops at the same time.

"Why is he behaving so curiously?" Honoria returned. "Of all your siblings I have always found Kit to be the most sensible, the most reliable. I am seriously concerned. Perhaps he is become ill and has the brain fever."

"He is merely kicking up a lark, which is not uncommon among young men his age," he responded, hoping he kept the irritation he felt from reaching his voice. She continued her gentle complaints but he closed his ears and instead concentrated on the sight of each happy face as the inhabitants of the sleigh waved up at him. He waved in turn, his heart full at being welcomed home so sweetly by each. His last view of the sleigh was of Merry, smiling up at him and waving, Beatrice held securely upon her lap.

Just as he closed the window, he watched Kit jump from the Yule log and race toward the front of the house. He wondered vaguely why Kit seemed intent upon entering the house as quickly as possible but his betrothed's final complaint diverted his attention. "Thank heavens!" she cried. "How grateful I am you closed the window. What a dreadful caterwauling! I hope they don't intend to continue singing once they are come into the house. It is all so—so noisy."

He was piqued as he looked down at her. He could not remember ever having been so irritated with her before, but how could she refer to the singing she had just heard as *dreadful?* He realized she wasn't being strictly critical of his family, for he strongly suspected that if a group of carolers had chosen to perform for them, she would probably have been equally as disenchanted with the whole of it.

As he watched her return to the sofa of green velvet, and again dispose the burgundy woolen skirts of her pelisse just so on the cushions, and place her slippered feet again upon the very center of the needlepoint basket of roses tacked upon the footstool, he wondered if he had ever really known her.

His thoughts and speculations could not continue down their course because the door suddenly burst open and Kit, snow dripping from his boots, strode in. "You will never guess, Hugo, what happened—in—the—oh, I am sorry! I didn't know!" He then bowed formally to Lady Hucklow, Honoria and to Sir Rupert.

"What manners, Kit," Honoria said in just that tone that could do nought else but bring an angry flush to Kit's cheeks. "I have never known you to behave so erratically," she chided, a single brow lifted in marked disapproval. "Of course, I don't doubt that while your brother was absent, Miss Fairfield has tainted you with her rather free manners, but you must agree it simply won't do to be bursting into chambers, now will it?"

Kit's chest swelled with repressed anger. Hugh was about to intervene, when Kit, between clamped lips, said, "My conduct has been inexcusable, that much I will admit, though I would much prefer to receive the dressing down from my brother than—than anyone else. But as for blaming Miss Fairfield, I cannot allow you to continue in your belief she is to blame, for she is not. And—and now I see by the hour I must dress for dinner." He again made his bows to each and quickly left the room.

"How extraordinary," Lady Hucklow said as the door closed behind him.

Hugh glanced from one rather disapproving face to the next and wished only that he had some pretext or other upon which he might quit the chamber as well. But no matter how hard he searched his mind, he couldn't find a single one. And worse. Because the evening had come so quickly upon him, he realized he would not be spared the necessity of extending to his guests an invitation to dinner. As it was he could do nothing else but ask Sir Rupert if he and his family should care to join them at table.

Sir Rupert saved him, however, saying that he needed to leave within the next few minutes. Hugh wasted no time in ringing for the butler.

When Siddons arrived, Hugh requested the baronet's coach and just as the butler quit the chamber, Merry arrived.

Hugh saw her pink-tipped nose, the happy glitter in her eyes, the warm smile on her lips and he felt as though a great weight had been lifted from his heart. Faith, but she was so pretty, her raven's hair a lovely contrast to her purple velvet gown. He knew the strongest urge to take her arm about his and to beg her to tell him every detail of the day's adventure with his siblings. He wanted to know all. He wanted to know everything she had done while he was away. Then he would tell her how his trip had fared and how pretty he thought the decorations in the entrance hall. Instead he politely led her into the room and stood back while she greeted each of his guests in turn. When she took up a seat he found himself strangely pleased that she had chosen to sit near his betrothed. He somehow thought— quite absurdly!—that he wouldn't experience so many improper feelings toward her if she was sitting beside Honoria. His betrothed's presence would remind him of his duties.

When she had politely recounted the day's adventure—a typical sleigh ride, an uneventful search for a Yule log—he reintroduced their former subject. "We were discussing the White Prince, Merry. Sir Rupert feels quite certain he will very soon have the outlaw in hand."

Merry felt her complexion grow quite cold and hoped with all her heart she did not betray the fear she felt. "Indeed?" she offered, attempting to sound disinterested. When she had seen Kit jump from the Yule log and race into the house, she knew he had impulsively intended to inform Hugh of their adventure with Jacob Wright. How her heart had quailed within her, for if Kit had revealed the poacher's existence in the presence of Honoria—who she had seen in the window with Hugh—she knew Sir Rupert would shortly be informed of the encounter.

Her only thought in making her way immediately to the library was to prevent Kit from revealing Jacob Wright's questionable activities. She had found Kit, however, in the hallway and to her relief learned that he had quickly made his escape before saying anything. He had then informed her that both Sir Rupert and Lady Hucklow were present. "And I would never say anything in front of Lady Hucklow," he stated simply. "She is nothing short of a vicious gabblemonger. And I never could abide Sir Rupert!"

Merry wanted to smile at Kit's quite caustic opinions of his brother's soon-to-be relations. She thought he wasn't even aware he had criticized them so roundly. But how nice it was to have him set aside his attempts to keep his tongue in preparation for his service in the church, and to unaffectedly state his not imprecise observations.

Knowing the den of lions she was about to enter, Merry was able therefore to compose herself. But upon Hugh announcing to her that the baronet believed he would soon be able to capture Laurence, her composure was in danger of slipping away from her again. She swallowed hard and clasped her hands upon her lap. "You have every confidence then?" she queried, hoping she might learn more of his scheme.

Sir Rupert smiled faintly. "With God's blessing I believe we shall very soon accomplish the deed."

The reference to a heavenly intervention with the strict purpose of slaying someone Merry loved dearly, brought a bit of warmth back to her cheeks. She smiled faintly in return as she responded as sweetly as she could, "God would not need to give such a blessing were the poor better cared for in England."

Sir Rupert would have immediately taken issue with her, but Lady Hucklow clearly felt it her duty to correct Merry. "What on earth are you speaking about?" she asked, stunned. "The poor better cared for? Why there is not a nation on earth with better tended poor than ours. Every village has in place a careful system of basic subsistence, or are you one of those misguided philanthropists who believe the poor are deserving of more than their daily bread?"

Merry pressed her hands tightly together, working strongly to keep her temper in check. She thought of the many families she had seen during the course of the past several years who had been misplaced by misfortune, families who lived in rags in the cold of winter; who suffered disease without hope of treatment, medicine, or a warm fire to ease their sufferings of blood and bone; of flour speckled with bugs; of roofs unable to hold back the rain. She could only respond with, "Have you seen the poor of whom we are speaking?"

"Of course I have. What manner of question is that, *have I seen the poor!* Every Saturday, before the Lord's holy day, Honoria and I deliver our baskets of bread to those in need, those who live by the beneficence of my husband's generosity. Do you expect we should do more? Well, I tell you now, you will hear no complaints from those dependant upon our lands!"

Merry regretted having engaged battle. Nothing could be gained by arguing against ignorance. At the same time, Laurence had informed her that the Dovedale estate was now one of the worst in the county in terms of the health of those tenanted upon the lands. She knew that Lady Hucklow, her niece and Sir Rupert had very definite ideas of the poor and because they varied so completely with her own, she merely responded, "I have little doubt whatsoever that your tenants who suffer are exceedingly grateful for the bread you provide them. I was not referring to those who are able to depend upon the bountiful hand of those to whom they belong, but rather those who have been completely dispossessed, particularly soldiers from the long war with France and their families, about those whose means of earning a living have been displaced by the opening of the cloth manufactures in the north."

"You refer to the cloth makers in Gloucestershire and the like," Honoria offered, entering the discussion for the first time. "You are mistaken, however. The mill owners with whom I have had occasion to speak have indicated that every effort is always made to move these workers and their families north where they would find employment."

Merry could have said so much—that to leave an ancestral home in one county, a hundred miles north to another, to leave behind friends and relations, to forsake an industry passed on from mother to daughter, from father to son, for a score of generations was no simple matter—but she clamped her lips shut. The subject was hopeless.

Therefore she waited silently, listening with polite inattention to Lady Hucklow's further diatribe on a subject of which she was ill-informed and cold-heartedly opinionated, until the family left.

Once they were gone, Merry quickly related to Hugh all that had transpired in relation to the poacher—her role, and Kit's quite gallant pursuit of Jacob Wright.

"Jacob Wright?" Hugh exclaimed. "The smithy's son?"

"Yes. He cannot find employment. His hands were destroyed at Waterloo."

"Dear God," he responded sympathetically.

"Just so," she said, staring down at her hands and trying to imagine, but failing to do so, just how difficult it would be to live without one's fingers and hands.

Hugh murmured, somewhat absently. "Still, he was poaching and it is a crime."

"You sound very much like Sir Rupert, Hugh. Tell me, you do not mean to give him into the hands of the baronet?" She watched him carefully, her heart suddenly anxious.

"No, of course not," he reassured her firmly.

She breathed a sigh of relief and he seemed taken aback.

"You thought I would?" he queried, his eyes narrowed as he watched her.

"I truly didn't know. You are so changed that I cannot guess at what opinions you might hold. But I do hope you will say nothing to Sir Rupert of Jacob Wright. I fear what he would do if he knew."

"I may not agree entirely with all your opinions, Merry, but I assure you that no one on my lands will be prosecuted—and certainly not hanged or transported—for fending for their families. I will not abide trafficking in profits—the selling of poached meats, mind. But feeding one's family, I can overlook a deer or two."

She rose to her feet knowing that the dinner hour was fast approaching and that she needed to change her gown. She addressed the other matter weighing on her mind. "Only tell me, did Sir Rupert seem completely confident he could bring down the White Prince?"

"Completely. He has a sensible scheme. It would seem the White Prince has erred in being quite so very well organized. But I won't trouble your head with the details."

"I see," she responded, her heart again constricting in fear for Laurence's life. She turned to go, but he stayed her with his hand, catching her upon the elbow and turning her toward him.

"You do not approve of me, do you Merry?"

Merry looked into his eyes and drew in a deep breath. "I don't know what to say. I think perhaps you have been so completely engaged in your own concerns for so long that you do not know what is truly going forward abroad. I wish you might have seen Jacob Wright. He is more bone than flesh. Hugh, he served in His Majesty's Army for ten years, has come home crippled, and receives not even half-pay for his devotion to England."

When Hugh frowned at her slightly, as though trying to determine in his own mind what the truth was, she bade him excuse her. "Or Cook will not forgive me for letting her day's efforts grow cold!"

She then hurried away to her bedchamber, wondering first if there was anything she could do to help Laurence, and secondly, trying not to be overly excited by the the memory of Hugh's expression when he had held the door to the library wide for her. It was just such an expression that, had they been alone instead of in the presence of others, they would have fallen into a brisk conversation. She had known a strong impulse the moment she saw him to begin chattering madly. How hard it had been to wait until his betrothed and her relations had quit the chamber to tell him all.

As Jeannette helped her remove her gown, she could not help but wish again that she had been given just a little more time to arrange everything than the mere three weeks remaining until Hugh's wedding. Goodness! Three weeks!

Chapter Fourteen

Dinner at Hathersage Park was served in the dining room on the first floor, a tradition passed on readily from generation to generation for a single reason—the domed chamber was by far the most beautiful in the entire house. The lofty, curved ceiling—the inside of the dome—was painted in deep, rich blues, greens and burgundies and portrayed a panorama of contented cherubs, draped in a dark blue silk and playing in a wooded dell. The chamber itself was round and quite expansive. Arched windows to the north overlooked a view of the beech trees along the drive and the easterly windows gave a spectacular view of a distant crag which dropped to a wooded slope, at the base of which a small stream crossed the north east acreage of the Rayneworth lands.

The windows were draped in a blue silk-damask, the color matching to perfection the cherubs's scant clothing. The floor was of a rich, polished oak covered by an unusual, round carpet which left four feet of the floor exposed around the perimeter. In the center of the chamber sat a unique round table about which the Leighton family had been gathering for over one hundred and thirty years. From the center of the ceiling, an elegant gilt and crystal chandelier hung in majestic splendour, pouring light over the family from its numerous candles.

Merry looked about the table enjoying the teasing and laughter which had been a natural result of the day's incredible

adventure. Spirits were high, even soaring. Besides, tonight Kit
was going to light the Yule log.

The only flaw in the familial setting was that Amabel was not
present. The afternoon's excitement had left her feeling poorly.
She was partaking of her meal in her chambers, but had sent
word to Judith that she would do everything she could to try to
join the family in the morning room after dinner—if not for the
whole evening, then at least for a few minutes.

But one facet of the dinner was proving to please Merry more
than any other thus far—the solicitous attention of the butler.
Siddons was at her elbow even now, begging to know if she
would like a poached sole filet. He stood behind her and spoke
quietly over her right shoulder, while next to him a footman
waited bearing a silver tray upon which were nestled several
finely cooked filets.

He alone served her.

He served no one else.

She felt the attention as acutely as if cymbals had been
shattering the air for the past fifteen minutes, from the time the
family sat down at the table.

Hugh watched his butler, his auburn brows arching in surprise, his fork poised at his lips, as he finally became aware of
Siddons' peculiar behavior. The butler carefully and elegantly
lifted yet another filet from the tray and tenderly placed it
beside the peas on her plate. Apparently satisfied that he had
attended to her sufficiently, he backed away, his eye watchful
upon her alone as he directed two footmen to attend to the rest
of the family.

Merry watched Hugh cast Siddons a curious glance, then
returned to the enjoyment of her meal. She comprehended
precisely what the butler was about—he was giving her a very
distinct message that he approved of her, so much so that he
was willing to risk the disapproval of his own master in attending to her exclusively. She could not imagine what Hugh
thought of her at this moment. Whatever his opinions, he did
not convey them.

"I was sorry to hear that Amabel has been taken ill again," Hugh said. "She had seemed quite well these few days past. I suppose it is the headache again."

Judith touched her napkin to her lips before answering him. "Nurse would not even permit me to enter Amabel's bedchamber to see her. Not that I wished to do it, for I vow I could smell the ambergris burning from her little china house. I despise that odor so very much. I cannot conceive how Amabel bears it, and so often!"

"I confess I was not aware of how greatly she suffers. In addition to her weakness then, she also must endure the headache?" Merry queried, her heart going out to Amabel.

"Indeed, yes!" Constance cried. "It is not at all uncommon for Bella to have the headache two and three times each sennight."

"I am sorry, so sorry," Merry replied. She heard Siddons' quiet voice in her ear again, "Do you care for a little more of the broccoli, Miss Fairfield?"

"No, I thank you," she returned quietly, turning to meet his gaze. His brown eyes twinkled at her in response. She smiled, adding, "You are very kind, Siddons."

"Thank you, miss," he responded.

"I should like a little more of the Madeira," Hugh called to his butler in a pointed manner.

Merry watched in some amusement as Siddons turned to one of the footmen and nodded by way of command. The footman immediately scurried to Rayneworth's side and filled his goblet. She saw Hugh's nostrils flare slightly as he directed a rather cold glance at his faithful retainer. But Siddons ignored him and once more stationed himself behind Merry.

Beatrice addressed her eldest brother. "I wish you had been on our sleigh ride today, Hugh," she began, setting her fork aside and lacing her fingers together beneath her chin. Her blue eyes gleamed with pleasure. "We had such famous fun. Did you know that Kit nearly murdered a poacher?"

Hugh, who had been sipping his Madeira, could not keep his

composure and came up choking. When he had coughed several times he finally said, "It would seem I missed a great deal of excitement by returning home after you had already gone. However, Beatrice—"

Merry knew that he intended to correct his youngest sister, but Beatrice could not contain her enthusiasm. "Oh indeed!" she cried. "Yes, you did—a great deal of excitement! But I am glad Kit did not kill Jacob Wright, because who would have fed his children? He has six, you know, and he is very thin. I thought he looked just like the scarecrow Cook put up in her vegetable patch last spring. Didn't you think so, Kit?"

Kit, who was seated beside her, smiled down at her fondly. "He was terribly thin, but quite strong."

"Weren't you terribly frightened?" Constance queried.

"Yes, Kit," Judith added. "Tell us what it was like! We saw you only at a distance, Merry and I, and the snow sprayed up about the pair of you as you tumbled around on the ground. I thought—well, never mind that, only I was so relieved to find you were not . . . not injured!"

"Funny, that," Kit replied, tilting his head at Judith, the appearance of his eyes quite faraway. "I wasn't afraid in the least. If the truth be known, I cannot remember feeling more exhilarated, save possibly once or twice when I took an impossible hedge on the back of Jupiter and actually came down safely on the other side."

Merry paused in cutting another bite of the succulent filet of sole and cast a penetrating glance toward Kit. She saw a glint in his eye as he looked into the past, a glint she only now realized had been missing from his expression. She stole a glance at Judith, seated at the foot of the table, and found that the elder twin was staring at her in return, a knowing brow lifted in an accusatory fashion.

Judith had been right after all. Somehow in the past several years, Kit, too, had lost his bearings. She turned her attention back to Hugh's younger brother. This was the Kit she had known, the boy who was now returning after a confrontation with a poacher to haunt the emerging man.

Kit returned from his reverie. "But there was no thought of murdering him, Beatrice. I am surprised you would think such a silly thing."

"But I thought that was what you did with poachers. At least, Lady Hucklow and Sir Rupert say that all poachers should have their necks stretched on Tyburn Tree. Where is that tree, Hugh?"

"Beatrice, I will not have you speaking in this truly wretched manner," Hugh countered firmly. "Young ladies do not speak of having *necks stretched* or anything like that."

But Beatrice did not express remorse. "But what do you think? Should Kit have killed him?"

"No, of course Kit should not have killed him."

"Then should he have been given over to Sir Rupert?"

Merry could not take her eyes from Hugh. An awful silence had come over the immense dining chamber. Even the cherubs above seemed to be staring down upon the current master of Hathersage Park, awaiting his answer.

He drew in a deep breath, a concerned frown between his brows. "There must be some laws upheld against poaching, Beatrice, as there must be laws upheld against anyone who steals from another, or injures another person in any manner."

"Then you do not think Merry and Kit did right by letting him go?"

Hugh turned to look at Merry and said, "Merry acted from the generosity of her heart, as did Kit. I cannot condemn either of them for that."

"Would you then have given him to Sir Rupert?" Beatrice pressed, still dissatisfied with his answer.

"I don't know," he said after a moment, again turning back to look at his youngest sister.

"Well, I wouldn't have," Beatrice pronounced firmly. "Who would then have fed his children? That is what Merry told us, that we must not tell Sir Rupert about Jacob Wright, because if we did there would be no one left to care for his family."

There was a decided shifting of feet, a rustle of silk dresses and a shifting of eyes. No one looked at Merry, except Hugh, and he glared at her. "Merry told you to keep a secret, did she?"

"Well, no not precisely," Beatrice responded candidly. "She didn't call it a secret. Besides, I wouldn't tell Sir Rupert anything. I don't like him. He looks like an eel."

"What?" Hugh cried, his attention drawn away from Merry by this strange description.

"Yes, I saw an eel once and its eyes looked just like Sir Rupert's black eyes."

Merry heard Siddons behind her choking on his laughter. What next would the child say? She had little doubt that Beatrice's observations would be quickly passed about the staff.

"I believe enough has been said about poachers and Sir Rupert," Hugh stated with finality. "We shan't discuss either, if you please."

Since Kit immediately brought forward a new subject— whether or not Hugh had had a profitable journey to Derby— Beatrice soon turned her thoughts toward her dinner.

Hugh was grateful for the shift in conversation. He was becoming deucedly uncomfortable with the whole business of Sir Rupert, the White Prince, poachers and the poor. Merry had been right about one thing—he had been so buried in his work that he truly didn't know enough of what was happening even in his own home wood to be able to judge properly. And the way Sir Rupert spoke of the division among the laborers, tradesmen and militia in Abbot's End, it almost seemed as though a riot were in the making.

He just didn't know what to think. Certainly in his youth his opinions would probably have led him to support the White Prince. But he was no longer young and naive. After having had to endure the struggles of the past three years, his whole perspective of life and the circles in which he moved had completely changed. He knew Merry disapproved of him, which led him back to Siddons and his extraordinary conduct toward her. What did he mean by it? He suspected it had everything to do with how she and Kit handled the poacher this afternoon. But he wanted to be sure.

So, after the ladies rose to leave the gentlemen to the enjoyment of their port and snuff, he did not hesitate a moment in permitting Kit to go with them.

"I hope you don't mind terribly, Hugo, but if you'll remember, we are to light the Yule log. Do come with us!"

Excitement shone in his eyes and almost Hugh was persuaded by his enthusiasm, but he felt a greater need to speak with Siddons. "I'll be along in a moment," he said.

"Should we wait for you, Hugo?" Judith queried over her shoulder just as she reached the doorway.

Hugh shook his head. "Do not delay Beatrice's pleasure a moment longer. She squirmed all through the last course. No, no, pray light the log without me. I'll be along."

Hugh watched his family quit the dining room as the footmen, under the watchful eye of the butler, began clearing the table. Before long, only Siddons remained in the dining room, carefully preparing a glass of port wine for Hugh.

He watched the servant meticulously perform this after-dinner rite and leaned his head against the tall back of the ancient, carved oak dining chair. He tried to discern the aging retainer's thoughts.

Siddons would have served three masters by now. He would have witnessed the house roaring to the rafters with thirty guests residing under the roof—along with their personal servants—for a summer's holiday. And he would have known the house quiet as a tomb upon the death of Hugh's grandfather and then his parents.

He had seen Hathersage in its finest hour forty years earlier, with the east wing completed and the gardens laid out in the formal rage of the times. He would have seen the Park in later times with the fifth viscount and his reckless cronies, drunken and swaggering, dimming the golden years into a red flow of

Madeira, port and brandy, a time when rumors abounded that Hugh's father and his friends held debauched revelries and drank wine from skulls. Absurd, of course, but his father was just roguish enough to have set all the gossipy Tabbies to caterwauling every manner of evil they could concoct within their fertile minds and dry bones.

Siddons would have seen, too, the encroaching poverty long before it overtook his father and the great house. Would he have said anything to the fifth viscount? No, he would not. He would have conveyed his opinions, however, in a dozen quiet, subtle ways which Hugh suspected his father could never have perceived. For all the fifth viscount's winsome, dashing ways and manners, he hadn't an ounce of perception in him. He could never have understood that his faithful friends were taking his money whenever they could—all through the gentlemanly sport of gaming, of course; hazard, faro, the horses at Newmarket. And poor Papa, he thought ruefully but not without affection, thinking himself at home to a peg when in truth, a dram of wine was enough to make him giddy and useless in his bets.

What did Siddons think the whole time his father was losing his fortune? Did he cast a shadow of disapproval over the men who frequented the manor, just as he had cast his shadow all through dinner tonight?

His thoughts having weaved themselves back to the extraordinary circumstance of Siddons waiting most particularly upon Merry forced him to speak. "So, Siddons, you approved of Miss Fairfield's conduct today," he said, picking up his glass of port about the bowl of the goblet, two fingers barely touching the stem.

Siddons stood to the side of the table and looked down at his young master. "Yes," he responded quietly but firmly, his gaze sliding away from Hugh respectfully.

Hugh frowned up at him, feeling irritated. "Now why the devil do I apprehend you have disapproved of *my* conduct? I was not even there today if you'll recall."

Siddons did not seem to want to speak. His lips were pursed tightly together and his brown eyes were fixed upon the fine blue draperies of one of the north windows across from the table.

"Come, man!" Hugh cried in exasperation, setting his goblet down on the table, sloshing the wine onto the fine white linen table cloth. "Your disinclination to answer my question is nearly as infuriating as your clearly expressed dislike of me."

Siddons shot him a surprised glance. "I do not *dislike* you, my lord. You mistake me entirely! I merely—that is, I cannot like what is going forward in your home, in the neighboring villages, in Abbot's End."

"In my home?" Hugh queried, bemused. "I don't take your meaning."

Siddons cleared his throat and very slightly shifted his feet. "Certain members of the gentry of late have been taking it upon themselves to be the law in this county," he said. Hugh knew now he was referring to Sir Rupert. "I—I cannot like all that I have heard of late, in particular as it affects—" He broke off, struggling with his thoughts.

"Speak your mind, Siddons. You cannot possibly be afraid to do so in front of me. I shan't repeat a word of what shall pass within these walls, I promise you."

"I have no such concern on that score, my lord. You are a good man and I could only wish that you had come into your inheritance just a few years earlier. But that is quite another matter entirely. The truth is, you won't like what you are compelling me to say." He eyed Hugh warily.

"My good Siddons, I did not like your insolence during dinner." He smiled faintly. "But that did not prevent you from doing just as you pleased this evening."

"Nay," he cried. "Let it never be said that an insolent word crossed my lips."

Hugh again smiled. "Insolence can also be expressed in one's conduct. And just what would you call a butler who refused to serve his master, and pointedly attended to the needs of one of his master's guests instead? And do not bother trying to tell me you had no such intention in mind, for I will not believe you."

Siddons smiled at last, his crooked teeth appearing then disappearing as his quick, comprehending smile faded. "As I was saying, you will not like what I am to tell you, but you've begged me to give you an answer and so I will. There are those who believe the White Prince is a gentleman—and more of a gentleman than Sir Rupert Hucklow."

Hugh stared at Siddons. Aside from the butler's disparaging comparison between the two men, he was stunned by his expressed opinion that many believed the White Prince to be a man of birth and breeding. "You are not serious. A gentleman? You mean, a gentleman by nature."

"No, my lord. A gentleman by birth, though most certainly a gentleman by nature, which he has proved in every instance of robbery. I've never heard that any of his attacks crossed the bounds of propriety."

Hugh considered this and thought back to his own initial impressions of the tall, soldierly man who had held a pistol to his postillion's head. "I must admit that he did have a considerably distinguished manner about him the night I was so handily stripped of my purse."

"And a great deal of good that purse accomplished—that is, I mean—I am certain that your *contribution* helped many who are suffering in these hard times."

At that Hugh rose from his chair, again irritated. He faced Siddons squarely. "Do you know I have grown sick to death with all the complaints of these *hard times*. However difficult times might be, with a little persistence and determination, I am convinced a man can turn any situation about."

Siddons lifted his chin slightly but spoke as he might to a thoughtless child, his brown eyes narrowed slightly. "If a man has both his hands, my lord, you have every right to that opinion. If a man has an education and connections, you can keep your opinion with great honor. Otherwise, I beg your pardon, but I must disagree, and a winter without coal in any

PRESENTING AN IRRESISTIBLE OFFERING ON YOUR KIND OF ROMANCE.

Receive 3 Zebra Regency Romance Novels *(An $11.97 value)*
Free

Journey back to the romantic Regent Era with the world's finest romance authors. Zebra Regency Romance novels place you amongst the English *ton* of a distant past with witty dialogue, and stories of courtship so real, you feel that you're living them!

Experience it all through 3 FREE Zebra Regency Romance novels...yours just for the asking. When you join *the only book club dedicated to Regency Romance readers,* additional Regency Romances can be yours to preview FREE each month, with no obligation to buy anything, ever.

Regency Subscribers Get First-Class Savings.

After your initial package of 3 FREE books, you'll begin to receive monthly shipments of new Zebra Regency titles. These all new novels will be delivered direct to your home as soon as they are published...sometimes even before the bookstores get them! Each monthly shipment of 3 books will be yours to examine for 10 days. Then, if you decide to keep the books, you'll pay the pre ferred subscriber's price of just $3.30 per title. That's $9.90 for all 3 books...a savings of over $2 off the publisher's price! What's more, $9.90 is your <u>total</u> price. (A nominal shipping and handling charge of $1.50 per shipment will be added.)

No Minimum Purchase, and a Generous Return Privilege.

We're so sure that you'll appreciate the money-saving convenience of home delivery that we <u>guarantee</u> your complete satisfaction. You may return any shipment...for any reason...within 10 days and pay nothing that month. And if you want us to stop sending books, just say the word. There is no mini-mum number of books you must buy.

An $11.97
value.
FREE!
No obligation
to buy
anything, ever.

ZEBRA HOME SUBSCRIPTION SERVICE, INC.

120 BRIGHTON ROAD

P.O. BOX 5214

CLIFTON, NEW JERSEY 07015-5214

Illnnlnllllnnnlllnlnlnlnllnlnlnlnlnllllnnl

of a dozen ramshackle cottages I know of on a certain neighboring estate will rob that man even of his life's breath, or worse—the breath of those he loves."

"Let it not be said that any suffer as you describe on our lands!" Hugh exclaimed.

"Nay, of course not. You've seen well to your tenants and for that reason you are greatly esteemed, more than you realize, by your peers and by the neighboring villagers. But there are some whose notion of kindness extends no further than a basket of bread once a week."

"Have you been speaking with Miss Fairfield?" he queried, suddenly suspicious, for it seemed to him that Siddons held views quite similar to Merry's, especially when he mentioned *weekly bread baskets*.

"If you mean has she swayed me with her opinions, I will say that we have not discussed any of these subjects. But when I learned that she had desired Jacob to go his way without harm, my good opinion of her was confirmed yet again. Master Kit also displayed great sense and the kind heart I've always known him to possess."

Hugh sat back down in his chair, frustrated by the whole of his conversation with his butler. To own the truth, much of what Siddons said made solid sense. He could argue with none of it, particularly since he would not have withheld the buck from Jacob either. It was merely that he was gaining a sense that his whole world had changed while he had been busy riding about his estate, pouring over his ledgers, and trying to determine whether or not he should reopen the Blue-John mine.

He thought of Sir Rupert and wondered if Siddons was referring to the baronet when he said that a neighboring estate's cottages were ill-attended to. Unlikely, he thought. Sir Rupert was a sensible man, and beyond his apparent disinclination to combine mercy with justice, surely he saw to the repairs on his tenants' properties and to the improvements of his land?

He again picked up his glass of port and took a long draught, ignoring the burgundy stain on the white cloth. Why did his life suddenly seem so very complicated, he wondered. He waved Siddons away with a slow gesture of his hand and thanked him for his opinions, but he wished to be alone for a time.

Siddons bowed and on his quiet, dignified tread, quit the dining room.

Hugh scooted his chair backward about a foot and stretched his long legs out in front of him. He faced away from the windows, his gaze drawn to the cherubs overhead. The setting for the childlike figures who gamboled about a green wooded setting was quite peaceful. The painting drew his mind into a state of reverie and he let his thoughts drift.

How much had changed in the past four years—his parents gone, Amabel in a Bath chair, the estate in shambles, even Puppy, who had followed him from grand chamber to grand chamber, had been caught by a poacher's spring-trap in the woods beyond the boundary of his property and killed. Some of the new mills constructed during the past ten years in the North Midlands had had their frames smashed by Luddites, men protesting the shift from cottage industries to mills. England seemed to have fallen into despair and chaos following Waterloo, his estate not less so because of his dear father's foolishness in trusting his boon companions.

He thought of the progress he had made and wondered how it had come about that tending to his own affairs would no longer suffice—that repairing the Rayneworth fortune was only part of what would eventually be required of him. Sir Rupert was pressing him, along with Siddons and Merry. But he didn't want a larger world. Hathersage was enough responsibility for any man.

The thought came to him awkwardly that somehow Merry was to blame for how complicated his life suddenly seemed. Honoria had been such a soothing balm in the press of his daily business. Her opinions had always been comforting, reassuring. For one thing, she consistently put forth the notion that Sir Rupert was managing the difficulties of the White Prince and other concerns in their shared neighborhoods so that he gave no thought to what had begun to consume every conversation of late—the capture of the White Prince. But Merry clearly did not approve of Sir Rupert, nor did Siddons, nor did even little Beatrice! Doubts had begun to destroy his peace of mind.

As his thoughts shifted about, he began to consider Sir Rupert and what precisely the baronet would have done with Jacob Wright. Would he have hanged him, as Merry believed he would?

Hugh didn't know what to think, except that the notion of a war hero being hanged for poaching so distressed him that he knew a strong desire to head for the stables and to take Jupiter for a hard run down the lane. But he couldn't—the lane was still deep with snow, night had fallen darkly over Hathersage, and the air was biting outside.

All he could do was sigh, and wish yet again that Merry had not come to his home. After all, if she had not insisted his family hunt for a Yule log, the poacher would never have been discovered and he would have been left none the wiser. His world would have been as it had been before she arrived.

Yes, somehow all his current distress and uneasiness was due to her presence, not least of which was the fact that ever since she had come he had dreamed more and more of holding her in his arms again. No matter how hard he fought the desire, it was always there.

Well, time would solve this dilemma as it had solved so many before. He had less than three weeks to endure her disturbing presence in his home, then he would be married and she would be gone. In fact, he would probably never see her again.

This last thought should have brought him some measure of comfort, but instead his heart felt heavier than he could remember.

As he finished his glass of port, he became aware of a beautiful harmony just barely audible over the jumble of his thoughts. He rose from his chair as one mesmerized, and headed toward the door.

Once in the hall, the singing became clearer, the harmony an exquisite and faintly familiar sound from years gone by. "O Come All Ye Faithful," echoed to him in wondrous waves, recalling to mind the vision of his siblings and Merry in the sleigh just a few hours ago, along with memories of past celebrations. He knew the voices well—Mrs. Penistone, Cook, Siddons and Colwich, the head groom.

He picked up his step and quickly made his way down the stairs to the morning room, his heart suddenly light again, as though the spirit of Christmas had reached out and placed a gentle hand on his heart.

Merry has done this, he thought. All former anger toward her somehow disappeared completely. In its stead was a sensation that forces were at work determined to rekindle his passion for life and his longings for love. What could he do for the present but surrender a little, if not completely? After all, in three weeks she would be gone.

Chapter Fifteen

When Hugh slowly opened the carved door of the morning room, the first sensation which greeted him, beyond the melodious sound of his staff leaders swelling their voices in song, was a rush of welcoming warm air. The heat from the blazing Yule log had already filled the large, high-ceilinged chamber. But as he slipped into the room and closed the door behind him, the delightful warmth was forgotten in the extraordinary vision which unfolded before him.

His throat constricted tightly, lending him the distinct impression he had wound his neckcloth a trifle too securely about his throat. He felt as though he had entered a world from his past, a world so sweetly familiar to the strings of his heart, it was as though virtuoso fingers had begun to pluck confidently at those strings.

A fire indeed blazed in the ancient, arched fireplace which was well-suited in size to the housing of a log which by tradition was to be lit on Christmas Eve and kept burning through Christmas Day. Of course it was not Christmas Eve, in fact nineteen days separated this evening from the night before Christmas. But the Rayneworth household had had a long tradition of keeping a large log burning upon the hearth for days on end—only observing the ritual of keeping the log in constant flames from Christmas Eve through Christmas Day.

For now, and for the next fortnight and more, the challenge

would be to keep it burning—and to not burn it all up—before Christmas Eve! From this time on, every member of the family took part in the diligent effort to stir up the embers, to add kindling and smaller logs, to eventually burn only one end of the log at a time, to sustain with great zeal a beloved, familial tradition.

Hugh swallowed hard, trying to keep the tears which threatened his countenance to overtake him. He was deeply affected by the sight of the log, by the musical voices raised in song, by his siblings and Merry clustered in chairs and sofas about the fire watching the servants sing so enchantingly.

And how charmingly decorated the chamber was!

Good God! When he had given Merry permission to lace the banister with a few greens and a half score of red satin ribbons, and when he had further agreed to permit her reign in the morning room, he had not expected to see a reflection of his mother's hand in the results. Lady Rayneworth always made a tremendous effort to transform her home with greens and ribbons, as apparently did Merry. Surely the yew maze had been stripped bare of its branches, for scarcely a surface or wall-sconce remained untouched by the Christmas spirit. Even the chandelier was draped with red ribbons and holly! Candlelight glimmered among the boughs and garlands from carefully placed candles.

How happy were the expressions on each face—Kit, Judith and Constance in winged chairs of red silk-damask near the fireplace, and Amabel in her Bath Chair beside the sofa. How completely Beatrice had taken to Merry, sitting on her lap and leaning her head against Merry's shoulder so that auburn curls mingled with black, silken ringlets. His heart swelled within him. His soul felt full, replete, even more content than when he had first caught sight of the same precious faces waving at him from the sleigh earlier that afternoon.

He felt as though he had come home after years of being away.

For a moment, as he looked at his family, he had the sensation that he did not even know his siblings, or perhaps more accurately, he had lost several years of knowing them since the burden of repairing the Leighton fortunes had been placed squarely upon his willing shoulders. How long had it been since he and Kit had taken Jupiter and Juno out of an autumn morning to ride and to hunt and to finish the day's shooting with a tankard at the Cat and Fiddle? A year? Two? Three? He could not remember.

And how long had it been since he had attended one of the assemblies in Chesterfield or Derby and stood up with either Constance or Judith? How pretty his sisters had become. But when had they transformed from merely passable chits just out of the schoolroom to young ladies of elegant demeanor and bearing as they were now? How had they achieved such elegance without a mother to guide them?

Good God! He needed to get them husbands, he realized with a start. It occurred to him that Honoria, as his wife, would be the proper woman to do so once they were wed, but somehow the thought of Honoria desiring to chaperone the exuberant Judith and the dramatic Constance all about a whirlwind of London gaieties caused his heart to give pause. She would dislike the task enormously.

His gaze returned to Merry. Now if she were wed, he knew she would be more than happy to launch herself into such a campaign.

As though sensing that his gaze was fixed upon her, Merry turned to look at him and smiled. His heart again rushed into his throat. Faith, but she was beautiful, her green eyes misted with the pleasure of the moment. He noticed that one of Beatrice's hands was laced within her own. He realized he had never seen Honoria once hold the child on her lap, or even touch her for that matter. Yet how easily Beatrice fit into the curves of Merry's womanly body. How firmly she still held his gaze. He saw his own children in her eyes. They would fill her arms just as Beatrice now did, and they would find every manner of warmth and succoring from her kindness, from her generosity, from the tenderness of her heart.

Suddenly, he wanted to be in those arms, to know her love, to hold her against him, to have her bury her black curls within the protection of his arms. He wanted her—in every way he wanted her. She leaned toward Beatrice and whispered something in her ear.

Beatrice quickly glanced toward him and seeing that he had come into the room she gave a little shriek, leaped off of Merry's lap and ran toward him. Hugh caught her up in his arms and lifted her into a full embrace.

Beatrice whispered, "Isn't the room lovely, Hugo? We worked ever so hard on it. I helped sew the holly together."

He held her close and kissed her cheek. "You darling, clever girl," he responded, whispering in return as he kissed her other cheek.

He didn't move from his place by the door since the quartet was halfway through the last verse. Beatrice slipped her arms about Hugh's neck and leaned her head against his. Hugh felt tears burn his eyes. He became acutely aware that how ever much he had been dutiful to his family, to his siblings by attending to the matters of their fortunes and the estate, he had forgotten how pleasurable it could be to simply *be* with his family—especially at Christmastide.

His staff finished the final chord of the carol and Kit led the family in a firm, enthusiastic applause. Beatrice squirmed from his arms that she might express her appreciation for their efforts with her own vivacious clapping. When the quartet bowed he moved forward toward them, and thanked them for their wonderful performance, after which Cook promised that very soon Christmas punch would be sent to the chamber along with an assortment of biscuits Mr. Belper's housekeeper had sent over from the rectory earlier that evening.

When the staff had gone, and only the family and Merry remained, Constance rose from her chair and could not keep from asking, "Only tell us Hugh, what do you think of our Yule log and of Merry's decorations?" She swept an arm in a wide, graceful arc encompassing the whole of the chamber.

He smiled upon Constance and moved to join her by the fire, where he slipped an arm about her waist and another about Judith's. "Everything is so beautiful and just as it ought to be at Christmas. You must forgive me if I have forgotten my holiday spirit these past several years and more, but I mean to do better. To begin with, I hope both you and Judith will be able to sport new gowns for your Christmas ball."

He didn't know when he had made the decision to permit his sisters the enjoyment of a ball they had so wished for and had so given up hope in having, but he rather thought it was the moment Merry, with Beatrice in her arms, had turned to look at him and smiled.

"Oh, Hugo!" the twins shrieked in unison, throwing their arms about him, fairly strangling him. "Thank you ever so much!"

He had never been so happily assaulted in his entire life.

Beatrice began turning circles and curtsying, going through the simpler steps of a country dance. Kit took her up as partner and, with his hand holding her small fingers, led her through the steps as he hummed one of Handel's tunes.

When the punch had been brought in, Hugh begged Siddons to bring as many staff members to the morning room as might wish to sing carols about the fire for a half hour or so. Merry immediately took up her station at the pianoforte and, as the servants began trickling into the room, the strains of the old Welsh tune, "Deck the Halls with Boughs of Holly," rose up in a swell of happy voices.

When the servants had gone and the family had stolen off to their respective bedchambers, Merry remained behind in the morning room standing with her back to the waning fire, her heart full of Christmas, surveying the wonderland she and Hugh's sisters had created. Most of the candles had guttered and she knew that when she finally left the room, Siddons would see that all the candles were carefully snuffed and replaced for the next evening. For the moment, however, she could not bring herself to leave the morning room.

Not yet. Not when the evening had given her everything she had hoped to enjoy when she first set out from Brighton to Derbyshire. She had wanted Hugh, as well. Of course she had wanted Hugh, but he was betrothed and there was nothing she could do to change that—at least for the present. But otherwise, she had found in the bosom of the Leighton children the very familial closeness and joy she had known four summers ago when she had spent an idyllic July and August at Hathersage Park. She had been the only child of her parents to survive. Three had died in infancy, and then her mother had died. Her father had never remarried and all that she knew of life and of being a woman she had learned from a beloved if eccentric aunt, and from her rather roguish father. She had never therefore known that so much pleasure could exist in the squabbles and giggles and mischief of a brood as large as the Leighton siblings. Perhaps because her father had been nearly as boisterous as Hugh's father, she had grown up with the same vivacious tendancies as Hugh and his brother and sisters.

From the first, when she, Judith and Constance had met at school, she had felt akin to them. When she had come to stay that summer, her joy had known no bounds.

To be here now, at another season of the year, to help the troubled family find a Christmas joy renewed, was a pleasure she could not begin to put into words, nor to measure—but it was very great. For that reason, she found herself reluctant to quit the chamber, to end the delicious flow of sentiments which had begun the moment Kit had lit the Yule log and had not as yet ceased.

She drew in a deep breath and let out a sigh so loud that in the quiet of the empty chamber it sounded silly. She could not keep from laughing at herself.

The door opened and Hugh, with his hand still on the doorknob, said, "So you have not yet retired as my sisters did? I heard someone chortling and now I find you are still here. It is past one o'clock, you know. Aren't you greatly fatigued from the day's adventures and celebrations?"

"No," she responded, smiling at him, thinking again how handsome he was. "And you oughtn't to stand there, you know."

"And why is that?" he asked, his brows lifted in curiosity.

"You are standing beneath the mistletoe and if you don't take care, I shall take advantage of you." How bold she was being.

He looked as though he would have said something, then stopped himself. He entered the room and closed the door behind him. "I know you are only funning, so I shan't come the crab over you for saying something so wholly inappropriate."

Merry wasn't sure why she did so, perhaps because he did enter the room and close the door behind him, but she took up a place on the sofa beside the fireplace and curled up in a most unladylike fashion in the corner of the sofa. Hugh didn't seem to mind in the least. He sat down on the sofa as well, not beside her of course, but an acceptable distance away, his gaze fixed to the steady blaze of the fire.

Silence reigned in the chamber for many companionable minutes. Only the crackling of the dry logs chose to attack the stillness of the air.

"I am so happy to be here, Hugh," she said at last. "You've no notion how greatly I delight in your family. I miss your mother and father, of course, but Beatrice seems to have taken to me and Judith and Constance never have enough anecdotes to please me, though they rattle on endlessly from sunrise to nightfall. Even Kit treats me as he would a sister. I wish I had grown up with my brothers and my sister, but I never knew them."

"I know," Hugh responded sympathetically. "I have not forgotten the many things you told me about your childhood, Merry. And I am glad you've come to stay for a few weeks. If

I did not seem welcoming at first, I hope you will forgive me."

"If you will forgive me for arriving without benefit of invitation."

"The day that my sisters's dearest friend must stand upon ceremony is the day we Leightons have become a hopeless lot."

Merry glanced at him and smiled, then looked away. It would not do at all to be looking at Hugo, not tonight, not given the way that her heart was full to overflowing already. How little encouragement would be required for her to throw all caution to the wind and confess her love for him. Instead, she kept her gaze pinned politely to the flames licking in blue, white and red at the blackened logs.

He began speaking then, of everything and nothing. Of the trials that had beset him since his father's death, of the solemnity of his house since they were buried in the family vault, of his hopes that his efforts would soon turn the tide of his family's fortunes that he might see his sisters well-settled in advantagous marriages. Of his delight that Kit seemed so mature for a young man of his years. Of his pleasure that Beatrice was such a loving, warmhearted, affectionate creature even though she had lacked a mother's care.

His greatest concern, however, was of Amabel, that she had not recovered as the doctors had at one time promised she would. Instead, she remained fixed in her Bath chair and suffered the headache so frequently that he found it increasingly difficult to forgive himself for the accident which had left her unconscious and feverish for a full fortnight.

Merry had known of the accident from the time it first happened. Judith and Constance had written to her of it. They had begged her to come, but she had been at her father's sickbed at that time, burying him the following month. With her own grief overtaking her she had been unable to support the Leighton family in theirs. She said as much to Hugh, that of all the twists of fortune to have suffered in her life, the one she regretted the most was that tragedy had struck them at the same time, making her support of his sisters an impossibility.

By now, the fire had been forgotten, and its safety in keeping her gaze from his face. She was turned toward him fully, her knees still tucked up beneath her, her eyes never leaving his as each spoke of the sadness which had beset them in the past several years.

When the clock upon the mantel chimed the hour in high, delicate tones, Merry cried, "My goodness, Hugh, do you realize it is three o'clock? Two hours have come and gone, yet it seems like only ten minutes have passed since you entered the room."

He laughed. "I cannot even recall having heard the clock strike two."

Merry rose to her feet and kicked out the skirts of her deep blue silk gown, smoothing out the creases one by one. She looked up from her efforts. "Isn't this silly of me," she cried. "As though it matters one whit that my skirts are crushed."

He stood beside her. "For such an adventurous young lady you always were inclined to dress as neat as a pin. I never could comprehend it."

She looked up at him, at the firelight gleaming on his auburn hair, his profile sharp against the still steady blaze of the fire which cast the remainder of his face in shadow. She knew an impulse to touch his hair, to smoothe her fingers across the coarse grain of his thick hair, her hand even responding by arching slightly up toward him. Instead, she sighed. "I'll bid you goodnight then, Lord Rayneworth," she said with a teasing smile.

"I'll be happy to accompany you up the stairs, Miss Fairfield," he returned in kind. "After all, it is quite late and at such an hour the former Leighton spirits are known to traverse the halls."

"If you are certain this is true, I shall be grateful for your company." When he offered his arm to her, she took it with a laugh.

They crossed the chamber together and, pausing before the door which led into the hallway, he placed a hand upon the knob only to let it fall back into place. He turned toward her, and glancing upward said, "A friendly kiss beneath the mistletoe, Merry, for old time's sake?"

Merry felt her heart leap within her breast. Could any kiss she shared with Hugh ever be *merely friendly?* She thought not, but the tenderness of his request prompted her to nod and smile up at him.

He placed his hands on each of her arms and leaned down to her, his lips but a breath away. He paused and she waited, wondering why he didn't kiss her. She felt his breath on her lips and her lips parted in a sigh. Her eyes were closed and she felt his hands slide from her arms to her back. As if responding on their own, her hands slipped easily about his back as he drew her into a firm, loving embrace. Only then did his lips find hers and he kissed her, a faint groan issuing from his throat.

How dear he was to her, as dear as bright sunshine after a month of rain, as dear as yellow daffodils springing to life after a late snow, as dear as a bountiful harvest of golden hay after years of famine. His embrace, the touch of his lips, brought a warmth surrounding her that even the chill of the winter night could not have dispelled. As she held him more tightly still, she felt the firmness of his back beneath the soft fabric of his coat. She stepped into him, a movement which brought another groan resounding deep in his chest.

She revelled in the closeness of his body, the feel of his lips and breath upon hers as he placed more forbidden kisses upon her cheeks, her nose, her mouth. She breathed in deeply, wanting his breath to mingle with hers that she might know a little of the oneness his betrothal was denying her.

His movements became more fitful, his hand sliding the length of her back to become a tight, breathtaking pressure at her waist. He held her against him as though he never wanted to be apart from her. She withdrew a hand from his back and slipped it about his neck, her fingers stretching into his auburn locks. In response, his own fingers were quickly laced among her black curls, kneading, searching, yearning. How much she wanted the moment to go on forever.

But just as this thought traversed her mind, a faint, quarter-hour ding from the mantel clock reminded her of the lateness of the hour and of her tardiness in coming to Derbyshire. Slowly, she began releasing him, disentangling her fingers from his hair, withdrawing her hand from about his neck and letting her other hand return to its natural but quite lonely place by her side.

He murmured a faint, "No," in protest. But she gently tugged at his sleeve. He released her at last, but did not at first look at her. Instead, he kept his gaze fixed to her arm which he again wrapped about his own in a protective manner. "I should explain," he began quietly. But she quickly placed a single finger upon his lips, which he sweetly kissed.

"I wish I had come to your home sooner, Hugh," she said.

Only then did he look at her, his eyes full of sadness. "I am beginning to comprehend that I have been something of a fool," he said, at last pushing the door open.

When Merry stepped into the hallway, a rush of cold air flowed over her, causing a shiver to run down her neck and side.

Had she come too late?

Chapter Sixteen

"It is so vulgar!" Honoria cried. "So—so common!" She closed her lace shawl over her bosom as though protecting herself from the sight of the morning room in all its Christmas glory. She stood near the doorway beside Hugh, her brown eyes wide, her mouth slightly agape.

Merry felt her cheeks tingle with embarrassment for Hugh and for Honoria. These words, spoken so spontaneously had said more of Honoria's disposition than any carefully prepared speech could possibly recover.

Constance had told Merry earlier that Honoria had been spending Sunday afternoons, following church services, with Hugh's family since the day she had accepted of his hand in marriage. According to Constance, Honoria's expressed intent had always been that she hoped by sharing the afternoon apart from her aunt and uncle, she might come to know the whole family better. Merry thought it likely she would come to know them very much better in the coming few minutes after such a wretched beginning.

"I don't like you," Beatrice returned hotly, glaring at her future sister-in-law. She had just finished helping Kit place another small log on the fire when Honoria delivered her speech.

"Beatrice!" Honoria countered. "Whatever your opinions might be, it is not considered polite to give them voice."

Merry would have intervened immediately, but Constance, who rarely came to cuffs with anyone, stepped forward and surrounded Beatrice protectively with her arms. "You ought more frequently to heed your own strictures, Miss Youlgreave!" she cried. "For I do not think you kept us in the least ignorant of your opinions where our decorations were concerned. And Beatrice worked for hours on the holly garlands upon the mantel. How unkind of you to call our labours *vulgar!*"

Kit was standing next to Beatrice as well and felt compelled to add, "We certainly don't think the satin ribbons, candles and yew branches either *vulgar* or *common!*" His lips were rather white and pinched as he stared back at Honoria.

Merry was not surprised that Honoria's cheeks turned a bright pink. Her first impulse was to intervene, to smoothe away the prickly reactions Honoria's words had caused, but she checked the impulse—it would do no harm for Hugh's bride-to-be to learn she could not give offense without the Leighton children expressing their dislike of it.

She glanced instead at Hugh, wondering what he thought of Honoria's spontaneous response to a setting he himself adored. He bore a slight frown between his brows and an arrested expression on his face as he watched his betrothed. If she thought he might make an effort to stop his sibling's counterattack, she was mistaken. As she continued to watch him, she realized he was too stunned to speak.

Therefore, when Judith joined the group in front of the fireplace, her countenance stormy, Merry felt compelled to rise from the sofa. "The entire chamber is much prettier at night," she offered, "when the candles are lit, which causes the shadows of the holly leaves to dance upon the wall. Do you intend to remain through the evening with your uncle?"

Honoria cast her a grateful glance and Merry found her heart going out to the young woman who was clearly out of her depth in the presence of so feisty an auburn array as the Leighton children. "No, I do not. My aunt is ill with a putrid sore throat and I must return to her. Thank you so very much for inquiring. Do you know I believe you are right when you say the chamber will show to advantage at night. I—I have always found that the glow of candles softens, er, everything."

From the corner of her eye, Merry could see Judith whispering something to Beatrice and afterward Beatrice dashed from the room.

"How extraordinary," Honoria said, watching the young child dart through the door leading to the servants' stairs. Again, her disapproval was marked, but not without cause. Even Hugh scowled at Beatrice's improper exit from the chamber and from the presence of a guest.

For the barest moment, however, Merry's attention was caught by the mistletoe which hung above the doorjamb. Memories from the early morning hours flooded her with unwelcome sensations and she could not keep from glancing at Hugh. He did not meet her gaze, but moved to Honoria's side and was even now begging her to seat herself on the sofa near the fireplace where the Yule log was burning brightly. She protested however, explaining that she was afraid a spark would catch in her lace shawl and set her ablaze. She chose therefore to sit on the sofa of red silk-damask farthest from the fire.

Merry could not keep from noticing that Hugh held her hand clasped in his. She felt terribly blue-devilled all of a sudden, wishing that Hugh was holding her hand instead of Honoria's and wondering how he would ever be happy with such a complaining female dangling about his coattails. She repressed a very deep sigh, and instead of taking up her seat on the sofa again—which would have placed her nearest to Honoria—she moved to a small writing desk near the southerly window.

Hugh seated himself next to Honoria and began speaking to her in a low voice.

Judith and Constance each moved to sit on the pair of winged chairs which were situated to the side of the fireplace. There, they immediately succumbed to a pile of magazines—*La Belle Assemblee*, of course—their most pressing task of the day to decide upon the gowns they would wear to the Christmas ball.

The *fete* had been set for two weeks time, the nineteenth, and if they hoped to have new gowns they would have to present their request to the modiste in Abbot's End as quickly as possible.

Kit seated himself in a chair near the fire but opposite the twins, disposing his long legs comfortably toward the flames.

Merry pulled a sheet of writing paper forward and began compiling a list of everything needed to be purchased or to be accomplished before the Christmas ball could take place. But it was a list from which she was easily distracted, by Judith's pulling a face at her sister's choice of gold braided trim, by Hugh bending his head near Honoria's in order to hear her whispers, by Kit first scratching at his elbow, then shifting in his seat, and finally tossing aside his book and jumping to his feet.

She was not surprised when he announced, "I intend to ride Juno this afternoon. Do you care to ride out with me, Hugo?"

Everyone was so surprised by his announcement, and by the obvious slight his invitation placed upon Honoria, that even Constance let out a small gasp. Every pair of eyes was instantly directed upon Kit.

Merry was able to see Honoria's profile from where she sat and, even at an awkward angle, she could easily discern that Honoria was displeased.

Hugh was angry too. "I don't know precisely where you put your manners since last night, but I beg you will retrieve them at once and apologize to Miss Youlgreave."

Kit brushed an impatient hand through his hair and said, "I meant no offence, truly," he said. "I merely wished to ask my brother to accompany me on a ride, but I forgot! I am sorry, indeed, I am." He then bowed to her and Honoria offered him a gracious inclination of her head by way of accepting his apology.

Shortly afterward, Kit excused himself from the morning room. Fifteen minutes later, Merry was able to observe Kit on horseback riding toward the home wood. She was intrigued suddenly. To her knowledge, Kit had not gone riding since her arrival and he had seemed quite restless all morning, squirming in the hard pews of the church during Mr. Belper's long sermon on the virtues of obedience. She held her pen in her hand and stared out at the cloudy sky. Snow still frosted the garden, though the yew maze—a little thin in spots—was no longer dusted with snow. She wondered how deeply the adventure of the day before had affected Kit and whether or not he would remain fixed upon becoming a clerk in Holy Orders.

Merry stared down at the paper in front of her. How her thoughts were rambling, first down one path then another, but each quite far from the Christmas ball. She withheld yet another sigh as thoughts of the kiss she had shared with Hugh the night before again assailed her. This morning he had apologized again, quite humbly, for kissing her. His words had been halting. "As though I could change a thing at this juncture— damme, I am sorry, Merry, for everything. Will you forgive me?"

Forgive him? She could forgive him for the kiss of last night—if it was in the least necessary, which it most certainly was not!—but she could not forgive him for having become leg-shackled to Honoria Youlgreave.

This time, she did not repress the sigh which had been building up in her the entire morning. Hugh turned slightly to look at her, frowning. "Is everything all right, Merry?" he queried.

She shifted round in her chair to see him more fully and said, "Yes, perfectly. I was arranging a list for the ball. I thought perhaps Miss Youlgreave would like to take part in making some of the plans." Only when she saw the look of perplexion on Honoria's face did she realize Hugh had not yet broached the subject with his betrothed.

He gave her a shake of his head, but it was too late.

"What ball?" Honoria queried.

From the corner of her eye, Merry saw Beatrice open the door to the servants' stairs and quietly enter the chamber. She knew then that mischief was afoot.

As Hugh began explaining his decision to permit the Christmas ball after all, Beatrice came around behind the sofa and before either Hugh or Honoria knew of her presence, she had dumped something in Honoria's lap.

Honoria shrieked, jumped to her feet and brushed the object from her skirts, shrieking a second time as she clutched her shawl to her bosom, then dropped to the carpet in a swoon.

Then Beatrice shrieked. "If she has fallen on Freddy he will be as flat as a sheet of paper! Oh, Hugo, please get her up at once! At once!"

"Oh, for heaven's sake," Hugh said, disgruntled as he scolded Beatrice. He found the lizard darting beneath the sofa, caught it, then bade his youngest sister immediately remove Freddy from the chamber. "You know she can't abide your pets! Now see what you have done! Go to your room at once and do not return until I give you permission."

Beatrice, in true Leighton fashion, merely gathered up her lizard and with her head held high, her countenance proclaiming victory, she strode from the morning room.

Hugh knelt beside his bride-to-be, patting her hand and speaking softly to her. The twins, completely unsympathetic, each moved to the back of the sofa and stared down at a female whom they informed Merry had fainted no less than three times in the past month alone. Merry rounded the corner of the sofa, her vinaigrette open, and joined Hugh in his ministrations.

Judith taunted her brother by addressing Merry. "You shouldn't have mentioned the Christmas ball, you know. That was the real reason she swooned!"

"Judith, hush," Merry whispered, biting her lip to keep from smiling.

Hugh glared up at his sisters. "She hardly fainted because of the ball and very well you know it."

Judith merely lifted a scornful brow. "I would not be so certain, brother dear."

And as though speaking her part on cue, like an actress at

Drury Lane, Honoria's eyelids fluttered open and she murmured, "Hugh, you cannot be serious about having a ball."

Merry dared not look at Hugh, but pressed her teeth deeply into her lip lest she betray her truly hoydenish amusement at the situation. She did steal a glance at Hugh and the irritation on his face, as he patted Honoria's hand a little more fervently than any lady could wish for, nearly set her off.

Fortunately, the butler opened the door and announced Mr. Belper. When he assessed the situation, he confirmed the truth regarding Honoria's propensity to faint.

"Oh, dear," Siddons said. "Has Miss Youlgreave swooned again? Shall I fetch the housekeeper, m'lord?"

"Yes, if you please, and the usual lavender water," Hugh responded.

When Mrs. Penistone arrived and directed Honoria to recline on the sofa with no less than three embroidered pillows behind her back, Merry stepped away from the sofa and joined Mr. Belper to stand at a polite distance near the fireplace. Hugh remained in front of his betrothed, still holding her hand.

Merry was about to make a comment on Miss Youlgreave's sensibilities when she noted that Mr. Belper's expression was quite fretful. He did not have a direct view to Honoria's face since Hugh's elbow or shoulder or his back frequently obscured his line of sight, so his head bobbed about in a curious manner.

Finally he turned to her and in a distressed whisper asked, "Do you think she is taken ill with consumption?"

"No, I don't think so," Merry responded. "I'm afraid Beatrice is to blame for her current indisposition. She dropped Freddy on her lap."

"Ah," Mr. Belper replied, then frowned. "Who is Freddy?"

"Her lizard," Merry whispered in return.

Mr. Belper had the good sense to chuckle a little. "Beatrice is quite high-spirited. Had she played such a trick on you, I have little doubt you would have enjoyed such an attention from Beatrice. But not Miss Youlgreave. She is not of your strong mind. She is quite delicate, actually." He smiled softly and sighed.

Merry looked up at the good vicar and was struck by how kindly he had spoken of Honoria. He was a good man, she thought. The sort of man who knew how to be a friend to everyone. That his heart beat for Honoria became more and more obvious to Merry.

As though to prove her belief, he withdrew a pressed flower from the book he was carrying. "Will you see that Miss Youlgreave receives this?" he said quietly. "She will recognize it at once, I'm sure. Last summer she admired the primroses that grow in abundance about the parsonage and I pressed this one for her. But now I must find Master Kit. He was supposed to be at the rectory at half-past one and it is nearly two I see, by the clock on the mantel." When he drew his silver watch from the pocket of his coat, he nodded. "Yes, two o'clock. I can't imagine what happened to him. He is always punctual."

"Indeed," Merry responded, a frown creasing her brow as she received the flower from him. "Kit was here until a few moments ago when he announced his intention of riding out. I did not know he had an appointment with you. But I'm 'fraid you missed him entirely. I saw him cross the field astride Juno."

Mr. Belper thanked her for her information, bowed to her, then excused himself. Merry thought it quite intriguing that Kit had apparently forgotten an appointment. She knew him well enough to know that he rarely, if ever, simply forgot an agreed-upon meeting.

When Honoria was sufficiently recovered, Merry placed the pressed flower in her hand and delivered Mr. Belper's explanation of why he had wanted her to have it. Honoria lifted the small, delicate yellow petals to her nose and sniffed, her gaze taking on a faraway appearance. "The primroses were so pretty last summer about the parsonage." Her fingers trembled as she spoke and a faint blush crept up her cheeks. In a whisper, she requested Mrs. Peniston to apply more lavender water to her temples.

Merry left her shortly afterward, her heart beating strongly in her breast. She quit the morning room, wishing to be anywhere but near either Honoria or Hugo. Hope was alive within her. Here was the very budding of love, but how was she to encourage sufficiently the match when only eighteen days remained until Honoria's wedding?

An hour later, while closeted in his study, Hugh received an unexpected visit from Sir Rupert. As the baronet seated himself in the Empire chair beside his desk, he informed him of some of the progress he had made during the prior two days, ending with the fact that he had been on the grounds of Hathersage Park for the past hour.

"What?" Hugh cried, unwilling at first to believe what Sir Rupert had just told him. He rose slowly from his chair behind the desk, staring hard at the baronet all the while. Sir Rupert was kind enough to repeat himself, after which Hugh rounded his desk and moved to stand squarely in front of him. He shook his head. "You are telling me that you rode onto my property, went directly to the stables and began questioning my head groom—all without so much as a by your leave?"

"Yes," the baronet answered baldly.

Hugh was dumbfounded. Never, no matter how sore the provocation, would he infringe upon the privacy of one his neighbors. He could comprehend any of his neighbors crossing his lands—making use of a style, or bridge or lane. But never could he condone what the baronet had done. "I beg your pardon, Sir Rupert, but I cannot credit that you were here, on my property, without informing me! I shall not mince words. You've gone beyond the pale."

The baronet lifted thin, white brows. "Discretion was critical," he responded by way of explanation, his voice even and clear. "I deemed it necessary to direct my questions to your servants without prior warning of my intentions. My sworn vow to bring the White Prince to earth must be my justification. You know how unreliable servants are. And you would be amazed the manner of prevarication I receive once they have alerted one another to my presence in any home." He shifted sideways slightly in order to remove a silver snuffbox from the pocket of his coat. The box bore a raised lid engraved with the image of a set of scales. Popping the lid open with the effortless skill of many years of practice, he offered some to Hugh. When Hugh refused, he took a pinch, placed the powdery grains at each nostril and sniffed strongly. "Ah," he sighed. "A much needed refreshment."

Hugh turned away from the baronet, his temper volatile in the face of Sir Rupert's lack of remorse. Harsh words kept rising from within his throat to burn his tongue but he bit them back. For some reason incomprehensible to him, Sir Rupert saw nothing wrong in his actions. It seemed incredible that the baronet felt himself justified merely because he was in pursuit of an outlaw. Perhaps it was that he felt the close connection between the families had given him a liberty he would otherwise not have taken. Yet Hugh could not help think that Sir Rupert was the last man on earth who would tolerate having his own servants questioned without his foreknowledge.

"The devil of it is, Rayneworth," he began, crossing his legs at the knee and relaxing into the chair of black and gilt, "—and I know you will be dumbstruck when I tell you as much—but every bit of evidence I have gathered points to a traitor here, in your house. I am become convinced someone at Hathersage keeps the White Prince supplied with knowledge of the comings and goings of the countryside."

If Hugh had been astonished by Sir Rupert's remorseless conduct, now he was indeed dumbfounded. "Someone here, in my home?" he cried, incredulous. "You cannot be serious!"

"Never more so," he said, his black eyes narrowed. "Do you remember my telling you a few days ago that I plotted on a map all the known incidents of attack?"

"Yes, you said that you could predict the next location by your map and that you had deduced the White Prince appeared to be conducting his activities from Abbot's End—spokes of a wheel, I believe you said."

Sir Rupert nodded, fingering his snuffbox thoughtfully, his eyes still narrowed. "I failed to mention that all these attacks are never more than ten miles distant from your house, how ever much they appear to radiate from Abbot's End. The outlaw travels but five miles to the north and west, yet more than fifteen to the south and east. That places your home in the very center of his activities." He gestured in a curt sweep of his hand outward, indicating Hugh's home.

"Are you absolutely certain?" Hugh responded, moving to stand by the fireplace where he leaned his arm on the mantel. "I know my servants well. Not one would use me so ill. Not one! I am certain of it!"

"We have all been misled," Sir Rupert said. "Consider the White Prince, for instance. He is believed to be a gentleman."

"I have heard such rumors," Hugh returned, giving hard consideration to all that the baronet had just told him. Someone in his house! Could it be possible? "And did you discover from my head groom the identity of the traitor?"

Sir Rupert shook his head. "No. I got the distinct impression he had his suspicions, but he would say nothing."

Hugh turned this over in his mind. Was it truly possible that someone he trusted was involved with the questionable activities of the White Prince?

"I can see you are distressed. But I wish to assure you that I shall very soon have the White Prince in hand and we shall have this dastardly business behind us. However, I do want your permission for members of the militia to follow any suspicious fellow who, in his flight, might choose to cross your lands or possibly *return* to your house. Will you agree to that?"

This was at least something, Hugh thought. Perhaps Sir Rupert was not entirely lost to neighborly consideration after all. "On the condition that I am notified immediately afterward, no matter how late the hour."

"Agreed," Sir Rupert responded, rising from his chair and replacing his snuffbox in the pocket of his coat. "And now, I must return to my wife. A putrid sore throat, or some such thing. Can't abide it when she's ill."

Chapter Seventeen

Late that night, Merry stole into Hugh's bedchamber, closing the door quietly behind her. Her heart beat loudly in her ears at the outrageous scheme she had concocted in response to Hugh's apparent ignorance of the state of the countryside. She intended nothing less than to persuade him to join her on the roads—two young men on a jaunt about the county, since she would be dressed in the same clothes she had worn during the White Prince's attack on his coach. She wanted Hugh to see for himself several pockets of poverty which Laurence had told her about during their conversation on her first day in Abbot's End. But at this late hour, it would not do to have Hugh calling for the guard in the middle of the night. Her scheme would surely come to nought and she would cast herself and Hugh in a terrible scandal.

No. She must be careful to wake him properly.

He was lying on his back with his pillow over his face, his body motionless save the slow rise and fall of his chest. He was in a comfortable sleep. She had intended upon gently speaking into his ear, but for some reason—probably the lateness of the hour and the adventurous nature of her plan—she was prompted to cross the room stealthily to his bed, climb onto the bed and creep across the small distance to his body. She then leapt on him, sitting on his chest as she placed both her hands on the pillow.

She had thought he might struggle a little, but she was not prepared for his strength as he sat bolt upright, dragging the pillow from his face, and immediately wrestling with her, tossing her over and throwing his weight onto the length of her body. She began whispering his name quickly and begging him to get up.

The whole of it was a sea of confusion to Hugh. He had been dreaming about riding across the valley on the back of a white horse and racing down a lane in the deep of night. He couldn't see where he was going and suddenly he found himself charging into thick shrubberies, his face, arms, and chest choked with leaves. Then he awoke, only to find himself being attacked in his own bed by a man, only not a man, a boy perhaps by the feel of the thin arms and legs flailing about beneath him. Then he heard the voice of the young woman who had robbed him alongside the White Prince, only her voice was genteel.

"What the devil!" he cried in a hoarse whisper. "Merry, is that you? Good God, what are you doing?"

He recoiled backwards, and though he wore a long nightshirt the intimacy of the moment startled him and he dragged his bedcovers all around him like a modest young maid.

Merry giggled and sat up rubbing her arms, for he had bruised her quite thoroughly. Oh, yes, awakening him rudely had achieved precisely the affect she had hoped for. He was in a sudden, astonished rage.

She quickly slipped from the bed and adjusted her neckcloth, her coat, the cuffs of her shirt, and began retying her breeches at the knees. Moonlight from the window poured across her back and she noticed how fine a gentleman's shadow she cast across Hugh's bed.

"Why are you dressed like that? Are you wearing some sort of wig?"

"Indeed, I am," she returned in a whisper. "It is coal black and when I settle Kit's hat low upon my ears, no one will guess that it is a wig. Now, do get dressed and be quick about it. We need to be five miles to the north by the time the dawn breaks.

I'll have the horses saddled immediately and don't worry—I have already spoken to your head groom. He says he'll saddle them but will wait for your approval before permitting me to mount Juno."

Hugh's mouth fell agape. "What are you about, Fairfield!" he called again in a hoarse whisper.

"Oh, Hugh! How very sweet of you, for you must know I like it above all things when you address me by my last name only. Indeed, I do. But hurry up, will you? It is nearly four o'clock and the servants will be rising soon. I don't want them to see either of us. Siddons knows where I am taking you and he means to put it about that I was called away to Derby, to visit my companion, Miss Yarlet, and that you are gone on estate business. Come. And try not to look like a lord, will you?"

"I won't move an inch unless you tell me what you are doing."

"Don't be a gudgeon! I'll not tell you a thing. You must trust me."

She did not wait for an answer, but ran lightly across the chamber, opened the door, peeked into the hallway, then raced for the backstairs. She heard his voice echo down the hall, "Fairfield, I won't do it!" but she ignored him.

Hugh closed the door and stared at the straggle of bedclothes which he had pulled behind him and now lay in a thick stream across the planked floor. He realized he still had one of the linen sheets wrapped around him like an ancient toga and with no small degree of disgust, let it fall to the floor. He could not imagine what she meant to do.

Good God! He still could not credit she had actually entered his bedchamber in the middle of the night and attacked him. He paused in his steps and a quite dishonorable thought entered his mind. He tried to picture Honoria dressing up as a young man and waking him from his sleep but the sheer impossibility of his bride-to-be daring anything so outrageous caused him to laugh. Honoria would prefer to fall into a decline than to disgrace herself in such a manner.

But not Merry. Faith, but she had been a game one from the moment he could remember. Enough bottom for the tallest hedge, the steepest hill, the longest ride. But where the devil did she mean to take him now? Well, he wouldn't go with her. He had too many tasks to attend to today, not to mention how truly scandalous it would be to spend the day in her company when she was dressed as a young man.

He sat down on the edge of the bed, his feet touching the cold floor. He kicked at the bedclothes hanging from the bed.

He wouldn't go. He had no intention of joining her on whatever mischievous errand she had in mind.

He couldn't go. What would Honoria say if she discovered he had done so? Of course he wouldn't be seeing her for a week. She and her aunt had gone to Derby to see to the final arrangement of her brideclothes. No, he couldn't go. He couldn't dishonor her so wretchedly.

He was sick of duty and honor, he thought distractedly.

He wasn't going.

Damme, he had to go!

He jumped up, turned and leaped up on the back of the bed, his heart racing with excitement. In two bounds he crossed the bed, jumped to the floor on the otherside and in another hurried bound tore open his wardrobe.

Don't look like a lord.

He had several blue hunting coats which had seen better days, and a pair of buckskin breeches that were stained in more than one place. He hoped the head groom had enough sense not to saddle Jupiter and Juno. Anyone who had the least sense about them would recognize either horse for the quality they were. Two horses normally employed on the farm would serve much better with which to travel in relative anonymity.

He quickly dressed himself and, once having made the decision to go, was anxious to be gone, so much so that in struggling to get his boots on he fell over backwards.

Much he cared as he laughed aloud, then checked himself. It would not do to rouse his family.

When he finally appeared before Merry, she scrutinized him closely and said, "You could have at least brushed you hair, Hugo!"

"Good lord! I was in such a rush. But what is this all about! Never mind, you may explain all later. Colwich!" He called for the head groom and a moment later he appeared at the end of the stalls, walking briskly toward them. "Though I don't know Miss Fairfield's scheme entirely, I understand we do not wish to attract attention. Do you have a pair of farm horses we can make use of today?"

Colwich was a tall, deep-chested man with a thick nose and keen eyes. "The very ones, m'lord," he responded with a quick nod of his head. "This way."

Colwich led him to two strong horses, a black and a bay. The two men immediately began to saddle them. A few minutes more and Merry was astride her horse, trotting alongside Hugh as they cantered in a northerly direction, down the lane heading into the home wood and the snow-laden countryside beyond.

Two hours later, Hugh stared at the dilapidated row of cottages. He moved his horse slowly along the High Street of the hamlet—if indeed the collection of a dozen houses could be termed even that. The deeply rutted road was a reflection of the misery all about him. He heard a baby squalling through the gray, early morning air.

"I believe Jacob Wright lives in the third cottage," Merry said.

"What?" Hugh returned in a whispered cry. "With six children?"

Merry nodded to his horrified look of inquiry.

The hamlet, hidden in a cleft of the valley to the north of his property, was a refuge for a number of impoverished families. Only one thin trail of smoke rose from the numerous chimneys. He could only suppose that coal was far too dear for many of the inmates of these hovels and stealing wood from the surrounding lands too great a risk.

He heard a scurrying above him and, looking up, saw a large

rat burrow its way into the thin thatching of a roof nearby. He shuddered inwardly. The snow from two days ago had been trampled thoroughly by small feet all about the cottages and was now mixing with the dirt of the road to lend a particularly seedy appearance to the hamlet. An ancient market cross at the top of the forgotten village was the only evidence that once a thriving community had existed here.

He wondered if this was where the White Prince disbursed his stolen largess. An ill-hung door squeaked open and a young, thin face peered into the growing light of dawn. Hugh tipped his hat to the boy, but received neither a smile nor a frown for his efforts. He was struck by the notion that poverty had robbed the child of both his tears and his laughter.

It also struck him that in the strangest way—until Merry's arrival—his own experience had not been so very different from the boy's, that for several years now he had been able to respond to life with little more than a shoulder ready for work. Neither joy nor sorrow had seemed to live in his chest—merely a daily, mindless drive to restore what had been robbed from him.

He had grieved for his parents, of course. But once he had begun ploughing his way through his own difficulties, strong emotions of any kind seemed to escape him.

Suddenly he felt overwhelmed by the child's suffering, because he knew equally as well what it was to live an impoverished existence. The sensations were too much of the moment. He gave his black gelding a solid kick and with little effort was trotting beyond the hamlet. Only when the village had been left far behind did he finally take a deep breath. As it was he gulped in the cold, snowy air, his breath leaving his body in a cloud of vapor.

Because of the vagrancy laws attached to the land, no one could simply move from village to village in hopes of finding a better life. Hugh knew that such laws protected the whole village, for without such a law, the poor would inundate a prosperous community and soon drain the almshouses of their funds. But when tragedy struck—when a job was lost, or the means of earning a living—where did a man go?

All that Siddons had said to him was beginning to make sense, certainly in light of what he saw.

In each village through which they passed as they began a journey in an arc to the north of his lands, he gained a sense that the well-travelled villages enjoyed a greater prosperity than those hidden and forgotten in the deep grooves of the lower Pennine mountains. It was to the latter that Merry took him. He wondered how it was she knew of the existence of so many pockets of misery. But she refused to divulge her source except to say that her work in Brighton and its environs had given her an understanding of how very much geography could play a devastating part on the ability of a village to feed itself—particularly when the crops were poor or, as in far too many cases, the landowner refused to take an interest in the welfare of his tenanted farmers.

"You will not see this manner of suffering in any of my tenants," he responded defensively.

"I know that, Hugh. Please don't think for a moment that I have brought you here to accuse you of wrongdoing, for I know very well that you have done everything possible to make your people comfortable during our country's most trying years. But the war, when it was over, bereft so many seamen and soldiers of their occupations, and the government has been so slow in taking appropriate measures to help them find a new place in our society, that even had the Corn Laws been repealed and cheap food allowed into our country, I don't doubt that a fair proportion of the suffering you have witnessed today would still have existed. And, like Jacob Wright, these valiant soldiers wanted nothing more than to return to their homes and families."

"What about the new factories here in the North?" he queried.

"One factory, Hugh, or even a dozen, as opposed to tens of thousands of soldiers and sailors. Besides, the factories hire women and children as well, or were you not aware of that? Of course they work for less than the men, so who is it the factory owners want to hire?"

He knew she did not require him to answer.

The day wore on and except for stopping at an inn for nuncheon and another inn at another village in the evening for dinner, they rested only to stop by a stream in order to water the horses before continuing the day's journey.

The sky grew leaden after dinner, and a chill wind from the north made a return to Hathersage impossible that evening. The horses were tired and it would be snowing soon. "I don't want to risk losing our way if this storm should prove violent," Hugh said. "We had best discover an inn close by."

But Merry objected to the scheme entirely. "For if it were discovered that I was a woman, along with your true identity, I would not want to think of the scandal you would bring down upon Honoria's innocent head. No, I have a better idea. There is a barn at the far reaches of this farm, stocked with some hay for the sheep in the dale. We can spend the night there, the horses can enjoy their fill, and in the morning you may pay the farmer for his trouble."

He agreed, seeing that her reasoning was sound, but still wondered how she knew Derbyshire so well.

She added, "But don't think we are finished with our travels. There is one last estate I wish you to witness for yourself."

Hugh frowned at her and searched his mind for all the lands through which they had recently travelled. "Hucklow's," he said at last, realizing through the mental map he had just created that Sir Rupert's realm, which marched along his own borders to the west, was the only land they had not traversed.

"Precisely so."

They came upon the barn, the night closing in rapidly about them, a chill wind causing Hugh to shiver even through his thick greatcoat. They led the horses into the high-ceilinged building, and noticed an immediate difference in the air. The barn was cold, of course, but nothing like the temperature outdoors. It was also dark as night inside. He bumped into Merry as he began easing his way along the stone stalls. He heard her laugh as she searched through a heavy bag she had had strapped to her saddle the entire day.

A few minutes more and the barn was aglow with a very dim light. "What the devil?" he cried as his horse turned to look at him. Over his shoulder, he watched Merry lift a small lantern near her ear and say, "I wanted an adventure but since I knew we might not be able to return to Hathersage, I thought it wise to pack a few provisions. A tinder-box, a candle and a small lantern."

He smiled at her foresight. "You would not have been so clever four years ago," he said, teasing her.

"Four years ago, I would not have dared kidnap you from your own bed."

"So you have grown both wiser and more brazen since I last knew you."

"Precisely so."

She hung the lantern on a nearby peg. Afterward they tended to the horses, stripping them of the heavy saddles and rubbed them down thoroughly with handfuls of straw while letting them graze on the well-stored hay. The barn smelled of the damp and of the earth and of the animals.

When the horses were properly tended to, Merry returned to her bag, from which she drew a thick wool blanket. He watched her, thinking that she looked completely like a boy with, he supposed, Kit's clothes hanging loosely upon her, disguising her womanly frame. The wig, of course, made the deception possible and with that thought he watched her tug her hat from her head, then with a quick jerk pull the wig from its place atop her curls.

The unveiling was not complete however. She flipped her head forward and bent over at the waist so that her long tangled curls hung in a cascade in front of her. She then set about briskly scratching her head and pulling at her locks until the curls disentangled themselves. As she flung her head backward, and the hair followed suit, he was greatly chagrined to note that her curls fell charmingly about her face and shoulders and trailed in ringlets down her back.

He couldn't help laughing, however, when she drew a brush from her bag and, dropping to the blanket spread out on the hay, began further easing the tangles from her hair.

"Was there anything you did not forget to bring on this supposedly madcap, impulsive scheme of yours?"

She paused in her brushing, resting her arms casually upon her knees as a boy might do, a pucker between her brows. "Only one thing—I forgot to steal some of Cook's apricot tartlets to tuck away for just this moment." She shook her head in disappointment. "For some reason, an apricot tartlet would finish this day to perfection." She then smiled up at him and patted the blanket beside her. "Besides, my scheme was not precisely *impulsive*. I gave it a great deal of consideration most of the night and only firmly decided upon it about three o'clock this morning."

"Why did you bring me, Merry?" he asked, although he felt he already knew the answer.

She smiled faintly. "You know of my sympathy for those caught in desperate straits through no fault of their own and, rather than argue for them, I wanted you to see for yourself the true state of those for whom the White Prince breaks the laws of the land. That's all."

He dropped down beside her, leaning back on his elbow, watching her as she continued to brush her hair. He could see she was exhausted so he was not surprised when she said nothing more.

His mind grew very loose and relaxed. His gaze travelled to the lantern hung safely upon a hook on the wall of the horse's stall, his eyes mesmerized by the steady light of the single candle. It was a stubby thing and would soon gutter, he supposed. He wondered if any of the impoverished people he had seen today had candles by which to rise from their beds in the morning, or by which to brush their hair in the evening. He sincerely doubted it.

When his eyes closed, he did not know. The day had been rigorous in the saddle, the up and down of travelling over hill and dale had brought his body to a place of immense but welcome fatigue. But sometime later, he awoke and was startled to find a stream of moonlight pouring in through a western window. Past midnight, he was sure of that. The storm had run its course, clearing sufficiently for the moon to flood his bed.

He had to squeeze his eyes shut once very hard in order to clear enough sleep from his brain to remember where he was. His bed. Only not his bed. He was too cold to be in his bed, he knew that much. He felt a body stir beside him and a sweet rush of awareness poured over him. He was in a barn with Merry beside him.

The moonlight permitted him to see her face, even in the shadows, and he knew a profound tenderness toward her. He watched her shiver slightly and then realized because he had fallen asleep like a big oaf, the blanket was beneath them both instead of over them.

Carefully, he moved off the blanket and wrapped the blanket about Merry. He heard her sigh in her sleep, and her body relaxed at the new-found warmth. He then rose up on his side and, reaching over her, pulled great mounds of straw toward her so that he was able to bank her body with the insulating hay. He then pressed his body next to hers, a movement which obviously pleased her since she reached an arm backward to him and pressed a hand to his face, her eyes still closed. "I love you, Hugh," she murmured in the cold stillness of the night. "I always have, silly man."

His heart began to ache as her sweet, sleep-laden words played themselves over and over in his mind.

I love you, Hugh.

I always have.

Silly man.

He laid his head down on the straw and felt her snuggle

closely against him, her back to him. He draped his arm over
her and, catching her arm, pulled her more firmly still against
his chest. She cooed her appreciation of the arrangement, and
fell further into her sleep.

He was warm now, warm from the feel of her body next to
his, warm from the honest impartation of her heart. He wanted
to ask her why she had never told him of her love and lifted up
to look at her, hoping his movements would wake her. If she
woke up, he would kiss her. But she did not even stir. The long
ride had taken its toll, and already her breathing was again deep
and even.

With the moonlight bathing her face, he could easily discern
her features, her lips and the smooth complexion of her cheeks.
He found himself wanting to press his lips against hers, not in
a passionate kiss, he thought with surprise, not by half. Desire
did not rule him in this moment as he thought it easily could
have. Rather, he found himself wanting to claim her for his own
by pressing his lips to hers, to say with the touch of his lips,
"You and every thought you possess, belong to me." Maybe he
even wished by such a kiss to draw into his spirit all the remarkable things she was—bold, compassionate, vivacious.

And she had said she loved him. Did he love her, he wondered? Or perhaps the question more accurately phrased was,
how much did he love her? How deeply?

He lay his head at last back against the thick mound of hay,
an arm slung backward behind his head. He stared out at the
starry night sky. The cool breeze which gently brushed against
the ancient stone building kept the stars twinkling brightly in
the great distance.

Today, he had seen a world he had not thought truly existed,
save perhaps in London. He knew the east end of the metropolis had long been a bed of extreme poverty and disease, of
mothers sitting on stoops giving gin to their crying babes, of
maimed, ragged soldiers, their uniforms visible only through
layers of grime, the same men begging pitifully at the edges of
civilization.

But his tidy lands, upon which he had moved, worked and over which he had slaved for the past three years, had escaped the ravagement of displaced soldiers and spinners, the terrible effects of the Corn Laws upon the smaller tenanted farmers, or the disastrous effects of the crop failures upon the subsistence of those already caught in the misfortunes of poverty—like Jacob Wright and his family.

So, the White Prince helped them all, Merry had said. He understood now this was the reason she had wanted him to see the state of Derbyshire for himself. He would not have credited her concern quite so forcefully without having seen the misery with his own eyes.

It was no wonder then that Abbot's End was a divided town—some extolling the White Prince as a hero, and others, like Sir Rupert, clinging to the view that regardless of the extent of the poverty involved, the laws of the land must be upheld. He believed that each side had a case, but where would justice fall once the White Prince was captured?

On the following morning, an hour past dawn, he rode beside Merry and saw for himself the condition of the hamlet nearest Hucklow's lands. He was sickened by what he saw—the thinness of the inhabitants, the empty air above the chimneys, the dilapidated condition of the buildings, the sounds of coughing coming from every other house.

Merry's voice, as she addressed him quietly, broke through his stunned awareness. "The land is rocky hereabouts. Their vegetable plots do not thrive. When the price of grain soars because of the Corn Laws, what can they hope for? Most of the men labor on the tenanted farms, tending to the fields, or the sheep. All of it is connected in a vicious cycle. When the farmers are charged increases in rent at the same time a crop fails, what hope is there for anyone?"

He could not give her an answer but in his heart he believed Sir Rupert would one day have much to answer for.

Chapter Eighteen

Ten days later, and only one day before the Christmas ball, Merry sat alone in the morning room. The clock had just chimed the midnight hour. Stationed in a comfortable, winged chair by the fireplace she paused in the quick flip of her mending needle to sigh and to stare into the fire. The Yule log was considerably shrunk, one end of it having been surrounded daily, as it was now, by smaller logs continuing to nip at its formidable flank. She realized by the diminishing light she was receiving from the fire she would soon need to place another log or two on it if she hoped to keep the blaze going.

Her neck and upper shoulders ached from holding her head at just that angle which needlework of any kind required in order to perform well. She rolled her head about slowly several times and rubbed her neck, but to little avail. She had been stitching a multitude of garlands of red satin ribbon, ivy, and holly together since early that morning along with Judith, Constance and Amabel. She wanted the ballroom to be decorated as prettily as the morning room and only a monumental effort would achieve her objective.

So it was midnight, she was alone, her neck ached—but how very happy she was. Her task was nearly complete and the combination of industry along with the pleasure the results of her labors would give Hugh's sisters was precisely the activity which delighted her most. The truth was, she was as excited about the ball as were the twins. For the past ten days, since she kidnapped Hugh from his bed and took him on a journey about the countryside, he had been wondrously tender with her, in word and deed. Frequently she had even caught him looking at her with just such a soft expression in his blue eyes that brought hope shooting skyrockets in her heart. She wondered what could have happened on the journey that might have prompted a shift in his conduct toward her, but she could think of nothing. Unless, of course, his awareness of the poverty about Derbyshire had moved him with compassion and some of that compassion had spilled over onto her.

Whatever the case, hope now reigned in her heart.

Therefore, since the journey, she had trebled her efforts in encouraging Mr. Belper's interest in Honoria, a scheme she had been finding surprisingly easy to accomplish.

During the past several days, she had had no less than six occasions upon which she had been able to closet Honoria and Mr. Belper alone together. Three times she had left them in the library pouring over favorite volumes of poetry. Once in the rose and green drawing room when Hugh had not yet returned from a brief trip to Chesterfield she had feigned the headache and begged Mr. Belper to tend to Miss Youlgreave. On another occasion she had led them into the yew maze, lost them and returned to the morning room by herself. And only last night— after the siblings had disappeared one after another and Hugh had helped Amabel to her bed—she had simply slipped from the morning room unnoticed by the pair who were happily engaged in practicing a duet at the pianoforte.

As she knotted her thread about another length of holly, she sighed. If only Christmas Day and the wedding were not a mere seven days away. She was confident had she more time, she could arrange everything to a nicety. As it was, would she truly be able to see Honoria's heart bent sufficiently toward Mr. Belper that Honoria would consider ending her engagement to Hugh? But she wouldn't think of that, not when it seemed so impossible.

So she doggedly provided Mr. Belper every innocent opportunity possible of engaging Honoria's affections.

Of course, the siblings unwittingly made her efforts quite easy, due primarily to their dislike of Hugh's intended. Whenever possible, Judith and Constance made an excuse to leave Honoria during her many visits to Hathersage, Beatrice by far preferred all her pets in the nursery to her future sister-in-law's company and Kit—well Kit was hardly about anymore. Amabel, by the nature of her weakened condition, was frequently sequestered in her chambers.

Her thoughts turned to Amabel, as she snipped another knot of green thread. It seemed so odd that the invalid would be perfectly well one day, though always somewhat listless, then laid upon her couch with a sick headache the next. Poor Amabel.

Poor Hugh, for she knew he still blamed himself for her hapless condition.

She let her needle rest finally, slipping the silver thimble from a perspiring finger and leaning her head against the soft fabric of the chair. She fixed her gaze languidly to the fire as her thoughts turned yet again to Hugh.

Since her escapade with him, he had begun conversing at length with her about the condition of the country and the increasing unrest of the populous. She related to him a speech she had once heard delivered by "Orator Hunt", a most persuasive speaker, upon the suffering of the poor in the provinces and in the cities and how the laboring classes were not represented in Parliament. He had listened intently to her and confessed a great regret that his own difficulties had served to separate him from his duties in the House of Lords for the past three years. He made a decision that he would come to London, if but for a few weeks of the season this spring, and attend as many sessions as possible while he was there.

"Which would greatly benefit your sisters, Hugh," she said enthusiastically. "I don't like to mention it, but I believe a little push on your part for either of them would see them settled in proper marriages. If you have not been entirely pleased with their conduct of late, you must comprehend that such high-spirited young women need to be busy about homes and families of their own. A lively infant or two and the demands of housekeeping would see both Constance and Judith safely separated from mischief."

He had nodded in agreement, stating that he would speak to Honoria about the prospect immediately. It was a day later, with a concerned light in his eye, that he revealed such a scheme, following so soon upon the heels of their nuptials, did not precisely agree with his bride-to-be. She had hoped they would spend the spring in Bath with Sir Rupert and Lady Hucklow, who had recently purchased a fine townhouse in Laura Place.

"Good God, Bath," he had cried, falling into a chair beside her. "A duller place does not exist. And as much as I might esteem Honoria's relations, three months would wear on anyone! Besides, I cannot possibly leave Hathersage for so long a time!"

Merry did not spare his sensibilities, but instead laughed at him, taunting him with the unlikely probability that he would very soon adjust to the rigors of married life with Miss Youlgreave. His irritation at her lack of sympathy lifted him back out of his chair with a promise that the next time she wished to ride out he would not go with her.

Merry had been riding out with him every morning since their return from the countryside, and she had loved every moment of it, as she was sure did Hugh. They rode the most mettlesome pair in the stables, Jupiter and Juno, hard across well-marked lanes, flying as fast as they could through slushy snow, their riding clothes a delightful mess by the time they returned. In particular, they enjoyed a hard gallop through the home wood and back. Only the easiest, friendliest discourses accompanied these jaunts. Twice Kit had come with them, leading each time, the strenuous exercise bringing a gleam to his blue eyes and a ruddy color to his cheeks.

Kit had changed, too, she thought. He did not speak anymore of his plans of entering Oxford in the fall or of his wish to take Holy Orders. More than once, Merry had found him lost in thought, a distressed expression on his face as he chewed his lower lip or ground his teeth. She tried once to approach him regarding his obvious discontent, but he assured her nothing was amiss, at least nothing about which he meant to trouble her head, especially not when she was so frightfully busy preparing for the ball. He did gently request, however, that once the ball was behind them, he had a notion he wished to discuss with her. Naturally, her curiosity had been rustled and she pressed him to open his budget, but he merely shrugged his shoulders and stubbornly refused to respond to any of her hints, suppositions or outright proddings. She would have to wait until after the ball to have her curiosity satisfied. That Kit seemed to enjoy having aroused her curiosity made him seem more like the young man she had first encountered some four and a half years ago.

She wondered if Hugh sensed that Kit was troubled, but she doubted he was capable of such a perception, since an event of greater significance now loomed on the horizon. Hugh had already confided in her the dreadful news that Sir Rupert believed someone within the walls of Hathersage Park was in league with the White Prince.

When he had first told her, Merry had instantly thought someone had discovered it was she who had robbed Hugh of his purse so many nights ago. But that didn't make sense, not when Hugh revealed that only a few nights ago, a member of the militia had actually followed a man, who had been witnessed at a most recent robbery, onto Rayneworth lands. The suspect had evaded capture, however, and a light snowfall had erased his tracks.

Merry felt ill whenever she thought of Sir Rupert's dogged efforts. This morning he had called upon Hugh with several of his supporters from Abbot's End. Hugh had told her the whole of their conversation—that each night for the past ten days some of the militia, as well as Sir Rupert, had been patrolling places of suspected activity in the surrounding villages and even as far as Chesterfield in hopes of capturing the White Prince. Twice they had nearly succeeded. It was only a matter of time, now. And worse, for once he was caught, he must be made to serve as an example; he must be hanged!

Merry thought of Laurence and tears of fright rose quickly to her eyes. She wanted to warn him of all that was going forward, but in her heart she knew he was already perfectly well informed. When he was not abroad at night, he resided in Abbot's End, in the very midst of the activities against him. He could not help but be aware of the mood of the militia nor of Sir Rupert's dogged efforts to hunt him down.

All this and a Christmas ball! How ironic, she thought as a tear slid down her cheek. She wiped it away quickly, unwilling to succumb to such truly unhappy thoughts and again picked up her needle.

Hugh stood in the shadows of the yew maze and waited. It was past midnight, he was sure of that. He was certain he had been outside, cloaked heavily against the cold December night air, his hat low upon his head, for over an hour, and he had quit his chamber at half past eleven. He had made a great show of seeking his bed before the ladies had gone upstairs for the night. Even now he could see that a glow of light still lit the morning room windows. He thought it likely one of his sisters had forgotten to snuff all the candles before retiring, or perhaps Merry was still tying up all that holly, ivy or whatever the deuce it was, with red ribbon. He supposed the ballroom would look quite pretty once it was fully decorated, but he couldn't remember having seen so much greenery all over the morning room floors than ever before—even when his own mother was caught up in a decorating frenzy. Really, it was like walking through a weed-ridden garden!

He stamped his feet, thinking he wasn't truly irritable over the ivy, it was Sir Rupert's arrogance that had vexed him so sorely. And damme, he hadn't much patience for the man anymore. The last part of his trek about the countryside with Merry had shown him more of that man's character than he ever wished to know. Over and over again, neglect had shouted to him from Sir Rupert's lands, neglect and harsh usage of his tenanted farmers. Since the trip he had made subtle inquiries and had learned that the baronet squeezed every groat he could from his farmers while roofs, walls and windows, even fences, remained unrepaired, and while every field was tilled, furrowed and planted when every good farmer knew the land needed to rest. Sir Rupert was relentless with them and ill feelings abounded on every side. The devil of it was, he had come to pity those dependent upon Sir Rupert.

But it was more than just the state of the baronet's lands which had brought about an unhappy opinion. Whatever the crime the White Prince was committing, and whatever penalty for that crime the outlaw was due under the law, Sir Rupert's wish to see him captured and hanged had come to seem to Hugh as entirely disproportionate to the suffering he had himself witnessed on his ride with Merry. When he tried to express his own mounting belief that until England was able to feed its own properly, she should not reject so hastily the efforts—however misguided—of such an outlaw, Sir Rupert had fairly called him a Jacobin for holding such an ill-judged opinion.

Hugh had then tried to address the matter of the Corn Laws and Sir Rupert had lifted a brow, stating with finality that those laws alone had made it possible for Hugh to sustain his own estate. Didn't his farmers get the highest price possible for their produce? Hugh had wanted to point out that with the harvest so poor, every groat went back into the farmer's lands, but he knew it was not his place or even his wish to take umbrage with the baronet.

Instead, he had asked for a detailed accounting of all that Sir Rupert had learned. When he revealed quite brusquely that one of his soldiers—yes, *his* soldiers—had followed an outlaw

back to Hathersage Park, Hugh had found the blood leaving his
face.

The implication was clear. If someone on his staff was involved, then someone he knew and undoubtedly held in either
affection or respect was in danger of being caught and hanged
alongside the White Prince.

After Sir Rupert had taken his leave, Hugh had waited in the
library for a full half hour, giving thoughtful consideration to
everything the baronet had told him. He had been forced to
conclude that there was indeed a possibility that someone in his
house was in league with the White Prince. Could it be Merry,
he wondered. Her beliefs were well-aligned with the actions of
the White Prince, but she had not been in Derbyshire all that
long, unless she had been living out a double life. But that
wouldn't fadge. He had more than one friend in Brighton who
wrote of her occasionally. She was fully engaged in a social life
there, and in doing good works in Sussex generally.

Who else? Even as he reviewed every servant who worked for
him, he could not think of one who had the ability to leave his
premises for long hours or days at a time without being missed
and disciplined for failing to work. He could think of no one, yet
Sir Rupert was quite thorough in his methods, and he doubted
that a mistake had been made.

So he waited by the yew maze, in the shadows, occasionally
stamping his feet. If the traitor knew of Sir Rupert's visit, it was
likely that the man attached to the White Prince would want to
make the baronet's visit known to his commander.

How long ought he to wait, he wondered as he balled up his
fists then released them, trying to keep the cold from inching
further into his fingers and knuckles.

Then he saw a brief movement, a flicker of shadow along the
windows and glass doors of the gallery overlooking the formal
gardens. One of the doors opened and a dark, masculine figure
appeared, slipping quietly into the night, turning at a hard right
angle away from the yew maze. He was heading in the direction
of the stables. To steal a horse? To meet someone?

On instinct, Hugh immediately left the cover of the maze and began running after the errant servant. Unfortunately, the snow was crusted hard and his boots resounded loudly in the still of the dark night. The man turned back, took one look at him and dove back to the door from which had emerged, disappearing quickly inside.

Hugh reached the door a long ten seconds later, running as hard as he could.

Merry heard the slamming of a door and was instantly filled with fright. She dropped her needle and thimble, rose quickly to her feet, the ivy and ribbons tumbling from her lap. She heard the quick footsteps as they approached the door of the morning room coming from the direction of the gallery. The door flung open, and in the darkness of the doorway, she had a brief glimpse of Kit's surprised blue eyes, then nothing as he backed out of the room pulling the door shut. She heard his footsteps race up the hallway toward the back stairs.

Merry could not imagine what was going forward. She took two steps toward the door then heard the second pair of heavier feet slamming against the planked flooring. These footsteps passed by the morning room, clearly giving chase. Who was chasing Kit and why? And why was Kit dressed as though he meant to go out at this hour of night?

She was still in a state of surprise when her limbs overtook her numbness and she bolted for the door. She threw it open in time to see Hugh, dropping his greatcoat backward off his shoulders, turn the corner and head toward the backstairs. Her gaze fell to the coat, and she listened intently for footsteps. She heard several, presumably Hugh's, then nothing. She waited, then returned to the morning room to retrieve a candle from the dining table. Afterward she moved into the hallway again and began a slow, quiet progress toward the coat. She strained to hear more movement, but no sound returned to her ears.

A moment more and she was picking up the coat from the

floor. Finally she heard Hugh's firm tread as he retraced his steps. He appeared at the end of the hallway, descending the servants' stairs. She held her candle high, allowing the light to suffuse the end of the adjoining hall, her brows raised in query.

He shook his head and shrugged his shoulders. She motioned him back toward the morning room.

Once inside, with the candle returned to its place on the middle of the dining table, Merry hung Hugh's heavy coat upon a peg by the door. Hugh sat down on the sofa, running a hand through his hair. He was clearly overset. He then sat forward, his hands clasped tightly between his knees, a heavy scowl on his face.

Merry seated herself in the winged chair near the fire and watched him, her heart beginning to pick up its cadence. She found herself in a quandry. Though she did not know the particulars of what had just occurred, she comprehended enough to know that Kit would not want his identity revealed.

Should she tell Hugh that he had been pursuing his brother? But why? What had Kit been doing?

Merry chose to ask instead, "What is going forward, Hugo? I don't understand. Who were you chasing?"

Hugh shook his head and rose abruptly to his feet. "The traitor Sir Rupert told me resided in my house. As to who this traitor is, I don't know. But someone left my house through the long, French windows not a moment ago. I meant to give chase toward the stables, but the man chose instead to return inside. I have no choice but to believe he is the same man the militia followed back to my house a few days ago."

Merry thought of Kit and she grew dizzy with fear. Was it Kit, then, who the milita had been pursuing?

Hugh was silent apace as he wheeled around first to stare at the fire, then to place a booted foot on the hearth. He leaned a hand on the mantel. "I didn't want it to be true but now I have no choice but to believe the whole of it—that I have been sheltering an outlaw. Merry, do you know more than I? Do you know who this man is? If this cursed house weren't so large, I should begin a search immediately, but I am convinced by the time I had opened and shut six or seven of the bedrooms, the traitor would be half way to Frogwell, having escaped down the backstairs again. Have you heard any gossip? Did you see anyone earlier moving about suspiciously?"

"No," she responded. This much she could say in all honesty, but how sorely her conscience prickled her. Yet she could not divulge Kit's identity. She could not! "The truth is, I cannot imagine anyone in your home behaving so disloyally to you." She thought of Kit and pressed her palms together to keep her fingers from trembling. Had Kit, from the beginning of her arrival—and two years prior—been dissembling, pretending to wish to take Holy Orders, but in actuality serving the White Prince? If he had been, he was certainly gifted with unsuspected theatrical qualities. And what of the change she had noticed in him recently? He would have no reason to alter his conduct even the smallest bit were he involved in so complete a charade. No, it seemed impossible to think of Kit connected to Laurence's activities. For one thing, she truly doubted Laurence would have permitted him to join his forces. On the other hand, she knew the Leighton will and, if Kit had been determined to help in Laurence's cause, nothing would have stopped him.

Lost in her thoughts, she absently leaned forward and began gathering up her materials, the ivy, her needle and thread, her thimble. As she began looping and stitching and weaving the garland together, a new fear caused her heart to beat strongly in her breast. If Kit was involved with the White Prince his life was now in as much danger as Laurence's.

Drawing a length of the ivy onto her lap, she asked, "I know it is not entirely my concern, but what did Sir Rupert have to say to you this evening? Did he recommend you try to discover the traitor yourself?"

"If you mean did he suggest I wait in the freezing air, hidden in the shadows of the yew maze, no. That notion came to me when I heard fumbling sounds outside the library just as Sir Rupert took his leave. Someone had been there, listening, eavesdropping. I am sick at heart to think that my home has been so ill-used and for so long."

Merry opened her mouth to say that she had seen Kit, that he was the one, but she couldn't speak the words. She wanted more than anything to speak with Kit first, to ask him why he had left the house surreptitiously. She chose, therefore, to keep silent. Tomorrow she would confront Kit.

She wondered now why, if he was involved, Laurence had not mentioned it to her. Or would he have felt he could have done so? It was all so confusing. "What do you intend to do?" she asked Hugh, as she rethreaded her needle.

He turned to look at her, the fire a warm glow on his face. "I don't know," he answered quietly. "I wish the ball were one or two days off. I have no wish to disturb my sisters' pleasure by oversetting the house by inquiring after an outlaw. I suppose I shall have to wait until Sunday before I begin trying to uncover the man, and then we shall see. But from all that Sir Rupert told me, it is possible he will have the White Prince in hand before the ball has ended."

"Sir Rupert does not mean to attend?"

"He will be here," Hugh responded slowly. "But the militia will be scattered about the countryside, waiting to see if the White Prince uses the ball to rob one or two of our guests."

Merry felt her heart turn over in her breast. How ironic that the Christmas ball—designed to give so much pleasure—might be the undoing of her dear friend. Again, she knew a strong impulse to try to get word to Laurence of Sir Rupert's schemes, but she thought it likely she might do more harm than good if she attempted to reach him now. Besides, she had little doubt Laurence was fully informed already, particularly if he had a compatriot living within the safety of Hathersage Park.

Chapter Nineteen

The first news to greet Merry in the morning was that Amabel had suffered one of her relapses and was laid up in her bedchamber with the headache. Merry was in the ballroom, helping one of the undermaids complete the hanging of the numerous garlands, when Judith informed her of the invalid's illness.

Merry was distressed at once, knowing how much Amabel had been anticipating the ball, how greatly she was looking forward to greeting a host of friends, many of whom she had not seen in years!

She immediately left Judith with the task of seeing the decorations finished and hurried to Amabel's bedchamber. Upon scratching quietly on the door, Nurse, her eyes weary with the fatigue of caring for the sick child, bid her enter. Dark lengths of fabric had been thrown over the windows to keep even a speck of sunlight from entering the chamber. The thick smell of burning pastilles permeated the room and for a moment made Merry's breathing difficult.

She covered her mouth and smothered a cough as she approached the bed. The only illumination permitted in the sickchamber came from a small candle on a wall sconce quite distant from the bed, the light shining in a dull pool on the far wall. The room was so dark that Merry had to creep forward slowly, reaching out a hand to feel for one of the four posters of the bed. Just as her fingers touched the carved wood of one of the posters, her foot struck an awkward object on the floor, knocking it over. Instinctively, she reached down to right the object and found her hands upon a boot. Setting it upright, she continued toward the invalid. She brushed her hands together and felt the grainy texture of dirt on her fingers and carefully rubbed away the grit.

"Is that you, Merry?" Amabel whispered, afterward emitting a faint groan.

"Yes, my dear," she returned quietly. "I have come to see if I might be of some assistance to you? Tell me you will be well by this evening. Amabel, you won't miss our Christmas ball, will you?"

By now, her eyes had become better adjusted to the dim light and she could see the frail hand stretched out on the bedclothes. She took Amabel's small hand in hers and patted it gently.

"I can't believe I've the headache again," Amabel said, sniffling. Merry reached up to touch her cheek and felt the wetness of her tears. As her vision adjusted further she could see the stream made by several teardrops down the side of Amabel's face, which disappeared into her auburn hair.

Merry slipped a kerchief from the pocket of her gown and dabbed at the tears and at her friend's hair.

"I don't mean to become a watering pot," Amabel sniffed again, sighing at the same time. Her hand was tucked beneath her cheek and she appeared quite forlorn. "It is just—that—I'm so scared."

Merry was a little surprised. "Why, whatever do you mean?" she asked, wiping at a fresh stream of tears. "The doctor says you are making improvements everyday."

"I know," Amabel whispered. She turned to look at Merry and held her gaze steadily, her expression grievously distressed. She did not seem to know how to give voice to her sentiments.

"What is it?" Merry pressed her. "Do you fear you are suffering from a greater illness—"

"No, no," Amabel interrupted hastily. "I'm sure you are

right and I am being absurd." She took a deep breath and squeezed her eyes shut. "I suppose I am just overset because I will not be able to attend the ball."

Merry's heart went out to her. For the first time since she had arrived at Hathersage, she realized just how difficult, how complicated Amabel's life was as an invalid—how easy it would be to let her fears overcome her common sense.

"Will you sing a carol for me?" Amabel asked quietly. "I should like it above all things."

Merry chuckled softly. "Are you sure, my darling? I have been known to inflict the headache upon even the stoutest listener with only a verse or two, nonetheless an entire carol."

She could see Amabel was slipping into a doze as the young lady smiled. "You have a very pretty voice. I wish Hugo was marrying you, Fairfield."

Merry felt an odd shiver course down her side at Amabel's use of the old nickname. All the siblings had called her Fairfield, and usually in the midst of a great adventure—like exploring a cave or a mine, or riding neck or nothing through the dale. At the same time, the child's expressed wish that she wed the man Merry loved, brought a wave of longing rushing over her heart. She wanted to voice her own opinion, *I wish he was marrying me, too.* Instead she began to sing in little more than a whisper, "Good King Wenceslaus."

Later that evening, Merry squeezed through a crush of guests at the entrance of the ballroom. She was leaving the finely crowded chamber in order to discover if she could see whether or not Hugh and his siblings had left their station in the entrance hall where they were greeting their guests. She made her way up the long passage from the ballroom at the back of the house and nodded to acquaintances all along the way. She kept a fan close to her cheeks for she had been dancing for the past hour, her gaze at times fixed politely upon whichever partner was escorting her about the ballroom, and at other times on the entrance to the long, rectangular room.

She had only one desire tonight, to dance with Hugh. Only where was he? Surely the family had performed their duties by now.

As she moved from chamber through antechamber to chamber, she could not help but be pleased with the results of her labors. By noon, the entire house had been in readiness, just as she had planned. Every garland, candle and red satin bow was in place throughout the ballroom and in various centerpieces throughout the main withdrawing rooms, all in imitation of the morning room. Surely sufficient Christmas greenery was displayed to lift even the lowest of spirits.

In the rose and green drawing room, a string quartet greeted the guests with music from centuries past, the sounds of the familiar strains undoubtedly serving to stir up distant memories of Christmas past in even the most aged of minds.

In preparation for the enjoyment of the ball, Merry had spent the afternoon in her bedchamber, resting, enjoying a light repast, partaking of the truly sensual pleasure of bathing—as Beau Brummell had so kindly taught the upper classes to do in a bath perfumed with rose-water—and finally dressing.

Jeannette, her maid, was skilled enough to arrange her black tresses in a lovely, knotted chignon atop her head. A spray of delicate curls framed her face and throughout the chignon was looped a long strand of pearls. Tucking a fine white ostrich feather into the base of the chignon completed her *coiffure*.

Among her many gowns, she had brought with her a cherry red velvet ball dress, which she had had made up last winter for a Christmas ball held at the Brighton Pavilion by the Prince Regent. It was an exquisitely designed confection bearing puffed sleeves and a bodice which would have been scandalously *décolleté* had not a ruffle of sheer tulle peeked up from the edge of the neckline in a teasing frill. The gown was caught up high at the waist and, because the back was gathered up tightly, also high at the waist, the gown tended to flow out behind her when she twirled to the strains of the waltz. She wore long white gloves, the prettiest white silk stockings and red velvet dancing slippers. A necklet of diamonds completed the ensemble. Even the maid clapped her hands together as she stood before the long mahogany mirror in her bedchamber.

"Oh, Miss Fairfield," she exclaimed. "You'll be quite the prettiest lady of them all."

Merry thanked her for the compliment, but somehow the maid's words brought her spirits turning sharply down—for an unhappy thought intruded. Even if Hugh thought she was pretty, what would it matter? If she could not somehow arouse Fate to intervene, Hugh would be married within only a sennight—a week from the ball.

She had given herself a sharp mental shake. It would not do tonight, of all nights, to dwell upon such an unhappy eventuality. Of course, she wished it wasn't true, but tonight he was not yet married and tonight she meant to have at least one last dance with him—a waltz if she could possibly manage it. Only, what to do about Honoria!

Now, as she travelled the distance from the ballroom to the entrance hall, she had only one object in mind—to beg a dance from Hugh. When she arrived there, only a handful of guests remained in line to greet their hosts. Merry stood in the recesses of the long chamber and looked at the family stationed side by side. The guests began with the services of Burton, which involved the careful relinquishing of hats, coats, capes and any other wintry garments employed to keep the travellers warm. They proceeded to greet Hugh, and in descending order of age, Judith, Constance, Kit and finally Beatrice—Amabel had not recovered from the headache afterall. The youngest Leighton beamed with pride, having been permitted to join her siblings when in fact she should have been relegated to the nursery for the whole of the evening. She was charmingly gowned in a beaded white satin dress trimmed with point lace that just touched green velvet slippers. Her hair was caught up in a green satin bow and she stood very proudly next to her brother and curtsied prettily to each guest.

Merry enjoyed looking at them all, at the happy expressions on each face, at the enchanting array of auburn heads. Only Amabel's absence detracted from the charm of the portrait.

Judith and Constance, for whom the ball had been especially designed, simply glowed. They were dressed dissimilarly, as befitted each young lady and their unique temperaments. Judith wore a striking ensemble consisting of a three-quarter length overdress of white beaded silk. The undergown was of a deep forest green and Merry thought the effect quite dramatic. Constance, on the other hand, wore white satin over which a sheer layer of tulle lent the appearance that she was surrounded by a beautiful mist, into which had been embroidered a scattering of holly berries and dark green leaves. Her hair flowed from a knot atop her head in a cascade of delicate curls, while Judith's coiffure consisted of a tight chignon with just a few curls upon her forehead. No one could deny how different each twin truly was.

As for Kit—merciful heavens, she had still not had occasion to speak with him about his suspicious conduct of the night before! Of course, when she had risen this morning, he had been first on her mind, but when she had tried to find him, she had been told by Siddons that Kit was out riding.

Had he gone somewhere he shouldn't have?

By the time he was known to have returned she was lying down upon her bed wearing only a warm nightdress and covered with a woolen blanket preparing for the evening's entertainment. From that moment until now, she had forgotten her need to speak with him and to have him, if he could, explain his bizarre appearance for that brief second, at the doorway of the morning room.

Well, perhaps she could speak with him later, she thought. But for now . . .

Her gaze drifted to Hugh, who was clasping the hand of the last guest he was to greet. He looked magnificent with his freshly starched shirtpoints just touching his cheeks and accentuating the handsome line of his cheekbones. He was dressed in black, following Beau Brummell's lead, a black coat which fitted his broad shoulders to perfection, a black waistcoat and black satin knee breeches, black stockings and black slippers. Only his shirt, shirtpoints and carefully arranged neckcloth were white accentuated by an emerald which sparkled from the folds of his neckcloth.

He spoke congenially and something he said made his last guest break into laughter. In turn Hugh smiled, a smile which caused Merry's heart to simply constrict with the pleasure it gave her.

Faith, but he would always be to her the handsomest man of her acquaintance. Everything about Hugh seemed designed to please her. Would she ever feel indifferent toward him?

She wouldn't think of that, not now. Now, she would simply enjoy this ball with him to the fullest and let the future care for itself.

Once the last guest had been ushered into the drawing room, he turned purposefully toward her, as though he had known she had been standing there waiting for him the whole time. He did not hesitate, but crossed the chamber to where she stood. He smiled down at her and for a moment, as he stood before her, he simply looked at her. She smiled in return, drinking in the affectionate expression she saw reflected in his eyes. She wanted to say so many things to him, to tell him she had been in love with him for ages, but she couldn't. Instead, her eyes suddenly filled with tears and he immediately complained, "How's this? Tears at our Christmas ball?"

"I'm sorry," she whispered as he touched away with his gloved fingers the tears that seeped from her eyes. "I don't know why I am crying. I suppose it is because——" But she did not want to finish the thoughts which stood poised at the very tip of her tongue.

"Because?" he urged her.

"Hugh, I missed you so much," she whispered. "These past years and more. You've no idea!"

There! She had said it. She had spoken words she should not have.

His expression changed, not quickly, yet not slowly, as though her words had drawn thoughts to his mind, feelings to his heart in a single motion. His lips parted—perhaps words now stood poised on his tongue—and his eyes grew very intense. He stepped toward her, a hand reaching to her and touching her arm in the tender place above the elbow. "Merry—" he began.

But he got no further. "There you are, Hugh," Judith cried, her voice fairly ringing out from the landing half way down the stairs. "And here is Honoria to dance with you!"

Merry instinctively stepped away from Hugh, frightened by the sight of his bride-to-be coming down the stairs. Hugh turned around and, seeing her, immediately moved toward the stairs leaving Merry in the cold shadows of the entrance hall.

She watched Honoria, begowned quite modestly in a plain, blue velvet gown. Her face was pale as usual above a white lace frill worn high about her neck, the only adornment to her gown. It seemed to Merry that she had seen nothing amiss as she greeted her betrothed. "We are to dance," she said. "Or so your lively Judith would have it. I suppose we should, Rayneworth. Everyone will be expecting it."

"Yes, my dear," he responded obediently, offering her his arm. He did not look at Merry as he took his bride-to-be down the hall.

Constance and Judith were quickly on either side of her.

Judith cried, "We are so very sorry, Merry! But it had to be done. We cannot get rid of Honoria for the night until she has danced at least once with Hugo!"

"And then he shall be yours for the remainder of the evening!" Constance whispered in her ear. They each slipped an arm through hers and pulled her down the same hall.

Merry whispered, "Whatever do you mean?"

"Never mind!" Judith returned, leaning toward her and hurrying her onward.

"The less you know, the better," Constance added mysteriously.

She knew they must have some mischief in mind, and truly she knew she ought to make an effort to stop them, but tonight was the Christmas ball and—and she was not of a mind to be serious, dull and responsible. As a footman passed by bearing a tray laden with cups of Christmas wassail, she joined the twins in descending upon the poor servant and rattling cups off the silver tray, nearly causing the poor man to lose his balance.

Forgotten were their veiled threats of mischief. All that she was concerned about for the present was dancing with Hugh.

An hour later, Judith and Constance sat one on either side of Honoria in the library. Judith pressed a kerchief damp with lavender water against Honoria's temples and Constance said, "Here, dearest Honoria, a little more of the draught and you will feel a great deal better, I promise you."

The twins watched eagerly as Honoria sipped the drink. "It is quite bitter—it tastes of laudanum."

"Amabel always uses it when she has the headache," Constance stated noncommittally.

Honoria smiled at each of the sisters in turn, quite lazily, her eyelids drooping. "I do not feel the pain quite so acutely, thank you."

A scratching was heard on the door and Judith eyed Constance eagerly over Honoria's head. With the gentlest push, Constance was able to shift Honoria onto Judith's shoulder, before she ran to the door. There, before her, stood the man for whom the twins had been waiting—dear, good, honest, trustworthy, dull Mr. Belper. She drew him into the chamber by taking his arm and giving the door a shove behind her with a slippered foot.

"Thank God you have come!" she cried, pulling him toward Honoria.

Mr. Belper began, "Whatever is it, Con—" He broke off suddenly. "Dear God, what is wrong with our sweet Miss Youl-greave?"

"Oh, hallo Edwin," Honoria called lazily to the astonished cleric.

Constance caught Judith's wide-eyed glance. Both young ladies mouthed the vicar's name at one and the same time, neither able to credit that Honoria had actually addressed Mr. Belper by his Christian name. Together they smiled and Constance did not hesitate to draw Mr. Belper to the sofa where Judith and Honoria were presently situated.

Judith explained in a quiet, concerned voice, "She has the headache and we have given her a little of Amabel's lauda-num."

"Ah," Mr. Belper responded with a knowing nod of his head. He then took up a station beside Honoria and took her hand in his. He patted her fingers gently, whereupon Honoria turned to him and said, "You were always so kind to me, Edwin. I shall never forget you, or the many presents you have given me over the past several weeks and months, and all the flowers you have sent from your own rose garden, and all because I commented once upon how prettily your roses bloom for you. You are by far the sweetest man I have ever known."

Constance bit the inside of her cheek to keep from laughing outright. She watched Mr. Belper's color rise upon his cheeks as he patted Honoria's hand in three quick successions and cleared his voice. "Well, yes of course. I'm certain I've done nothing more than any gentleman would do in the face of your obvious desire—that is, your enjoyment of my roses." He glanced nervously from Constance to Judith and back again.

Judith then cleared her voice, and encouraged her sister to speak by waving at her with her free hand.

Constance took up her part readily. "Mr. Belper, my sister and I truly hate to discommode you in any manner, but would it be possible for you to tend to our dear sister-to-be? You see, if we are not in attendance upon my brother's guests, especially when Hugo was so kind as to give the ball especially to please us, I greatly fear we shall arouse his rightful wrath. Do we ask too much in begging you to sit with Honoria until she is feeling more the thing?"

She cocked her head, adopting the most pleading expression she could summon, and smiled innocently upon her hopefully unsuspecting victim.

Mr. Belper regarded her seriously, for a long moment, before answering. "It is of course not quite appropriate that I remain alone with Miss Youlgreave. But since we are in the library after all," and here he paused to glance about the large chamber, "I see no real harm in it and . . . and you must see to your guests. I shall be honored to be of service to you."

Judith gave the limp Honoria a shove and before Mr. Belper knew what was happening to him, Honoria's head was buried tidily upon his shoulder. It clearly seemed the most natural of effects that his arm should slip about her thin shoulders.

"Thank you ever so much!" Judith cried, rising to her feet. "Whatever would we do without our dear Mr. Belper. We shall return shortly to see how you are going on."

"Yes, thank you, indeed!" Constance added.

With that the twins linked arms and fairly ran from the chamber, satin skirts and silk skirts swishing side by side. They repressed their devilish giggles until they were far enough from the library not to be heard. As they tripped lightly down the stairs, they gave way to squeals and chortles which quite naturally brought a swarm of handsome young men rising up to greet them, begging for dances, each in turn, until the entrance hall rang to the rafters with the sounds of youthful flirting and laughter.

Chapter Twenty

How appropriate it was, Merry thought, that as the clock struck twelve, Hugh finally led her out for the waltz. She wasn't certain in the least what midnight had to do with the appropriateness of the moment, but there always would be something magical and pressing about the twelfth hour, the hour dividing day from day. As though midnight represented the onward thrust of time and of change, an element wholly outside of one's control. There was only one response to midnight—surrender.

So she gave herself to dancing with Hugh, endeavoring to keep her fears at bay, fears which reminded her that less than a sennight now—six pitiful days—would see Hugh taken from her forever.

As he settled her in a place among the dancers on the floor, he held out his hand to her and, with a smile, she placed her gloved hand in his. They stood thusly, along with at least thirty other couples, awaiting the commencement of the music. From the corner of her eye, she could see the violinist give the nod of his head and the dip of his bow. Sweetly, the vibrant waltz began.

She stepped into the marked rhthyms of the dance in harmony with Hugh, and from that moment she was caught up in a sense that this dance with him would be magical. Her fears could no longer touch her.

"Did I tell you how pretty you look in your red velvet,

Merry?'' he queried softly, leaning toward her ear as he spoke. They were very near the orchestra at this turn of the dance.

"Thank you," she whispered back into his ear. For the barest second her cheek touched his, since he was still close. Did she imagine he drew her closer to him at the same time? Was it his sigh which touched her face and brought a shiver racing down her neck? They turned, paused, turned again.

Beyond his shoulder, at the far end of the ballroom, she vaguely discerned Judith and Constance enjoying the attentions of several lively young gentleman, though more than one appeared to be half-foxed.

They turned, paused, turned again. Her heart beat strongly as she gave herself to the dips and sways of the music. Hugh drew her attention back to him, and from that moment he did not take his eyes from her. She could only return his gaze for moments at a time, for the mere looking into his eyes brought every fine emotion rising within her chest and a strong, pleasurable dizziness would assail her. She sighed with contentment. This was what she had wished for all afternoon—a dance with Hugh.

Then another turn, another pause, a quick turn again. His eyes always watching. What was he thinking, she wondered, as her own gaze fluttered back to his for a moment. She wanted to ask him, at the same time she did not want the dance to be interrupted by words. She wanted only to feel his hand upon her back, to feel the pressure of his hand as he guided her about the floor, to be swept into the dance by his mastery of the movements, to take full pleasure for this brief time in being with him.

Would she ever dance with him again?

She squeezed her eyes shut refusing to let the question dwell in her mind. She pushed it from her thoughts and again concentrated on the moment, on his nearness, on the steady beat of her heart. She opened her eyes, looked up at him again, and smiled. Her heart was full of gratitude that she had been granted this dance. He smiled in return, still watching her intently.

She knew there were other dancers on the floor, she could see the brief wisps of colorful silks and satins in predominate whites and reds and greens, as other couples whirled by. But her attention was all for Hugh. The exercise of the dance had brought a sheen to his complexion and a glow to his eyes. The waltz was a vigorous affair.

He drew her a little closer to him, and one turn in three she felt the pressure of his leg against hers. He whirled her steadily, again and again. She danced with him as though they had practiced their steps together for months and knew each other's every nuance of movement. She realized his clasp upon her hand had become stronger, more demanding. She returned the pressure of his hand. He whirled her more forcefully still. The music rose and swelled. She saw the beads of perspiration on his brow and how his eyes bore into hers as though he was commanding her to read his thoughts. She no longer looked away from him, but returned his gaze steadily. She realized she wasn't breathing and took a breath, but it seemed only the smallest, lightest breath would come. She felt dizzy and strange, not like she would swoon, but that were he to lead her from the floor and give her the smallest hint he desired to kiss her, she would likely fall into his arms.

This thought forced her eyes to close as in rapid succession she gave herself to every memory of having been kissed by him. How many times, including their flirtation of four years ago, had he kissed her? A dozen? How wicked! How utterly scandalous! How sublime!

How strange that she could so easily follow his lead with her eyes closed. She wished the dance would go on forever. Would he want to hold her in his arms forever?

Hugh looked down at the woman in his arms, her eyelids closed. How easily he guided her even when she was dancing without sight. He felt consumed with guilt that he had not ordered the guttered candles in the chandeliers relit. He had wanted the chamber dark when he danced with Merry. He was being very wicked and well he knew it. But from the moment he had caught sight of her earlier in the entrance hall, standing to the side of the chamber, waiting for him, he had wanted only this moment with her.

Faith, he did not even known if Honoria was nearby, but then he had not seen her for hours. He thought it likely she had retired to a chair in a quiet corner of one of the drawing rooms. She had not wanted the ball and during the only dance they had shared—a simple country dance—she had confessed to having a headache. The worst of it was, of the moment, his thoughts were not with her. Only with Merry.

With Merry, he was behaving scandalously. But hopefully the dim lighting, the crowded ballroom floor, and the flow of champagne, wine and brandy would serve to disguise his truly wretched conduct. In a moment, he meant to lead her from the floor, before even the orchestra had played its final notes. One more turn about the floor . . .

When a loud crashing sound, along with the curses of several young men, erupted near his twin sisters at the far end of the ballroom, when he saw that all eyes were directed toward an ensuing melee, he wasted no time in guiding Merry quickly through the doors of the ballroom across to a hallway which led to an unused antechamber.

Merry did not demure, but walked quickly beside him. "What is it, Hugh?" she queried almost groggily, as though she had been awakened from a dream.

"Several of Judith's beaux have begun brawling for her favors, I fear."

"Where are we going?" she asked, as he drew her arm about his and pulled her close beside him. Once down the deserted hall, he opened the door to a dark antechamber and fairly shoved her inside.

"Hugh!" she whispered. "Whatever are you—"

She got no further, for he suddenly took her in his arms and kissed her soundly.

Merry began to protest, pressing her hands against his chest, because she feared discovery and scandal. But when she realized he was doing precisely what she had dreamed of for the entire day, she surrendered. Sighing deeply, she threw both her arms about his neck and held him close. She breathed his name upon his lips, and he responded by catching her up tightly about her waist. She felt herself pressed to the length of him. Even her shins touched his. He turned her bodily around and she felt the door against her back, then his body pressed more firmly into hers.

The sensation overwhelmed her in its intensity and her love for him transformed into a wave of passion that poured over her like the blast from a blacksmith's forge. She felt as though her body was merging with his, that though they were fully clothed and no intimate caresses were exchanged that still she was giving herself to him, completely, without reservation.

He kissed her lips again and again, then her cheeks and her hair. He spoke her name and again kissed her fully on the lips. She felt unaccountably hungry, desirous, clinging to him as though her very breath depended upon his nearness.

Then his kisses slowed and his lips drifted away so that he leaned his forehead lightly against hers.

Merry's breathing was still uncertain and shallow. All of her love for him was united in this moment as she stroked the nape of his neck with agitated fingers.

"Merry," he whispered, his breath also uneven. "My darling Fairfield. Whatever am I to do without you?"

Merry squeezed her eyes shut, the pain of his words a wave of torment over her heart.

She knew then he had been kissing her goodbye.

A moment later, he kissed her on the forehead and quit the chamber.

She waited in the dark recesses of the small chamber, where dimly outlined she could see that Holland covers had been thrown over a harp and a pianoforte. Instruments without music.

How long she stayed within the chamber she did not know, but she suspected it was over an hour before she finally emerged. She had found herself not wanting to leave. Her mind had become very dull. Her heartbeats had slowed. Her hands were now cold.

When she finally did leave the room, it was to discover that most of the guests had departed the ballroom, and at least half had already quit the house. Apparently, the disturbance which had caused Hugh to risk taking her apart from the guests had alerted the older, steadier guests to the circumstance that enough fun had been had by all—the time to depart had arrived.

Coaches were still being called for, capes, hats, and coats retrieved from Siddons' capable hands, carriage rugs wrapped tightly about the ladies's laps, and a stream of vehicles was wending its way into the night.

Still feeling a trifle dazed, Merry avoided the entrance hall where several young gentlemen were flirting noisily with Judith and Constance. She moved instead to the rose and green drawing room. There, at the far end of the chamber, she saw that Hugh was deep in conversation with Sir Rupert and three men wearing greatcoats, whose pink noses and cheeks spoke strongly of their having just come in from the cold. By the expression on Hugh's face, the worried frown between his eyes, the strong working of his jaw, she knew that something untoward had occurred. She thought of Laurence and of Kit. Panic began rushing through her. Her head began to pound with fear. What if either of them had been captured?

She did not hesitate but skirted the several remaining clumps of guests who were still awaiting their carriages, and approached the group. She heard Hugh ask, "But are you certain this fellow quit my house? You mistook one of the guests, surely."

"He went down to the stables, m'lord, saddled a horse and rode quickly through the home wood. We followed him, hoping to be led to the White Prince. He knew his way. We were able to track him part of the way, but lost him—until he returned. Somehow he caught sight of us and disappeared to the east. We couldn't find him. One more thing—shots were fired tonight. Some of the militia are sick to death of being made sport of. I tried to stop them, but tempers are high."

Sir Rupert addressed Hugh, "With your permission we wish to continue searching the countryside for this conspirator. Will you agree to it?"

Hugh nodded. "Of course, but pray instruct your men to cease making use of their pistols. What is one man against so many?"

The men present agreed and Sir Rupert began delivering his orders, but Merry had stopped listening. Her heart was constricted with fear. It could only be Kit, she thought. What if he has been shot, or killed? It would be her fault for not making a greater effort to speak with him, to confront him.

But Kit had been in attendance at the ball.

Relief flooded her, but only for a moment.

But if not Kit, then who? A servant acting on his orders? Possibly. There was only one thing to do—she must speak with him now, to confront him about his activities of the night before, to discover the truth. Knowing that neither Hugh nor the men surrounding him had even noticed her presence, she left the rose and green drawing room by way of the entrance hall. When she did not find him among the young men still flirting with Judith and Constance, she asked the latter if she had seen Kit recently.

Constance, her eyes glittering with happiness at so much masculine attention, waved a hand toward the stairwell. "I saw my brother go up not five minutes ago. He was looking for Mr. Belper."

Merry thought a funny expression passed across Constance's face upon mentioning Mr. Belper's name, but when one of her beaux stole her fan from her, the younger twin's attention was immediately diverted.

Merry lifted her skirts and began making a quick ascent.

She found Kit a few moments later storming away from the library doors. "Merry, I am glad I have come upon you! You are the very person I wished to see. You cannot imagine what is going forward in that—that den of iniquity!"

Merry raised her brows, stupefied by Kit's demeanor. If he truly was in league with the White Prince and if he had been involved in some mischief only this evening, surely nothing of greater consequence—however shocking—could possibly have claimed his attention. Nothing it seemed pointed to Kit's involvement with Laurence, save his inexplicable appearance last night in the darkened doorway of the morning room, some time past midnight.

She was about to ask why he was in the boughs when the door of the library opened and a red-faced Mr. Belper emerged. He was wringing his hands as he approached Kit and said, "My dear boy, you much mistake what you saw! 'Pon my soul, I would do nothing to harm Miss Youlgreave. The poor child has been violently ill since early this evening. I have been in strict attendance upon her by your sisters' request. Whenever I tried to rise from the sofa to ring for a servant, she fell into a bout of tears. I—I couldn't leave her side for a moment. Do come see for yourself."

"Her head was upon your shoulder," Kit countered, his brow stormy. "And you were caressing her hand."

"Whenever I tried to remove my hand from hers or to adjust her head away from my shoulder—where, I entirely agree with you, it most certainly did not belong—she whimpered pitifully."

"Well I think there's something havey-cavey about the whole of it!" Kit cried.

When at that moment a white-faced Honoria appeared at the doorway of the library, called weakly for Mr. Belper, then promptly swooned upon the carpet in the hallway, Kit's misgivings were entirely allayed. Mr. Belper was with her instantly. Merry watched the vicar lift her easily into his arms and take her back to the sofa. With Kit in tow, she followed after the good reverend.

So this was Judith and Constance's scheme! As she watched Mr. Belper lay Honoria gently on the sofa, she realized she could not have concocted a better plan herself.

Merry gave two hard tugs upon the bell-pull and told Mr. Belper she would soon have Mrs. Penistone tending to Miss Youlgreave. She also suggested that it might be wise to have the young lady removed to a bedchamber where she could be attended to properly. Mr. Belper agreed whole heartedly and Kit, a little shame-faced, begged his mentor's forgiveness.

Twenty minutes later, after Honoria was taken to a bed-chamber and Mr. Belper had quit the library, Merry held Kit back by a slight pressure on his arm. "Stay a moment, Kit," she said. "There is a matter of some importance I would put to you." She then begged him to answer one question—had Hugh chased him through the hallways last night?

"Whatever do you mean?" he asked, blinking at her, clearly astonished. In fact, he looked so stunned, so bemused that had she not actually seen him, she would have begun to doubt he had even been there.

"Kit, please, this is most urgent. Pray, attend carefully to me. Did you not leave the house last night? Then, upon turning back abruptly, pause at the door of the morning room? Remember? You looked directly at me, before bolting for the stairs. Don't tell me you were sleep-walking for I will not believe you."

Kit frowned at her. "To my knowledge, I have never walked about in my sleep. As for the rest, Merry, I haven't the faintest notion what you are talking about."

Merry blinked back at him. She had no reason not to believe him because Kit would never lie to her. Her thoughts turned inward as her gaze slid from his face. Who then had she seen in the doorway of the morning room, if not Kit? She looked back at Kit, scrutinizing his face—his arched auburn brows, his straight nose, the unmistakeable Leighton features. If he had

had a brother nearer his age and build, and in possession of the same features, she might have been able to presume she had erred, that she had seen not Kit, but his brother. But Kit didn't have such a brother, only four sisters.

Was it possible she had seen Judith or Constance? Beatrice was too small and Amabel was an invalid. Was Judith or Constance a member of Laurence's army?

She narrowed her eyes and Kit smiled broadly. "What are you thinking about Merry? Your face is pinched up like a dried fig."

"I am trying to make something out and I am having a most wretched time doing it!"

"Well, perhaps I can help. What do you mean, when Hugh was chasing me? Was someone in the house? A stranger, perhaps?"

"Not a stranger. I was convinced until now that I had seen you." She continued to look at Kit and brought back to mind the image of the young man she had seen in the doorway. What if it had been Constance or Judith dressed up in Kit's clothes? Who most ressembled Kit? Neither, really, she thought with an absent shake of her head. Of all four sisters it was Amabel who bore a keen resemblance to Kit. In fact, strikingly so. They were also nearest in age, little more than a year separating them.

Amabel.

Her mind began swimming about unsteadily as a most bizarre notion came to her. *I am so afraid,* she remembered Amabel saying only this morning. At the time, Merry had thought the invalid was expressing a fear she had contracted consumption or some other dread disease. She had been crying, as well. If not a disease, then what had she been so afraid of?

"Now what maggot has got into your head?" Kit queried. "For I can see your thoughts shifting about on your face, one upon the other. What is it, Merry? I don't like to mention it but you look very queer of the moment."

Merry lifted a hand and turned away from him. She then bid him goodnight, attempting to convey to him that she had made a silly mistake, she had imagined something that had not happened, and if she seemed in an odd humor it was probably due to the enormous fatigue she was experiencing. The successful Christmas ball had quite taken a toll upon her. If he seemed distressed by her words, or her actions, she ignored him. For the present, she had to uncover the truth, and her suspicions of what the truth might be were causing her to feel quite ill.

Amabel.

Her mind was now completely obsessed with a possibility that was as remote as it was absurd.

She left the library and began a steady progress toward the family's bedchambers, mounting the stairs to the second floor, her red velvet skirts in hand. Her mouth was dry and her heart was a heavy thud in her chest. She did not hesitate, but went directly to Amabel's room. She did not knock but gave the door a firm shove and walked in, her heart now hammering against her ribs.

She heard Nurse's snores. The chamber was still redolent from the use of perfumed pastilles, and a single candle still burned steadily in the sconce opposite the bed. Because of the dimness of the chamber she waited a full minute for her vision to adjust before she ventured further into the chamber. She could see Amabel's shape beneath the bedcovers, just visible through the partially drawn bed-curtains.

Then she was mistaken.

If Amabel was asleep in bed, she must be mistaken.

She knew an impulse to turn and quit the chamber.

Clearly she was mistaken.

Yet some instinct told her she was not. As she approached the bed, she remembered tripping over the boot the night before.

Amabel's boot. A boot that had had dirt on it. A boot that had been out of doors.

But Amabel couldn't walk. She was confined to a Bath chair.

She stared at Amabel's outline and watched for movement, for the rise and fall of her chest, but she saw nothing. Only then was she moved to quickly cross the remaining distance to the bed, to flip back the bed-curtains and stare down at Amabel.

Still there was no movement and she touched the tousled hair on the pillow. It slid away.

A wig.

A pillow for shoulders and chest.

No Amabel!

"Nurse!" she called sharply.

The snores ceased abruptly as Nurse jumped to her feet. "Whatever is amiss, Amabel? Are you returned so early, then? Oh, my! Miss Fairfield! Oh, dear, Miss Fairfield! Oh, dear, oh, dear."

"Returned from whence?"

"I don't know," the flustered woman countered, wringing her hands. "I don't know anything!"

"Where is Amabel?"

Nurse began to cry and flopped back down in the chair pressing her apron to her face. "I knew t'would come to this one day. I told her not to do it."

"She can walk, can't she?"

Nurse blubbered and sobbed and nodded her head. "Yes, for the past year—almost two, in fact—only don't tell a soul, I pray you won't. Miss Amabel will be that angry, she will."

"I am not concerned with her temper," Merry responded urgently. "It is her life which concerns me now."

"What—what do you mean?"

"One of Sir Rupert's aides followed Amabel back to the home wood from wherever it was she had gone. Apparently shots were fired. She could be hurt or worse! Now tell me, when did you expect her home? It is half past one now."

Nurse wiped her face and ceased crying. "Merciful God, she should have been home by now. If she is dead I will never forgive myself."

"If she has been able to sustain her deception as an invalid for so long, she cannot be without a great deal of cleverness. Most likely she realized she was being followed and chose to hide for a time until she could return safely. So no hysterics, mind!"

"I pray you are right, Miss," she returned, swallowing hard and sniffling.

Merry sat down on the edge of the bed, trying to think, to piece together all she knew in order to best decide how to proceed. "There is only one difficulty. I heard Sir Rupert order his men to search the countryside thoroughly for the outlaw—for Amabel. We need to find her before anyone else does. She could be hanged for her crimes if she is in league with the White Prince and if they find her first—well, she could get hurt. She is helping the White Prince, isn't she?"

Nurse nodded, her lips quivering. She again began weeping quietly into her apron. Merry watched her, feeling very little sympathy for a woman who had conspired to place Amabel's life in jeopardy, however unwilling her part may have been.

"I suggest you remain here and please let me know if Amabel returns. I mean to speak with Lord Rayneworth immediately."

But upon these words Nurse bolted from her chair. "Oh, do not!" she pleaded. "Pray do not! His lordship will never comprehend his sister's devotion to the White Prince! Never!"

"She's right, Merry!"

Merry turned toward the door and saw Kit's frame filling the doorway. He entered the room and closed the door behind him. "Hugh would never understand. He is too much under Honoria's thumb to comprehend anything of compassion upon the poor and suffering. And he would never understand why my sister has done what she has done. But I do! God help me, I do!"

He approached the bed and as his face came into the light, Merry saw that his eyes shone with an expression which she had thought lost to Kit. "Did you know of her activities?" she asked, staring up at him in wonder.

"No," he said ardently, shaking his head. "But by God she has more bottom than all of us put together! Imagine, pretending to be crippled for a year and more! It is unbelievable. And no one would have suspected a thin girl in a Bath chair to have been the one to support so fully the White Prince. And I—" here he paused, his expression euphoric "—and I was too far down the wrong path. But never mind that! We've got to find her and I believe I know where she is. I'll go to her now. Presuming she's hiding, she'll be at the caverns to the northeast. She knows her way about the caves as well as any of us and the militia would never find her there. Besides, it looks like it might snow soon and whatever tracks she's left behind will soon be covered up."

Merry rose from the edge of the bed and took Kit's hands. "Sir Rupert's men said shots have been fired. You don't know what you will find once you get to the caverns. We should talk to Hugh, tell him—"

"Hugh will feel obligated to tell Sir Rupert and then where would we be?"

She acknowledged this much was true. "Then let me go with you."

He lifted an imperious hand. "From what you have said, Merry, your life would be put in jeopardy and I can't permit that. Amabel is my sister and I will go after her. Please don't argue or—or I will be forced to bind you up with a rope and lock you in the jericho!"

Merry smiled faintly but she could not laugh. She was too sick with fear for Amabel's life and now Kit's safety that she could do little more than respond with, "Go then! But if she is not at the caves, come back quickly before the militia find you and mistake you for the White Prince. Shots have already been fired."

"Don't worry. I know she is there. We always used the caves for hiding. If you go deep enough, no one can find you for days."

"How long will it take you?" she asked.

"Even if she is hurt, we shan't be gone above an hour. And I promise you, if she is not there, I shall return."

"I'll give you an hour then," she said, her heart constricted in her breast. "After that, I'll confer with Hugh. And Kit, take a tinder-box and a candle, at the very least."

"Agreed," he said and, placing a kiss on her cheek, left the room on a quick, firm tread.

Chapter Twenty-One

Merry remained in Amabel's bedchamber waiting for Kit to return with his sister. He had left shortly before two o'clock and some minutes ago the clock in Amabel's bedchamber had struck the hour three times.

She felt as though her nerves were near to shattering. Kit had not yet returned and more than an hour had passed. She didn't know what to do or to think. Nurse was snoring again, the lateness of the hour the victor against her weariness. Should she tell Hugh of his siblings' mischief? Should she wait?

She paced the floor, her limbs readied for action. She tried to keep her mind calm. She knew the distance to the caverns which were situated at the edge of Rayneworth's lands to the northeast. A stream flowed nearby, disappearing underground just a half mile beyond the caves.

One thing she knew for certain, Kit should have been back by now, unless there was trouble.

Wait a little longer, she adjured herself. Just a little longer. She heard footsteps in the hall.

Kit.

She crossed the room on a quick tread, pulled the door open and stepped out into the hall. Behind her, the clock chimed the quarter hour. In front of her, Hugh stood, bearing a candle and staring back at her in surprise.

"What is it?" he asked. "Who were you expecting, for I can see you are disturbed. Why are you in Amabel's bedchamber?"

He stepped toward her, his voice low and firm as he added, "Whatever has gone amiss you may tell me! Is it Amabel?"

Merry deliberated within her own heart precisely what her next course of action ought to be, but only for half a second. She closed the door behind her, entered the hall swiftly, and began to move toward her chambers.

"Come!" she commanded him in a hurried voice.

He did not hesitate to follow her, nor to enter her bedchamber—a most improper arrangement—nor to close the door behind him when she bid him do so. She crossed the room to her wardrobe, threw the door open and reached swiftly for her heaviest cape. Throwing it about her shoulders she said, "Draw near while I tell you what I have to say. You will not like it and if you were fainthearted I daresay you would quickly fall into a swoon." When he stood next to her, she began to speak in a low whisper, informing him of the true state of Amabel's health, the deception she had been enacting for nearly two years, and lastly about her involvement with the White Prince.

He was stunned, grievously so, the look of horror on his face unlike anything she had ever witnessed before.

"There is more, Hugh," she said, pulling three bandboxes from the top shelf of her wardrobe and letting each fall to the floor. She dropped to her knees and tore the first two open, discarding as suitable headgear a satiny pink confection and a straw bonnet. The last bandbox held a green velvet bonnet with wide white ribbons. As she tugged the hat over her black curls, and began tying the ribbons under her chin, she looked up at him over her shoulder and said, "Amabel has been gone all night. Kit went after her. We both believe she is in a desperate case. When I heard earlier that Sir Rupert and his men were searching the countryside for the man who left, then returned to your estate earlier, only then did I realize there was a connection between the *man* you were chasing last night and the one who ostensibly left this evening. Hugh, that man was Amabel! I saw her last night—she had intended upon going through the morning room to the backstairs when she saw me. I thought it was Kit, for she was dressed like a man and looked just like him—at least in the dim shadows of the doorway she looked like him." She rose to her feet and, finding her half-boots of brown kid from deep within the wardrobe, kicked off her slippers and began wiggling her toes inside. She was unsuccessful and it was necessary to sit on the chair near the foot of her bed and work the snug-fitting boots onto her feet. Hugh followed behind her, keeping pace with her every movement.

"Why didn't you tell me last night that you had seen her?"

"I didn't know it was her. I thought it was Kit and whatever mischief he was up to—and you may imagine I never thought he was informing for the White Prince—well, I couldn't expose him to you until I had confronted him. I had meant to speak with him this morning but I didn't see him, and all this afternoon I was secluded in my chambers preparing for the ball. So you see there seemed nothing *desperate* to tell you last night. Perhaps it may seem wrong in me to have avoided exposing Kit to you, but I just couldn't't!"

He drew close to her and leaned down. "Thinking like a true friend, eh? All right, I can understand your keeping your silence then but what about an hour ago when you learned that my sister—however incredible it seems!—was *the man* Sir Rupert and his men have been hunting? Do you not know that there are over a dozen men of every stamp looking for her? And many who, in the heat of the chase, might not hesitate to fire upon her?"

"Why do you think I'm telling you now? Kit bade me wait until he could bring her home himself. He thought it best to keep mum because if we were to tell you of Amabel and her activities, your knowledge would place you in a difficult position with Sir Rupert. He said he knew if she was in trouble she would hide in the caverns, which is where we are to go now."

"We?" he queried, his voice at full force.

"Do be quiet, Hugh! Your future wife is in the bedchamber across the hall. She will not like to discover you have been in my room in the early hours of the morning."

"As though I give a fig for that in this moment when my family is tumbling down about my ears! Good God, I wish I'd known! All right, then. I won't repine about your having kept your silence. What is done is done."

"I think we should take the curricle. The lane is not much travelled to the northeast and if Amabel is hurt—" She could not continue, but drew in a deep breath, sudden tears smarting her eyes.

"Yes, yes," he responded. "I must get my coat and put on a pair of boots myself. All right, I won't prevent you from coming along."

"You know you couldn't, even if you wished to."

He looked down at her and smiled faintly. "You always were a game one, Fairfield."

Merry had completed fitting her boots to her feet and, taking hold of his hand, gave it a squeeze. "I shall meet you in the stables. Hugh, hurry."

"You may depend on it," he said, quitting her room.

Fifteen minutes later, with only a single, quite feeble carriage lamp to show the horses the road, Hugh cracked his whip expertly over the matched pair. "Don't be frightened," he said to Merry. "If I know anything it is this lane. I have travelled it a hundred times in the past year alone—I know every inch of it!" He laughed softly if bitterly, "But I own I never expected to put my knowledge to the test for such a reason as this!"

Merry was not frightened about how swiftly he was moving the curricle down the lane, only by the horrible thoughts which kept dogging her mind no matter how hard she tried to ignore them—of Kit, of Amabel, wounded or dying. She clenched her teeth together, holding back the panic and tears which after so much suspense in awaiting Kit's return had finally begun to overtake her.

But she would not panic now. Not when she might be needed.

The caverns were only three miles from the house, a distance which even at full bore still required the curricle nearly thirty minutes to achieve. The terrain was rugged the closer the curricle got to the caverns. The lane rose up and dipped down, rounded stiff bends with shallow drops on one side, then the other, trees rose up to disguise the next twist of the road, and the lane was slushy and rutted in places. But all of this Hugh knew, as he quickly encouraged his horses along.

At the entrance to the caves, only blackness greeted them and the drift of the icy stream nearby. If Kit had indeed made use of a tinder-box and candle, it wasn't evident. Hugh brought the carriage close to the footbridge and bade Merry tend the horses while he quickly crossed the bridge, his footsteps a dull echo on the water below. Then he disappeared into the mouth of the cave.

Merry had jumped from the curricle, her half-boots landing in crunchy snow. The air was biting cold on her cheeks as she went to the horses' heads and talked quietly to them, their steamy breath hot on her face.

The waiting soon became excruciating. How many minutes passed, she couldn't tell. Fifteen, twenty? During all that time, she scanned the three converging lanes and as much of the land beyond which her gaze could see. Tall beech trees and gnarled oaks obscured most of her view. She listened and looked and listened again.

Suddenly, in the distance, coming from the north, a flickering light appeared.

"Oh, dear God," she breathed aloud, her breath fogging in the cold night. The light was but a half mile away. Surely they could see her carriage lamp as well. There was only one thing she could do. She had to extinguish the light. But how then would they see sufficiently to get back to Hathersage without driving off the road to land in a shallow ditch or at the bottom of a cliff?

Hugh had said he knew every inch of the lane. They would soon discover whether it was true or merely a boast. She rounded the horses and, opening the top of the lamp with her gloved fingers, blew out the flame.

The snow at her feet was slushy. She suspected Sir Rupert's men had already been at this location once before. By morning's light, the curricle's tracks would be visible. Anyone would be able to follow their trail back to Hathersage—if indeed they were able to get back before being caught.

She did not want to leave the horses, but she felt she had to find out what was happening within the caverns and, if possible, to let Hugh know that someone was fast approaching. She bid the horses to stay where they were—much good that would do if they became startled!—and ran to the entrance of the caverns. She called out Hugh's name and warned him that they were being pursued. For a moment, there was no response, only blackness. Then she heard Hugh's voice, though it was obvious he was still deep within the cave. "Turn the carriage around to face the lane back to Hathersage."

Never had his voice been so reassuring, or his words. She hurried back to the curricle, falling twice, striking her knees painfully against the hard, crusted snow. She winced at the pain but kept going. She felt a wet drop on her cheek, then another. She looked up and felt more drops, only not drops, but flakes—welcome snowflakes! She blessed their good fortune as she groped for the horses. The snow began to fall rapidly as she climbed aboard the curricle and slowly turned the entire equipage in what she hoped was the proper direction. It was very dark and without the lamp impossible to see but a few feet in front of her.

To her right, she again caught sight of the light. It was brighter now, closer. How much time did they have left by which to steal away?

Hurry, Hugh! her mind cried.

A moment later, she heard a scuffling behind her and the sounds of Hugh, Kit and Amabel struggling in the snow. She heard Amabel whisper, "He is bleeding. They'll follow his tracks if he stains the snow."

"We can't concern ourselves with that now. We must trust that the snowfall will cover all."

The next moment, she felt Hugh leap up beside her, and extend an arm down to Kit. "Can you make it? Kit, you must try! Someone is but a quarter of a mile off. We can make it if you'll give me your hand and leap up."

Merry could see nothing, but the next moment Hugh leaned back heavily into her and Kit groaned loudly, his voice catching on a thick sob. Hugh fairly threw him into her arms and Merry held him tightly.

"Get him home," she heard Amabel say from the ground. "I'll find his horse and be along directly. Do not concern yourself with me."

Hugh cracked the whip and the curricle moved swiftly into the lane. "You did well to extinguish the light," he said. "I only hope I know this road as well as I think I do."

Merry looked behind her. So little was visible in the night, with the clouds so dense and the snowflakes falling thicker and thicker each moment. Suddenly a shape loomed up behind her and she could just barely discern Amabel astride Kit's horse. Amabel passed the curricle by and soon disappeared.

Merry held onto Kit as Hugh guided the carriage home at a slow trot. Only once or twice did he narrowly run the horses into a tree, and once almost missed a bend that would have taken them into a ditch. But more and more, the land opened up, putting the dangerous portion of the drive behind them. Fifteen minutes more saw them skirting the edge of the home wood, and a few minutes more brought lights from the great house flickering in the distance.

Merry was never more grateful for anything that she could remember than the sight of Hathersage. Only then, when the outlines of the house could be discerned through the falling snow, did Hugh at last give his horses their heads. They seemed to know that a warm stable was nearby for they responded readily to the sound of his whip. A few minutes later, the head groom had the team unharnessed and was leading them into the stables.

Amabel was ready as well, with one of the stableboys by her side. Merry expected her to help Hugh with Kit but instead, as soon as Hugh had Kit in his arms and was carrying him up to the house, she watched in amazement as Amabel, along with the stableboy, began hauling the curricle into the coachhouse. She understood then what Amabel was about and immediately followed behind to help.

The three of them together wiped down every inch of the curricle, drying off every watery snowflake from the body of the carriage and cleaning the wheels of any sign of mud and travel debris. Afterward, fresh hay was strewn about the floor of the entire coachhouse.

In complete fascination, Merry then followed Amabel to see what next she would do. How strange it was to see her dressed as a man and walking about. Walking! She went not to the house, but into the stables, where she checked each of the horses over carefully for even the smallest sign of mud or debris and instructed the head groom to again spread fresh hay onto the floor. When she was satisfied, she turned to Merry and spoke in a determined manner. "The snow is falling briskly enough so that our tracks will be fully covered by now. I know you will say nothing of this for you are acquainted with the White Prince and . . . and I know you wouldn't want to do him harm." Her expression changed, a sadness overtaking her. Smiling faintly, she said, "Pray come to the house and I will tell you all."

Merry was completely amazed and followed behind the younger woman as though she was being carried along solely by Amabel's will. They trudged up to the kitchen entrance of the great house and, once inside, Amabel bade her remove her half-boots. She then addressed Cook, who was waiting nearby. "Have my brothers come in?" she queried.

"Aye," Cook responded, appearing grave, but not in the least surprised.

"See to the boots, then, or all will be lost. It's the first thing they'll check, as you know."

"Yes, miss."

"Is my maid about?"

"Yes, of course, Miss."

"Send her to my chamber. She will need to brush Miss Fairfield's clothing as well."

"Yes, miss. At once."

Again, Merry was stunned. Cook took her orders from Amabel as tidily as any soldier. Clearly several staff members were fully conversant with Amabel's activities. Only it wasn't Amabel at all, Merry thought distractedly as she again blindly followed Amabel's command to follow her to her bedchamber. They were both now in their stockinged feet.

Once inside, Nurse's snores provided a strange backdrop to the tale which Amabel began to spin. As she spoke, she undressed herself, removing her mannish clothes, beginning with her neckcloth. "I was aware from the first Laurence was the White Prince."

Merry looked at her, tilting her head. Memories flooded her of the first night she arrived in Derbyshire—of the attack upon Rayneworth's coach. "You were there that first night," she exclaimed, stunned. "I presumed the soldier with Laurence was a young man. But it was you all the time, wasn't it?"

She nodded as she finished unwrapping the white linen cravat and let it drop to the floor. She laughed suddenly. "How thoroughly Hugh kissed you, too—and he, betrothed! I was never more shocked, especially since he is so changed! At the same time I was glad of it, and hoped that you would come to Hathersage. And so you have! Honoria will never make him a proper wife! Never!"

Merry felt herself blushing and was grateful that the chamber was still only barely lit by a single candle. Amabel stripped off her coat and began unbuttoning her waistcoat of black superfine, then quickly removed it. Merry shook her head as though trying to clear her vision. Was this the invalid? How energetically she moved!

"When did you discover you could walk?" she asked.

"About a month after the accident," Amabel responded, unflinching.

"What?" Merry cried. "That was nearly two years ago! You've been two years in a Bath chair? How have you born the deception? I cannot begin to conceive of how difficult it has been to do so!"

"Then you will comprehend the depth of my regard for Laurence and my belief in his activities." Amabel stepped out of her breeches and slid into a warm, woolen nightdress. "Besides, you cannot imagine how many larks I have kicked up in the past two years! A hundred, at least. It was worth every moment of my daily confinements in the chair. Each time Nurse alerted the family that I was suffering from the headache, I was free to roam about my bedchamber as much as I wished. And except for tonight, she has been a most watchful guard." Since Nurse chose at this moment to snort quite loudly, Merry could only laugh along with Amabel.

Merry again turned her attention back to Amabel. She was still so amazed that she felt as though she must be in the midst of a dream. "But Amabel, how could you have deceived Hugh when you must know he has always blamed himself for the accident, and for your supposed inability to walk?"

At that Amabel lost some of her conviviality. "There were so many times for his sake I wanted to end the charade, you've no idea! But I couldn't, not when, because of my invalidish state, I could learn from Sir Rupert everything Laurence needed to know about his schemes to capture him. And Merry, I would have done anything to have continued play-acting for Laurence's sake. You know yourself what a great work he has done among the poor in Derbyshire. I know that he has saved lives because of the money he was able to disburse. Of course, his efforts are not entirely selfless—you know how sorely Sir Rupert used him."

Merry nodded, finding it impossible to condemn Amabel for her decision to remain a cripple in appearance for so long. "You will have a difficult time convincing Hugh that you did what was right. But enough of that—tell me what happened tonight."

Amabel explained that she had been carefully picking her way back to Hathersage Park when she came upon Kit riding on horseback. "I had been at the cavern just as he supposed I was. I called to him and he quickly lifted me onto the horse, insisting I ride in front of him, instead of behind. He immediately spurred his mount away from the caves heading west. I didn't know why he made me sit in front of him or why he had hurried his horse away until I heard a shot, and Kit slumped forward against me. I quickly took the reins and, because I knew the country so well, I eluded our pursuer—besides, who could track anyone on a night like this! It was impossible. I had hoped to get him home, but I saw more lights coming from the north and knew my only hope was to get him back to the caves. I hid the horse, meaning only to settle Kit, then return to Hathersage when Hugh arrived. I was never more grateful for anything than the sight of his face! Though I promise you I have never seen him more furious than when he looked at me. I doubt he will ever understand or forgive me."

"You are right on both scores!" Hugh said stiffly.

Merry jerked her head toward the door and saw that he was standing in the doorway regarding his sister. His face was a hard mask and, in the dim candlelight, had Merry not heard his voice first she would certainly not have recognized him.

"Will you excuse us, Merry?"

Merry rose from the bed and said, "Yes, of course, but tell me first how Kit fares."

"He will do," was his curt response.

Merry did not attempt to glean more information from him. Instead, she quit the room and closed the door behind her. Though she felt a numbing fatigue in her limbs—by now it was past four o'clock—she did not consider for a moment retiring to her bedchamber. Instead, she went directly to Kit's room. When she opened the door she saw that Cook was lifting him up at the shoulders and one of the maids was helping him to sip a draught of laudanum to help him sleep. She crossed the chamber and looked down into his drowsy blue eyes. He sputtered down a little of the liquid and then smiled at her. "Got her home safely, Fairfield. Told you I would!"

"You were always full of pluck, Kit. By the sounds of it, you saved her life."

He nodded. "Just before I found her, I discovered three men waiting for her. After I lifted her onto my horse, I heard the pistol shot."

"I'm very proud of you, but now you must rest."

Cook laid him gently upon his pillow and he sighed, still not taking his gaze from her. "You must help Hugo to understand. He's very angry with Amabel, though he shouldn't be. She's got more courage than the rest of us Leightons put together. Please, Merry, speak to Hugh."

"I will," she assured him. "But not tonight. Best let everyone get a little sleep. I promise you I shall intervene, if it proves necessary."

Kit chuckled. "Oh, it will, have no doubts on that head." His lids began to grow heavy and Merry left the bedside beckoning Cook to follow her, which she did.

"Tell me in truth precisely how he is," she said, once they were in the hallway.

"He's got a pistol ball lodged in his shoulder, but even his lordship dunna believe he's in mortal danger. Of course I've 'ad Siddons send for t' surgeon, though God help us all if 'tis learned why he's come."

Merry looked at her thoughtfully for a moment then said, "I shall see that it is put about that Amabel required the surgeon's attention, and when it is learned that she has miraculously begun walking again, who will suspect he came for any other reason?"

"Bless you, t'will do to a nicety. Lord, protect this house.

Now off to bed wi' thee. I've 'ad the maids build up a fire in thy chambers and thee'll find a warming pan already heating up thy sheets. 'Tis been a long day."

"Indeed," Merry responded. She turned from Cook and headed toward her bedchamber but before she had reached her door, Nurse emerged from Amabel's room, sobbing.

Merry felt her heart go out to the servant who quite clearly had found herself trapped between Amabel's will and Hugh's anger. "I've been let go," she explained on a sob. Merry would have tried to console her, but the servant quickly headed toward the stairs and her bedchamber in the garrets above.

Chapter Twenty-Two

On the first floor of Hathersage Park, between the library and the domed dining room, was a chamber Merry enjoyed above all others and one which today had become her refuge. The family called it Lady Rayneworth's drawing room because when their mother had been alive, she had favored the chamber as well.

Merry was there now, looking out the middle of three long Elizabethan windows which had a direct view of the yew maze and the home wood beyond. The snow lay in pretty drifts a few inches deep on the ground, covering the formal gardens and the maze with a beautiful roundness. In the early afternoon, with a deep blue sky and a bright sun overhead, the snow simply sparkled. Without a single footprint to mar the soft layer of snow, the appearance of the garden was magical and serene— in strident contrast to the current temper of the master of the house.

She squeezed her eyes shut, trying to press back the realization that so much had changed since the near-tragedy of last night's adventure. But the thoughts came—of Kit tossing about feverishly in bed, of Amabel walking about the halls startling everyone, of Hugh ready to pounce upon anyone who dared to so much as look at him.

She turned quickly about, refusing to think about Hugh for the moment. Soon enough he would come to her and she could only imagine with what hostility he would view her part in Kit's injury.

She set her gaze and her mind to appreciating yet again the beauty of the chamber. The entire room was panelled in a finely grained mahogany which covered the walls and the ceiling. It was beautiful wood, rich and masculine in appearance. Deep burgundy velvet valances, fringed in gold, had been hung upon brass rods at the top of each window. Velvet panels of the same fabric hung to the floor to the sides of each window and were drawn back by thick tasselled gold cords. Situated just behind the velvet panels, yet covering the remaining exposed portions of the windows, thin white muslin draperies caught the brilliant afternoon light and diffused it gently into the chamber.

In keeping with the stately appearance of the window coverings, furniture reminiscent of ladies in heavy velvet gowns and wide, white ruffs about the neck, sat majestically throughout the long chamber. The chairs and sofas were heavily wooded and intricately carved, each covered *en suite* in the same burgundy velvet. Two large tapestries hung on opposite walls adjacent to the windows, each depicting Elizabethan ladies at their labors—one with their music, the other with their needlework.

Lady Rayneworth had taken her books to this chamber, novels of romance and intrigue. Merry thought it quite likely that with logs ablaze in the grate, with a wild spring storm beating upon the windows, with night's dark shadows dancing upon the panelled walls and the tapestries, one's imagination could take flight.

When Mrs. Penistone had learned that Merry adored the chamber, she had made certain a fire was always readied upon the hearth—a lovely gesture which of the moment had provided her a peaceful place in which to await Hugh and his wrath.

She moved to stand by the large fire, her back to the blaze that she might warm her fingers and the skirts of her midnight blue velvet morning gown. She thought with a smile that if she might not be justified in Hugh's sight by her involvement in events of the night before, at least he could not find fault with her appearance. Jeannette had drawn her long, coal black hair into a knot atop her head, leaving a riot of curls free to cascade all about the knot and several long ones to trail just past her shoulders. A ruching of sheer tulle rose up high on the back of her neck and travelled in a gentle slope over her shoulders to a pretty scoop low on her bosom. The waist was high and tightly gathered in the back so that, like her ball gown of the night before, a billow of fabric trailed behind her when she walked. The sleeves were long and warm, a narrow band of tulle ruching peeking out from the hems at each wrist. About her neck she wore a gold locket. Inside the locket was a treasure she had kept for four and a half years—a lock of Hugh's auburn hair, which she had mischievously stolen from him while he was sleeping in the apple orchard on Well-Dressing Day.

She opened the locket now and touched the curl, smiling fondly down upon it. How long ago that day seemed, when the family was young and whole. They had travelled to Abbot's End to view the five wells in the town, each of which supported a large picture made up of flowers, mosses, and leaves pressed into wet clay—all in thanksgiving for the water. After the viewing, they enjoyed an *al fresco* nuncheon in the family's orchard and Hugh had fallen asleep. Amabel had offered up her scissors for the task and would have done the deed herself had Merry's courage faltered. But Merry had delighted in stealing a lock of his hair. He had slept soundly through the delicate procedure, awakening only to Amabel's uncontrollable giggles.

Merry shuddered as she closed the locket with a snap.

She had taken refuge in Lady Rayneworth's drawing room because Hugh and Amabel were brangling in his study on the ground floor—and had been doing so for the past two hours. Even from the morning room, their raised voices could be heard.

Once Hugh was finished with Amabel he had already informed Merry he meant to speak to her, that he was sorely disappointed in the part she had played with regard to the previous evening.

She wasn't trembling precisely, but her heart did seem to be sitting in her throat more often than not as she awaited his arrival. Would he forgive her for not telling him that Amabel was abroad last night? From this vantage point, Kit's wound was entirely her fault.

Sufficiently warmed by the fire, she crossed back to the middle window and again looked out upon the snow-laden garden. The truth was, her conscience smote her heavily. If Kit had died, his death would just as surely have been on her hands as if she had held the pistol herself, primed the pan and pulled the trigger.

Fearful tears burnt her eyes and she brushed them quickly away. She could only be grateful that Kit had not died. The surgeon had pronounced him to be safe from danger. He had withdrawn the pistol ball and cleansed the wound, but a fever had already taken hold of him. When she had visited him late in the morning, he had been turning fretfully in his bed, shifting from side to side, pushing Mrs. Penistone's capable hands away as she tried to cool his brow with a cold, damp linen. He was not delirious. Kit knew her when she spoke to him, and the only encouraging aspect of his appearance was that he said, "Tell Mrs. Penistone that I'm not a child to be coddled, damme!"

He had smiled weakly at her. "We had such famous fun last night, didn't we Fairfield?"

She could only nod, her gaze misted over by a sudden profusion of tears as he again pushed the housekeeper's hand away from his face.

"I'll come to you later, Kit," she had said. "And do let Mrs. Penistone tend to you or very soon you will have Cook to answer to."

"Good God!" he had cried in response. "Hadn't thought of that! I am sorry, Penny," he said, addressing the housekeeper with the nickname he had given her when he was quite young. "I'll do better. See if I won't!"

Afterward, she had descended the stairs only to hear Hugh and Amabel tearing into one another in his study. She had covered her ears as she strode past the chamber on her way to the morning room. Neither of the twins nor Beatrice were about and, since every once in a while Hugh's angry voice could be heard all the way from his study to the morning room, she finally picked up her cup of tea, stole up the backstairs and closeted herself in Lady Rayneworth's drawing room.

With her gaze still fixed upon the gardens outside, she was surprised to see Honoria emerge from what would be the long gallery directly beneath Lady Rayneworth's drawing room. She was clad in a thick fur cape, the hood drawn closely about her pretty face, her hands tucked deeply into a matching muff.

Honoria. How very surprising to see her walking out in the snow since she was a lady who neither enjoyed exercise nor the cold. She was careful, however, to stay in the center of the gravel paths as she made a slow progress about the snow-buried flower beds. Perhaps Honoria had come downstairs only to hear Amabel and Hugh caught up in profound disagreement and had decided to seek a refuge of her own.

Then she saw another figure emerge from the west.

Mr. Belper.

Merry's heart paused in its steady beats.

Honoria and Mr. Belper. An assignation? She laughed, thinking it highly unlikely. But if not a prearrangement, then chance? To Merry, that seemed equally as unlikely. An innocent word let fall from Honoria's lips in the library of the night before—*I shall take a walk in the gardens if the sun is shining tomorrow*—and Mr. Belper picked up the fallen words.

Merry nodded to herself. Yes, Mr. Belper would certainly avail himself of fallen words.

She watched Honoria pause and turn toward him. He lifted a hand in greeting and she could see even at that distance that he held in his uplifted hand several roses, a product of his warming houses.

In spite of her belief that some attachment—even if unacknowledged—existed between the pair, she was still stunned, her heart now leaping within her breast. Here were possibilities and more, only . . .

The strong drift of her thoughts was interrupted by the opening of the door to the chamber. A rush of cold air greeted her. She stiffened, believing Hugh to have arrived, but instead a young voice broke the stillness of the chamber.

"Merry," Beatrice called to her. "Cook said you were in mama's room and here you are. Do you mind a little company? It—it is very noisy belowstairs." Her eyes were wide with concern.

"Of course I don't mind," she responded, smiling. "Please, do come in and close the door quickly, mind."

"It is warm in here. What are you looking at?"

"Mr. Belper is arrived and has brought some flowers for Honoria. Yellow and pink roses."

Beatrice joined her by the window and stared down into the garden. "He is head over ears in love with her, that is what Judith says. I wish Honoria would marry him instead of Hugo. Do you think she will?"

"She cannot. She is betrothed to your brother."

This simple answer seemed to satisfy Beatrice and the scene below, as Mr. Belper took Honoria's arm and began to walk up and down the paths with her, soon lost her interest. She turned back to Merry and, biting the inside of her cheek, queried, "Why is Hugh coming the crab over poor Amabel? I heard him fairly shouting at her in his study. Merry, I've never heard him so cross before, with—with anyone!"

"Yes, I know," she said, slipping an arm about Beatrice's shoulders and giving her a squeeze. "But Amabel, well, she did something that hurt your brother very much and—and I daresay it will take some time to mend these hurt feelings."

"Is he sad, then? Why is he yelling if he is sad?"

Merry could only chuckle a little. "Must you be so very precocious? Hugo is also quite angry with her because she played a little prank on him."

"What did she do?"

Merry knew she was treading on prickly ground and smiled at the young girl. "I'm 'fraid you must ask either Amabel or Hugh for an answer to that question."

Beatrice appeared as though she wished to argue the answer out of her—in true Leighton fashion—but at that moment the door opened again, quite abruptly. Hugh stood in the doorway, his brow thunderous, glaring at her.

Beatrice looked from Hugh to Merry. "Oh, my," she whispered. "Did you play a prank upon Hugh, as well?"

"Not precisely," she whispered back to her conspiratorially. "But it would seem your brother feels he ought to come the crab over me as well!"

Beatrice, full of mischief, whispered, "Should I get the *Times*, for I don't think he has been entirely broken of his bad habit!"

"Beatrice!" Hugh cried. "That is quite enough."

Merry gave Beatrice another hug and queried, "Do you mind leaving us for a few moments? Perhaps now would be a good time to seek out Amabel—I believe she has a surprise for you."

"A surprise?" she cried.

But before Beatrice had taken two running steps toward the door, Amabel appeared just behind Hugh. "Hallo, Bea," she said quietly, moving past her brother and walking toward her youngest sister.

"Bella!" Beatrice squealed, running at Amabel and embracing her. "You can walk! It's a miracle like the ones Mr. Belper speaks of in his sermons."

"Well, not precisely a miracle, scamp. Come with me to the morning room and I'll tell you all about it."

Hugh spoke for the first time, his words crisp and hard. "Not everything, surely!"

Amabel glared at Hugh over her sister's head. "Beatrice shall know everything I wish her to know."

Merry was shocked at Amabel's defiant manner and was not

in the least surprised that Hugh's complexion rose to equal the quick angry flush which now covered his sister's cheeks.

He would have given full voice to his arguments but Beatrice said, "Bella, did you know we are to have a lot of bad luck? Siddons said so because the Yule log went out. Did you know it went out?"

"No, did it?" Amabel returned, her attention shifting entirely away from Hugh. "Then we shall have to see to the log immediately." Amabel drew Beatrice into the hallway and firmly shut the door behind her.

Merry remained standing by the window, surprised at how calm she was. Somehow Beatrice's innocence and playfulness had dulled her anxieties, reminding her that not every happenstance in her life was within her control. All that had occurred the night before—how much of it would she have changed merely because Hugh didn't like her choices? In hindsight, she would probably have gone with her first instinct and told Hugh all about Amabel rather than let Kit search for her first. At the same time, as she reviewed her conversation with Kit—and his plea that she refrain from involving Hugo until he could try to help Amabel first—she knew she had wanted him to go, without Hugh, to prove his temperament once and for all.

But his life had been placed in jeopardy.

Yet, he had not died.

Somehow the whole of it made sense to her and had become acceptable to her.

So it was, when Hugh advanced into the chamber, his jaw working strongly, his lips for the present clamped shut, she was able to relax, to breathe, to let him be as angry as he wished to be without her knees turning to water. His hands were clasped tightly behind his back, causing the tails of his coat of blue superfine to angle sharply away from his buff pantaloons, his present choler giving his complexion a warmth which contrasted sharply against his finely starched, neatly tied, white neckcloth, and his gleaming Hessians threatening every piece of furniture by which he passed, his movements quick and menacing in response to his ire.

The rich auburn color of his hair, brushed *á la Brutus*—how fitting!—matched his temper this morning. Just as it had matched Amabel's temper and just as it had matched Kit's unwillingness to be coddled, as well as his referring to having been wounded by a pistol ball as *famous fun*.

They were a feisty lot, she thought, not being able to refrain from smiling fondly at Hugh, no matter how angry he was of the moment. Not for the Leightons to exist mildly, not for the Leightons to refrain from mischief and adventure, not for the Leightons to discuss their differences with amicable good humor.

"I can't imagine why you are smiling, Miss Fairfield," he began coldly as he marched toward the tapestry which portrayed Elizabethan ladies singing and playing their lutes. "I assure you I can find nothing about which to laugh or smile this morning—specially since I nearly lost my brother last night! Or do you find it amusing that my sister has been traversing the countryside with an outlaw for goodness knows how many years and ill-using every acquaintance hereabouts by evoking undeserved sympathy? By God, when I think of the many gestures of kindness extended to her over the past two years, I could wring her neck."

"Well, I suppose you could do that," Merry responded with mock seriousness. "But I daresay it wouldn't answer. You would very likely be imprisoned, and then where would your family be?" She clasped her hands behind her back, taking up his posture.

He whirled around, now facing the opposing tapestry of Elizabethan ladies and their needlework. He paused, glared at her again, and breathed harshly through flared nostrils.

She thought he had the look of a fire-breathing dragon of the moment as he marched toward her, toward the smiling ladies and their needles. She suddenly thought of Mr. Belper and Honoria in the snowy gardens below. She did not want Hugh to see them in case he unwittingly disturbed their *tête-a-tête*. Therefore, she crossed quickly in front of him, forcing him to come to an abrupt halt as the skirts of her deep blue velvet gown brushed against his Hessians. She heard him growl—at least his displeasure in her movements sounded very much like a growl! She hid her smiles as she moved to stand again in front of the fire, turning toward him.

This time he approached her, holding her gaze steadily. "Your lighthearted demeanor shocks me, *Miss Fairfield.*"

She ignored his criciticm and his formal address and responded instead, "Beatrice said you were giving poor Amabel a rather severe dressing down."

"*Poor* Amabel?" he retorted. "There is nothing *poor* about that child!"

"She is not a child," Merry returned quietly.

"No! Not by half," he responded through clenched teeth. "And neither are you, which only makes me wonder how you came to be so shatterbrained as to have let Kit go in my stead last night! But I did not come to brangle with you about my brother—Kit is not mortally wounded, and I must be content with that! But what I most particularly want to know is—what is your connection to the White Prince? Do you know who he is, for he has much to answer for and by God, he will answer to me. How dare he jeopardize the lives of my brother and sister! He may choose to risk his own life for a cause he believes is right and true, but I cannot forgive him for nearly costing Kit his life, nor Amabel hers. Tell me who he is! Amabel stubbornly refuses to do so, but she has given me to understand that you are acquainted with him as well. Is it true, Merry? Do you know the White Prince?"

She blinked back at him, wondering for only a brief moment whether or not tell him the truth. She sensed that there was no reason now to withhold Laurence's identity, particularly because of last night's near-tragedy. Instinctively, she nodded by way of answer.

"Who is he?" Hugh's voice was flat and cold.

Merry tore her gaze from his impassioned face. She thought of Laurence and of Sir Rupert and of the militia. Because she was convinced the whole situation was driving to an inevitable conclusion, because Kit had been wounded, because Amabel could have been hurt, or worse, she replied, "Laurence Somercote."

Hugh appeared as though he had been struck hard across the face. His complexion, which had been high, now paled ominously. He stared at her in disbelief, then shook his head. "Laurence Somercote is in the Colonies where I have heard he has purchased land. He has built a new life for himself after he was disinherited. This much is spoken of everywhere. He can't be here in England. He can't be the White Prince."

"He is. The stories you heard were tales he put about himself. I knew nothing of his identity until I came to Derbyshire a fortnight past. I, too, thought he was living in America. But all this time, he has been residing in Abbot's End, supporting a disguise even more difficult to sustain than Amabel's. I only wonder that he was not discovered earlier. I chanced upon him my first day in town, the day before I came to Hathersage. He told me all and—and he invited me to join him in robbing a certain nobleman of his purse."

Hugh stared at her for a long moment, through her, remembering. "I kissed you!" he cried at last, utterly astonished. "It was you I kissed. It was you all along!"

"Yes," she responded in little more than whisper.

"All of this is too incredible to believe!" He threw up his hands in a gesture of despair, then turned to face her, leaning toward her, his blue eyes intense. "I have been surrounded by deceptions and disguises. Tell me everything, Merry, before I go off in a fit of apoplexy!"

Merry took a deep breath and began a recounting of all that she knew, of all Laurence had told her of Sir Rupert's wicked scheme regarding his inheritance, and that she had had no contact with Laurence since her arrival at Hathersage save for a brief encounter in Abbot's End nearly a fortnight earlier. She then reiterated just how thoroughly ignorant she had been regarding the true state of Amabel's health until last night.

When she had completed her history, he shook his head, his expression bemused. At last, as though beginning to accept the truth of the situation, he sat down on a heavily carved sofa by the fireplace. Merry watched his face, wondering what he was thinking, what he meant to do next.

He seemed completely befuddled. "And you were the White Prince's compatriot who robbed me! Incredible." Chuckling softly, he continued, "It is no wonder then, that while I held one of Laurence's soldiers in my arms, I was deluged with memories of you. I suppose part of me knew it was you I was embracing. The devil take it, Merry, you could have been hurt! I could have had a pistol hidden nearby. Faith, I could have struck you with my walking stick."

Merry shook her head. "No, you wouldn't have," she responded, dropping to her knees in front of him, and placing a hand gently on his arm. "You knew I was a woman from almost the first, I saw it in your eyes. And you would never have harmed a female. Besides, your postboy was in jeopardy, and you would not have risked his life either. Do not think so little of my abilities to suppose I could have misjudged your character. I was in no risk of injury and well you know it."

"There is always a risk," he said, narrowing his eyes.

"Perhaps, but of the moment I felt it was a risk well worth the taking, though I will confess to you that had I known of your betrothal—which I did not—I would never have kissed you."

He leaned back into the sofa and sighed deeply. "I have grown fatigued with trying to make sense of everything. Amabel says she is in love with Laurence. How is that possible?"

"I am not surprised. She always was in love with him—even as a child of twelve she used to dangle at his coattails. She followed him everywhere, joined him in all manner of mischief, much as I, at sixteen, could not seem to keep from staying close to your side."

A swift expression of pain crossed his face. "That was a long time ago," he said.

She watched him, her heart yearning for him. After a moment, she asked, "What do you mean to do now, Hugh?"

He pressed his hand against his forehead and closed his eyes. "First, I intend to see Amabel enrolled in Miss Teversalls's Select Seminary. That much is certain."

Merry was stunned and wanted to protest, for nothing was surer to provoke Amabel's volatile temper than a threat to separate her from the man she loved. But she held her tongue. Now was not the moment to argue with Hugh. Instead, she let him continue.

"As for Laurence—good God, Laurence! I still cannot believe he is the White Prince. We used to fish the River Dove together! I wish I'd known of his circumstances before he set off down this road. I could have helped him then!"

"I am not so certain," Merry responded. "Sir Rupert brought witnesses against Laurence. I don't know how he achieved it, but it would seem the tide of popular opinion was set against Laurence from the start. It was all cleverly and wickedly accomplished. Besides, if you'll recall about that time your parents had been deceased for over a year, you were embroiled with all of your father's creditors in a terrible battle, and Amabel suffered her accident. No, I am persuaded even had you been informed, there would have been precious little you could have done to help him."

He looked at Merry and searched her eyes, as though in the searching he could begin to comprehend the implications of Laurence's assertions. "Accepting that Laurence was cheated out of his rightful inheritance, then—"

She knew what he was wondering and she finished his thought, "—then Sir Rupert Hucklow is a man without a conscience, a man possessed of a vile, wicked character. A thief, in fact."

"How great an irony," Hugh responded. "But tell me this, can Laurence prove his assertions?"

"There is a man in Abbot's End—a solicitor who has admitted, while in his altitudes I believe, to having lied about Laurence's supposed involvement with the opera-dancer."

Hugh shook his head. "What a cursed bumblebroth," he said at last. "Is Laurence aware how close to discovery he is?"

"I don't know. Did you ask Amabel? For you must remember, I haven't spoken to Laurence at length since the day of my arrival in Abbot's End."

"Amabel says he is fully conversant with every movement of the militia—and of Sir Rupert's."

"Hugh, you must go to him, speak with him. If you were to extend your support, you could persuade him to reveal his identity before he is hunted down and killed. Perhaps then the solicitor could be persuaded to speak the truth." She squeezed his arm and leaned into him. "He is one man against so many. And Sir Rupert, once he learns that Laurence is the White Prince, will have every reason to wish him dead. I fear for Laurence, for his life. Kit's injury is proof enough that neither the militia nor Sir Rupert will exercise either good sense or self-control."

"I will see what I can do," he said at last. But when he rose to his feet, his gestures, his quick movements as he strode toward the windows, became more and more agitated. "I wish that none of this had happened! Damme, why must I do something? Kit is safely at home, I mean to send Amabel away as soon as I am married and—good God, Honoria is walking about the gardens with Mr. Belper! And for some time, too, by the appearance of all the footprints in the snow. By the looks of it, there is not a single flower bed they have not passed by! How very curious! I didn't know she took pleasure in his company."

Merry waited, her breath compressed in her chest, wondering if he would take umbrage at his betrothed having been so long walking about with the good reverend.

But when he turned around, he gave no indication of harboring even the smallest suspicion or disapproval.

"You were saying?" she queried, hoping to turn his attention away from the interesting pair below.

"Merry, I just want everything to be as it was before—well, as it was before you arrived, though I don't mean to give offense. Kit's future was all but settled, but of late he seems to have become disoriented. And now Amabel! Even I seem to have lost some of my ability to make careful judgements. Well, all of that shall change. I shall attempt to intervene in Laurence's predicament—though I can't imagine what I can hope to accomplish at this late hour." He sighed. "In six days, I shall take Honoria to wife and all of this, including my heinous and quite despicable advances toward you, will be forgotten."

Merry could have said many things. But all that came to her truly unconscionable tongue was, "I would never consider your advances as either heinous or despicable, Hugo. Halting, at times, ill-timed, perhaps, passionate, yes, but never heinous or despicable. Oh, you mean because you are betrothed to Honoria! How silly of me, well yes, I suppose one could construe that when a man kisses a lady, while he is engaged to yet another lady, he is behaving in a despciable and heinous manner. Yes, I do see your point, but somehow given the extraordinary nature of the situation, I would never be quite so harsh."

She curtsied to him briefly, cast him a challenging smile, then quit the morning room.

Hugh watched her go, feeling both piqued and pleased at one and the same time. When the door had closed upon her midnight blue velvet skirts, only then did he permit himself the luxury of smiling. How greatly she pleased him, in every way, from the coal blackness of her hair and the rich green of her eyes, to her dignified countenance and her teasing, taunting manners in his presence.

These thoughts caused him to sigh again, wishing for the hundredth time that Merry had not come to Hathersage to so thoroughly cut up his peace.

Besides, precisely what had she meant by *halting?*

Halting, indeed!

Chapter Twenty-Three

For several hours that night, Hugh tossed in his bed trying to determine how best to proceed. When he finally fell asleep in the early hours of the morning he was still confused. However, when he awoke, it seemed that during the time sleep had dominated his mind, he had been able to sort out the difficulties before him and he now knew what he ought to do. But would Laurence Somercote listen to him?

Before leaving the house, he visited Kit in his bedchamber and found to his surprise that his brother was faring better than he had expected. "You are looking well," he said, smiling down at his brother's pale face.

Kit extended a hand up to him. "Do sit down, Hugo. I—I have something I wish to say to you. Only, in private." He glanced up at the housekeeper, who was stationed on the far side of the four-poster bed, who in turn looked to Hugo for her orders.

He waved Mrs. Penistone away and once the door was closed upon her, he queried, "Now what is all this?"

He rolled his head on the pillow to better see Hugh. "The church is not for me!" he blurted out. "I can't take Holy Orders as I once thought. I—I wish you to purchase a pair of colors for me. Ever since, well, I suppose ever since Merry came to Hathersage, I've slowly come to realize that I'm no more suited to the church than a grasshopper is to the sea. The truth is I've always wanted a career in the army and besides, Boney was shipped off to St. Helena a long time ago and it isn't as though I will be required to face the French in battle as I would have three years ago."

Hugh stared at him greatly surprised, his heart sinking. So he had not been wrong in supposing that something was amiss, that Kit had been distressed about something for days.

Kit took Hugh's hand and pressed it. "Well, brother, what do you say?"

"I say you are still suffering from the fever and once you are fully mended we can discuss your future. But not now."

"I haven't the fever, Hugo," he stated firmly. "And I want you to know that I will have a career as a soldier, whether you purchase a pair of colors for me or not. I grant you I was willing to submit to your notions a year ago and more because I felt sorry for you, for myself, for Amabel, for all of us. I thought it was my duty to please you and to take the safer path and enter the church. But all of that is changed. It changed the day Merry took us on the hunt for the Yule log and I battled a man so emaciated that my stomach turns upside down when I think of it. Laurence had enough bottom to strike out as he felt was necessary, and never let it be said that a Leighton has less pride and ability than a Somercote, or any other family in Derbyshire. You may choose to remain closeted behind the hedge and rock borders of Hathersage but I will not. I will not!"

His impassioned speech had tired him and he closed his eyes, releasing Hugh's hand.

Hugh stared down at his brother's tousled red hair, at the strong Leighton features, at the mulish set of his jaw. Kit was wrong—he did not *choose* to remain behind the thick hedge and dry-stone wall borders of his estate. That role had been forced upon him by his father's gaming debts. But it would seem, regardless of his inclination to concentrate solely upon the restoration of the Leighton fortunes, he would not be permitted to do so any longer.

"Rest easy, Kit," he said at last, patting his brother's arm. "We'll talk again, when you are feeling more the thing."

Kit opened his eyes to look at him, a pained expression on his face. "You will consider it though, won't you? I don't mean to be brangling with you—but, dash it all, this is important to me!"

Hugh smiled crookedly. "When was it you came to determine I was such a complete ogre? Of course I will consider purchasing you a pair of colors, but not before you are fully recovered from your wound."

Kit returned his smile. "I always knew you were a right one. But admit it, Hugh. You would not have been so easily swayed had not Merry come!"

"I'll admit nothing of the kind," he retorted, rising from his chair.

He left the sickroom shortly afterward thinking Kit was probably right—he would not have considered it before Merry had come to Hathersage.

He would have gone immediately to the stables had not Amabel intercepted him in the long gallery.

"How dare you!" she cried, bursting through the doors that led to the morning room. "How dare you forbid me the use of the horses!"

"And why do you think I did that, Amabel?" Hugh asked, impatient that she should be so ready to argue with him, to attack him.

Amabel pursed her lips together. She could not give him answer as she strode angrily toward the long French windows that overlooked the formal gardens and the yew maze.

"There, you see," he said. "You know me well enough, don't you Amabel, to believe I might have a solid reason for my orders. Don't you think I have your interests at heart? And give me a little credit for knowing precisely what you would do once you had got astride a horse!"

"I must see him," she responded, turning back to him, her arms folded tightly across her chest. "I must!"

"If you wish to send word to Laurence, you must let me do it for you."

"You can't get word to him, Hugh. You don't understand. Sir Rupert would do anything at this juncture to seize the White Prince and he'll be watching everyone who leaves your house." She placed a hand at the back of her neck and squinted her eyes shut. "I must get to him, Hugh. To tell him if I can."

Hugh moved to stand beside his sister. "I didn't say I meant to get word to him," he responded quietly.

Amabel looked up at him, anger again flashing across her face. For a moment she did look just like Kit and he could readily comprehend why Merry had mistaken Amabel— dressed up in a man's apparel—for her brother. He smiled at her quick temper, at the lightning flashes in her eyes. "You are such a goosecap, Bella! Always quick to rise to the fly. As it happens, I mean to seek out Laurence myself. I believe I know how we may resolve the entire predicament."

The sudden change in Amabel's expression, the light of hope which quickly suffused her face, was worth it all, Hugh thought. She threw her arms about his neck and hugged him hard. He felt her chest constrict on a string of sobs which broke his heart. He drew back from her. "No tears, now!" he adjured her. "Not when I mean to attempt to set everything to rights!"

"You are the best of brothers, Hugo!" Amabel cried, sniffing loudly as she held tightly onto his arms. Looking up into his face, she said, "I do love him, more than you will ever know! I intend to wed him, too, so long as, so long as—" Her voice became suspended with tears.

"Darling Bella! I will do all that I can to keep Sir Rupert and the militia from harming a hair on his head."

She swallowed hard and nodded several times in quick succession. "I know you will," she breathed. "Oh, Hugh, will you ever forgive me for, for all that I've done to you? I used you so ill, more than anyone else, for you were always so attentive to me when all the time I was only pretending to be ill. I saw that you blamed yourself. Hugo, forgive me!"

All of his former ire toward her dissipated upon her plea that he forgive her. "It is enough now to know that you are well, that you can walk! And you are right, I blamed myself so completely for what happened to you."

Amabel, still holding his arms, said, "I never did! Never! I remember it all, tumbling over and over, and do you know what? God help me, I enjoyed every minute of it! Do you see how hopeless I am?"

"Yes, you are a Leighton born and bred and we none of us can escape our heritage."

"Nor can you," Amabel returned quietly, looking up at him earnestly. "Hugh, you mustn't wed Honoria. You mustn't!"

Hugh shook his head. "It is not so simple, is it?" he queried.

At last Amabel released him, her expression full of sorrow. "I suppose not. I only wish there was some way you could be released from your betrothal."

Hugh smiled, straightening his shoulders. "That is another matter entirely," he returned firmly. "For the moment, I must do what I can for Laurence."

Amabel's eyes again filled with tears and just before he turned to go, she again cast herself upon his chest and embraced him. He held her tenderly for a long moment.

"Oh, and Hugh," she said, again drawing back from him. "Would you please permit my nurse to remain with me? She is not to blame for my obstinance and you have quite slain her heart."

Hugh laughed. "Yes, she may stay. Of course she may stay."

"And what of Miss Teversall's?"

Hugh rolled his eyes. "Merry said you were no longer a child and I suppose she is right. Do as you please, then. I daresay you would simply run away from that good lady's establishment anyway."

The answering, impish smile on Amabel's face was sufficient

proof of his suspicion and, pinching her chin, he quit the gallery
and headed for the stables.

That same afternoon, Honoria sat in the morning room of
Hathersage Park, sipping tea from a cup Judith had just handed
to her. Though she had returned to her home yesterday, following her peaceful walk with Mr. Belper about the snow-shrouded
formal gardens, she had come back to Hathersage today in
order to speak with Hugh about their forthcoming wedding
breakfast. She didn't want the chamber in which their nuptials
would take place to be absurdly dressed with greens and red
ribbons.

She was surprised to find upon her arrival, however, that
Hugh had gone to Abbot's End, for he had said nothing to her
about doing so the last time she had spoken with him. But that
was just as well, for she could put to use his absence in becoming
better acquainted with his siblings.

While she sipped her tea, she kept her gaze pinned to the
band of pink silk, decorated with tiny flowers, which ran the
length of her pelisse from neckline to hem. On the band, she
had embroidered two dozen infinitesimal roses, a task which
had required three weeks of steady effort. She was proud of her
needlework, though she cherished every notion that this sort of
pride was not of the offensive sort, for she despised what was
haughty.

She glanced up from the band of her pelisse and looked at
little Beatrice quietly playing spillikins on the hearth. Beatrice
had told her earlier that she had wanted to play spillikins with
her brother, but that Kit had suffered a fall from his horse and
was now recuperating in his bedchamber, his arm in a sling.
The mere mention of the sling had bespoken pain. She quickly
shifted her gaze away from Beatrice. She couldn't abide physical pain.

Thoughts of pain forced her to consider her forthcoming
marriage. She would be expected to fill up Hugh's nursery. Her

betrothed had already expressed a desire to have several children. It wouldn't do at all to let him think she would tolerate bearing more than one or two heirs, and she wanted to speak to him on the subject as soon as possible. She sipped her tea and swallowed hard. The thought of being required to endure the rigors of childbirth nearly sent her swooning. She blinked three times in rapid succession and set aside such wretched thoughts.

She turned to look at Judith, who was enrapt in that vulgar magazine of ladies' fashion, *La Belle Assemblee*. She lifted a brow, hoping to give a small hint of the disapproval she felt. Judith was so very headstrong and absorbed with every vanity imaginable. She actually wore pearl eardrops and it was still early in the afternoon! The thought of an unmarried young lady adorning herself so lavishly, and that so early in the day, caused her to shudder.

Her gaze drifted to Constance. She had always felt of all the Leighton children Constance showed the most promise. Unfortunately, she was too firmly sheltered beneath Judith's wing to make any real progress. Once she was married to Hugh, however, she hoped to see the twins separated—perhaps Judith could be shipped off to her Aunt Phillips in Bath while she made efforts to ingratiate herself with the most sensitive of Hugo's siblings. Then perhaps Constance's thoughts could be guided down a more serious, more profitable path.

Since Amabel was pacing by the window, just beyond Constance's shoulder, there was nothing for it but to let her gaze slip over that shoulder and onto Amabel.

She felt a wave of nausea assail her which she could not explain, save that the sight of Amabel walking about was completely grotesque, a sight her delicate constitution found nearly impossible to endure. She expected at any moment to see Amabel collapse, with hysterics to follow, and where would they all be then? She felt dizzy and tore her gaze from Amabel and again sipped her tea. She would be so grateful once her nuptials were complete, then she would be rid of Amabel—Miss Teversall's Seminary would be of enormous benefit to her.

Merry's voice intruded, "Are you feeling well, Miss Youlgreave?" she queried gently.

At least she was certain Miss Fairfield thought she had spoken gently, but there was something about her voice that positively wrenched Honoria's nerves. She kept from wincing only by the strongest of efforts and turned slowly to regard her fully in the face. "I am perfectly well, I assure you. I am not used to seeing Amabel so—so lively and quick in her movements. I find I am still utterly amazed by her astonishing recovery."

Merry turned to look at Amabel, who paused in her pacing and in turn met Honoria's gaze.

Somehow in that gaze, Honoria felt that Amabel disliked her. This knowledge so surprised her that when she set her teacup back on its saucer, it clinked. She never clinked her china.

Oh, dear. She looked at the clock on the mantel—still surrounded disgustingly by all that holly and red satin ribbons— and saw that she had been sitting for twenty minutes with the family. Her own sense of decorum required another ten before she could make her excuses and leave, or perhaps inquire after Mr. Belper.

She sighed faintly and let her gaze drop to the fireplace where the Yule log, now a third of its original vulgar monstrous size, still blazed in the hearth. What a terrible waste, was all she could think. Well, once she was mistress of Hathersage, there would be no more Yule logs. A tidy fire on Christmas Eve, made of rotting wood from the forest, most certainly would suffice to lend all the Christmas cheer necessary.

"Would you care for a macaroon?" Merry again addressed her. "Cook baked them fresh this morning."

Honoria repressed a sigh of exasperation. She knew Miss Fairfield was being polite, but couldn't the young lady see that she was of a delicate constitution and that her digestion was overset by anything sweet served early in the afternoon? "No, I thank you," she said firmly, and set her tea cup, this time, in perfect silence upon its saucer.

Somehow, her ability to control this small, polite mannerism, brought some of her peace returning to her. She could even endure being with the children another five minutes longer than necessary. She was just about to smile thinly and ask Beatrice if she was progressing on her reading, when the young child turned to her and queried quite abruptly, "Are you in love with Mr. Belper?"

She did not know how it happened!

She did not even know it had happened until suddenly Miss Fairfield, Judith and Constance were all huddled around her, pulling at her gown with soft cloths and exclaiming over her green silk pelisse, saying that the housekeeper had a recipe which would surely remove tea stains from silk.

Utterly bemused, she looked down and saw that her cup was gone from her hand and that tea had dripped down her skirts and had settled inside one of her green leather slippers.

"I don't understand," she stated, looking about the faces gathered around her. When they had helped her all they could, it was Miss Fairfield who assisted her to rise from the sofa and afterward who led her toward the housekeeper's chambers.

Truly she would be so happy when she and Hugh were married, for then she could get rid of each of these children, one after the other. And what was it Beatrice had said to her? She couldn't recall precisely, but she rather thought it was something about Mr. Belper.

Fancy that! A question about Mr. Belper caused her to spill her tea! How was that possible?

Chapter Twenty-Four

Hugh found Laurence, in the guise of the beggar named Gates, sitting on a mound of straw in the stables behind the smithy. Laurence did not know he had company, for he was leaning against the stone wall, his arms crossed over his knees and his forehead pressed against his arms. Amabel had told Hugh of Laurence's costume, and he could even recall now having seen the hunchbacked beggar roaming the streets of Abbot's End many times. But the truth was, if he hadn't know of the disguise, he would have sworn a beggar was sitting before him.

As he looked down upon his Derbyshire friend, all the anger he had felt for him in jeopardizing his brother and sister somehow vanished. In light of his costume and the identity he had had to sustain for over two years, in view of his disinheritance and of the great work he had done in Derbyshire, he found himself both compassionate and awestruck. He wondered how he would have fared under similiar circumstances. Probably not half so well.

Still, he couldn't resist funning a little.

"You there!" he barked at Laurence. "Have you not sought the White Prince for a little relief from your sufferings? He took my purse, you know, nearly three weeks ago. Surely, he could spare a shilling for you and at least a new coat!"

Laurence looked up at him from brown startled eyes. To

Hugh's surprise, he quickly rose to his feet and, just as Amabel had done earlier, latched onto his arms. He neither pretended to be Gates, nor tried to explain his actions. Instead, he addressed his most immediate concern. "Tell me how she fares!" he whispered, his expression desperate. "The militia found blood stains in the caverns to the northeast of Hathersage. Is she dead? She cannot be dead!"

"Good God," Hugh returned, unaware that Laurence might have been kept in ignorance of what had occurred on his lands. He shook his head. "No, she is not dead. She is perfectly well, I assure you." He then glanced behind him, fearing to be overheard. "But Kit left the house to rescue her and is now abed. The surgeon removed a pistol-ball from his shoulder. He had gone—quite without my knowledge—to rescue Amabel."

Laurence released Hugh immediately, dropping back down onto the hay and again leaning his head against the stone wall. "Thank God! When I heard the militia recounting their adventure near the cavern—and not a word from Amabel! You've no idea how vivid my imagination can be! But Kit was hurt. Hugo, I am sorry—I never meant, not in a thousand years—!" His eyes welled up with tears. "I told her not to come to me again—that the whole situation was likely to disintegrate at any moment. But she would come!"

"Of course she would," Hugh responded. "She loves you and she is a Leighton."

At that, Laurence smiled faintly. "We brangled endlessly about her involvement in my campaign. I forbade her a hundred times—"

"—and she disobeyed you. More bottom than sense."

"Yes, but I have loved her for it and if I can ever extricate myself—" He broke off, unable to continue.

"As it happens, that is why I am here," Hugh said solemnly. "Amabel has told me everything—as has Merry—and what I wish to know is where I might find the solicitor who you believe to have perjured himself."

Hope gleamed suddenly in Laurence's eyes. "His name is

Mickles. Geoffrey Mickles. His offices are in Church Street. You may ask any of the shopkeepers for directions. He is well known—though of late not quite so prosperous in his business as in former times. He prefers drink to work."

Hugh nodded. "I mean to go to him immediately. But once I have him in hand, who can best serve your cause where the law is concerned?"

Laurence fell deeply into thought. After a moment, he said, "You must try to get Squire Cubley to believe Mickles. He is the local justice of the peace and also leads the militia. He is greatly respected, but for the present he fully supports Sir Rupert. I am convinced were he to know the truth, however, he would best be able to help me."

"I'll go to him now," Hugh said. "Don't worry. I'll be quick about it!"

Four hours later, with night hard on the countryside, Merry waited with Amabel in the rose and green drawing room. She was sitting in a winged chair near the fireplace where a tidy blaze warmed and lit the expansive chamber. Amabel sat on the sofa opposite her, a deep frown on her face, her thoughts drawn inward, her blue eyes misted with tears as she stared at the geometric carpet beneath her slippers.

Merry watched her, fear rising and dipping in her breast like a kestrel on the hunt. Time was passing too swiftly. Hugh had not yet returned from Abbot's End and he should have been back long before nightfall.

Conversation between the ladies had ceased a half hour earlier. Suppositions as to what Hugh had been able to accomplish, or whether Sir Rupert had finally captured Laurence, had become both painful and fruitless. All the ladies could do now was wait.

When a running step was heard in the black and while tiled entrance hall, Merry immediately leaned forward in her seat. Amabel rose to her feet and whirled around to face the doorway. Siddons appeared out of breath, his complexion red from his exertions. "What is it?" Amabel cried.

He swallowed hard, his face pinched with fright. "They have him, Miss. Colwich is just now returned with news from Abbot's End. He could not find Lord Rayneworth. The whole country-side it would seem is pouring into the town upon news of the White Prince's capture."

Merry rose from her seat and moved forward to quickly slip an arm about Amabel's shoulder. She heard Amabel whimper and watched her swipe at quick tears on her cheeks. "We must go to him, Siddons. Now!"

"I'm having the barouche brought round even as we speak. You'll want your capes and I've sent Jeannette for them both."

"Thank you," Amabel whispered. Together, Merry and Amabel moved to the entrance hall to await the coach and Jeannette.

A half hour later, cloaked in a cape and bonnet, Merry peered through the front window glass of the barouche, her vision diminished by the rise and fall of the horses' heads in front of her. She could see that the highway leading to Abbot's End was becoming increasingly crowded with villagers. It would seem that from miles around, word of the capture of the White Prince had brought his supporters flowing into the small market town.

As the High Road straightened in its approach to the town, she could see that a long string of rushlights kept the cloudy dark night from obscuring the road.

"It is a riot," Amabel cried, clutching Merry's arm. "I can hear the shouting even from this distance. I am frightened. What if Sir Rupert has already succeeded in hanging Laurence!"

"You mustn't think about that!" Merry cried. "Besides, if the number of folk hurrying in support of Laurence has any significance, the baronet will not be permitted to work his mischief. Not tonight!"

The closer they drew, the more the highway grew clogged

with people on foot, smaller driving vehicles, and one or two coaches. When they were within a few hundred yards of the bridge, Amabel let down her window and called to a man nearby. "What has happened, Jacob!"

Merry leaned forward and saw that the man was none other than Jacob Wright, supporting one of his young sons upon his shoulder. Amabel couldn't hear him because the crowds were swelling all about the carriage and great cries were going up everywhere. Amabel leaned out the window while Jacob drew near the coach, walking along beside it as the barouche crossed the bridge.

After a moment, Amabel drew back inside and repeated what Jacob had told her. "Sir Rupert discovered the White Prince in the stables behind the smithy not two hours ago. When word was spread that he had been captured, his supporters ran out into the countryside, beckoning any who could come to meet him in the town as quickly as possible. You can see what an effect we have achieved," she added, not without pride. "They are coming from as far away as Chesterfield to the northeast and Matlock to the south! He is beloved, Merry. Only we must get to him! Jacob said his identity as Laurence Somercote is now known as well. Sir Rupert will want him dead!"

As the postillion pressed the Rayneworth coach forward, Merry saw that the crowd was parting respectfully. She heard Rayneworth's name evoked by the masses and as she and Amabel passed by, she could hear the disappointment in the same people when it became known Hugh was not within the barouche.

"My brother has the esteem of the people as well," Amabel said. "His care of his estate has earned him a fine reputation. I just hope he can stop this madness before Laurence or other innocent people are harmed."

Merry glanced at Amabel, wondering how it was at sixteen the young lady was more grown up than Judith or Constance. She looked all about the crowds and realized that many women and children had thronged into Abbot's End—many innocent people indeed!

As the coach approached the market square, Merry felt ill with fright. The combined voices of the crowd were a constant pressure on her ears. Cries and jeers abounded. She heard Rayneworth called for over and over. "There must be five thousand and more collected here!" she exclaimed. "And the militia are mounted and bearing swords! Dear God!"

"Rayneworth, how do you find the outlaw, Laurence Somercote!" came the cry over and over as their coach moved forward, followed always by the resulting moan of disappointment at Hugh's absence. Where was he?

She felt the crowd swell up about the barouche as though it was a living being unto its own. She thought how easy it would be for such a crowd to run riot, giving over to instincts as far from concern for life and property as anything could be. Fear worked at her heart until she could scarcely breathe.

When at last the crowds parted, and the barouche moved within the square, the sight which greeted Merry's gaze caused her to feel violently ill. Sir Rupert stood on a tall scaffold—some fifteen feet in height—supporting wooden gallows. Beside him with a noose about his neck was Laurence, his face bloodied and almost unrecognizable.

She heard Amabel gasp and Merry immediately turned and grasped hold of her arms, then pulled her into a tight embrace. Amabel cried into her neck, sobbing uncontrollably.

"He is still alive, Bella," Merry whispered. She could see that his feet were still planted firmly on the planks of the scaffold. Every now and then he shifted his head as though attempting to rid himself of the noose. He appeared to be only half-conscious.

Hugh worked his way down Church Street holding firmly onto the arm of Geoffrey Mickles. He wasn't afraid Mr. Mickles would escape his grasp, but he had a great concern that the increasing pressure of the crowd would succeed in separating them.

From the time he had left Laurence in the stables until now, he had felt himself trapped in a nightmare. Time had become a most hated enemy. He had gone to Mickles' office, only to find Mickles had left for the day. Where could he be found? His clerks shuffled their feet and cleared their throats. A pub or the taproom at one of the towns inns—the Dophin perhaps, or the Cat and Fiddle.

Mickles was a drunkard.

When at last he had found him at the farthest reach of the town, at a seedy hostelry overrun with rats and mice, he had taken the man bodily from his table, hauled him outside and forced his head into the freezing waters of a rain barrel by the front door.

Mickles had come up sputtering, spewing and fighting. But by now, when Hugh had just learned that Sir Rupert had captured Laurence, he was prepared for a fight and gave one fiercely to the unsuspecting Mickles. Of course it was hardly a fight. Mickles was more than half-foxed and a few agile steps to the left and right of the solicitor prevented him time and again from planting a facer. Hugh, on the other hand, felt his fist connect quite handily with Mr. Mickles' jaw.

When at last Mickles was lying flat on his back in the snow and gasping for breath, only then did Hugh explain his errand. The bout of fisticuffs had succeeded in clearing Mickles' head and he was able to listen to Hugh, watching his face in the growing gloom, his expression increasingly sobered.

"I'll not hold the truth back a moment longer," he said at last. "Take me to Squire Cubley who heads the militia. He'll want to hear what I have to say and he's the only one who can stop Sir Rupert now."

When at last Hugh pulled Mickles into the square he was horrified by what he saw. Sir Rupert was calling to the crowds to permit him the justice he had sought for the past two years— the hanging of the criminal and outlaw, the White Prince. The baronet subdued the swaying crowd before him with the even, firm tenor of his voice. "Laurence Somecote has used you ill—all of you! His schemes are now clear! What did he hope to achieve by pretending to be the hope of the poor? His inheritance returned to him by your good graces? I say, he has held back that which was stolen from families of birth and breeding to feather his own nest and to mock me. I say hang him! Hang him for making a mockery of the laws of England and of us all!"

A violent cheer of agreement rose high into the air, above the thatched roofs of the brown-stoned buildings, into the dark, snow-laden sky above. Hugh felt the vibrations of the cries through his chest. Mickles muttered he had come too late, too late!

"Not too late!" Hugh returned, dragging him toward the scaffold.

A second cry rose up into the air, countering the first. "Long live the White Prince!" was repeated again and again.

Hugh could see the militia mounted on their horses, swords raised. A few minutes more, a little more provocation, and the whole square would become a twisting, mauling riot. But what chance did the crowd stand of surviving an onslought by a mounted militia? None.

Sir Rupert again appealed to the crowd, speaking in his clear, even voice, ennumerating Laurence's supposed crimes, both as the previous heir to Dovedale Manor and as the White Prince. Hugh could hear the confusion in the crowd. Sir Rupert was a persuasive man.

If only he could reach the scaffold. A few steps more. A cry began going up about him, "Death to the White Prince!" The militia along with Sir Rupert's supporters took up the chant.

Hugh finally found the steps up to the wide scaffold which several of the militia were guarding. When he was recognized as a man who Sir Rupert had said would support him, he and Mickles were let pass, but he found the stairs and the scaffold, once he had reached the top, to be unsteady. He could only hope the platform would hold. He drew the solicitor forward.

At the same time, his appearance on the scaffold had a startling effect—the crowd in quick stages grew quiet and his own name was picked up and carried into the air.

He looked out at the sea of faces before him, lit by rushlights scattered through the crowd. He was overwhelmed by what he saw, by the confusion in the masses, by the affection and respect with which his name was cried. Then he saw his barouche, and Amabel and Merry within. His sister was drawing back from Merry's shoulder and met his gaze. She then leaned out the window and called something to him, but he couldn't hear her. She then gestured far to his left.

He followed the line of her arm and saw a sight which sickened him. Good God! Sir Rupert and his men had brutalized Laurence. He would not even have recognized him. His face was swollen, purple and bloodied. His lips were torn and bleeding. He swayed on his feet. The noose was tight about his neck. He might as well have been unconscious.

He wanted to go to him immediately, but he knew he had to address the largest concern before him—giving evidence as to why Laurence as the White Prince should not be hanged.

"That man deserves to have his case heard!" Hugh shouted, gesturing toward Laurence. "I have a man beside me who can testify to a great evil—one which must be rectified before judgement can be passed upon the White Prince!"

Hugh looked at Sir Rupert and brought Mickles forward. When the baronet saw Geoffrey Mickles, his complexion paled. Hugh thought it likely all would be settled quickly, but Sir Rupert immediately began to laugh. "What can a drunkard testify to, except the quality of the ale served at the Dolphin?"

A general laughter rippled through Sir Rupert's supporters.

Hugh waited only a moment before calling to Squire Cubley. "Hear him out, Squire! His testimony provides Laurence Somercote with a pardonable excuse for taking to the high roads on his mission of benevolent thievery. Whatever the White Prince has stolen from the nobility and the gentry—and I am one of them—he has given back to the poor, earning his own subsistence at the smithy. Hear what Mr. Mickles has to say, I beg you!"

The crowds were restless but subdued, looking from Squire Cubley mounted on a black horse near the scaffold and back to Hugh.

The squire was a large man with keen brown eyes, graying hair and a thick neck. When he spoke, it was clear he was angry. "If you mean to argue that Mr. Somercote was cheated out of his inheritance, Lord Rayneworth, you are fair and far off the mark!"

Hugh was prepared to respond, but Mr. Mickles cried out, "Sir Rupert Hucklow bribed me to falsify Laurence's father's will! But what the baronet does not know is that I have a copy of the true will hidden in my office! I won't live with the deception any longer, not when I have seen with my own eyes the poverty Sir Rupert has brought to the Somercote lands!"

At his words a profound hush came over the crowd. The implications were clear—if Mr. Mickles could produce the original will, Sir Rupert would be ruined.

"I'll see the will!" Squire Cubley called out, his expression astonished. "If the will proves true—"

But he got no further, for at that moment Sir Rupert pushed past Hugh and dove at Mr. Mickles. "You miserable, lying—" He caught Mickles high at the waist and brought him heavily to the floor of the scaffold. The hastily erected structure began to sway. Many of the ladies screamed. Hugh immediately turned toward Laurence and saw that the noose had tightened about his neck and he had lost his balance. He caught Laurence firmly about the legs and lifted him off his feet, giving the noose slack, but it had already tightened. Several of his supporters near the front of the scaffold lifted one of their men the fifteen feet to the scaffold floor. A moment later, he ripped the noose from about Laurence's neck. Hugh held Laurence against him to keep him from falling over. Laurence coughed hoarsely and gasped for breath.

Only then did Hugh turn around to witness the struggle at

the far end. The scaffolding was still unsteady and the movements forced Hugh and Laurence to fall to their knees. The scaffolding was coming apart.

Suddenly, at the far end where Mickles fought with Sir Rupert, a support gave way, the corner slanting ominously and the nearby crowd thrust backward as the two men toppled from the scaffold.

Another hush rolled through the crowd. Hugh left Laurence to see if he could help Mr. Mickles. With the aid of the men below, they lifted him down to the stone cobbles. He pushed his way to Mickles and Sir Rupert. What he found shocked him.

Sir Rupert was dead, blood seeping from his head, which had struck the cobbles when Mickles landed on top of him in the fall. Mr. Mickles stood beside him, staring blindly down at the baronet.

Hucklow is dead, someone nearby stated. The news was then quickly lifted up to the crowds and made known to all. Hugh kept Mr. Mickles with him and, after delivering a few quiet orders regarding the removal of Hucklow's body, he headed back to Squire Cubley and said, "Attend me, Squire. Let's see this miserable business laid to rest with all due haste!"

Squire Cubley agreed, appointing the militia to move forward and provide horses for both men.

Sometime later, the crowds were informed of the findings— witnesses to the signature of Laurence's father confirmed the will in Mr. Mickles' possession to be true. Laurence's lands would be returned to him. He then went back to the market square, at which time he made a speech to the crowd, however difficult it was to speak with his lips thickened and cut, promising a careful accounting of the monies he had taken as the White Prince, along with a promise that every tuppence would be repaid from the Somercote estate to those from whom he had stolen.

Though there remained many who wanted a harsh judgement against Laurence, Squire Cubley wisely dictated that reparations would suffice and any who held a complaint could see him privately to argue the matter. Since the squire was known to be a brute of a brangler, Hugh doubted that many would come forward to deliberate his judgements.

When the crowds began to disperse, Hugh drew Laurence toward the barouche and saw the White Prince carefully placed within the arms of his sister.

Hugh caught Merry's gaze, now brimming with tears and affection, and queried, "Do I still disappoint you?"

She laughed a watery laugh and responded, "Do get in, silly man!"

A moment later, the barouche was heading back to Hathersage Park.

Chapter Twenty-Five

Merry was not surprised that the aftermath of Sir Rupert's death was immediately felt throughout the county. Once Sir Rupert's crime of cheating Laurence of his inheritance was proved, Dovedale Manor was speedily returned to Laurence. He in turn made all haste to disburse those funds which he had promised to the crowds following his near hanging. It was to the credit, however, of the majority of the victims of his benevolent crimes that they placed the reimbursed sums within the jurisdiction of the local magistrates, for the benefit of the poor and suffering throughout the county.

Hugo did not hesitate to permit Amabel to accept of Laurence's hand in marriage, though he insisted she wait until she was seventeen before her nuptials could take place. The union of two families, so highly valued in Abbot's End and the surrounding countryside, brought a wave of congratulations flowing into Dovedale Manor, and best wishes showering Hathersage Park.

The day following the near hanging, Sir Rupert was buried by Lady Hucklow's request in the churchyard of St. Michael's in Frogwell, far from the disturbing place of his death at Abbot's End. The funeral was brief, the burial even more so. The widow was supported by Honoria, Hugo and Mr. Belper. The ladies now resided beneath Hugh's roof at Hathersage Park since

Laurence had taken up his rightful residence at Dovedale Manor.

After the funeral, Lady Hucklow retired to her bedchamber for the remainder of the day and the next, a time she spent, along with her abigail, sewing a proper black mourning gown and veil. Two days before Christmas, she rejoined the family party, a somber, tearless woman, strangely indomitable of will in face of the terrible disgrace her husband's crime had brought upon her.

She behaved as though nothing untoward had happened, inquiring as she always had upon the health and activities of everyone with whom she conversed. Merry would have held such conduct in the supremest of admiration had she not reason to suspect that Lady Hucklow's lack of grief was an indication that her marriage to Sir Rupert had been merely a useful one. Now that the baronet's death brought the marriage to an end, her object was to begin anew, a plan which involved getting her niece married expeditiously, regardless of the proprieties. Normally, a death within a family of this magnitude required all celebrations to be postponed until a proper grieving period had been observed—six months at the very least.

But Lady Hucklow knew her duty—to herself and to Honoria. The marriage would take place as planned. She was adamant on that score. "Honoria need not suffer for Hucklow's indiscretions," she informed Hugh with a firm nod. "You may depend upon your marriage taking place on Christmas Day."

Merry had heard her pronouncement with a sinking heart. Had a period of mourning been observed, and the wedding delayed, Merry was confident Honoria's fledgling affection for Mr. Belper could be properly encouraged to blossom. As it was, even the few days remaining until her nuptials would be spent not in Mr. Belper's company, but rather in tears and quiet distress. Sir Rupert's death had affected Honoria more profoundly than Lady Hucklow.

Merry comprehended enough of Honoria's temperament to understand that the young woman felt keenly the disgrace of Sir

Rupert's crimes. She had her opinion confirmed when, in a moment of uncharacteristic candidness, Honoria revealed her sentiments to Merry. "If I had the courage," she began, dabbing at her tear-stained cheeks with a white kerchief, "I would end my betrothal to Rayneworth. I have brought such a scandal upon him—he can only despise me now."

Though Merry was aware that for the sake of her own desire to see Hugh's betrothal to Honoria brought to an end she should encourage Honoria in her thinking, she found she could not. No matter how much she desired Honoria to relinquish Hugh, she found she simply could not permit her to continue in such ignorance of his character. "As though Rayneworth would give a fig for such a thing," she said, holding Honoria's gaze steadily. "He is a gentlemen, not just in the proper connotation of the word, but in the goodness and rightness of his heart. He would never hold you accountable for your uncle's conduct, nor would he despise you for it!"

Honoria smiled weakly. "He is very good, then, and I am quite wicked because I would have despised him, had the situation been reversed. Had one of his relations committed so great a crime, I—I would have ended our betrothal." She had then dissolved into tears.

As Merry watched Honoria weep, she could only think how great an irony it was that Laurence's salvation had been her own undoing. Of course she was beyond content that her dear friend was now residing in Dovedale Manor, but the cost to her had been great. Honoria now needed Hugh, and his consequence, more than ever before.

On Christmas Eve, Hugh sat in the morning room with his family, along with Merry, Lady Hucklow, Honoria and Mr. Belper. The diminished Yule log—still sizeable by any standard—was now completely surrounded by smaller logs and its fierce blaze set aglow the red and green chamber. In the quieting of the countryside and of his house, he had found many hours with which to ponder all the changes which had arisen in his life since Merry's arrival some three weeks earlier. He frequently had felt as though, in those three weeks, he had lived a lifetime and was even now embarking on a new life. His outlook was altered—he was certainly no longer unaware of the needs of his community, nor was he indifferent to the role he was being asked to play in the coming months and years. He had already spoken to Honoria of his intention of taking his place in the House of Lords this spring. If he had expected an argument, he was mistaken. Honoria's spirit had been greatly affected by all that had transpired. She was now entirely meek, and would make him a perfectly dutiful wife.

That was the rub. He didn't want a dutiful wife. He wanted Merry. He smiled to himself, knowing that were he to take her to wife, she would be forever kicking up a dust over any subject which distressed her—the poor and needy, for instance, or child labor legislation.

He sighed inwardly, his heart heavy. But there would be no Merry beside him down the years, unless . . .

But he couldn't ask Honoria to release him. He couldn't! She had been slain by Sir Rupert's crimes and Lady Hucklow was depending on her to sustain her consequence before the world.

Yet to wed Honoria when he was now convinced they truly did not suit seemed a terrible mistake. His family was too bent upon mischief of every kind to ever make Honoria comfortable. Surely, she must know that by now!

So, he had to try, to see if there was the smallest possibility she might willingly release him. Therefore, when Honoria bid the family good night, he followed her. When he had closed the door behind him, he called to her. "Honoria, wait a moment," he said. "Will you come into the library with me? There is something I wish to ask you."

She did not meet his gaze as she nodded to him, her eyes downcast. A great sense of pity overcame him as he watched her solemn expression. He gently offered her his arm and guided her across the entrance hall and up the stairs.

Once in the library, he closed the door behind him and saw her seated on the sofa near the fireplace. Afterward he took up a seat next to her and possessed himself of her hand.

She still did not meet his gaze. He wondered what she was thinking or whether she suspected what he wished to say to her. She was such a mystery to him, her life an internal one, lived within her thoughts and only occasionally extending itself outward. Were two more ill-suited?

"There is no simple way of placing my request before you, Honoria," he began, caressing her hand lightly.

"Have I not been sufficiently attentive to you?" she asked hurriedly.

"No, no, that is not at all the case. You've been solicitous in your attentions."

"I see," she returned quietly. He frowned down at her, wondering why she had asked such a question. She continued, "Then I don't comprehend why you feel it necessary to speak to me now, if I haven't failed to attend to your needs well enough to suit you."

He sighed. Clearly, she had discerned his purpose.

"You have been sufficiently attentive to please the hardest of men and I trust I am not of their number. Will you not look at me?"

Honoria flitted her eyes over his face twice and finally permitted her gaze to rest upon his. She stated her case simply. "I can't break off our engagement, Rayneworth, even though I know it is what you wish. I—I have nothing now, don't you see that? And my aunt needs me to secure her place in society by wedding you. Besides, the only happiness I have ever known in my life has been here at Hathersage. I—I can't permit you to take that from me."

"You have found happiness here?" he queried, stunned.

"Yes, very much so."

He found himself unable to believe her. He searched her eyes, trying to find even the smallest evidence of dissembling, but he could not. She appeared to be speaking the truth from her heart.

He released her hand slowly. Her gaze fell to contemplating her own hands, which she now clasped tightly upon her lap. He rose from the sofa and crossed the room on a slow, absent tread to stand before one of the windows. He looked out upon the rise of the home wood over the hill beyond. His gaze drifted up into the dark, starry night sky. He wondered absently when it would next snow. Siddons was predicating a fresh layer to grace Christmas Day.

We need a fresh layer of snow, he again thought absently. For the roads had become an ugly, muddy mess since the near riot in Abbot's End. Everywhere the tracks of coach wheels had tracked the mud into the melting snow. There was nothing pretty about mud. It was messy, and if you walked in it and dared to enter the house without scraping your boots on the boot brush by the back door, both Cook and Mrs. Penistone were likely to bite your head off, nobleman or no!

He smiled faintly, valuing as he never had before, the easy nature of his household, yet knowing that Honoria's presence was likely to end the conviviality of his home. How had it come about that he had actually offered for a woman so ill-suited for his home? Until Merry had come, however, he had been lost to himself. The real wonder was that he had not made more such grievous errors.

He glanced back at Honoria and caught her staring at him, her eyes full of panic. The look of fright in her eyes settled his mind completely. From this moment on, she would be his wife and he would tend to the delicacy of her nerves and her disposition with every ounce of energy and kindness he had within him.

Therefore he smiled at her and extended his hand toward her. "We have always rubbed along together tolerably well, you and I, Honoria. And given our mutual willingness to be attentive to one another, I am sure we shall very soon show the world how a marriage ought to be conducted."

Honoria rose from her seat and smiled faintly, which was her way, as she came toward him. She did not take his hand, but instead walked into his arms, a small, tender act which bent his heart toward her. He was touched, deeply so, as she embraced him and laid her head upon his shoulder. He held her tightly to him.

Merry had thought the library empty when she opened the door and found Hugh cradling Honoria in his arms. She had come to find a new book for Beatrice and had been stunned to discover anyone in the room, nonetheless the man she loved embracing his bride-to-be. She opened her mouth to speak, to excuse herself, and to retreat, but something in the look in his eye gave her pause as he held her gaze above Honoria's dark brown locks.

Entreaty? No.

Despair? Yes.

Only then, when she had properly understood the look in his eye, did she slip back through the crack of the open doorway and back into the hallway, her heart weighed down to her toes. He had no need to tell her what had just transpired.

She leaned against the wall of the hallway, her hands pressed into the wall for support.

"To come so far—" she breathed, tears starting to her eyes. How ironic that the restoration of Laurence's fortune should be the demise of her chance for any future happiness.

She did not know she was not alone, until Mr. Belper's voice broke her unhappy reverie. "Miss Fairfield?" he queried solicitously. "You are looking quite pale, and are those possibly tears I see in your pretty green eyes?"

She swallowed hard as she turned her gaze upon the good vicar of Hathersage. She smiled a watery smile and placed a hand upon his sleeve. "Lord Rayneworth is closeted with Honoria. There was a time when I thought—"

"Honoria?" he asked gently.

She looked up into his eyes and saw a look of pain drift into them and settle down for what she was certain would be a long visit once Hugh and Honoria were wed. "Yes," Merry responded. "Her situation is disastrous and he—he was offering her solace."

His arm fell beneath her touch and he looked away. "I—I am so very grateful for her sake that she is betrothed to a man of honor." He fell silent, his gaze staring off into the future. He seemed to forget her presence entirely. After a full minute, he blinked several times, then cleared his throat. "Do you know," he began softly, "I have just remembered a task left undone at the vicarage. You will excuse me, won't you, and should Lord Rayneworth ask for me, please tell him I have retired for the evening. I shall see you then on the morrow. Good night."

Not once did he meet her gaze as he turned away and walked slowly down the hall toward the stairs.

Merry was about to leave the vicinity of the library herself, when she chanced to glance down and saw that good Mr. Belper had dropped something, a little lace kerchief wrapped about an object, which upon untying the kerchief proved to be an ancient coin—probably from one of the caves or mounds found on the Hathersage estate. She wanted to call after him, but she stopped, looking at the kerchief which she realized must have been Honoria's, for it bore her initials in a beautiful lavender thread. It would seem he had brought the coin to give to Honoria—a parting gift perhaps?

Merry's heart ached, for herself, for Mr. Belper. Hugh and Honoria would be married tomorrow, on Christmas Day, and there didn't seem the least likelihood that anything could at this late hour prevent the wedding. She moved away from the library, to the landing by the stairs and beyond. She wanted to be alone in her distress, at least for a few minutes before Beatrice claimed her for another story. She went directly to Lady Rayneworth's drawing room where she closed the door and immediately lit a fire in the grate. She wanted to cry, to give herself over to the release of shedding all the tears that were of the moment compressed in her chest, but she couldn't—not when she would need to return to the morning room and fulfill her promise to read to Beatrice.

She was about to draw a chair near the fire when a scratching was heard on the door. It must be Beatrice, she thought, wondering how she could explain to a child that she needed a little time alone to compose herself. Taking a deep breath, she bid the child enter.

She was surprised then, to see Hugh open the door. "May I intrude?" he queried gently.

"I thought you were Beatrice," she responded with a smile. "I was sent to the library to fetch a book, if you must know. But yes, you may intrude. Please come in. Is Honoria with you?"

"No, she was not feeling very well, as you may imagine, and has retired to her bedchamber. Events of the past several days have taken a harsh toll. I don't think I ever quite understood until now her delicacy of mind and spirit."

He closed the door behind him and entered the room.

Tears rose to her eyes, but she held them back. Hugh wore a resigned expression, though not an entirely unhappy one. He knew his duty and Merry knew him well enough to comprehend that he would not repine, he would do all he could to make the best of a difficult situation. His devotion to the restoration of the Leighton fortunes was sufficient proof of that.

He moved to join her by the fireplace. "I've come to say good bye to you, Merry. I don't know when it will be that I shall see you again, or ever truly enjoy your company as I have had occasion to on this visit of yours. Tomorrow will be busy from the onset and, with the ceremony at ten o'clock, I know I will have precious little time to speak with you then."

He placed a booted foot on the brick hearth and she could see he was struggling to keep his composure.

"Take me away, Hugh," she said on a whisper, placing her hand on his arm. "Gretna Green is not far." She could barely see him. Her eyes were misted with tears.

He laughed, placing his hand on the mantel and leaning into it as though he was holding the bricks up all by himself. "Would to God I could," he replied. "But I know you, that you are only funning."

She wanted to assure him she was never more serious, but he was right. As much as she knew a penchant for adventure, never could she participate in one that would so destroy another person, as an elopement would certainly destroy Honoria.

She moved closer to him still. He turned to look down at her and covered her hand with his own. "I love you, Fairfield. I always shall. I've been the worst fool these many years, pretending that my sentiments toward you were a brief, reckless kind which would surely pass. Instead, I have to bid you good-bye instead of welcoming you into my heart, my home, my bed. I'm sorry, my darling. I tried to ask Honoria to release me from the betrothal but, given the circumstances of Sir Rupert's death, she has come to depend entirely upon me."

"I understand," she responded. "I comprehended as much when I found you holding her in your arms."

"Merry, I am so sorry. I would have given anything to have been released from this betrothal that I might spend my life seeing to your happiness, but it cannot be."

"Don't fret yourself," Merry returned, lifting her other hand to touch his cheek. A tear slipped down her cheek.

"Please don't cry," he whispered and leaned toward her to kiss her cheek. "I can't bear your tears right now." He kissed her other cheek.

Merry closed her eyes, reveling in the feel of his lips upon her skin. "Kiss me, Hugh," she whispered.

He did not hesitate and quickly placed his lips fully upon hers. The warm, sensual touch radiated through her soul, filling her with a low, murmuring vibration that forced her to draw closer and closer to him until he held her locked in a tight embrace. She felt the full length of him pressed against her as his kisses claimed more of her. His arms encircled her waist, the pleasure and wonder of his affection drying her tears, easing the lonely pain of her heart and filling her with the joy his love would always bring to her.

Memories of the past flowed over her again, especially of Hugh kissing her beneath the mistletoe and again in the draped music chamber the night of the Christmas ball. Even if she wished to do so, she knew she would never forget him, or his love for her. Would she ever know such happiness with another man? How impossible that seemed.

A moment later, he drew back from her, searching her eyes and face as though wishing to commit each feature to memory, and without another word quit the chamber.

She stared at the door for a long time, transfixed by having been kissed by him. Only after a long moment did she turn away from the door, back to the fire which was now burning brightly on the hearth. She realized suddenly that she was still holding the kerchief and the coin in her hand. She looked at it blindly for a time.

Mr. Belper was in love with Honoria and every instinct told her that Honoria was not indifferent to the kind vicar. Setting aside the truly horrid fact that only fourteen hours remained before the wedding was to take place, she finally drew forward a chair and sat down to think, to plan. Here was a situation that required a sensible solution—and she was nothing if not sensible. Even if her efforts failed, she must attempt to remedy the whole of the situation before all was lost!

There must be something she could do.

The door opened upon this thought and Beatrice entered the chamber with a book in hand. "I found *Arabian Nights!*" she cried, obviously pleased with herself. "It had fallen down behind my bed."

Merry extended her arm toward the child, and Beatrice quickly took up her favorite place on Merry's lap.

Time enough, Merry thought, to construct a new scheme. For now, Beatrice needed her. "One tale only," she said. "Then you must be off to bed before Nurse begins to complain of the lateness of the hour."

Beatrice responded by snuggling her head closely into Merry's shoulder.

Chapter Twenty-Six

Late that night, Merry and Mrs. Penistone trudged the snowy path which connected Hathersage Park to the lofty vicarage several hundred yards to the west of the great house. The housekeeper went before her, carrying a lantern. The slow sway of her steps was reflected in the unsteady light as it travelled from short hedgerow to snow-covered stone, to an occasional beech tree. During the spring, Honoria had told her, the path would be a delight to behold since Mr. Belper had planted hundreds of bulbs along the gravel path. But in early winter, only the snow greeted the light from Mrs. Penistone's lantern.

Hidden deep within the pocket of Merry's gown of burgundy velvet was a blank sheet of paper which she hoped would change her future and Honoria's forever. If it did not—well, she would not think of that! For the present, she ordered her thoughts, concentrating fully on the task at hand as she again reviewed carefully in her mind her quite scandalous scheme.

Mr. Belper's housekeeper, Mrs. Trent, had already been forewarned by Mrs. Penistone that Merry would be arriving to speak with the good reverend. He, of course, was in complete ignorance of her intended visit. If Mrs. Trent was not wholly conversant with Merry's scheme, Mrs. Penistone's higher rank as housekeeper of Hathersage encouraged Mrs. Trent to be biddable.

When Mrs. Penistone pounded the brass knocker on the

gabled front door, Merry did not have to wait long—the house-keeper was always grateful for the attentions of Mrs. Penistone. The aroma of fresh-baked brambleberry tartlets and tea further bespoke her toad-eating relationship with the housekeeper of Hathersage Park.

Mrs. Trent excused herself to make known to her employer that Merry had arrived. She returned quickly, dipping a curtsy to Merry. "He will be 'appy to receive thee, miss." She appeared as though she wished to say more, that she perhaps thought the visit highly irregular, but she refrained.

Merry turned to Mrs. Penistone. "Please be ready when I need you, Mrs. Penistone. You may tell Mrs. Trent whatever she needs to know regarding the purpose and nature of our call. Just be prepared to enter when you hear me say, *You must come to me at once.*"

Mrs. Penistone nodded in comprehension then prodded the bewildered Mrs. Trent to lead Merry to her employer.

Merry entered the bachelor's drawing room and saw at once that Honoria would heartily approve of his taste in decor and furniture. The room was sparsely decorated *en suite* in a royal blue silk-damask which hung from a pair of windows facing the lane, and covered both a winged chair and a sofa before the fireplace. Three smaller tables supported gleaming silver candlebra but otherwise did not display even a small ceramic figurine for adornment. The polished wood floor was bare of carpets, the mantel held only a candlestick. Above the mantel was a portrait of a woman who, because of her resemblance to Mr. Belper in her thin, sensible smile, could only be the good reverend's mother. At one end of the chamber, a small cabinet held a collection of books and at the other end, between the windows, sat a polished pianoforte of rosewood. The lack of ostentation, of any attempt at expression through the selection of furniture, the straight legs of all the pieces, including the chair and the sofa, so much seemed like a proper setting for Honoria that more than ever, Merry was convinced even in her mischief she was on a proper course.

Taking a deep breath, she plunged into the cold waters of her scandalous scheme.

"I am so very sorry to disturb you so late in the evening, Mr. Belper," she began, pretending to be greatly agitated as she wrung her hands, and began pacing the space between his chair and the pianoforte. For effect, when she reached the pianoforte, she plunked a high note twice.

Mr. Belper lifted his brows in astonishment. "Whatever is amiss, Miss Fairfield, for I don't hesitate to tell you I have never before seen you so distressed. You are in general a young lady of such equaniminous spirits—even in the most trying of circumstances—that I can only suppose the worst. Has Honoria— that is, has someone fallen ill? Lord Rayneworth, perhaps?"

He stood beside the winged chair and regarded her intently.

She could not resist plunking the high note again and observed that he flinched. She repressed a smile. Were two better suited than Honoria and Mr. Belper? Well, there were two, but she would not think of that just yet.

"You mistake my fretful manner entirely. No one is ill. Unless of course you call a sickness of the spirit an illness. You see, I have left Miss Youlgreave prostrate upon her chaise-longue, lavender water at her temples, poor child!"

Such whiskers! Merry was not in the habit of lying so brazenly. She hoped Mr. Belper could not see that beneath her skirts her knees were trembling.

Mr. Belper, however, was far too caught up in his own concern for Honoria to be aware of Merry's dissimulation. He started like a frightened animal, taking a quick step forward, his hand outstretched. "What is wrong with her?" he cried, his eyes wide with sudden horror. "Rayneworth has not jilted her, has he? Is she fallen into a decline?"

Merry lifted her chin. "Lord Rayneworth is a nobleman in every sense of the word! Of course he has not jilted Miss Youlgreave. How could you even think such a wretched, dishonorable thought?"

Mr. Belper sank down into the winged chair, a hand to his

brow. "No, of course he has not. You were very right to admonish me. Rayneworth is a man of great honor, just as you have said."

Merry watched him, thinking that never was a man more hopelessly in love than Mr. Belper. "I wish he had jilted her," she stated baldly.

"What?" Mr. Belper exclaimed, looking up at her. "How can you speak so?"

"Had he done so, Miss Youlgreave would now be free to pursue the real object of her heart." There! She had made the beginning for which this visit to the parsonage was designed. Only, God help her if she had misjudged the interest Honoria had shown in Mr. Belper.

"The real object of her heart?" he queried, leaning forward slightly in his chair.

Merry needed no further encouragement. She crossed the room to kneel in front of the vicar. "You cannot be ignorant of the true state of her feelings, that for a long time she has been in love with you! She was telling me as much, not an hour past." Oh, how her conscience bit at her. She shouldn't be saying such things to Mr. Belper. Still, she pressed on. "Honoria loves you, but she feels bound in honor to Lord Rayneworth. As much as he would never end the betrothal, nor is she capable of doing so, unless—unless—" She let her gaze drop dramatically away from the stunned vicar, her words hanging in the air.

"Unless?" Mr. Belper breathed like a man struggling for air.

"Unless you speak with her yourself, now, at once, and convince her she must break off her betrothal to Rayneworth!"

"Now?" he queried, dumbfounded. "When it is nearly the middle of the night?" The clock struck the hour—it was midnight.

She pulled the sheet of paper from the pocket hidden within her gown and placed it on his knee. "You must send for her. I know she will come to you and I will take the letter directly to her myself. Don't you see? She has hitherto been uncertain of your love. She must know the depths of your sentiments. You do love her, don't you Mr. Belper?"

"Well, yes, of course," he stated as a matter of course. But once he realized the words had been spoken aloud, that the true state of his heart had been exposed, a quick blush suffused his cheeks in stark contrast to the white of his neckcloth.

"I knew it!" Merry cried, rising from her knees and clapping her hands joyously. "Then it is all as good as settled! You must write to her now."

"But—but what of Rayneworth! This will be a most dreadful blow to his heart to have his beloved Honoria—"

Merry lifted a hand to silence him. "Do you wish to see her spend the remainder of her days in complete misery with Rayneworth? For if you have not seen her unhappiness, I have! His lordship may be noble and he may be a gentleman, but he cannot make her happy—of that I am convinced!"

"As am I," he returned firmly. "I do not mean to disparage Lord Rayneworth's fine character, but Honoria is so delicate, so refined, so pure in her sensibilities, so—"

"Yes, yes," Merry interrupted hastily. "I don't mean to be uncivil, but time is become a great adversary of the moment. Will you write to her?" She crossed to a small cherrywood writing desk near the door, picked up a pen from the tray and handed it to him.

At last Mr. Belper courageously rose from his winged chair, moved to stand beside Merry, and took the pen from her.

"What will I say to her?"

Merry appeared to ponder his question. "Let me consider the matter for a moment," she said innocently, as though she had not already decided what needed to be in the missive. "First, do not address the letter to her, but rather begin," and here she spoke quietly, lest Mrs. Penistone mistake her cue, *"You must come to me at once.* Yes, write that down and let me see if I can determine what next you ought to say."

She heard the scratching of his pen, and when the scratches

ceased, she picked up the sheet of paper and read quite loudly, "You must come to me at once."

Bless Mrs. Penistone, for the door suddenly burst open and Hugh's housekeeper appeared, her countenance thunderous. "You blackguard!" she cried, wagging a finger at Mr. Belper. "How dare you seduce Miss Fairfield in this truly libertine manner! I knew something was amiss when I saw her stealing from the house secretively. And here is the proof I need." She tore the letter from Merry's hand and read over the single sentence. She then drew very near to him and said, "You enticed Miss Fairfield to your home with this imploring love letter! I trust you realize now what you must do—having compromised a lady. I suppose it will be just as easy to have two weddings tomorrow as one. Come, Miss Fairfield! I shall escort you back to Hathersage at once!"

Merry followed Mrs. Penistone in mock obedience. She cast a final, hopeless glance toward Mr. Belper and quit the room close upon Mrs. Penistone's heels.

When the two ladies were far down the path, and nearly half-way to the great house, Mrs. Penistone queried, "I don't understand precisely why you didn't simply have Mr. Belper speak to Miss Youlgreave. Couldn't all have been settled more easily in this manner?"

"I considered it," Merry returned. "But Mr. Belper and Miss Youlgreave are each of such a proprietous disposition that I feared, even if they admitted their love to one another, it would occur to neither that Honoria should simply end her betrothal to Lord Rayneworth. No, they must be shocked into action. I am persuaded that the moment Honoria learns I am to wed Mr. Belper, her horror will be so great she will confess all before she is even aware she is in the act of confession."

Mrs. Penistone shuddered, "I hope you are right, else we will never be permitted our comfortable fires again!"

* * *

The next day, Merry joined the family in the library, along with Honoria and Lady Hucklow. She sat upon the sofa opposite the fireplace, while Lady Hucklow sat in a winged chair nearby. Hugh and Honoria stood before the mantel speaking in low tones to one another. Judith, Constance, Amabel, Beatrice and Kit—who wore an interesting sling—stood near the windows overlooking the yew maze, their presence in the chamber acutely noticeable because they were quiet—an unusual circumstance for the Leighton siblings. It was clear to Merry they disapproved of the wedding.

The ceremony would commence once Mr. Belper arrived. He was fully fifteen minutes late, a circumstance which caused Merry to wonder if he was shaking in his boots in dread of having to wed her. She smiled to herself. She had left the poor man in a dumbfounded state, believing today he would be forced to marry her. How horrified he had appeared! She would have taken exception to his obvious dislike of the notion had the expression on his face not amused her so. Poor Mr. Belper. But if all went as planned, he would soon be thanking her, only where was he?

For the present, the assemblage could only await his arrival.

Merry glanced about the chamber trying to divert her thoughts from the sight of Hugh and Honoria together. If she dwelt upon the possibility they would end the hour as man and wife, her heart became a painful thudding in her breast. She could not let such thoughts overtake her, so she tried every manner of diversion which presented itself. The chamber would suffice for now.

In honor of the bride's dislike of decoration, the library had been left bare of any traditional symbols of the nuptial knot—not a single flower was present to celebrate the day. Merry thought that were this her wedding, flower-filled vases would stand proudly upon every table, upon the generous mantel over the fireplace, and would be laced through her hair in summery, jubilant fashion. Rose petals would have been scattered over the carpet so that the entire chamber smelled of spring and life and love. She would want the world to know that she loved and was loved.

These thoughts brought her gaze back to the bride's pale face. Honoria appeared numb and almost disinterested in her surroundings or her future husband as she stood beside him and answered his polite questions in monosyllables. Her expression was somber and her gaze was directed at a solemn angle to the floor. At least she was pretty in white, her high-waisted gown a lovely confection of silk and Brussells lace. But were she to wed Mr. Belper instead, would her features be more animated? Would a smile enliven her listless expression?

Merry hoped so. She continued to watch her, wondering what Honoria's thoughts were. Did the bride regret her forthcoming marriage? Did she have any thoughts of Mr. Belper at all?

Merry could not know. Honoria was a great mystery to her. She could only hope that once the vicar arrived, and the remainder of her scheme was set in motion, that the truth of Honoria's heart—whatever that might be—would make itself known to all.

She could not be easy. Though she knew Mr. Belper loved Honoria, almost to distraction, what were Honoria's sentiments?

When footsteps were heard ringing down the hallway, her heart began to hammer strongly in her chest. The door opened at last and there was not only Mr. Belper, but Mrs. Penistone as well.

Hugh was surprised by his housekeeper's appearance and said, "What is it, Mrs. Penistone? You seem distressed."

Mrs. Penistone curtsied slightly to Hugh and said, "I am here at Miss Fairfield's request."

Hugh seemed surprised and directed a questioning gaze toward Merry. "If you've no objection," Merry said, "I—I have a particular reason for wishing Mrs. Penistone to be with me at this time."

He narrowed his eyes slightly, paused for a moment, then agreed to it. "Very well," he said.

Mrs. Penistone then moved to stand behind the sofa upon which Merry was seated.

Mr. Belper begged pardon nervously for his lateness, glancing briefly at Mrs. Penistone in what Merry could only determine was a terrified manner. He explained his tardiness to Hugh by saying that his hat had blown off in the wind twice and he had had to chase it through the icy snow.

"We have not been waiting long," Hugh said kindly. "But I'm sure you understand we are quite ready to begin. So, if you would oblige us?"

Mr. Belper again glanced toward Mrs. Penistone, who Merry knew was enjoying her role immensely. Only when the vicar opened his mouth to begin the ceremony did Mrs. Penistone finally intervene.

"You are forgetting, Mr. Belper, what we discussed last night. And though Miss Fairfield was unwilling to press you, I feel I am duty-bound to see that all is as it should be."

Mr. Belper swallowed hard. "I—I daresay the matter to which you refer can be discussed after the ceremony."

"But my dear Mr. Belper," Merry said, rising from the sofa and crossing the chamber to stand beside him. She slipped her arm through his, much to the astonishment of everyone else present. "Do but think how very romantic it would be if you and I were married alongside his lordship and Miss Youlgreave. We have only to send Kit to fetch the good reverend from Abbott's End, and I've little doubt he will join us shortly to set everything to rights."

"What the devil—" Hugh began, "—I mean, when was it decided you were to marry Mr. Belper?"

Merry lowered her lashes provocatively and whispered, "When I responded to his plea that I come to his home last night. It was very late, nearly midnight, and I know unbecoming of me. But he seemed so very impassioned!"

"But I never—" Mr. Belper began. Merry pinched him hard

to keep him from speaking. "Ow, er, that is . . ." he sighed in resignation. "Miss Fairfield did call upon me last night."

"And here is the letter he sent her," Mrs. Penistone said, "all but begging her to attend him at the parsonage." She held the missive before Honoria's gaze. "I saw Miss Fairfield leave Hathersage at a most scandalous hour and felt it was my duty to follow her, to see that no harm came to her. Of course, I had always believed Mr. Belper's affections were engaged by another lady, but then most gentlemen can be so whimsical. Imagine when I found them alone in his drawing room, standing quite close together. There is only one thing to be done— Mr. Belper must, as a gentleman of honor, wed the lady he has so thoroughly compromised."

Honoria gasped and grabbed the missive from Mrs. Penistone's hands. "Is this true, Edwin?" she queried, tears starting to her eyes.

Merry watched Hugh look down at his bride in surprise as he repeated, *"Edwin? You call him, Edwin?"*

Mr. Belper responded to Honoria's question. "Yes—that is no—that is, I don't know any more! I am completely turned about. I never meant to compromise Miss Fairfield, but I do know my duty, however odd the circumstances." He glanced at Merry askance. "Will you do me the honor of becoming my wife?"

Merry gave his arm a squeeze. "What a kind man you are," she said, smiling fondly up at him. She then turned to Honoria and asked, "Don't you think I shall make Mr. Belper a very good sort of wife? Of course, since I am very rich he will not need to remain at Hathersage a moment longer. In fact, once we are become man and wife, I daresay you will never see either of us again, unless of course you will visit us at Brighton and perhaps go sea bathing with us. You will like to sea bathe, won't you, *Edwin?"*

Merry was enjoying herself hugely.

Mr. Belper swallowed hard. "I don't like the ocean overly much," he said, the reality of what his life would be like married to Merry being brought home to him in a most unhappy manner. "And—and as for leaving Hathersage immediately, my roses—" He gestured behind him in the direction of the parsonage.

"Well, who gives a flying fig for a rose or two," Merry cried. "With my fortune you may purchase a dozen a day from the vendors along the Steyne. Don't be such a goose, *my love!*"

Merry apparently had said all that was necessary to accomplish her purposes, for at that moment Honoria simply crumpled up into a heap at Mr. Belper's feet. He, of course, could do nothing less than drop down beside her, lift her tenderly onto his lap and begin a speech which brought even the Leighton children gathering round. "My dearest, my darling Honoria! Are you all right, my little pet, my turtle dove, my sparrow!" He placed a kiss upon her forehead. "Please wake up! Did you injure yourself? My darling! My darling!"

Merry looked at Hugh, who shifted his astonished gaze from the scene at his feet to her. He blinked several times in great surprise. "So this is what Honoria meant when she spoke of knowing happiness at Hathersage!"

Merry placed a hand upon her cheek. "What a coil," she said facetiously. "I can't imagine how to resolve this most puzzling dilemma."

Only then did he seem to comprehend the whole of her mischief and burst out laughing.

Honoria's eyelids fluttered open. "Is that you, Edwin?" she queried, clutching at Mr. Belper's arm. "My darling, you can't, you simply *can't* marry Miss Fairfield. She will make you do everything you dislike most, promise me, I am well-versed with her notions of fun and amusement! And you will not like your home at Christmas tide! It will be strewn with yew and holly and—and red bows!"

Merry should have been offended, but somehow she couldn't be since Mr. Belper took Honoria's gloved hand and lifted it to his lips. "I shan't marry her," he said, "But I fear you will have to break off your betrothal to Lord Rayneworth, as much as you dislike doing so."

"Well!" Lady Hucklow erupted, suddenly rising from her chair and making her presence known. "Of all the absurd starts! And why is it no one has consulted me on this matter?"

Merry felt her heart quail within her breast. Would Lady Hucklow fail her now? Would she hold both her niece and Rayneworth to an engagement which by law she had every right to?

"Lady Hucklow," she began earnestly. "Please, do but consider—"

But her ladyship would not be denied. "Silence," she said. "You are quite a mischief-maker, aren't you! Well, I have no intention of continuing any association with Hathersage, so I will say only this—Mr. Belper, if you choose to marry my niece, you must give up your living here. Yes, yes, you may see to the packing of your roses if you truly wish for them. My brother in Bath has a living which is due to come open at the end of the year and which I know he will be happy to give to you. That is what I require."

"I will do as you wish," Mr. Belper said. "I have found the woman I wish to marry and, though I will regret my associations at Hathersage, I most willingly accept of your kind offer."

"Then all is settled. Honoria, do get up from the floor. I wish to begin packing at once. The sooner we are gone from this absurd house, the better. Everyone is gone mad here." She then took the missive from Honoria's hand, read it and crumpled it up. "Of all the ridiculous starts!" To Hugh, she said, "You are released from this betrothal! Good day!"

Hugh bowed to her. "As you wish."

"As I wish," she countered, round-eyed. "As I wish? What I wish was that my husband was still alive, but he is not. I wish that my niece were to enjoy the consequence of being Lady Rayneworth, but she is not. No, Lord Rayneworth, I don't believe anything of the moment is *as I wish*, except," and here she softened a trifle, "except that Honoria does seem to love the fellow and I suppose for that I must be grateful! And now, if you will excuse me, I now have every *wish* to be gone from Derby-shire!"

Once they left the chamber and the Leighton children were left to ponder the great good fortune of having rid Hathersage of Honoria Youlgreave forever, Judith cried, "I shall tell the head groom myself to prepare the carriage!"

Constance added, "And I shall have Cook prepare hot bricks for their feet and baskets of food for their journey."

Amabel cried, "I must send the stableboy to Laurence at once and tell him that he may come to Hathersage Park for dinner this evening."

Beatrice cried, "I shall bring my pets back to the morning room!"

One by one, the girls hurried from the chamber. Only Kit remained. "Mr. Belper has been a good friend these many months and more," he said quietly. "I have come to esteem him. He was always kind to me."

Hugh clapped him on the shoulder, "You might wish to give him a parting gift—perhaps that volume of Plato which you recently received in the mails."

A smile overspread Kit's face. "I believe you are right. Not much use for Plato in a horse regiment."

"No, not much use by half," Hugh agreed.

When Kit had left the room, only Hugh and Merry re-mained. Hugh smiled down at her, his hands on his hips. "Well done, Fairfield," he said. "And so tidily, too. How was it, though, that I didn't know my bride-to-be had tumbled in love with the dullest man ever set on God's earth?"

"Because you couldn't imagine her not being madly in love with you," she countered, also placing her hands on her hips. "You were always a bit arrogant, you know, and set up in your own conceit."

"Are you sparring for a fight?" he queried.

"Yes, a very long one," she answered. "I expect a victor will not be declared, either, for many years to come."

"Yes," he responded, his voice low, as he stepped toward her and drew her roughly into his arms. "For many years to come." He then kissed her and there was nothing for Merry to do but slip her arms about his neck and return kiss for kiss.

About the Author

Valerie King lives with her family in Glendale, Arizona. She is the author of more than ten Zebra Regency romances, including *The Elusive Bride, My Lady Vixen, Captivated Hearts* and *A Lady's Gambit*. Valerie is currently working on *Vanquished,* a historical romance set during the Regency period which Zebra Books will publish in August 1995. Valerie loves hearing from her readers and you may write to her c/o Zebra Books. Please include a self-addressed stamped envelope if you wish a response.

ZEBRA REGENCIES
ARE
THE TALK OF THE TON!

A REFORMED RAKE (4499, $3.99)
by Jeanne Savery

After governess Harriet Cole helped her young charge flee to France—and the designs of a despicable suitor, more trouble soon arrived in the person of a London rake. Sir Frederick Carrington insisted on providing safe escort back to England. Harriet deemed Carrington more dangerous than any band of brigands, but secretly relished matching wits with him. But after being taken in his arms for a tender kiss, she found herself wondering— *could* a lady find love with an irresistible rogue?

A SCANDALOUS PROPOSAL (4504, $4.99)
by Teresa DesJardien

After only two weeks into the London season, Lady Pamela Premington has already received her first offer of marriage. If only it hadn't come from the *ton's* most notorious rake, Lord Marchmont. Pamela had already set her sights on the distinguished Lieutenant Penford, who had the heroism and honor that made him the ideal match. Now she had to keep from falling under the spell of the seductive Lord so she could pursue the man more worthy of her love. Or was he?

A LADY'S CHAMPION (4535, $3.99)
by Janice Bennett

Miss Daphne, art mistress of the Selwood Academy for Young Ladies, greeted the notion of ghosts haunting the academy with skepticism. However, to avoid rumors frightening off students, she found herself turning to Mr. Adrian Carstairs, sent by her uncle to be her "protector" against the "ghosts." Although, Daphne would accept no interference in her life, she *would* accept aid in exposing any spectral spirits. What she never expected was for Adrian to expose the secret wishes of her hidden heart . . .

CHARITY'S GAMBIT (4537, $3.99)
by Marcy Stewart

Charity Abercrombie reluctantly embarks on a London season in hopes of making a suitable match. However she cannot forget the mysterious Dominic Castille—and the kiss they shared—when he fell from a tree as she strolled through the woods. Charity does not know that the dark and dashing captain harbors a dangerous secret that will ensnare them both in its web—leaving Charity to risk certain ruin and losing the man she so passionately loves . . .

Available wherever paperbacks are sold, or order direct from the Publisher. Send cover price plus 50¢ per copy for mailing and handling to Penguin USA, P.O. Box 999, c/o Dept. 17109, Bergenfield, NJ 07621. Residents of New York and Tennessee must include sales tax. DO NOT SEND CASH.